DEADLY FAE DUOLOGY

BOOK 1

WHISPERS AMONG THORNS

CASSANDRA ASTON

For every woman who's ever wanted to fling a dagger at a man when he pissed her off.

CONTENT AND TRIGGER WARNINGS

This book is a work of fiction. No part of this book should be construed as true or accurate; no people or animals were harmed in the creation of this story. Whispers Among Thorns is intended for mature readers and is recommended for 18+. Mature content and triggers are listed below.

- Graphic descriptions of torture and death
- Allusions to rape and other acts of sexual deviance
- Open door spice
- Biting and blood
- References to fae, fairies, and other fantastical creatures
- Explicit language
- Mental and physical issues described
- Addiction
- Family abuse/trauma

Please use caution when reading.

SPRING

LAKES & STREAMS

OCEANS & SEAS

FAERIE

PROLOGUE

PRINCE AEGON OF OCEANS AND SEAS

I ripped the bit of parchment in my hands into ribbons, glancing coolly at my first in command.

Ceto bowed low, tentacles wrapping around one another in agitation. I had selected my first in command for her cunning wit and her dominance over other sea creatures, but nothing would spare her from my wrath should any more of my nephew's plans come to fruition.

"Tell me this news is speculation and nothing more."

Ceto's body contorted, growing smaller. "Would that I could, Your Majesty, but it has been confirmed. He has formally aligned with Spring."

A current of frigid water tore through the room, unleashed by my uncouth outburst of emotion. Ceto shriveled until she was unrecognizable as a squid, favoring a sea snake more than a monstrous creature of the deep.

"And what of my marriage to the autumn princess? Have the arrangements been made?"

Ceto nodded, bobbing in the water.

A school of silvery prey fish gusted by, carried on a current of my making. Whipping out my tail, I speared several, stuffing them into my mouth. Ceto hovered before me, watching the sea floor as the tiny fish crunched loudly between my teeth.

"Call Aslik and Dagon. Our timeline has just moved up."

Ceto's tentacles brushed the floor, and she was gone.

In the silence of my sea castle, I slid a sharp nail between my teeth, picking them clean and awaited my two deadliest assassins. A lumbering beast cast shadows overhead and I leaned back staring up as it passed.

In the murky distance, something approached at a rapid clip. The dark, grey outline divided, splitting in two as a pair of massive bull sharks halted inches from my face. They delighted in terrorizing all the creatures of the sea.

Normally, I would punish such behavior, but the occasion called for just such creatures. Aslik and Dagon grinned, rows of sharp teeth on display.

"I need you pets," I crooned, patting Aslik on the nose. "My nephew has grown too ambitious for my liking. It's time we remind him of his place."

Aslik snapped at my fingers, narrowly missing flesh and I growled at him. His black eyes widened and he backed up, fearful of the greater predator in the room.

"Go, make trouble for my freshwater kin. I have a wedding to attend."

ONE

SAV

The city was a cage, and I was its prisoner. Heat pressed through the cracked windowpane, sticky and suffocating. Humans called Central Park beautiful. Their little Garden of Eden amidst the urban jungle. I saw only man-made cages for plants and carefully culti-vated paths for its inhabitants. Nothing about this place was free or wild.

Like the hedges lining the sidewalks, I was being groomed into what humans expected me to be. Molded a bit more each day into a human version of my once lethal self. I would have preferred to vanish from memory rather than rot in this prison, but that was not to be my fate.

Sighing heavily, I rose from my perch in the window and edged around the dorm-style bed to the single closet that housed all my remaining possessions. One thing New York City was short on was space, and our proximity stacked against the ever-rising tension mounting between two species, stifled in the sizzling heat of summer.

I pulled the solid green apron off its hook—my uniform—and tied it behind my back in a tight knot. Not only was I trapped here, but I was required to hold a job. A mandatory step in the assimilation project to help fae and humans coexist. Work for a folk, especially for those of us who were not part of a Faerie court, was limited.

If you knew the right human or had the right kind of magic, positions in modeling or television were prestigious and paid well. I knew precisely the wrong humans, not that I would lean on them for a favor, especially with my magic bound.

Assessing myself in the mirror, I considered inching up my skirt for the briefest moment before dismissing the idea. Although it was guaranteed to get me better tips, the urge to draw blood would be fierce when someone inevitably tried to grab my ass, and then I would be fired. And jobless fae weren't awarded housing. There were more of us than there was space, and only those who proved their willingness to participate in the program were given a place to cram their possessions in.

Tonight was a full moon, and that meant I was more likely to threaten violence. Oddly, full moons on the human side were almost as unpredictable as in Faerie. Men behaved as though they had trace werewolf genes hidden in them, howling at females and starting fights that turned bloody quickly on the nights when the moon hung round in the sky. The same sky we looked upon back when I lived in Faerie.

With that in mind, and because I didn't give a damn what any human male thought of me, I swung my long auburn hair into a topknot. I stared into the mirror at dull hazel eyes. Human eyes. Once, they had burned amethyst in moonlight. Now they barely sparked, like Faerie had been bleached from me. When I was cast into this realm, I'd used the last remnant of my power to glamour myself to look human. Now, even if I wanted to, I couldn't change back.

I tucked a loose strand of hair behind my ear, trailing my fingers down to the dusting of freckles on my chest. Mab knew why, but men always stared at them. *Assholes*. But it meant better tips, and I had my eye on a few human gadgets that cost money. Money—a foreign concept in a land built on bargains, but bargains were illegal here.

Grabbing my house key, I slipped into a pair of heels—invented by men to torture women, no doubt—and stepped out the door.

In the hallway, I wedged myself against rough unfinished wood as an ogre shoved past me, not bothering to make room.

"Hey!" I demanded. "Share the hall!"

He grunted, ignoring me.

My fists tightened at my sides as I pushed off the wall. If I'd had even a fraction more power available, I would have blasted him across the hall and left him whimpering for his mommy, but in my current condition, he would only feel a tickle.

Bounding down the back stairs, I moved quickly to the bottom floor, thrusting open the emergency exit door, and squinting against the harshness of the fading daylight. In Faerie, the sun always grew hazy as the day reached its end. In the human realm, it was a brutal tyrant seeking enemies to flay alive should you look upon it.

Heels sinking into soft grass, I crossed the manicured lawn surrounding the housing, built just inside Central Park for our kind. If I could have left this park to settle anywhere more remote, I would have, but the deal we'd made with humans only granted us living quarters in designated areas—as though they knew we would suffer most trapped among all this iron and it delighted them.

I trailed the back of the building, cutting through the uninhabited part of the park to avoid running into any humans as I left Central Park. Something stuck to the bottom of my shoe, and I leaned down, tearing the scrap of paper, sticky from someone's gum, free and rolled my eyes. *Keep Harlem Human* glared up at me in bold neon lettering.

Just another day living among people.

Fae'z In Harlem was a seedy interspecies bar just a few blocks away, on what people referred to as *the wrong side of town.* Its flashing neon lights had been broken in some act of vandalism a few weeks ago by anti-fae faction members—in the early hours of dawn—when the bar was closed, and no one was around to retaliate. The AFF were cowards.

Sam, a man with the right politicians in his pockets, had built the bar three years ago, hoping to capitalize on humans who would pay extra to gawk at our kind. It had been hastily constructed, cutting as many corners as possible, and was wedged uncomfortably between two derelict buildings that housed the city's poorest residents. My least favorite thing, the unisex bathroom. Sam called it a uni-species bathroom, claiming it increased cohabitation and the city inspector had allowed it. It had been used for so many dirty deeds I wouldn't piss in there if I had a full hazmat suit on.

Stepping inside the windowless bar, the dark momentarily swallowed denizens lingering from the day shift while my eyes rapidly adjusted to the low light.

I smiled at Brixz, who was nursing a drink after work, as I slid behind the counter. His hunched shoulders and pinched expression could have been a mirror to my own dejected mood, but Brixz didn't have my luck in blending in. His green, slightly slick-looking skin clashed horribly with the powder blue button up uniform he wore for his front desk job in my building.

Grabbing his cup, I refilled it. "Hey Brixz, bad day?"

He frowned up at me, his heavy brow folding thickly into a z across his forehead. "Damn riots making my day shit. They broke a window this morning and been throwing bricks at all the fae comin' in and out of the building," he grumbled.

I straightened. "I saw no riots outside our apartment."

He took a long sip of his cup before shrugging. "They were at the front door. Did ya go out the back again?"

I wiped down the bar, biting my lip. I had, but the crowd couldn't have been as large as Brixz described or I would have seen or heard something. Maybe. My hearing was better than a human's, but the glamour dampened some of my ability to hear as well as I had before. Just another thing I lost when I was forced out of Faerie.

My stomach soured. It wasn't the first time the Anti Fae Faction had targeted our building for one of their demonstrations. When would enough be enough? In three years, their actions were only escalating.

Last week, Clover, a fawn who worked weekends, hadn't come in. When I'd gone to check on her, she barely cracked her swollen lids and didn't bother getting up from her bed. She'd been cornered on her way home and beaten within an inch of her life. I had reported it to the Inter Species Human Fae Alliance, but as far as I knew, nothing had been done about it. She was expected to return to work this weekend. A stipulation if she wanted to keep her housing. Luckily, our kind healed quickly.

Curling my fingers into a fist, I scrubbed the countertop with more force than was necessary. The paint meant to give it the look of marble was wearing away under my ministrations, and the cheap plastic underneath peeked through.

I glanced around. "Where's Juniper?"

"She poured me a drink half an hour ago," he said, head tipped into his cup. "Haven't seen her since."

It wasn't like Juniper to disappear, and we didn't have a back room. A cold stone settled in my stomach. Like me, she avoided the restroom here at all costs. *She used the bathroom somewhere else;* I reassured myself. Goosebumps rose along my arms, and I rubbed them. Scanning the dark room again, I turned to the bar's single occupant. "I'll be right back. Okay?"

Brixz mumbled into his cup as I untied my apron, set it on the counter, and stepped outside.

Moving down the cracked sidewalk, I raced the several blocks it took to get from the bar to the front of my building, heart pounding in my chest. The electricity in the air, charged with violence, pricked the hairs on the back of my neck. I hadn't felt it before, hadn't seen them as I followed the forest's unpaved path to work.

Now, the sheer size of the crowd stole my breath. A mix of bitter anger and disgust roiled in my gut as they raised signs and shouted slurs outside my building. Had Juniper been caught up in this mob? Was she lying in a heap, unconscious as they trampled her body in their frenzied state?

My heart crashed against my ribs, drowning out the world around me as I strained to see through packed, sweaty bodies. Picking up my pace, I smacked into the hard expanse of a chest. Peering up, I swallowed as a male with dark slashes for eyebrows and raven hair falling nearly to his collar bone frowned down at me, his glare burning behind mesmerizing emerald eyes. The sharp cut of his jawline, smooth skin and tall build could have

8

marked him as one of the high fae of our court, but the way his shoulders curved uncomfortably said otherwise.

Those unique eyes widened as he took me in. "Excuse me," he said in a rumbling voice, stepping aside to let me pass.

Flinching as his utterly human smell permeated my space, I backed up.

His beauty had momentarily distracted me from the other signs of his humanity. Folk attempted to blend in with humans—far outnumbered and bound by so many laws, we could scarcely breathe around them—but grunge attire and a blatant disregard for hygiene. Never. Millennia of polish—and pride in our appearance—could not be wiped away simply for the sake of appearing human.

I sidestepped the man, banishing him from my thoughts, and scanned the ever-growing mob for any sign of Juniper.

As I drew near, the words to their chant became clear. The famous line they'd graffitied on every alley and building in Harlem was the slogan of the Anti Fae Faction. "We don't need no assimilation," cleverly twisted from the lyrics of the song Another Brick in the Wall, rang in my ears, making me want to stab something.

While I quietly plotted my escape from this new hell, some humans made their feelings public. I felt like shouting back at them that we didn't enjoy living among them either. That they agreed with me did nothing to raise my opinion of them.

I skirted the crowd, searching for a satyr with curling horns and a mane of sandy blonde hair, when a man stepped up onto an overturned crate, megaphone in hand. Steel-gray eyes swept over the mob and his lips twisted cruelly.

Heat boiled in my veins as my gaze landed on a face every creature knew. Dane Clyde, the leader of the Anti-Fae Faction and the self-proclaimed slaughterer of our kind, raised his hand and the crowd fell silent. He had personally led over a dozen riots through the streets of New York City and claimed responsibility for the brutal murder of several low fae who were courtless and lacked high fae protection.

A jolt of terror shot through me when I spied blonde curls bouncing near the front. I surged forward as she turned, and I caught a glimpse of her very human face. *Not Juniper.* Exhaling a breath, I stopped. I may look human—mostly—but to someone like Dane, or his fanatics, I wasn't sure my glamour would fool them. I wiped a sweat slicked palm on my skirt and continued around the crowd, sticking to the shadows where the man with dead eyes, leading his very own crusade of torment, wouldn't see me.

Dane cleared his voice and from the corner of my eye, I saw the raven-haired man I had bumped into—still standing across the street—cringe visibly.

Holding a megaphone to his mouth, Dane shouted, "Grotesque monsters plague our city, take our jobs and frighten our children." Shouts of agreement rang out from the gathered horde. "We stood by, waiting for our lawmakers to come to their senses and banish these creatures back to the hell they came from, but have they listened?"

My gaze traveled the crowd as the spark of violence in them ignited into a flame of rage. Heat radiated through me. They were vile, pitiful beings fueled by fear, and if my magic had been free, I would have reveled in their deaths. The fire clawing at my ribs wasn't just for tonight, though. It was for every veiled threat I'd been forced to endure since the night I'd been cast out. Since the day my magic was bound.

Mumbles from the people.

"I said: Have they listened?"

"No!" everyone yelled.

A satisfied smirk twitched at his lips. "Now is the time to take matters into our own hands!" As he shouted, fevered cries rose.

Dread pooled in my gut, dousing some of my rage as he pointed behind him at my building, and bellowed: "Tonight we tell the malignant creatures who live in our world, that they can go back to Hell!" With his last statement he waved a bottle I hadn't noticed, stuffed with a bright flaming cloth in the air, and the mob lit their torches.

TWO

SAV

I swore when Dane's bottle smashed against the untreated wood of my poorly constructed building and flames licked greedily along the wall, scorching a path upward. I sucked in a breath, trying to slow my frantic heart as I searched for a way through the tightly packed mob of sweaty bodies. There were fae inside. Children. Casting another glance over the crowd, I inhaled sharply and turned, racing around the side of the group to the back of the building.

Ice slid down my spine as I gaped at the long iron bars crossed over the door and screwed into place by massive bolts. Trapped. They were all trapped. My mouth dried. If Juniper had gone inside, she would be stuck now, along with all the others. Their only chance was to push through the angry mob at the front.

Sheer luck, or Mab, watching over me from wherever she was, had made me leave my window open that morning.

Backing up, I took a running jump—thanking the stars I hadn't lost my fae strength when my powers were bound—and caught the edge of the third-floor sill, digging my fingers into the sharp plastic encasing my window. Wedging a foot against the wall, I pushed up and heaved myself through the opening, rolling into a crouch on my bedroom floor.

I dove for the satchel stashed under my bed and swung it over my shoulder. In the closet, I grabbed my pearl hairbrush and leaned in to peer at the shelves in the back. A loud thud had me spinning around to find that my window had fallen shut. *Damn.* I darted to the window, digging my nails in. "Come on," I groaned, muscles straining as I pulled. "Damnit!"

Shouts and cries from the hall made my stomach sink, and I flung my apartment door wide, halting as a stampede of wild creatures crammed together in the narrow space. Second-floor residents shoved their way up, fourth-floor residents frantically pressed down, and my floor was trapped between.

A tangle of limbs pressed in on all sides, all sweaty skin and sharp elbows. Terror was a living thing, climbing up my spine. I spied some of the daintier fae turning red, wedged between larger, bulkier creatures. If someone didn't take command of them, fae would die before they ever faced the mob.

I whistled loudly in the door frame, not venturing into the hall. Some of the pushing slowed, and several fae turned to face me. "Listen to me!" I shouted, lacing my words with authority. "We can't go out the front. We'll need to go through the windows on the first and second floors."

"The windows are sealed," someone called from the other end of the hall. A child wailed, and the crowd pushed again.

My heart spasmed, terror clawing at me. All sealed? Magic. It was fae magic. But how? Why? *No.* It couldn't be. It had to be the heat from the growing fire causing the plastic encasing the windows to seal themselves shut. No fae would do something so cruel to their own kind.

There was no time for speculation. Creatures shoved one another— panic seizing them—as the heat surrounding us pressed in and smoke began to swirl its way up the stairwell.

Coughs and sputtering cries from the first floor rang in my ears as they pushed harder, forcing everyone on the second floor up. Fae spilled off the stairwell, crammed against walls, and at the end of the hall an urisk spread four arms wide and forcibly swam through the mass of bodies.

Yells of pain and protest erupted in his wake and a fawn's eyes rolled into the back of her head as she collapsed into the folk pressed into her. Someone shoved her off, and she slumped below the mass of bodies, disappearing.

"Stop!" I shrieked as I searched desperately for any sign of her. I stepped into the hall, wedging my elbows into the bigger creatures, freeing some of the smaller fae trapped against walls and giving them space to breathe.

I slid a dagger out of my bag and pressed it into the back of a gremlin who growled at me, but made room and I reached for the fawn at my feet. Thankfully, her eyes were open again, and she grabbed my hand, pulling herself up. "Stay close," I told her, spinning around to fight through to the stairs.

Some of the bigger fae forced the others aside, but as I pulled more creatures up, pointing my dagger into the backs of those in my way, they began to make space. Heat licked at my feet and rising smoke burned my lungs, but I cleared a path, inching down the stairwell. "Has anyone seen Juniper?" I asked as I pushed through them, down the narrow stairs to the first floor.

Two large orcs I didn't recognize shoved through the crowd and positioned themselves beside me. "Haven't seen her since she left for work this morning," the first said. I glanced at him, tugging at the shirt clinging to my sweaty skin.

I was simultaneously relieved and terrified that she wasn't in the building with us. Was she alright somewhere far from here, or had something terrible happened to her? The sinking feeling in my gut said it was the latter, but until we were out, until we were free of the humans who had gathered to watch us burn, I would pray to Mab my friend was safe.

A troll, small for his kind and still in his construction uniform, blocked the door. I peered up at him. "What's wrong? Why aren't you going out?"

"The fire's too hot," he said in thickly accented English.

"The windows are sealed, and the back doors are barred with iron. This is our only way out."

The troll flinched and leaned away from the exit. His forearm was singed black, the skin burned away, and I had to assume he'd already opened the door once.

Broad shoulders pressed tight to my sides as the pair of orcs beside me leaned their heads together, whispering in their language. Although I'd spent most of my adult life among at least some of the orc soldiers at my former court in Faerie, I'd never learned the orc dialect. My gaze darted between their dark brows furrowed over matching broad noses bisected with so many scars, I had no doubt they had been members of some guard before they'd been forced to live in the human realm.

"They'll be waiting for us," the one to my right said to me.

I nodded.

Blazing heat grew hotter, suffocating the cries and protests of the fae at my back, and the smoke was thick enough I had to squint through watery eyes to see. We'd need to be fast when the door swung wide. We couldn't harm the humans, couldn't do much to defend ourselves against their iron weapons and guns, but we weren't made to bend, and it was this or let the fire burn us.

"Don't waste your time fighting!" I called to the writhing bodies crushed against my back. "Push through them and run!"

The orc soldiers beside me straightened, nodding to one another, and without a word, they turned, ramming their shoulders into the troll between them and the door, and all hell broke loose.

The door flew off its hinges, taking down a wall of humans in one go. It shouldn't have been possible, but I'd thank Mab for that small mercy later.

The troll crashed to the ground, consumed by the wall of fire just outside the door, and I screamed as his skin turned black and his eyes rolled back in his head.

The pair of orcs beat a path forward and a stream of bodies carried me on their tide. I tried to fight them, to force my way to the troll who had slumped over onto his side and was no longer moving, but the press of their bodies carried me farther away and I spun around, dodging a meat cleaver as it swung for my head.

Soot and ash drifted on a phantom wind and the heat pressing in from all sides singed my bare shoulders and calves. The smell of burning flesh was enough to turn my belly, but I had no time to waste on the foul scent of burned skin as I ducked a metal pipe and danced out of the way of what must have been an old bayonet from the First World War.

Panic rose in the crowd and screaming began. My stomach soured as I dropped to my knees to avoid another crushing blow from a human and sent a prayer to Mab that those screams were in fear and not pain. I couldn't waste time worrying about what happened behind me as burly men in makeshift armor charged me.

My orc companions fought the magic that restricted them from harming humans, shoving against the crowd, and making a path for us to escape. Orcs were the least affected of our kind by iron and they took blow after blow to the forearm and chest as they pressed the angry mob back.

A nymph child huddled on the ground wailing, and I bounded for her, scooping her into my arms just as a human woman with a jagged bit of glass lunged for her, swiping. I stumbled back, wrapping my arms around the child, and nearly tripped over a satyr sprawled out on the ground.

"Juniper!"

I dodged the human's second swipe, kneeling to help the satyr to her feet. Not Juniper. She wrapped an arm around my neck, and I stood, turning with the child in my arms and the satyr's shoulder draped heavily around my neck.

I ran as fast as I could with a hobbled satyr and a nymph, but even with them, the human was no match for my speed. Setting the satyr against a tree, I handed her the child. "Have you seen Juniper?"

I searched her face for any sign of recognition. "Look out!" she shouted, and I ducked just as a flaming torch swung for my head.

"Burn fairy bitch," a man roared, spittle flying from thin, red lips.

His eyes were wild with desperation, and ice chilled my veins. Dangerous. People were dangerous when they were caught in the throes of bloodlust. I had seen it many times over the centuries. Small altercations that catapulted into war when the rage that lived in human hearts overtook them.

He swung for me again, narrowly missing my head, and I moved out of his reach. He followed, putting more distance between himself and the pair I'd just saved. I had to get him away from them. To give them a chance.

"Come on then, catch me if you think you can." I grinned, all teeth, and backed up, never taking my eyes off him even as I watched the fae slinking behind the tree and making their escape from the corner of my eye.

Blistering heat scorched my back, and I didn't need to turn to know I was too close to the bonfire that had been my building. My satchel was a thin barrier between skin and the raging inferno incinerating my temporary home.

The man grinned and my stomach twisted at the sick pleasure he would get from watching me catch fire if I got much closer. "Nowhere to go," he sneered, waving his torch in my face.

My legs shook. We were dying. And no one would come for us. Not my court or any of the fae.

"Voooorrraaaalllinnnnn." Someone to my left shouted, and an orc barreled into the man, knocking him to the ground. It roused some long-dormant part of my soul. It was a war cry. A rally call to our people. My gaze landed on the orc, blood pumping in my veins, urging me to take up a sword and cut down our enemies.

"Run, Lady."

My heart rate ticked up and this time it wasn't the fire or the battle that had fear filling my lungs. "I'm not–"

"Go."

Curling my hands into fists, I glanced around, breath coming in rapid pants. Everywhere I looked, fae fought instead of running, trying and failing to beat an enemy they couldn't injure. An ogre, twice the size of the group surrounding him, screamed as massive spikes were driven through his arms and chains went taut as men swung hammers overhead, spiking him in place.

Bile rose up my throat as I spied an orc so bloodied, I only recognized him by the blue uniform he wore. "Brixz," I breathed and took a stumbling step forward.

A flaming torch whizzed by my ear and someone shouted: "Get that one! She's escaping."

I glanced around, terror coursing through my veins as a dozen humans charged me, raising pitchforks and other iron weapons.

I backed up, turned and ran.

Tears streamed down my face as I ran. Because I had no choice. Because I was too afraid to stay. But I heard their screams long after I left the park.

THREE

SAV

I pressed against the alley wall, heart battering my chest. I'd seen the flames. Heard the screams. They were dead. No fae could withstand iron, and nothing living could survive a fire like that. A desperate part of me wanted to go back for them, to help them, but bound as I was—magickless—I was as pathetic as a human.

I had to regroup and form a plan, but first, I needed to stow my bag somewhere until I was sure it was safe. There was only one place to hide it. The bar.

Crossing cracked pavement, I glanced up and down the path, ensuring none of the people from that horrid scene had strayed this far. I dashed behind the counter, taking out the box labeled onions, uncloaked its masking spell, and dumped my satchel inside. I didn't like leaving it there, but if humans got ahold of it, all hope was lost. My gaze darted to the empty stool where Brixz had been, and I gasped around a pained breath. An image of his ruined face flashed through my mind.

I bit back a sob. I would not cry. Brixz needed me to keep it together. I had to find Juniper and figure out how to help all the captured fae. To demand retribution for what they did to us.

Giving the cloaked box a quick once over, I nodded to myself and stood, moving to the door. I glanced over my shoulder, grimacing at the empty space. How had I spent three years working here, allowing humans to paw at me and gawk, to leer and make jokes at our expense? How had I sat by and waited for this to happen?

●→)(↩♦∧♦♦●

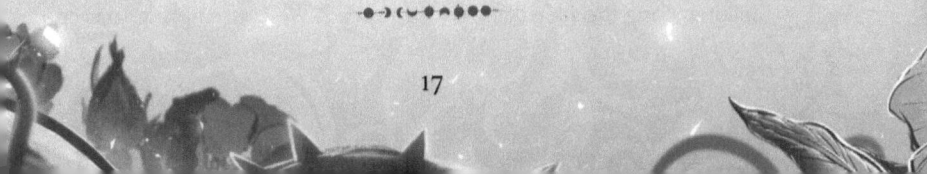

I moved quickly, darting behind a building across the street from Central Park.

Flames stretched high into the sky as my former dwelling was consumed. The fire's tendrils reached for me, choking the sky with an oppressive haze. It burned my lungs, tasting like ash, and I drew shallow breaths, scanning the poorly lit space.

It was truly dark now and the thick smoke filling the air made it hard to see from this far, but park lights refracted off metal chains and nets wrapped around fae of all kinds. I could just make out their shapes as humans overwhelmed the burned and battered folk still struggling to escape the fire ravaged building.

My fingers twitched at my sides as the need to do something, to help them, took hold of me.

A large ogre who had fought his binding more than any of us, clearing a path through people with relentless force, was slumped in defeat, thick metal chains sizzling against his muscled arms.

Fury burned in my veins as despair clouded his vision and he sagged against his manacles.

Sparks leaped from the building and still no human fire trucks or ambulances arrived. Morbidly, I wondered if any would or if the humans would risk widespread destruction if there was even a slim chance the flames might turn south and wipe out the pockets granting access to what remained of Faerie.

As my apartment crumbled, large chunks of burning debris crashed to the ground. The fighting paused as people and fae alike dodged out of the way to save themselves. Smoke blackened the sky, blotting out the waning light, casting the world into eerie darkness.

A human screamed.

I squeezed my trembling hands into fists. I should be the one to make them scream, to revel in their demise. My gaze landed on a shape I recognized, and fury blazed to life in my chest. Dane Clyde would die by my blade. That was a promise I made to the stars and felt the magic accept my bargain.

Heat sizzled in my veins as he sent hand signals to a few militant looking men and women who grabbed their victims by their chains and nets and began dragging them away. Most of the crowd—fae and human alike—was too busy dodging flaming debris to notice their exit as they took mostly smaller creatures, ones who were easier to carry, leaving the larger folk behind.

I skirted around the building, dashing across the street, keeping Dane in sight.

Snaking along the alley behind Central Park West, attempting to keep a safe distance from falling debris, I swore when they rounded a corner and disappeared.

I sped up, darting into an alley, when a voice rang above the crowd.

I already knew the voice, but undiluted power dragged my gaze to her and I glared up at Morgan, Emissary of the autumn court. Black wings beat rapidly, floating several feet overhead, and blood-red eyes raked over the carnage with the same lack of empathy she'd shown our kind when the laws were passed that banished low fae here.

Morgan had a choice. She came because she wanted what so many of the high fae coveted above all else. Power. In the human realm, there was no one to challenge her. No one to stop her from lording her position over the creatures we were meant to protect. She was given magic, as all high fae were, to protect those beneath her. Instead, she used her station and her gifts to install herself in a role greater than she would have ever achieved in Faerie.

I would have spit in her face if her magic wasn't currently compelling me to stand perfectly still.

"Good Humans," her ethereal voice chimed. "Do not fear, we, the autumn court, will protect you from this disaster."

I ground my teeth. Leave it to Morgan to use this tragic situation to further her own agenda. She snapped pale fingers, and the flames evaporated. Several people gasped. Smoke hissed and choked the sky as the wood continued to collapse in on itself.

She may have been willing to put out the fire, but there was no way a high fae would clean up that mess. "You see," she said. "We turn our cheek to the hands that slap us and provide this gesture of goodwill to show that peace above all else is what we desire with you."

Was she serious? She was going to let them get away with this?

All across the park, people dropped their shovels, swords, and chains and stared up at Morgan.

"Return to your home, humans. Fae who have been displaced, we bid you return to Faerie through the appropriate court access point and receive instruction on your new dwellings." Golden curls framed her face, making her look ethereal as she floated above us all.

I snorted. Only Morgan could make a command sound like a request. The humans may have believed her magnanimous bullshit, but not one of my kind mistook her words for anything other than a summons from their court.

They were expected to return to Faerie. Or else.

She disappeared, and her magic released me.

I glanced back into the dark alley, but Dane and his band of bigots were gone.

My ear twitched as the buzz of murmured voices at my back grew louder—angrier—and I whipped around. The humans she had just saved debated what to do next. Folk were hunched in on themselves, arms secured behind their backs. Some had stakes through their hands and feet, pinning them to the ground.

She hadn't freed them. She hadn't *fucking* freed them.

I scanned the creatures, searching for Brixz or Juniper, but the air was too thick with smoke and the humans had clustered too densely around them for me to tell. These people weren't members of the AFF though, perhaps they would disperse peacefully. As I watched with growing unease, my stomach sank. They wouldn't. What was worse, I was bound. If they killed them right now, I could do nothing about it.

The magic of her command was already beginning to chafe. The compulsion sank into my chest. Every step away from the park sent sparks down my spine. Go home, it whispered. Go. Home.

I *would* return to Faerie, demand we do something about Dane, and free our kind. I would do what Morgan clearly had no intention of doing. But first, I needed to help as many of the fae in Central Park as I could before Dane came back to drag them away, or kill them where they lay.

I left Central Park, turned down Birdie Path, flipping the finger at the NYPD precinct as I passed by several officers huddled inside, and broke into a jog.

Reaching down, I wrenched a shoe off each foot, tossing them into a nearby bush. Bare feet slapping against pavement, I ran around the back of the Met building and down Fifth Ave. A soft chant started in my head as a smile spread across my face. *We don't need no assimilation.*

FOUR

SAV

The ogre crouched farthest from the mob, chains hanging against burning his skin, would be the perfect distraction—if I could free him fast enough. Touching iron was as painful for me as the next fae though. I'd need something to pry those cuffs off and there was no better place to find just such a tool than a museum.

I peered through the window, scouring the dark hallways, and grinned. An exhibit on ancient weapons was only a thin bit of glass away. The best thing about the Renaissance era was its fanciful armor and weapons. Deadly but beautiful.

I drew on the dregs of magic available to me. Sweat broke across my brow as I traced the glass with a sharpened nail.

"Appreciate it." I told the suit of armor holding a gold encrusted sword from somewhere between the seventeenth and eighteenth century, as I slid a hand through the circle I'd made in the glass. This jewel embellished beauty was exactly the sort of thing you might find in Faerie.

The sword was heavy in my palm, but it didn't burn or drain my limited power. The pommel was pure gold.

Continuing around the building until I was just behind the ogre, I leaned close and whispered against his back: "I'm going to free you. Hold still."

The ogre gave the slightest lift of his shoulder, a sharp sizzle sounding as skin met chains. Ogres had it especially bad with iron. Poor fellow.

I slid the sword through one link in the iron chain and hoped it was the stronger of the two. I twisted only twice before it gave a pop and slid apart, grimacing as the slackened chain slid down the ogre's arm, burning him all the way to his wrist.

Looking up, I exhaled softly. The humans still had their backs turned. I twisted again. Cheap iron. It snapped with a pop, clattering to the ground. Their mistake. The second chain clattered to the ground and although the sound was deafening to me, the humans hadn't seemed to notice.

I backed up, ducking behind the building as shouts rose over the sound of a loud roar. Slapping my hand over my mouth to hold in a manic laugh, I settled for imagining humans fleeing in terror as he charged through them. But though his roar was frightening, the ogre wasn't. Harming a human in the human realm was a death sentence if he'd agreed to the laws enacted by the Inter Species Human Fae Alliance, and he must have. All creatures who lived in the human realm had agreed to them.

I poked my head out from behind the building and scowled. The humans had picked up weapons and charged the fae I'd just freed. If they captured him again, I wouldn't save him twice.

As the crowd jabbed at him with their makeshift weapons, I seized the opportunity to slide behind a tree and get close to the next bound fae. Trapped in a birdcage, a small pixie whimpered softly.

"Are you okay?" I whispered.

She nodded, but one of her wings was bent at an odd angle. "If I get the cage door open, could you fly out?"

"I don't think so," she squeaked and tried to lift the damaged wing with little success.

"Crawl out onto my hand and I'll carry you." I leaned over the top of her cage, angling the sword so that it fit between the cage door and the frame. It popped open easily, and she climbed into my hand.

"Watch out!" she yelped just as a hand landed on my shoulder, spinning me around. I dropped the pixie, and she darted behind a tree.

Three humans loomed in front of me, chains in hand. "What do we have here?" one asked. He sneered at me, and I smirked, raising my sword and stepping back on the balls of my feet.

"Come on then, boys." Loosening my grip on the pommel, I twisted toward them.

They grinned. "What a pretty face you have, fairy. Maybe we won't take you straight back to the boss," one man taunted.

The very idea of these filthy, stinking human pigs touching me sent white hot anger burning through my veins. I flicked the sword with two quick motions, and his pants dropped to his ankles. He looked down, frowning, and his two friends laughed. I used the moment of distraction to hook the chains from ugly number two's grasp and toss them several feet away.

"Hey," he bellowed.

"Oops, you dropped that." I winked.

The third little pig charged me, and I aimed my sword directly at his male parts, relishing the thought of running them through with this five-hundred-year-old bacteria infected sword. Humans died easily from those sorts of things.

He was coming too fast and couldn't stop in time.

The magic binding me from harming humans kicked in, jerking my arm to the left and ugly fell on me with all two-hundred-fifty pounds of his girth. We went down hard and grubby hands wrestled my arms to my sides. I threw my knee into his groin and bared my teeth. At least this much I could still do to a human.

The others dropped beside him, pinning my legs to the ground, and the iron chains were clamped around each bare ankle. I mustered what remained of my magic and threw a glamour over my legs, hiding the damage the chains did as they burned into my flesh.

Piggy number two looked confused. "She's not affected by the iron. Are we sure she's a fairy?" he asked the others. They inspected my legs and found nothing but unmarred skin stretching all the way up to my short leather skirt.

"She tried to free the fairies. She must be," said piggy number one.

"Let's have a look at those ears," said piggy number three.

I sent a silent thanks to Mab that I'd had enough magic to glamour my ears when I came to Earth as all they found when tugging aside my loosened knot of hair, were a pair of innocently round lobes.

"What the hell?" Piggy number three stumbled back.

"Even if she's ain't a fairy, she's a fairy sympathizer," said piggy one. He was clearly in charge of this band of losers. "Let's take her to the boss."

They pulled me to my feet roughly. Dark spots danced at the edge of my vision as the iron burning my ankles sent blistering sparks of pain shooting up my calves and I imagined all the ways I would slice off their bits if they ever dared enter my realm.

My gaze shifted past them to the battlefield where our kind had lost this night.

Groups of humans encircled burned, scraped, and bleeding fae. Low park lights cast shadows across the humans' dirt and blood-streaked faces. Even with the magic binding us, we'd put up a fight.

Ash and charred wood clung to everything, painting a dismal scene of the place we'd called home for a brief period. The sour feeling in my stomach hardened into disgust as I watched men and women talking animatedly, laughing and slapping one another on the back while my kind bowed their heads in defeat, the bodies of our brethren visible through the rubble.

The stench of burned flesh hung heavy in the air, making me sick. I counted several dozen fae staked or chained in place, and Dane had taken at least twenty more. It was impossible to tell how many he had captured this night–including me.

I let out a breath when I saw that the ogre I had freed had not been recaptured. With any luck, he had continued running and escaped to...to where? Where could any of us go now that Dane had burned one of the few fae housing units to the ground?

If he was lucky, one of the courts would offer him refuge in Faerie until they decided what to do for the displaced fae. I scanned the wreckage, throat tight. Had anyone else made it out? Was anyone left to tell the courts what happened?

Would my sister hear the news and intervene? There was no love lost between us, but I had to hope that someone had escaped tonight and would bring word back to her. The ache burned up my throat, a scream ready to be loosed on the world. The humans may have wielded the swords, but our kind had let the injustice play out.

Movement near the tree caught my eye and a small green slipper peeked out from behind a thick root. I averted my gaze immediately so as not to draw attention to the pixie hiding there and looked over my shoulder at piggy number one. "So," I said, swallowing the disgust choking my lungs. "Is this where you take me to meet your fearless leader?"

His ugly sneer matched the hate in my heart, and I grinned at him. His meaty hand flew, and I braced as it crashed across my face, and he dragged me toward the alley behind the MET. So much for respecting human women.

FIVE

JACK

I stepped out of a convenience store and began stuffing granola bars in my pockets as I hurried down the sidewalk.

"Watch it," a man grumbled, knocking into my shoulder as he barreled past.

I shifted sideways, ignoring the tension coiling in my shoulders, and slid the final two granola bars in my pockets. I had more important things to worry about today than brawling with someone over cramped sidewalk space. A horn blared, and I jumped out of the way as a cab sped through a red light, nearly taking out everyone crossing.

For as long as I'd lived in New York City, it had been a tempest of boiling tempers and cultural incongruities, but when the fairy realm collided with ours and creatures from another world took over Central Park—creating pocket entrances between our two worlds and erecting fairy houses—the underlying friction had erupted into all-out hostility.

While the fairies intrigued and even enchanted some of us, the vast majority of humankind had let their fear of the unknown settle deep into their bones. Now, the dissidence in the air was so thick, on some days, like today, it was hard to breathe. Our city was alive with roiling anger and panic; a tinderbox ready to ignite at the slightest provocation.

Turning off one-hundred and eleventh, I cut through the park, and slipped into the alley, scanning the dark before reaching in my back pocket to pull out a wrench. Tipping my head back, I scanned the dingy brick facade of the Anti Fae Faction's side entrance for any signs of life. All the windows in the narrow alley were dark, most of the curtains pulled tight to hide the illicit activities that took place inside.

Across from the eight-story apartment building the AFF had confiscated through squatter's rights when all the people surrounding Central Park evacuated, was a derelict building only used by Xcess junkies and the occasional drug lord. No one ever stayed long.

That my mom had survived nearly a year was unheard of. Anger twisted in my gut as I ran my gaze over the empty building.

Seeing no signs of life, I pried the massive bolts securing the secret entrance to Dane's compound loose and set the bar silently against the wall. With Dane and his men occupied by the riots, it was my chance to time an evacuation. The warehouse wasn't quite ready yet, and I wanted at least one practice run before we put the fairies' lives in danger with the actual event.

I traced the path I'd take between the side entrance and our makeshift recovery center twenty-two times, checking my phone several times. Twenty-two was half the number of prisoners being held here and based on their injuries, I'd planned to take two at a time.

It was less than five blocks each way and on my last trip between the two buildings, I checked my phone. Sixty-nine minutes. Better than last time, but unless Dane was attempting something ostentatious like tonight, I needed to drop it to under an hour. Getting some out wasn't good enough. I had to rescue them all.

Although I wasn't ready to spring them just yet, I couldn't leave them with nothing and I had a little time left. Dane had gone all out tonight.

On light feet, I moved down the narrow stairs—once used to receive packages and goods—into the inky cellar where Dane's magical prisoners were now held. Running a hand over rough brick, I relied on the smell and the press of their strange presence to guide me as I descended. A board creaked underfoot, and I winced, but after a moment, when I heard no one coming to investigate, continued on my path. I inhaled a shallow breath as I reached the bottom step. No matter how often I came here, I would never be used to the scent of burning flesh and creatures forced to live in their own filth.

In the near dark, my gaze roved over the dozens upon dozens of cages of all sizes, tossed haphazardly against one another, housing Dane's *prisoners*. Heat swam in my veins. What gave him the right to incarcerate others? I supposed it was the blatant apathy of the general population who turned a blind eye to all he did. Who cheered him on to continue.

A steady drip of some unknown liquid was the only sound in the dim room. The creatures were deathly still, although I knew they weren't dead. Their shadowy outlines stood like statues and only their otherworldliness permeating the space—barely contained within the dingy walls of this dark basement—told me they were still with us.

I scanned the wall opposite mine where an empty folding table and plastic chairs sat. Jim, Oliver and Brian were out, as I'd known they would be. Dane only trusted a select few with guarding the prisoners or even knowing about them, and I'd seen all three at the riot. His trusted trio were likely rounding up the latest batch of prisoners to be brought here. To add to the already dizzying number of creatures he had captured these many months.

Pushing down the simmering anger, I approached the cage closest to the bottom of the stairs. They seemed to sense my moods, and I didn't want to agitate them any more by bringing my rage with me. Black shining eyes met mine and something like a smile crept onto the treelike creature's face. She couldn't eat the granola bars, but my presence cheered her.

"Jack," a fairy whispered, and another repeated my name. Soon they were all shuffling in their cages to face me. I grimaced. There were so many compared with the last time I visited, and the food I brought wasn't enough. It also put a dent in my plan. Unless I could carry three at a time, I'd need a bigger window of time to evacuate. That or convince Leo, my best friend, to take a more active role in my plan.

A satyr who hadn't been here two nights ago slid her tufted hand through the bars, careful to avoid touching them, and I handed her a stack of granola bars. She passed them to those closest to her.

An enormous creature with skin charred all along his back didn't turn to me when I approached. Didn't acknowledge my presence. My stomach threatened to heave as I took in the sight of all his terrible burns. He was new. Probably brought in earlier today to ensure their plan went off without a hitch. Dane enjoyed stacking the deck in his favor before he executed a mission. It was what made him an effective leader.

My jaw locked as I crouched beside the cage. Soon. Soon I would put an end to all of this.

"Hey," I whispered. "I know you don't know me and you probably don't trust humans, but I want to help." I held out the bar, but he continued to ignore me. Iron burned into his already blackened skin, sizzling. "I'll leave it here. Don't let the guards see it. They'll punish you."

I moved to the darkest corner of the room at the very back, trying hard to ignore the crumpled form of the creature I'd spent more than a month convincing to trust me enough to take what little I could offer, and held two strawberry oat bars out.

Cool, scaled skin brushed my palm as a nymph snatched the food from my hand and moved deeper into the shadows and away from me. They didn't eat meat, which I'd learned the hard way when I'd tried to bring down food from the kitchens, but the ones with scales would eat fish and fruit. I hoped the strawberry bars would be close enough.

"Give me your wrappers," I whispered, holding my hand out. The wrapper crackled loudly, and a ball of plastic hit the side of my face. I couldn't blame the creature—any of them, really—for any of the harsh things they said or did. They hated us for the way we treated them, and we deserved it. I wouldn't tell them what we were planning, though. If Dane interrogated them—if he learned of my plan—these creatures would never be free.

Boots scraped loudly at the top of the stairs, and I glanced around the room, giving them all a warning look. I didn't need to warn them, though. They all had far better hearing than I did and in moments, most were handing their wrappers to the satyr who waited by her bars for me to come around.

She handed me the pile, and I crammed them in my pockets, wincing when the sound scraped against my ears.

"I'll be back soon. Next time I'll bring medicine," I whispered, and several creatures looked at me with so much hope in their eyes, something twisted in my stomach. I hated leaving them down here, hated watching them suffer with every fiber of my being, but Dane was no fool. When we came for them, we had to be ready.

Racing back up the stairs, I set the bar over the door and screwed both bolts in place.

When I was sure no one had heard or seen me, I stepped out of the alley and rounded the corner to the AFF headquarters' main entrance and knocked three times, paused, knocked twice more, paused and knocked again.

Six

Sav

They yanked me along, rough hands biting into my arms. I didn't fight. Not yet. Let the idiots lead me to their lair.

A plain black door with a thick metal bar bolted across it, just a few feet into the alley, appeared to be our destination. The bolt looked far too large for humans to lift without the aid of magic.

I tried to peer over Piggy number one's shoulder as he produced a wrench from somewhere inside his jacket and began twisting the bolts that held the metal bar in place. It came loose and, with some disappointment, I watched as the bar lifted easily.

No magic use happening here. The "iron" clattered to the ground—plastic. My lip curled. The door swung open, revealing narrow stairs leading down into a dank room. Iron permeated the space, and a low headache settled behind my eyes. This was their true defense. No fae would willingly enter this place.

Piggy number two swiveled his head around, leering at me as we descended the steps and I painted a look of indifference on my face, praying to Mab I wouldn't retch right here in front of them. He was still looking back at me when the horror of the next room came into view.

Cages of all sizes were crammed into the space, leaving very little room to stand and in almost every one was a creature. Some were small, like the pixie I had just released, while others were so large the bars melted into flesh where it burned them. If the smell of iron had not overpowered me, I would have noticed the acrid scent of charred fae flesh immediately.

Now, though, faced with so much misery, I forced the bile down.

Piggy two smiled at me, revealing broken craggy teeth that might have

29

given a goblin a run for his money. I shuddered, gaze shifting to an emaciated fae in the corner, and my heart shattered for the kelpie who had clearly been here for some time. Kelpies were wildly powerful creatures. They could have only caught him with a bargain.

My gaze jumped cage to cage. Scorched skin, split lips, eyes dulled from pain. Something in my chest cracked. This wasn't new. They'd been doing this for far longer than we'd guessed. I searched their faces, memorizing them and making a silent promise to avenge them all. Ogres, wilden, dryads, satyrs, nymphs, hobgoblins, and even a troll were packed into every available space.

My gaze landed on a sandy-haired satyr. "Juniper," I breathed.

Her shining honey-colored eyes locked on mine, and I watched her mouth the word *Shit*. I gave an infinitesimal shake of my head, and she averted her gaze. The three piggies pulled me to the closest empty cage, grabbing a ring of iron keys from the wall and unlocking it.

"Aren't you going to take these chains off?" I asked, shaking my leg at them.

Piggy number one scoffed.

"It's not as if I can escape a cage. Do I really need both?"

He raised an eyebrow. "You deserve those chains, fairy lover." He spat in my face and slammed the door, locking me in.

I leaned casually against the bars without allowing my skin to touch them. If I could continue to convince them I was human, perhaps they would eventually let me go, but I could only keep up this charade so long, sitting in a cage surrounded by iron.

They paid me no more attention as they crowded around a small table in the room's corner. Piggy number two opened a mini-fridge and pulled out three beers. They sat, drinking and joking as if the sight of tortured, starving fae was commonplace. And for them, perhaps it was. Murderous thoughts danced through my mind, and I entertained myself by picturing each one screaming, begging for his life as I scraped sinew from his bones, slowly roasting him on a spit.

"It's no use," a silky voice said in my ear. I knew better than to turn toward it. The pitched voice was deliberately intended to elude human detection.

"How long have you been here?" I asked, glaring at my captors.

"Three days, six hours and nine minutes," she hissed. "And not once have we been let out of these cages. Not to pee. Not to eat. Not even when we die."

I turned at that, staring at the wood nymph whose deep brown, bark-like eyes were cast down, gazing at the broken branches that hemmed her feet. Her forlorn expression sent a chill down my spine.

"Some have died here?" I whispered.

She raised a finger, which once would have been suffused with budding seedlings and growth, but was now brittle and dry, pointing it toward the darkest corner of the room. My hand flew to my mouth.

"It can't be," I stammered. "How?"

"She died the day I arrived," the nymph breathed. I heard the sorrow in her voice.

A tear came unbidden to the corner of my eye. I had underestimated these humans. Killing the winter hag was no easy feat. Mab would raze this place to the ground—if she were still out there. But Faerie hadn't seen her in years, and every court was crumbling without her.

The door flew open, shaking me from my thoughts and two more men stepped in, one holding a small birdcage and the other dragging a large gray-skinned urisk behind him. His tusks, sliding between charcoal lips, were sharpened to points, and the metal at each tip gleamed wickedly in the light cutting through the inky dark from atop the stairs. He bucked against their hold, but the iron chains around his thick arms hissed when they dug into flesh. I scanned his leathery skin for any sign of the deadly weapons his kind wielded, and exhaled a long breath when I saw none, despair settling on my shoulders like a heavy blanket.

They set the small cage housing the pixie I'd tried to save before down beside me and I winced as she stared up at me and began to sob.

"Don't cry," I whispered. "We'll get out of here."

She turned away from me, her broken wing curling tightly against her back, and sniffled loudly for such a little creature.

My attention flew to the urisk as he struggled against the men in earnest. He wrenched one arm out of his shackle, tossing it to the ground. As he did, two sets of arms sprouted on his back, and he used them to grab two by the neck.

Piggy one shouted orders even as he gurgled in the urisk's tight grip. Piggy three grabbed the pitchfork leaning beside him and began jabbing it at the creature. The urisk swatted it away with little effort as he throttled the two men he'd come in with. He roared as Piggy One plunged a knife deep into his side and flung him at the brick lining the room. A crack sounded before Piggy One slid down the wall, eyes fluttering closed.

Piggy Three was inching around to his blind side. "Look out!" I shouted.

The urisk whirled, knocking Piggy Three to the floor, holding fast to Piggy Two who was turning blue in his fist.

I marveled at his ability to harm the humans, wondering how he made it to Earth without making the bargain that forbade him from harming them. Perhaps he was just that strong. Was he fighting it? Could we all?

Something twinkled across the room, and my lips stretched into a grin when I spotted the sword I'd used earlier. It was out of reach, though, and I didn't have enough magic left to do anything besides glamour the burned skin around my ankles.

The wood nymph next to me extended her arm, pushing her branches toward me. A small green bud appeared on her forearm. I held my breath as it slowly sprouted and stretched into a sapling.

Wood nymphs, who could normally raise an entire tree in a few days, found themselves severely diminished in the new world. The effort she expended now was immense and proved just how powerful she once was. The sapling had thickened into a branch, and she extended it to me through the bars.

"I don't want to hurt you."

"You cannot harm me more than they already have." Her gaze dropped to the branches piled beneath her.

"Are you sure?" I held my breath, touched by her desire to aid me.

She nodded.

Gently, I wrapped my fingers around her forearm and bent the wood. It gave a crack and came free.

Her breath hitched, but she didn't cry out. Sap welled from the jagged break, and with shaking fingers, she tucked a leaf from her tangled hair over the wound.

I dipped my head to her in appreciation, and turned to my bars to pry them loose, glancing up as one piggy stumbled into the wall and collapsed. Sliding the malleable wood between iron, I wrapped it around them. On my butt, in the dirt, I lifted both legs, resting a bare foot against the bars, wincing at the burn, and tugged.

It didn't budge. I pulled again, straining against the pain scorching the soles of my feet and I wished for the barest moment I hadn't tossed the shoes I was wearing earlier. The bar gave slightly, and I let out a small whoop.

Chairs and weapons flew in all directions as the urisk continued to fight his attackers, who were all standing again, but I gritted my teeth and pulled harder. The iron was truly bending and sweat trickled down my back as searing agony radiated across the pads of my feet, but I kept pulling.

A loud crack rang out, and at once everything stopped.

I looked up, loosening my hold on the branch.

The urisk released the three men he now had hold of, wrapping his arms over his middle, and all five humans looked up.

A shadow blocked the light at the top of the stairs. Heavy boots thudded loudly. Then his face emerged from darkness. *Dane Clyde.* He leveled his gun toward the urisk and deftly fired three more shots. The urisk dropped so quickly, those bullets could only be made of iron.

I scrambled back from the bars and tucked my branch behind me.

Dane swaggered in, shaking his head at the men struggling to climb to their feet. "I bagged that urisk for you myself. What have I told you about allowing one to free a hand?" He tsked. "If we are to win this war, we must outthink the beasts."

The three piggies looked anywhere but at their leader, while the other two humans leaned heavily into the wall, faces pale. They picked up broken chairs and righted the table, stepping over the dead creature.

Dane turned his attention to the cages, crowding the room with his massive ego. His gaze landed on me. "What do we have here?"

"She's a dirty fairy-loving bitch," Piggy One spoke up.

"She's human?" Dane asked incredulously.

"We caught her trying to free the beasts in the park."

Dane stepped closer, staring down at me, and I lifted my chin. He inspected my unblemished skin beneath the chains around my ankles and stroked his stubbled chin. "How could you betray your own kind?"

My throat was sticky and dry, all my standard snarky replies stuck to the roof of my mouth.

Piggy One glared at me. "She let loose that ogre that clobbered Connor. Jack had to take him to get stitches."

"Did you?" he asked me.

I squared my shoulders, meeting his gaze. "Would you treat a dog the way you've treated the fae?"

"A dog can be trained. And when a dog bites his master, you put him down."

I bit my tongue so hard I tasted blood.

Dane smiled, but it was a cruel smile, full of sharp angles and teeth. "What is it then? Was he your supplier? Are you an addict?"

I could have laughed. He thought I was one of the human groupies who had become addicted to Xcess? I showed none of the signs, but perhaps in my current state...

Humans felt invincible for the short while Xcess coursed through their veins. But it exacted a heavy toll. Most went mad within a few weeks of its continued use, and none had the power to resist its call once they had a taste for it. Its unexpected ability to awaken the latent magic almost all people possessed to a fractional degree made them feel immortal. But it lasted only as long as it survived in their system. The moment it metabolized, a mundane human was all that was left, leaving an ache for the magic they didn't have.

And I knew something about how that ache felt. It was no wonder they paid top dollar.

"I don't do drugs." I snapped.

"You have a fairy boyfriend, then?" He tilted his head. "Or girlfriend?"

I glared up at him. "I already told you why I was freeing them. They are alive, and no cre—animal deserves to be in a cage."

"Come here," he commanded and reached behind him to grab the keys from the wall. I leaned forward, careful to only allow my covered shoulder to brush the bars as I did.

He unlocked the door and held a hand out to me.

I swallowed down my revulsion, hesitating for only a second before I slid my hand into his outstretched one. For the briefest moment, I imagined wrapping both hands around his neck and squeezing. I imagined ramming my thumbs through both eyes and pressing until blood ran down my fingers and his screams filled my ears.

He pulled me up gently for a man who had just killed someone in cold blood and left his corpse to rot on the floor. He brought my face within inches of his own and stared deeply into my eyes.

I stared back, counting to four in my head, then I averted my gaze, careful to look in the opposite direction from the dead urisk.

He grabbed my chin, twisting my head to the left and checked my ears.

"We checked that first. You think we're stupid?" Piggy One called out.

Dane ignored him and turned my head right for good measure. He pushed my hair more gently this time, trailing his finger down my cheek as it dropped away. My breath caught in an imitation of a flustered human, and my stomach turned as I smelled his pheromones, delighting in the dominance he thought he held over me.

It was a genuine effort not to roll my eyes.

"I think this one just needs a little re-education," he said softly. "Let's bring her upstairs and give her a proper introduction to our group."

I did everything in my power not to turn and look at Juniper, or the nymph who had given a limb to save me as they led me, still in chains, out of the room where I belonged and into the viper's nest.

SEVEN

JACK

I shoved another granola wrapper into the trash, collapsed onto my bed, and let the ceiling blur. Worst day since the realms collided, and that was saying something.

When my mother died, I thought that was rock bottom, that life couldn't get any worse. I was wrong. The discovery of creatures should have been exciting. It should have been a reason to celebrate. With the formation of the Inter Species Human Fae Alliance, rules were put in place to keep us safe and ensure a peaceful coexistence, but instead, the ISHFA had only given people like Dane power.

I had never fit in—not in high school, not in med school, not here. Being six-four with only one true desire, helping people–even after the world was on fire, hadn't won me many friends.

A knock sounded at my door, and I sat up. "Yes?"

"Jack. Kyle's asking for you in the kitchen."

I winced at Alice's cloying voice, but stood, tugging down my shirt and stepped through the door.

In the hall, I side-stepped her, ignoring the hopeful look in her corn-flower-blue eyes. She trailed me and my skin prickled as I felt her gaze on my back. I resisted the urge to whip around and tell her to stop.

It wasn't just that she wasn't my type physically. Her devotion to Dane and his cause turned my stomach every time I thought of it. Of the horrible atrocities the AFF committed on the fairies, simply because they differed from us. I'd never feel anything but disgust for the people who lived here, and Alice was no exception.

In the kitchen, I glanced around before moving to the corner and dumping my trash into one of the larger bins. I tossed a few paper towels on top and set my trash down beside it. Alice stepped through the door, opening her mouth to speak, but I cut her off before she could spout some new nonsense about Dane's greatness or worse, her feelings for me. "Hey Alice, if you're going back up, would you take my trash can to my room?"

She beamed at me, grabbed the bin with far too much enthusiasm, and disappeared into the hall.

"Better watch out for that one. Give her a kind word and her stuff will be moved in by the weekend." Kyle slid his spatula under a slice of bacon and flipped it.

"She's harmless." I forced a grin, but the bacon sizzling behind Kyle was too loud, reminding me of burned flesh and my stomach soured.

Kyle slapped me on the back. "Got a tray o' food for a new guest. Dane wants me to take it to her, but I'm slammed. Can you bring it up for me?"

I nodded, taking the tray from the counter. Another person joining Dane's group. Every day more came. Every day, more people hated the fairies enough to give up all their worldly possessions and move into the compound.

"Oh, Jack! I almost forgot."

"Yeah?" I turned in the doorway.

"She can't leave her room."

I arched a brow. "What?"

"She was caught trying to free the fairies. Dane wants her to stay here until she's learned her lesson."

A chill ran down my spine. Then something else bloomed beneath it. Hope. Fragile and reckless. Someone else was fighting back. I schooled my face into neutral indifference even as my heart picked up speed.

Living so long among the fanatics at the AFF, I'd almost given up hope that there were any honorable people left apart from my two best friends, Grace and Leo. Every day I listened to the vitriol that spewed from AFF members' hateful mouths and nodded, pretending I agreed with them all so I could gather the information we needed to put a stop to Dane for good. But if a person had been caught trying to help the fairies, perhaps we could recruit her to our cause.

Currently, we were a party of three, not nearly enough to accomplish all we planned, but it had been too risky to attempt bringing anyone else in with us. Though some people had welcomed the creatures, the tide had been shifting and the violence brimming under the surface made those who might have once spoken up fearful of being caught on the wrong side of a war.

I couldn't remember the last time I felt this pull toward something that wasn't survival.

EIGHT

SAV

Upstairs was only slightly better than the basement. The same sour odor permeated every surface of the derelict building. Walking the halls was like playing a game of Tic Tac Toe except you had to jump holes rotting through the floor.

I stumbled awkwardly, hoping I was doing a fair impression of a clumsy human, and kept my eyes pinned on my feet. In truth, the soles of my feet hadn't entirely healed yet and walking on the angry flesh still burned.

Dane led me to a room near the end of the third-floor hall and pulled a silver key from his pocket. He unlocked the door, ushering me inside.

One mattress was tossed on the floor, and across from it, a narrow bed on a thin wooden frame was neatly made. I didn't need to ask which was mine. My mattress had no sheets, the window was barred with iron, and the closet door had been removed from its hinges. So only a slight downgrade from the home this man had recently evicted me from.

Dane cleared his throat.

My gaze shot to the vile being crowding the doorframe.

"You have a roommate. Alice should be back later. Dinner is at eight in the lobby. I'll let you settle in tonight, but tomorrow morning, you will begin your re-education."

"So, I'm a prisoner?" I asked, darting a quick glance up at him before staring down at the stained floor.

He smiled that same cruel smile. "Of course not. But we wouldn't want you to go wandering around anywhere you shouldn't, setting any monsters free." His eyes danced with dark amusement. "Think of this as a

39

temporary situation. Once you learn the truth, you will understand why it's too dangerous for them to live among us."

I frowned at my feet. "But it will be impossible for me to sleep tonight with these heavy things on." My words dripped with honey.

He stepped into the room, and I flinched. The scent of the arousal that wafted from him made me grimace. I had known this was a sick human, but this...Anyone who got off on the fear of others was wretched. And he called us monsters.

I planted my feet as he continued toward me.

He pinched my chin, thumb digging into my jaw. My blood flared hot —but I didn't look away fast enough. His grip tightened. My error in judgment might cost me, but I couldn't bow to this demon.

He swallowed whatever he had been about to say. "You're a strong girl," he said. "You will manage it." He turned and left the room.

To my surprise, he didn't lock the door behind him.

I sank onto the bed, taking deep, calming breaths. It was so much worse than I thought. I wasn't just in one of their camps, this was their headquarters. If they found me out, there would be no escape. I'd be right back where I started, rotting in a cage until my jailers scraped out my remains to make space for a new prisoner.

With the binding on my magic and on my ability to harm a human, I was helpless without the aid of a fae army. The realization settled into my bones. I owed it to the fae below my feet to help. I owed it to them to escape this place and bring back an army to rescue them.

❖ ❖ ❖

My stomach was in knots as I thought of everyone just below, starving and in pain. Shuffling onto my side, I lay my head on the vile-smelling mattress and closed my eyes to think. I would need the aid of the courts. Morgan had been of no help. With Mab still missing, I would be at the mercy of one of the princes or princesses for support.

Autumn wasn't an option. They'd sealed their borders years ago. Summer. Never. That left Winter or Spring. I scoffed aloud. Winter. I would go to Winter.

A knock sounded at the door, startling my eyes open.

"Yes." I bit the words out sharply.

"I have your dinner," came a smooth male voice.

"I'm not hungry." A long pause followed, and I wondered if he'd left.

"I can leave it outside," he finally replied.

I huffed and got up, throwing the door wide.

My stomach twisted as I opened the door. *Him.* The stranger from the riot. So he *was* one of them. My fingers clenched the tray tightly as I slammed the door in his face.

"I hope you like it," he called through wood.

I yanked the door open and shoved the food back into his still raised hands. "I don't want this. I want nothing from you." I glared at him.

"I get it. I wouldn't want anything from anyone at the AFF either, but you'll need food to keep your strength up," he whispered as he glanced over his shoulder.

I eyed him, taking him in under harsh false light. He was tall, as I'd remembered, raven hair falling in waves to shoulders that nearly filled the doorframe. None of that was what captured my attention, though. His eyes, a deep emerald, sparked with barely contained fury and the yellow starburst surrounding his irises gave them the appearance of a fae's. *Beautiful.* I grimaced, banishing that horrid thought from my mind.

"Come in." I backed up, giving him plenty of space to enter. Was I wrong about him? He looked human, dressed human, but there was something...

Balancing the tray in one hand, he stepped through the door and into my small room. Electricity charged the air, making the tiny hairs on my arm stand on end. He smelled like pine and woodsmoke and something dangerously inhuman. I told myself to stay focused, but my body hadn't gotten the memo.

I backed up, dropping to the low mattress.

He moved with me, sitting on the bed across from mine, knees bending awkwardly in the small space, and held out the tray of food.

I took it, setting it down beside me, and picked up the stale bread, tearing into it with my teeth.

Dark brows rose and some of the anger simmering in his eyes banked as his lips tipped up. "Glad to see you haven't lost your appetite."

"You said I needed my strength." I ran a hand down my thigh, wiping crumbs from my tanned skin. His gaze dropped to my fingers, tracking the movement, and I bit back a smile. Typical man. I could use that. "You know what I really need?"

Piercing viridian eyes shot to my face. "What's that?" White teeth flashed, and for the barest moment, his sharp edges softened. I wondered absently what had happened to make him so hard.

He's human. I reminded myself. *It doesn't matter.*

"The key to these chains." My gaze fell to the chains still burning against my red, angry flesh. He couldn't see it or smell it. Glamours were useful that way, but they didn't hide the pain that made me want to weep when I thought about it for too long. At least it drowned the tug of Morgan's summons to return home.

A raven brow shot up. "Why *did* they chain you up?"

I ground my teeth. "Never mind. I don't need your *help*. You can find your way out, I'm sure. The door's right there." I leaned for the tray and pain spiked sharp and bright as the iron scraped bone. I bit back the scream clawing its way up my throat.

"Are you hurt?" he asked, and there was genuine concern in his voice.

I scrambled desperately for something to say that wouldn't draw attention to my burned flesh. "One of those men must have hit me harder than I thought. My head is pounding." I rubbed my temple for emphasis.

"I can get you some aspirin." He leaned closer, gaze scouring my head for said injury.

"No," I gasped, leaning back. "I just need a bit of air. It would help clear my head. I'm feeling...Dizzy."

I shifted my leg, attempting to move the iron away from the bone that was screaming in agony, and his gaze slid down my bare skin. Toward the chain. Alarm bells sounded in my head. Had my glamour slipped? Would he see what I truly was and drag me back downstairs?

Reaching for his hand, I laced my fingers through his. "Could you take me...outside?"

He looked up, searching my face. His heart beat rapidly in his chest, but I couldn't tell if it was because he had figured out what I was or if he was considering breaking his faction's rules.

His gaze dropped to my mouth and my fingers tightened around his reflexively, warmth flaring to life in my chest.

I released his hand, scooting back. What was wrong with me? He was my enemy. My fingers were cold and clammy, and I squeezed them into fists. I had to get control of this situation. This human man was the first person here who hadn't treated me like...a fae.

I had to use that.

He looked away, jaw tightening. "I...can't." Something flashed in his eyes and his gaze fell on me again. "Why did you free those fairies tonight?"

My heart rate picked up speed. He knew about that. Damn. So much for asking for his help. Like all the other cult members here, he probably assumed I deserved this punishment. "I...Wasn't. Those men called me a fairy, and they were going to lock me up." I glanced at my leg. "Is it a crime to fight back against your attackers?"

He searched my face for a long moment. "So, you weren't helping them?"

I forced a laugh between my teeth. "Why would I help those animals?"

He stood, moving to the door. My chance was about to walk out and leave me alone. I hopped up and didn't need to fake the shake in my knees. The pain of the chains overwhelmed my senses, and desperation weighed me down, pulling me toward a spiral of anxiety. I would be trapped here in AFF headquarters and all the fae below–the ones who were counting on me–would die.

"Ow," I cried, falling to the floor and sniffling softly.

He knelt beside me, resting a hand on my back. "Is it your head? Let me get you some water. Or aspirin."

I looked up, wiping a tear from my cheek. At least some of the pain wasn't an act. I *was* desperate for his help. "If I could get these chains off, I could rest for the night. Maybe then I'd feel a little better in the morning."

"Yes." He sounded more confident this time. "Wait here. I'll be right back." He stood, rushing from the room.

My shoulders slumped, some of the tension bleeding from me. Let him come back. Let him believe I was broken. When night fell, I'd be gone.

NINE

SAV

Heavy footfall pounded in the hall, and I looked up when dark curls swung into the room. He was back, kneeling beside me, and my heart sped up when he lifted my leg, placing it atop his thigh. Panic flared. Would the glamour hold, or would blood soak into his jeans and give me away? All thoughts fled as iron scraped over virgin skin and veins bulged along my neck with the effort of holding in my tortured scream. In moments, the key was turning and one leg was free.

"What do you think you're doing?" a voice demanded from the hallway. I had been so focused on the pain that I hadn't heard the approaching woman who now framed the doorway. She was thin and mousy with no curves to speak of and a pale complexion that made her seem sickly.

The man beside me looked up, startled, and a guilty expression crossed his face. He said nothing as they stared at each other.

"I'm getting your dad," she declared, breaking their silent standoff, and spun on her heel.

"No!" He dropped my leg, leaving the other chained, and ran after her.

The haughty girl storming away explained a lot. He had been dragged into this cult by a girlfriend or a father, or both.

Clipped words wafted down the hall and away from me. She didn't trust me and neither did their fearless leader and he was an idiot, blah blah, blah. I got the sense that this was more of a lover's quarrel than genuine concern. They were far enough now that I couldn't make out their conversation, which also meant they wouldn't hear me.

It was risky. The odds of escape on my own were far less likely than the eventual help from the green-eyed man, but relying on a human would never be my first choice.

I stood, rolling my free ankle. The damage was severe, but it was healing. Some magic remained buried in me, after all. Or perhaps as a cruel joke, my sister had not bound my healing magic to ensure I would suffer long in this world with no easy escape into the after. I could imagine her doing just that.

I stepped into the hall and moved in the same direction I'd heard the voices go. The loose chain scraped over linoleum, making enough noise I half expected someone to dart out of one of the many doors I passed and wrestle me to the ground, but I couldn't risk touching it and burning my hands. Harsh fluorescent lights illuminated faded wallpaper and molding corners along my narrow path. My ankle throbbed, vision swimming, but I didn't stop. I couldn't.

How I wished for the wood nymph. What destruction she could bring to this horrid prison. I choked on the thought. My cage paled in comparison to the one that sapped her life just a few floors below. I picked up speed. Those creatures needed me to escape. They needed me to bring down this place and its vile leader.

I came to the end of the hall looking left, then right. The halls were identical to the one I'd just come down with nothing to distinguish one from another. It was a maze of tan doors and stained linoleum floors, and I wasn't sure I'd ever escape.

I went left, begging Mab for aid in choosing wisely as my heart beat a frantic rhythm in my chest. Too slow, I was moving too slow. I picked up my pace, wincing as the iron bounced up and down on the bone of my ankle and bit back a shout of pain when it sliced through skin.

I heard it then, feet stomping at a clipped pace as they neared. Glancing around, I tried the first two doors near me. Locked. Damn. My hands were slick as I squeezed the next, finding it locked too. As the pounding of feet grew closer, I swallowed hard and leaned against the wall, sucking in labored breaths.

Dane Clyde rounded the corner, eyes landing on me. The man and woman who'd left to find his dad came next. Dane closed the distance, getting right up in my face. I held my breath, leaning back to put as much space between us as I could in the confined hall.

He gave me a hard stare before bending down and inspecting my free ankle. The pair behind Dane said nothing as he spent several moments looking over my bare skin. His gaze crawled up my leg and stalled on my chest. Disgust curdled in my stomach.

"Jack," he called without turning his gaze from me. The man with emerald eyes, Jack, stepped forward. "Do you know why this girl is staying with us?" Dane didn't wait for an answer, barreling on. "She was caught freeing the fae animals at the protest today."

Jack's eyes met mine, a look of admonishment in them for my earlier lie. "Does that give you the right to chain her?" He raised a brow at me when he asked the question. What did that mean? Had he wanted me to free them? Would he have helped me if I'd told the truth?

The pause that followed hung heavy in the air.

Dane's voice was steely when he answered. "We have more than fifty monsters in cages just below our feet. What do you think would happen if this fairy lover released even a handful of them?"

Jack said nothing, his gaze hard on the back of Dane's head. For a moment, I wondered if this human hated Dane more than I did. The rage radiating off him in thick waves was enough to make me swallow.

I pressed against the wall, desperate to be free of both of them—of all the humans I'd been forced to endure these three years in their realm.

Jack's gaze flicked back to me, some of the fury in his eyes banking, and Dane swore, spittle landing on my cheek. "If she freed even *one* of them, we could all be dead, Son."

Son? Evil incarnate had spawned a child, and it was...Jack? That couldn't be right. I looked between them. Strong jawline, impressive height for a human male. Same dark hair, although Dane's was cropped short and graying at the temples.

It was true.

Revulsion rolled through me. I had asked Dane Clyde's son for help. I was going to be sick.

The group was all watching me now and every moment that ticked by felt one closer to the bars sealing me in this hell forever. I had to do something, had to find a way out of this mess, even if it meant playing along.

I slumped to the floor, tears rimming my lashes. "I just... I can't stand to see animals hurt," I whispered. "Even the ones that scare me."

Jack moved toward me, but Dane held up a hand. "She's playing you, Son."

The lack of emotion in his voice and the immediacy with which he had seen through me caught me off guard. I covered my surprise with another sob.

"She's scared," Jack said and tried to push past his father.

Dane held him fast. "She sees your soft heart and plans to use it. But listen to me, I can help her understand how dangerous those monsters really are. Don't you want me to help her?"

Fear bubbled up my chest. The man was far too cunning for his kind. I wasn't entirely sure I wasn't in some sort of trap of his making.

Jack stopped resisting his father's hold, and his jaw set in a hard line. "You can't treat people like animals, *Dane*."

My gaze swiveled between them, waiting to see how it would play out.

My stomach sank as Jack shoved his father's shoulder and marched down the hall. Away from me.

"Alice, take our new guest back to your room so she doesn't get lost. If she behaves herself, perhaps tomorrow night we'll show her to the showers and a change of clothes. Tonight, let her sleep in her filth to remind her what she'd done." Dane said.

The mousy girl with dishwater brown hair and too-large eyes stepped forward for the first time since Dane had arrived. She held out a hand to help me up, but I didn't take it as I balanced against the wall and stood.

"Just go." She tried for an authoritative tone, but there was a tremor in her voice.

Narrowing my eyes at her, I pushed off the wall and turned, limping forward.

"Wait." Dane's voice was low.

I froze, ice leaching into my veins as I held my breath.

He strode down the hall, taking up more space than was necessary as he nudged past us and his big hand fell heavily on my shoulder and spun me around. He leaned down and plucked the loose chain I had been dragging from the floor. "Your leg, please."

I bit the inside of my cheek and lifted my leg obediently, setting my foot on his thigh. My spine straightened as I glared down at the top of his head. He secured the metal around my still-healing ankle, and I imagined three painful deaths for him in the time it took him to finish.

He stared pointedly, waiting for me to remove my bare foot from his leg.

Hot blood pounded through my veins, lighting a fire in my belly that begged for his death. I made that silent promise as he stood, brushing off the dirty footprint I had left behind. I would *kill* Dane Clyde.

"Have a good night, ladies," he said.

I smiled. Not for him, but for the promise I'd etched into my heart. And a fae always kept their promise.

TEN

JACK

I turned over in my bed, punched the pillow, and closed my eyes. The woman's wild eyes haunted me—the way her foot trembled on Dane's thigh, how she bit back the embarrassment and pain. I'd never forget the iron clamped around her ankle... or the fury that lit her face.

Though my temper had gotten the better of me, I couldn't help the urge to turn back. I'd stopped at the end of the hall, watching as Dane ordered her to place her foot on his thigh and heat sizzled in my veins when he clamped the chain around her leg once more.

She *had* been helping the fairies. Of course she wouldn't admit it to me. She was in chains for it, and I was just another AFF member to her.

I jabbed the heel of my palm into my pillow again, resisting the urge to march back to her room and release her right now.

When she'd asked for my help, I'd been gutted. It wasn't in my nature to sit by while anyone suffered, but such an overt act of defiance would undo all my work. Dane was intent on making a lesson out of her and if I freed her now, my cover would be blown. With Alice as her jailer, I couldn't do anything at present, but I wouldn't leave her behind when I freed the fairies beneath Dane's compound.

--●→(↲●▲◆●●-

Eyes sliding open, I blinked a few times, waiting for the room to solidify into recognizable shapes. My first thought was of the woman trapped here. How had she slept? On a dirty mattress on the floor with chains around her ankles, it wasn't hard to guess.

Sitting up, I rubbed my neck. I never slept well after my mom passed, but ever since I'd left college and moved into the now AFF headquarters three years ago, I was lucky if I got four hours a night. When I moved in, it was meant to be temporary. I hadn't known what Dane was up to. When I arrived and learned he wasn't just squatting in a building near the pocket entrances to Faerie—he was organizing a revolution against the creatures —I knew I had to stop him.

When I learned he had taken prisoners, it became clear he must be shut down for good.

The linchpin to my plan was my anonymity. No one would suspect the son of the AFF leader of duplicity. At least not as long as I wasn't caught. That meant I couldn't risk helping the fairies escape until the rest of my plan had been set in motion. The day I freed them, I would need to leave this place behind, knowing it would all fall.

I dressed quickly, sliding on a pair of jeans and a black tee. I wanted to be out of the compound before anyone was truly awake.

Slipping out the side exit reserved for high command and...me, I crossed the street and stepped into my favorite morning coffee shop.

"Jack!" Leo called.

I frowned as I stepped up to the counter.

"What's a matter?" Leo leaned his elbows onto the glass counter and although there was a line of customers, gave me all his attention.

Leo was my first real friend in the city, and when I'd told him of my mad plan, he hadn't blinked. A former naval intelligence officer, he'd been eager to put his hacking skills to use, doing something good. It didn't hurt that he owned the coffee shop across the street from AFF headquarters, which made it the best place to meet. We never communicated via text or emails, knowing all too well how easy it was to hack devices. We discussed everything in person after the room was swept for bugs.

We'd learned a lot about Dane's operation since Leo joined my cause over a year ago, and most recently, Leo was tracking the source of large payments Dane had begun receiving over the past several months. Before, Dane relied on the money donated by AFF initiates to fund his mission. That he now had a new source of funds from an anonymous donor worried us all.

"Coffee. three sugars." It was code for 'we need to talk.'

Leo jerked his head to the side, letting me know some of my father's devotees were already here. I glanced left and grimaced when I spied his three armed guards perched around a high top, sipping coffee. Oliver, Jim, and Brian always traveled in a pack. Of course they were here. They were likely celebrating their night's success. Disgust simmered in my gut.

"I just got a shipment this morning. I'll be right back."

I dipped my chin. "Take your time. I need to use the restroom."

Leo went first, and I followed, moving past the restroom to his office.

I closed the door behind me and waited in silence as Leo swept the room. He nodded, giving the all-clear, and I moved to a chair in the corner. "Dane has a woman chained inside the compound for attempting to help the fairies last night. I have to get her out when we free the others."

Leo's thick brows bunched over his nose. "I have something more important."

I straightened. "Did you find the source?"

He nodded. "It's much worse than we thought."

My stomach dropped. I'd speculated over who the new donor could be for weeks, naming several outspoken celebrities and political figures who might be eager to see Dane carry out his campaign.

"The money is coming from Janet Glassdon."

My throat went dry. Worse was an understatement. My knuckles turned white as I gripped the chair arm. "Janet Glassdon. Co-council leader of the Inter Species Human Fae Alliance? Why? Why would she want Dane to succeed? She helped create that council to ensure peace between our kinds."

Leo shrugged. "Took me a long time to trace. It was buried under so many dummy corporations I almost didn't find it. But she slipped." He shook his head. "They always do."

Prying my fingers off the chair arm, I stood, stuffing my hands in my pockets and paced the room. Janet Glassdon was the last person I'd ever expect to support my father. She was extremely vocal about her views on the alliance and instrumental in pushing forward cohabitation laws. She'd also been the first to initiate the no interspecies relationships laws, but she'd claimed that was a law fairy kind had instituted. One necessary to ensure peace.

This blew all my plans to shit. Stopping Dane was one thing. Taking down ISHFA. Impossible. I ran a hand through my hair, continuing to pace. "She must be working against the council." I looked up. "Start digging up anything you can on Janet. We need to find out how deep this goes." If Janet was working against them, we'd add her to the list of people to take down. If she wasn't…Taking down the entire council would be insurmountable with our limited resources.

Leo nodded, tapping a finger against the counter. His nervous tick. "I'll tell Grace. She'll want to know."

I tugged my phone out of my pocket, checking the time. "It's early. She won't be up yet. I have a few things to do this morning. Let's meet again tonight?"

Leo frowned, a scar bisecting his right eyebrow, showing starkly with the movement. "Phones, Jack?"

I shoved it in my pocket. "Habit. Won't happen again."

I waited, counting to ten before leaving the room after Leo slipped out and grabbed my coffee from the counter, not meeting Leo's eye as he rang another customer up.

I stepped out onto the street and stuffed a hand in my pocket, fishing out my phone. It was three hours until the pharmacy where Grace, my only friend from undergrad, worked and I relied heavily on her to provide meds to treat the injured fairies. Grace was the first to join the cause, following me home one morning after I'd made yet another run for supplies. She'd thought she would bust an Xcess distributor, but had even more to say when she learned where I lived. I'd had no choice but to tell her the true reason I lived at the compound.

She had demanded to help and wouldn't take no for an answer. She made deliveries to Dane's other prisons around the city when she could, but those were heavily guarded and a lot harder to get into. We planned to free those creatures after we took Dane down. Now, knowing there may be others involved in his scheme, I wasn't sure how much longer they would have to wait to be freed.

Crossing into Central Park, I did something I hadn't done in three years; I left the main road and stepped onto the running path.

People weren't expressly forbidden from leaving the main roads in Central Park, but it was risky. There were four fairies living in the park who weren't bound by the rules ISHFA had put in place that protected people from fairy magic. They were guardians who lived just outside the pocket entrances to Faerie, inside a protective shield meant to keep the magic of Faerie from spilling into our world. I'd never seen them before, but we learned all about them in Dane's re-education class.

I broke into a light jog as my arms prickled with goosebumps. When we moved to New York, Central Park was always crowded. Now, people rarely entered the park, especially near the water. This close to the JQO Reservoir, I felt the otherness of this place.

Something not of Earth startled from the trees, flapping overhead and I ducked on instinct. It flapped great leather wings as it moved, carving a path over the reservoir and away from me.

I picked up my pace, cutting through the grass onto East Drive. The North Woods should be safer than the lake, considering they were under the Seelie Court's jurisdiction, but something about this part of Central

Park unsettled me. It was one of the many reasons I usually avoided it. Today, though, I needed to see just how far my father had gone.

Leaving the road, I followed the path to the cohabitation housing built for fairies living on Earth. Black clouds puffed into the sky long before I reached the place where the several-story building sat only yesterday. The air was heavy with ash and the smell of charred wood.

The building was gone. Nothing remained but blackened wood and smoke. The home of hundreds, erased like it was never there. Charred bodies lay scattered and my knees hit dirt before I knew I'd dropped. I pressed my fingers against the cool, burned skin beside me. I couldn't tell what type of creature he'd been. Even the name tag affixed to his blue button-down was too melted to read.

Vision blurring, I looked up, scanning the scalded earth for any signs of life. No one moved. All was still and silent. For these creatures, I had come too late.

Scrubbing ash from my lashes, I stood, taking in my surroundings.

The largest of the fairy buildings had sat at the edge of the woods, backing up to the main road, close enough that any of the condos across the street could have caught fire in the blaze. Miraculously, they hadn't.

A line of scorched earth cut too cleanly across the grass.

Someone had made sure only the fairies burned.

ELEVEN

SAV

Although it was late when I finally made it to the room that was to be my cell, I had slept fitfully. Alice's malicious glare had bored into my back as I faced the window and tried to think of anything other than the pain in my legs and the fae below who undoubtedly had a worse night than me.

When I woke, blessedly, she was still asleep. I sat up, stretching. My too short skirt was twisted around my waist and I tugged it down, straightening it over my hips. It wouldn't have been my first choice of outfit had I known where the night would take me.

I inspected the glamour on my ankles for any cracks in the facade. So far, it was holding. Smooth tanned skin was all anyone would see if they checked my legs. I stood, and the room spun dangerously. Sinking back onto the mattress, I pressed my palms to my temples, groaning around the pounding of my heartbeat in my head. Prolonged exposure and Morgan's summons were beginning to take their toll.

Inhaling deeply, then exhaling, I centered myself and gained inner clarity to separate my mind from the physical pain. I wasn't new to pain, even if my enemies had never used iron as a form of torture before. I dug deep, searching for the magic, hoping any small kernel would respond and help me block it. Nothing. With the iron wrapped around my legs, what little I could use was completely locked away from me.

Standing again, I wobbled but steadied myself.

Pale blue eyes met mine when I glanced down, and I started. She could have given the fae a run for their money in terms of stealth. Her pupils dilated. That was rage.

Human women never warmed to me. That was a fact I had learned quickly when forced to assimilate, but this was something else. I stretched my lips over pearly white teeth in a dazzling smile. As expected, her cheeks burned crimson.

This felt personal. She saw me as a threat. Good. I was.

She sat up, pulling her covers with her. "You don't fool me," she seethed. "I saw the way you pawed at Jack last night. But he's not interested in you."

This human was chatty in the morning. I liked her better at night. "I don't know what you mean."

She rolled her eyes. "I saw you acting all hurt. Jack can't stand to see anyone in pain. He's sensitive that way, but don't think for one second it means he's into you."

Yes, human girl, tell me more. "I want to go home to my family," I whimpered, a tear forming along my lashes.

Her grip on her blankets loosened, her brows furrowing. "Just watch the videos and Dane will explain everything. Once you understand, you'll be free."

"Were you trapped here too?" I asked, concern lacing my words.

"What?" she sputtered. "No. I came here after..." she trailed off. I waited, widening my eyes. She sucked in a breath. "It doesn't matter. I came because something had to be done to...To those assholes." Some fae creature had played with this little mousy thing. It was there in every word she was too embarrassed to say aloud. Good. "We should go down," she finished.

The crimson staining Alice's cheeks burned down her neck and though I'd love to stay to watch her relive her pain-filled memories, I would never escape this place if we didn't get moving. Gesturing for her to lead the way, I stepped into the hall and followed her through the same dismal hallway from the night before, reaching an emergency exit around another corner.

We moved down two flights of stairs to the building's lobby, now lined with rows of cafeteria tables. It was standing room only in the packed entryway and more people were trickling in by the minute. They came down stairwells and hallways, piling in until I was crammed against Alice's shoulder and the air became suffocatingly hot. The front door, which was what I had truly wanted to see from the inside, was painted over with piles of rebar, cement, and old demo materials wedged against the entry points.

Dane climbed on top of a reception desk and whistled sharply, two fingers at his lips, to draw out a piercing sound. Reluctantly, I followed everyone's gazes, drawn to that magnetic pull he seemed to have. The room silenced, all eyes on him.

"Welcome Followers." His voice boomed over the quieting crowd. "Yesterday." He paused for effect. "Was the turning point in our war." Shouts rose in response. "You." He spoke over them, and they quieted again. "You are the heroes of the hour. You showed the monsters we will *not* stand by any longer. We will not lose our jobs to them." Bellows of agreement. "Our husbands." More yells of agreement. "Our families," he finished soberly.

A hush fell. "Yesterday we said: No More! And they listened." This time, the cheers were deafening. He raised a hand. "But the work is not done. Today, they rebuild. Today, they will erect another home for the monsters that have invaded our world. Our city. We cannot stop now. Now we must act."

He pointed to a person in the crowd. "Ben. Lead a team today to try again to gain access to the Seelie court. Take four of our best. If we know how to get in, we can attack them on their own turf."

"Shut it down from the inside!" Ben shouted.

"That's right," Dane called back.

"Elizabeth—Fifth Ave. Remind the ladies who really prowls the park." She grinned.

"William—re-education. Evan—supply run. Let's move."

People dispersed, heading to their tasks for the day.

Dane climbed down from the desk. "Oliver, Jim, Brian, with me. We have a job to do."

Finally, I knew the names of the three little pigs. There was power in a name. I would not forget theirs.

William approached me. He was an overly cheerful cultist with a round belly and shining bald spot in the middle of his long, tangled hair. "Hi, I'm Will."

"I don't care."

He was unperturbed by my dismissal. "Dane tells me you fell in with a bad crowd and just need a little history lesson in what fairies are really like."

I stared at him. Yes William, please educate *me* on my kind.

"Well, it would be nice if I at least had a name to call you," he grinned, and his full round cheeks reddened.

I smiled. All teeth.

He stepped back.

Play nice, Sav. My smile softened into something sweeter. "I'm Sally." These humans would get my real name when they carved it from my bloody tongue.

"Sally." He swallowed. "Do you want to come with me and the other new recruits?"

57

"There's absolutely nothing I'd rather do, Will!"

He didn't catch my sarcasm.

Will led me and a group of five others to a room on the first floor with folding chairs and a projector.

I chose a seat at the back, even though there were at least a dozen chairs in the room. The initiates all sat at the front. A few cast glances at my chains. I rattled them at a lady who looked like she probably had ten cats waiting at home for her. She clutched her purse tightly and turned to face the front. I slouched in my chair, swallowing a pained cry at the new spots the iron touched. Will fumbled around at the front before the light flicked on, projecting a number four onto the screen. My little show had cost me, but it was worth it.

He passed me, going to the back of the room, and flipped off the lights.

On screen, black and white images of old Shakespearean plays flashed.

"We have always known about them," a voice spoke. "Legends embellish their best qualities. They are sexy, smart, powerful.... Dangerous" The screen changed to pictures of fae captured in and around Central Park, then to someone's shaky camera footage of a kelpie swatting at a child as he leaned over the lake. An ogre ripping a door off its hinges to enter a retail store. A harpy grabbing a homeless man's bucket of money and running down the street.

These were old videos. In keeping with the first laws enacted when we came to Earth, before they started imposing stricter ones. But honestly, what was the problem? The man looked perfectly healthy after the exchange. No harm done.

Then a picture of the Bitter Wraith, beautiful and terrible in white robes, with eyes so black they would suck the souls from any who gazed upon her without permission. The screen changed. It was Brixz, sitting benignly at a desk, reading a newspaper.

Brixz, whom I hadn't seen in a cage when I was taken below. Did it mean they'd left him to recover, or that he was dead? I tasted bile as I thought of the kindest fae I knew laying bloody outside the building he'd been forced to live in for three years. And these humans dared to use his image to promote their zealous propaganda.

Rage boiled in my gut, making me see red. They were evil, vile beings, and they deserved a slow death.

"As you can see, the legends were wrong," the voice went on. "These abominations are not gods to be feared or worshiped. They are not even the all-powerful creatures we once believed them to be." A drawing of a dark being, red eyes glowing, appeared. "We thought they were the stuff of nightmares."

Then a picture of Morgan, emissary to the autumn court, flashed on screen. Beautiful, ethereal, inhuman.

"But they are not what we thought." The screen flashed back to Brixz, and I squeezed my fists—nails slicing into my palms—relishing the pain as blood dripped through my fingers. "They take our jobs." Then an image of Vogue's July cover with Uncle Robin, bare chested, ears pointing, in all his glory, staring intently into the camera. He would have loved knowing even the AFF were watching him on screen.

I would have laughed if I had the stomach for it. Once, Robin Good-fellow had glamoured himself to look human and become the world's most famous actor. He reprised roles in some of the top films of the early two-thousands, aging his glamour appropriately, but when our realms collided, exposing the truth of our kind, he used the worst time in the history of the fae to gain more fame by coming out.

Leave it to Uncle Robin to profit even from our tragedy.

A man sitting close to his girlfriend wrapped his arm protectively around her. I rolled my eyes.

The screen flashed again, and this time, all five recruits gasped. In a cradle, where a rosy-cheeked human baby should be lying, a scaly green creature with glowing eyes stared menacingly back at the camera.

Who made this video? Did they even know what a changeling looked like? If that was a changeling, I was a unicorn. At that moment, my gaze met Will's. He had been watching *me*.

I covered my mouth in horror.

"We didn't ask for these monsters to come to our world; terrorize us, stalk us, steal our children, our husbands, our families..."

This sounded familiar.

"Our government receives favors from the high fairy courts." The image changed to Morgan sitting at a restaurant with humans in suits. A few people in the front row whispered. The screen flashed and this time it was Alder Hawthorn, prince of spring, shaking hands with the President of the United States.

"We cannot wait for our government to act. The time for waiting has passed. We must act now. We must seize our future back."

The last words were in Dane's voice.

The video ended, leaving the room in darkness. William fumbled around in the dark and I watched the creatures, blinded by their own weakness, clasping hands tightly, sitting rigidly. It was the first phase of their brainwashing. How easily human minds were muddled.

The lights flickered on, and William coughed. "I know you're all here because you want to make a difference." His eyes found mine. "Over the next seven days, you will train rigorously in the areas of weapons, fairy weaknesses, and combat. Once you've completed this training, you will be tested to prove your capabilities. Your assignments will be based on your test results. You may be assigned to tasks here at Basecamp like me, or you may join our field teams. No job is too small." His gaze swept over the room. "Questions?"

When no one spoke, William cleared his throat. "Let's all break for fifteen and meet in room one-twelve on the first floor."

I slid my chair out, scraping the ground, and a few humans glanced my way. *Be on your best behavior,* I reminded myself and stood clumsily, smiling at the group. I shuffled out behind the rest of the new recruits, turning left in the opposite direction of the main lobby.

"Sally," William called behind me. I kept walking, moving as quickly as I could with the iron chains shortening my step significantly. "Sally," he called more loudly, and I heard him picking up his pace.

Gritting my teeth, I slowed, turning and pasting a look of confusion on my face. "Did you call me?"

William caught up to me, leaning to catch his breath. "Hey! Yes. Sorry. You can't go that way. You'll have to stay with the group, I'm afraid. Dane's orders." He straightened, inhaling deeply. "Just until you've proven you can be trusted without the um..." he glanced down at my ankles.

I dropped my gaze, following his line of sight. "Yeah, I'll have to sit out during training today, I guess," I muttered, sounding put out.

"That's okay." William smiled. "I heard you handled your own out there against some of our guys. You're probably well ahead of the rest of this group in the hand-to-hand combat department." He gave me a pat on the shoulder, and it took a monumental effort not to snap at his fingers in response to the unwelcome touch. Something in my eyes must've slipped, because he yanked his hand back like he'd been burned. "You can be our scorekeeper."

TWELVE

SAV

Training was painful. Not literally. It was painful to watch. How humans became so populous confounded me. Cat lady, that's what I'd taken to calling her, would be dead in her first actual fight. Of that, I had no doubt. The couple—I named them Hansel and Gretel because they actually looked related—obviously hadn't lifted a sword a day in their lives and came away with bruises even though they were using wooden practice bats.

A man whom I assumed had lost a family member and blamed the fae for it—I didn't have a name for him yet—was the only decent fighter in the bunch, and he was too afraid to hurt anyone.

That left Jackie O. I named her that because her attachment to her pearls reminded me of the late Jackie O who had weaseled a string of enchanted pearls out of the grasp of the former winter court prince. The prince must not have told her that all fae bargains required payment because she'd looked devastated when payment was collected. The cost? Her husband's life. My Jackie O fought like she had someone to kill for, but her ferocity was no match for a lifetime of sedentary behavior, and try as she might, she was no knight.

It was a sad bunch, but did they need skill when we were unable to harm them?

After weapons training, we had lunch. My gaze roved over mundane human faces, searching for the one that stood out among the crowd. I needed those keys, but Jack was nowhere to be found.

The rest of the day, we watched more brainwashing videos, toured the building, and crammed into the makeshift dining hall for another horrid evening meal. The surrounding humans looked exhausted and the steady drain from the iron around my ankles left me feeling zapped as well, so it took little effort to imitate their fatigue. I yawned loudly, earning a few glances from those who had been avoiding my presence.

A hand touched my shoulder, and I jumped. I really must be losing it to allow someone to sneak up on me. I turned, peering up at Dane.

He smiled that artificial smile I had come to recognize as his pontification smile. I glowered back. No amount of acting could have prepared me to fake sweetness with this man after a long day of bullshit.

"You look tired, Sally." His tone suggested he didn't care one bit. "But I have another task for you tonight before bed. Come with me." He stepped back, waiting for me to rise.

I stood and made a show of fumbling with my chains before extricating myself from the bench.

His smile never wavered as he turned and walked to the side exit, and as I followed, the three little pigs fell into step beside me. Their jeering faces left a queasy feeling in my stomach. We exited the building onto the same street we'd entered from the night before, but this time, we came out farther down the alley and were immediately at ground level.

I marked my surroundings, looking for other entry and exit points as we made our way to the main thoroughfare. New York was always crowded, but if the humans passing us thought it was strange that a lone female in chains was being escorted by four men, they didn't show it. Not one passerby stopped to give aid or check on my well-being. And I looked like a human, for fuck's sake.

We turned again, and as I feared, we were headed back to Central Park. Plumes of black smoke wafted into the air, blocking out the night sky and all the stars with it. My stomach flipped as the reason for this trip became clear. Stationed in front of the billowing charcoal cloud were three forms, shackled and staked to the ground.

The first was an ogre. At least eight feet tall and slick with his own green blood, he looked as though all the fight had been bled from him. He swayed, his labored breathing audible from across the park and his unfocused eyes told me the iron shackles protruding from each arm were having the desired effect.

The next, a pixie with a wing bent at an odd angle, was no longer crying and that broke me more than her tears had.

I struggled to stifle my protest.

Dane's hawklike gaze zeroed in on my face, and I put three-hundred years of fae court training to work as I schooled my expression into neutral disinterest, swallowing down the anger roiling in my gut.

The last was a satyr with sandy blonde hair, but she was too bloody to make out any discernible features. The world skidded to a halt as my blood froze in my veins. I couldn't see her face, but I knew. I knew with every ounce of my being it was Juniper.

As we moved, the three little pigs tightened their circle around me, and Jim gripped my biceps.

I fought his hold.

Dane gave a shake of his head, and the grip loosened. To me Dane said, "the best way to overcome a perversion is to rid yourself of the temptation."

A lump rose in my throat as my gaze shifted from the scene before me to Dane.

Holding a microphone to his lips, Dane said to a gathering crowd stopping on the street: "We have a demonstration for you." At his projected words, more stopped to watch. "Yesterday, we stood up for humanity." He paused. "Tonight, we show you that the thing you fear can bleed."

Without preamble, he produced a knife from under his jacket and sliced across the front of the large ogre's pecs. Green spilled down his chest in a thick line and he roared, swiping blindly at Dane.

Dane easily dodged the swing.

"You see," Dane said to the audience. "They look fierce, but they bleed just as we do." He stepped closer, slicing again. Deeper this time. The ogre howled in agony. He moved behind him and swiped across his ankles. "When you get them on their knees," he shouted as the creature dropped. "You realize they aren't so tough."

My blood ran cold at the sick delight in his eyes.

The crowd closed in, their gasps of surprise changing to righteous outrage. Shouts of: "Finish him," and "Kill him, Dane," rose and my stomach roiled again, threatening to spill my dinner at my feet. Although ogres were strong, their capacity for healing was severely diminished by iron, more so than any other fae-kind. In sick fascination, I wondered if Dane knew that and selected this creature for that very reason.

Dane circled around the slouching ogre, slicing his ear cleanly across the top, removing the point. The crowd cheered and bile climbed up my throat.

The ogre bellowed a mournful cry, reaching for his ear, but the chains jutting from each arm just above the wrist did not have enough give for the reach. He whimpered and my heart fractured, crumbling to bits in my chest.

The crowd was growing more frenzied, and they elbowed each other for space for a better look at the wounded creature. More people stepped out of their homes and off the street to watch. Phones raised as humans recorded Dane's show and the ogre's end.

I yanked against Jim's grip, but a second arm closed around mine and dirty nails dug in, holding me still.

Dane stepped back, letting the growing mob take his place and too late, I realized his plan. A vile grin twisted his lips as they grabbed the pixie's cage, and she was tossed between them. The small creature banged against the bars, her wings destroyed, her skin popping and sizzling each time she crashed against the cage bars.

"Stop," I breathed, wrenching my arm from Jim's clammy grip. I fought the crowd to get to the fae being tortured by this mob.

Brian, Jim and Oliver tried to stop me, but I had ducked into the melee, and they were too large to squeeze in after me. Shackles slowed me down, but I dodged between sweaty bodies, moving out of their reach. The little pixie was far into the mob now and I could see between pushes and shoves that the ogre was not moving on the ground.

I dashed for the satyr, sinking down beside her. "No, no. Juniper."

She wasn't moving and dirty shoe prints covered her back. The press of sweaty bodies crashed into us in their frenzied attempts to kick or punch the ogre. Madness had taken them, and their bloodlust would not be sated for long. Soon, their attention would fall on Juniper.

I dragged my shirt over my head and wrapped it around the stake, pinning her chains to the ground. I yanked it free, exhaling a breath of relief. Dropping the iron rod, I covered her chains with my shirt as a foot landed on my ankle, and I cried out, shoving them away. Arms and legs wedged into my back, and I pushed against them, throwing my body over Juniper's, protecting her from the crowd.

A kick to the side of my head made me see stars, and I glanced up, dazed. Through blurry vision, I spied the three pigs pushing their way toward me. Adrenaline pumping, I jumped to my feet, twisting hands through the shirt wrapped around Juniper's chains, and began dragging her, shoving humans aside as I limped away, still bound in my own manacles. If they reached us, it would be both our ends.

"Hey! She's helping that one escape," someone shouted, and several people turned in our direction.

Squaring my shoulders, I barged through people as kicks and blows fell on me. A man grabbed Juniper's horn, trying to wrench her from my hold. I pulled with what little remaining strength I had, breathing hard as I kept pushing through the mob.

Then I was through the crowd and out the other side.

Juniper was still not moving, and I had no time to wonder how bad her injuries were.

Dane called out to the mob to stop me and slowly, they changed tack, unifying in one common goal.

Tightening my hold on the shirt wrapped around the chains at Juniper's wrists, I dragged her toward the bar. If there was anywhere else safe in the human realm, I'd have taken her there, but the AFF was directly in my path to the pocket entrance to Faerie and humans would never offer shelter to one of my kind.

Juniper bounced over rocks and debris, but I had no time to carry her, especially with my own shackles slowing me down. I turned left, leaving the park, the mob tight on my heels, and took another left and another. I dashed into the bar, desperately begging Mab to cloak us from the angry humans who were out for blood.

The bar was dark and deserted, and I ran to the back, pulling Juniper with me, and slammed the unisex bathroom door shut behind us. I slumped against the shit and piss-stained wall, listening for any sound of my approaching demise. My heart clattered against my ribcage as I tried to hear over its pounding.

After a lifetime frozen in the filthy room, I lifted on groaning knees, stiff from the odd angle I'd crouched in, pulling Juniper up with me. She would never heal with iron spiked through her body. I glanced down at her battered face, grimacing at the mottled bruises and gashes, knowing some of those had been my fault.

"I'm sorry Juniper," I whispered.

Her steady pulse gave me hope, but a wave of sorrow hit me hard and the sob I'd been holding in since this all began tore its way up my throat and I leaned back, letting it out.

Wiping my shaking palm on my skirt, I took a few steadying breaths and assessed the damage to Juniper's wrists. Bile burned the back of my throat as I inspected the flesh melted away around the massive bolts jammed through bone. Would she recover from wounds like these?

Tugging the fabric of my shirt out from under the chains around her ankles, I swore as her flesh bubbled. I wrapped my shirt around one enormous bolt head spearing her wrist, and twisted. The grooves scraped bone and sinew, and blood oozed into the fabric. Twice, I had to stop to expel the remaining contents of my last meal.

The first bolt came free, and I let out a small whimper as thick, dark blood chased it, quickly saturating my once-white top.

I let the bolt drop and got to work on the second. It took more time to work free, using a shirt so sodden with blood. My grip slipped more than once, and my gaze darted to the alarming puddle of green pooling under her first injury.

It came free with a popping sound and fell to our feet. I leaned into the wall, catching my breath. I shouldn't have been this winded, but my own shackles were sapping my strength.

The door to the bar banged open, and ice slid down my spine.

"This way. She must be around here somewhere. Search next door. I'll check in here."

Silently, I slid my full weight against the door.

"The apartment building?" another voice asked.

"Yes, you idiot. Check the laundry chutes, dumpsters, alleys, every-where. She wouldn't have gotten far dragging a half-dead fairy with her," the first voice called back.

Shit. Shit. Shit.

I should have tried to take my shackles off first. At least then I would have been stronger in a fight. And there would be no other way out of this than a fight. No back exit. No window to crawl through.

"Go with Brian. I'll check in here." A voice I recognized. There was a beat of silence. "You can go, Oliver. My dad asked me to help search."

Feet shuffled, and the door closed. My breath caught in my throat, and I thanked Mab with everything I had that humans couldn't hear heart-beats. Mine was pumping wildly out of control. Jack was a big guy, but I could take him. If he was the only person out there blocking my escape, I'd win. I just had to bring him down without harming him.

"Sally. It's safe to come out. I won't hurt you."

I tensed, muscles coiling in my abdomen and thighs. Gently, I let Juniper slide to the floor, mumbling a silent apology, hoping she wouldn't get sepsis or an STD.

"I saw what you did tonight." Poorly constructed wooden floorboards creaked under his larger than average feet. "I don't agree with my...with Dane. What he did was wrong."

Juniper's eyelids fluttered, and her lips parted on a soft moan. I knelt, cupping trembling fingers over her mouth.

"Sally, I don't blame you for helping the fairies." Another creak on the floorboards, closer this time. "I want to help them, too."

Sliding Juniper away from the door, I tugged it open and stepped out into the light.

Jack grinned, and it lit up his entire face. He took a step forward, but I held up a hand.

"Why didn't you try to stop him?" Did I care? Did it matter that this human was no different from any of the others? I supposed it did.

Jack tensed, his shoulders bunching. Emotions warred across his face.

I let the silence hang between us.

In typical human fashion, his lips parted, and he wet them before saying. "It's...complicated."

Wrong answer. Slow death it was. I'd drag him back to Faerie and end him. Painfully.

His eyes widened. He must have seen something in my expression because he held up his hands, palms out. "I won't let him imprison you again."

"So you'll help me, but you would never aid a fairy. Is that it?"

Hands still outstretched, he took another step toward me. "That's not true."

"Then help me." It was risky. It was so damn risky—especially after he'd left me with his father the night before—but some stupid part of me wanted to believe he meant those words, and I didn't have many other options at the moment. I stepped back, pushing the bathroom door wide, and revealed Juniper's unconscious form sprawled across the floor.

His mouth fell slack as his gaze moved from her prone shape to my ankles. "Did the iron do that to her?"

I bit back a dozen vicious retorts, swallowing before saying: "Can you help her?"

He reached into his pocket, produced a key, and dropped to one knee. Instead of going to Juniper though, he gripped the iron shackling me and shoved the key into the keyhole. He did the same for the second and metal clattered to the floor.

It was an adrenaline shot to the heart. Every bit of available magic flowing through me raced to the injury, and I squeezed my fingers into fists to keep from checking if the points in my ears were back.

In moments, the flaming agony in my ankles dulled to a cool burn, and I exhaled softly. My gut twisted and I darted a glance at Juniper. Her wounds were healing far too slowly, and the massive bolts tearing through her were likely the cause.

Jack's gaze lingered on my bare skin. "You don't have any rub marks."

"There's no time for that." My heart sped up at the slow rise of Juniper's next inhale. "She might die."

Jack jolted, his attention going to my co-worker and maybe friend of three years. He knelt beside Juniper, pressing two fingers to her throat, and looked up, eyes meeting mine. "Her heartbeat is dangerously slow."

"We have to get the iron out of her." I picked up the green bit of fabric that was my shirt, remembering I was in only a bra in front of this human, and he hadn't glanced at my breasts once. I'd waste energy on that thought later. Now, I lifted Juniper's leg and wrapped my soaked shirt around the first bolt, twisting.

Jack tugged his t-shirt over his head and exposed ridiculously sculpted abs. I ignored them as he covered the second bolt with it, following my lead, and began turning.

This close, I could smell his hot breath exhaling sharply as he worked. It wasn't unpleasant. *Strangely.*

The bolt in my hand came free, and I tossed it on the floor. Jack's bolt came loose a few moments later, and we sat back.

Come on Juniper. Please wake up. Her wrists had stopped bleeding, but ugly, torn skin was taking far too long to heal. Blood ran down her legs, soaking the floor. I laid my finger tentatively against her cheek. Not burning as it had been with so much iron in her system. My chest lightened. If we could escape the AFF, she would recover.

"Let's get her out of the bathroom before she catches something," I said. "Help me?"

I could have carried her myself. My energy was returning as my injuries healed, but I didn't think the son of my enemy would aid us if he knew what I was.

He scooped Juniper up in his arms, surprising me. Even with my strength still returning, I was strong, but satyrs were heavy, and this man had just picked her up like she weighed nothing. He set her down atop the bar and I slid into an empty chair, gaze lingering on the pool of blood forming under Juniper's legs.

Jack followed suit, sitting across from me.

I glanced at the door and back, biting my lip. Exposed as we were, if someone walked through the door now, there would be no escaping, but I was desperate to give Juniper a little more time to heal before we left the bar.

Jack's gaze followed mine. "They won't check here again. They trust me."

I looked back at him. "I'm sure they do. The son of Dane Clyde probably runs that cult."

He frowned, eyes boring into mine, and I looked away. He was a conundrum. He should be dragging me—dragging us both—out the door right now, but instead, he seemed to genuinely want to help. I watched him from the corner of my eye, gauging the tense set of his jaw and rigid posture. I saw no weapons on him, but he was tall and well-built. He likely assumed he could take me easily. Little did he know, I was twice as strong as any human on my worst day.

Juniper's eyelids fluttered wildly, and my nails tapped a nervous rhythm over flaking paint on the plastic tabletop. When Juniper woke or at least stopped bleeding, I'd need to get her out of here and as far from AFF headquarters as possible. She needed to be in nature to speed the healing process, but Central Park wasn't safe. In the concrete jungle that was New York City, there weren't many places with trees.

"Do you want my shirt?" Jack's question tore me from my thoughts.

I glanced at him.

His gaze was on my face, but the pink in his cheeks told me they hadn't been a moment before.

"Never seen a bra before?" Good. He wasn't chivalrous. If he had been, I'd be forced to find something redeemable in this human.

His bronzed skin flushed crimson and his heartbeat tripled in speed.

I bared my teeth in a mockery of a smile. "I think your shirt might need a wash."

"Right." His gaze shifted, with some effort, to Juniper. "Do you have anywhere to go that she would be welcome? I can help you carry her."

My nails drummed faster. I didn't have a plan for this part. Humans had human dwellings. People to return to. I needed to rid myself of Jack before he figured out I didn't and realized I was no human at all.

Juniper stirred, and I sat forward. Her eyes opened, and she tilted her head, turning watery yellow eyes to me. "Hey, girl."

THIRTEEN

SAV

I waggled my eyebrows at Juniper, but schooled my face into neutrality when Jack's gaze swiveled to me.

"Do you know the satyr?"

My eyes widened. "What?"

Juniper struggled to get her elbows underneath her and pushed herself up.

I darted from my seat, rushing to help her up. "I'm pretending to be human," I said under my breath in Elvish.

Juniper shot me an incredulous look but accepted my hand as she swung her legs over the side of the bar, whimpering softly.

"Are you okay?" Jack asked *right* fucking behind me.

Ice shot down my spine.

He held out a hand, and Juniper took it, sliding off the countertop. She staggered, but after a moment, she straightened and thrust her shoulders back, tugging her fingers from his. She gave Jack an odd look before searching my face.

"We can't go out there," I said, glancing at the blood on Juniper's legs. "They'll finish what they started."

"Do you have anywhere to go?" Jack asked.

"Just Faerie," she said, eyes narrowing. "Now that my home is gone."

Jack's body radiated heat against my back, a furnace boiling my blood, and I leaned closer to Juniper. "We can't get to Faerie. They have Central Park surrounded."

"*We?*" Juniper's mock affront would have made me snort if Jack wasn't standing so close. "I'm not going anywhere with you humans."

71

Jack cleared his throat. "Oh. I thought you knew each other."

Juniper's gaze slid over my shoulder. "Why? Because I called this one girl? I call everyone what they are. Boy."

Jack let out a startled laugh. "You know I want to help you."

His heat was pressing in again, making my pulse pound, but unless I wanted to climb in Juniper's lap, there was nowhere to go.

"Why? Because you brought me food one time? Human help got me into this mess in the first place."

She shoved past me, knocking me into Jack's chest.

They knew each other. That much was obvious. And I thought I was the only fae getting tangled up with a human this week.

Juniper marched for the exit.

"Wait," Jack said, and she halted, hand hovering over the handle.

She eyed the two of us with enough contempt that I felt it might not all be an act. *Damn. What did I do?* "I'm going to Faerie to report what happened to the courts. Then we'll see how brave your little faction is."

She turned on her heel once more and yanked the door wide, storming out. Jack ran after her, but I hesitated. It swung closed behind them, blocking my view of the outside world.

Juniper had some big balls I'd give her that, but images of her torn, bloody flesh and the green stained bolts on the bathroom floor sent terror shooting through me. One didn't survive as long as I had by making rash decisions, like charging into the middle of the AFF after nearly becoming a demonstration for Dane Clyde's propaganda. I knew deep in my bones if she went out there now, she wouldn't survive it this time.

I bit my lip. I'd spent less than an hour in those iron cages, and it was worse than anything I could have imagined, but Juniper could die if they caught her a second time. For some immeasurable period, I was frozen between doing the right thing and saving my own ass.

I cursed under my breath, squared my shoulders, and went after her.

She might hate me later—but at least she'd be alive to do it.

FOURTEEN
JACK

The brave little satyr marched out of the bar and straight into Jim's waiting arms.

He grabbed her, wrapping a sweaty hand around her neck. She bucked and kicked in his hold, but she was weak from blood loss and gave up quickly. Her wide eyes met mine and I read the betrayal in them. I swallowed hard, guilt twisting in my gut. I couldn't tell her I didn't plan this, not in front of Jim or any of Dane's soldiers.

"Jackie. You actually did something right for once?" He squeezed tighter. "Where's the other one? The fairy loving bitch?"

"The other one's human," I spat, an edge of protective energy lacing my words.

Jim tilted his head to glance at the satyr. "We'll get her. Your dad's got plans for her."

Heat sizzled in my veins at the threat in his words, and I bit down hard on a retort. I had a choice to make: Help the satyr and blow my cover, or let Jim take her and add her to the growing list of creatures I needed to break out. It was a risk I couldn't take. Not yet. "Let's just go before this one escapes."

Jim's thick eyebrows slouched low, and he looked me over. "Where's your shirt?"

"I lost it," I grumbled, and shoved his shoulder, stomping past him. At any moment, Sally might walk through that door, intent on helping the satyr, and I wasn't willing to put myself in *that* situation again. The last time she'd been in danger, when Dane had her trapped in his compound,

I'd considered something reckless. Something that could have cost me my whole mission.

I didn't look back as I left the bar, crossing the street and retracing my earlier steps toward AFF headquarters.

"Let me go," the satyr demanded, wriggling furiously in Jim's arms. He'd released her neck and wrapped his arms around her biceps. She stomped a hoof down hard on his foot and he howled in fury, squeezing her arms tightly.

I glanced over my shoulder, biting back a grin. She was a vicious little thing.

She hadn't said it, but Sally and the satyr knew each other. The look that passed between them wasn't as cleverly disguised as Sally thought. I understood her reticence in admitting it, though. Especially to the son of Dane Clyde. I had so many questions for her. Why was she helping them? How had they met? What else was she willing to do?

Movement at the corner of my eye caught my attention. I glanced to my left—to the alley behind the bar. A mop of deep auburn hair, swept up in a bun, ducked back and I swore internally. The small bit of hope I'd had that she wouldn't come after the satyr died.

"Jim. Hold up."

He grunted as the satyr landed an elbow to his gut, but stopped beside me. "What is it, Jackie?"

I ground my teeth at the nickname. "I think I saw something."

Jim glanced around and I moved to block his view of the alley. "I'll go check it out. Wait here."

"Like hell," he groused. "I gotta get this one back to base before she gets loose."

I nodded. "Alright. I'll catch up."

He pulled the satyr with him, glancing back as if he'd reconsider, but she rammed a horn into his side and he dragged her away, mumbling curses.

I waited till he crossed the street before turning, circling around the back of the bar from the other side and sliding up beside Sally.

"Hey."

"Shit!" she shouted, eyes going wide. "How are you so quiet?"

I shrugged, and her gaze slid past me. "Where's the satyr? Don't tell me you let him take her."

I balled my hands into fists at my sides. "I didn't have a choice." Sally's face contorted in pain and my chest spasmed. "Look. I'm working on something more important than one satyr right now." I ground my teeth together, unwilling to say more. She'd tried to help them twice, but that wasn't enough for me to put complete faith in her yet.

Her mouth pressed into a thin line, and the rage wafting off her could have melted steel, but after a moment she swallowed. "Then I'll get her out."

She turned, and I grabbed her arm, panic flaring through my gut. "You can't."

She wrenched free from my grip, lean muscles along her forearm yanking loose with far more strength than she looked like she possessed. My gaze fell to her ankles. I had to check again to remind myself that no fairy could withstand iron the way she had. She was petite compared with my much taller frame, but that didn't mean she was weak. I needed to remember not to underestimate her.

Sally made to dart past me, but I caught her around the waist and pressed her back to the wall, leaning down to whisper in her ear as voices drifted toward us. "Think for a minute. If you go after her, you'll be captured. Dane will lock you up and force you to do terrible things."

The voices grew louder, but my focus was stolen by her breath puffing against my bare chest. Her lace bra rubbed against my skin as she heaved in and out. Every muscle in her body was tense in anticipation of a fight. Hers was a body honed by years of training. I knew it well. When my father began his crusade, his sole mission had been to make me into a killer. Too bad for him, it was the furthest thing from my dream. Like mom, I'd wanted to help people. To heal people. Taking life, any life, would never sit well with me.

Shadows stretched across the alley as members of the AFF passed by, and I leaned over Sally, covering her smaller body with my own. Her floral rainwater scent drifted up, invading my senses. It reminded me of early spring when dew clung to blades of grass before the sun's warmth baked it away, the softest hint of honeysuckle lingering on the air.

Sally's lips grazed my chest as I wrapped an arm overhead, shielding her from sight. I tried and failed to ignore the images her lips against my skin conjured. She moved and I blinked, inching backward to give her space.

Her thigh slid between my legs, and my thoughts took a turn toward indecent. Perhaps she didn't want to—"Uggggg," I groaned, slumping forward and cupping my balls as her knee slammed into me.

Sally seized her moment and slid out from under me, stepping back, leaving me to bend forward, cradling tender flesh.

"If you ever think of trapping me like that again, it will be a knife next time instead of my knee," she warned.

"Sorry," I wheezed out.

She crossed the alley, putting distance between us and, with some effort, I straightened, still holding my crotch.

"You're right. I can't free her myself, but the satyr had a good point. If the fae courts knew Dane was holding fae captive. Torturing them...They would have to send aid. I need to go to Faerie. To tell them what's really going on."

She said *Faerie* with a strange lilt that made my head fuzzy, but perhaps that was just the blood rushing to my balls.

"Humans can't go to Faerie."

She eyed me, gaze dropping to my hands cupped protectively over the area she had injured. "You stay. I'm going."

She leaned out of the alley and the bun atop her head wobbled precariously to either side before she righted herself again. Her light hazel eyes studied me. They were an unusual color, but more than that, they held an ancient grief that didn't match her youthful face.

She couldn't be over twenty-five, but those eyes. They said she was ageless.

Her nose crinkled. "On second thought. I need you to come with me."

I nodded, already having come to the same conclusion. If she thought I was going to let her try to find a way into another realm alone, she was sorely mistaken.

"But first, I need to get something." She darted from the alley and ducked around the corner, stepping through the door to the bar so fast I blinked, rubbing my eyes.

In moments, she emerged with a bag slung over her shoulder and a T-shirt on that said: Fae'z in Harlem .99 cent Fridays, stretched over the lacy black bra I'd never forget if I lived a thousand years. She tossed a white bit of cloth at me, and I held up a shirt that read: Fae'z in Harlem do it better.

"Thanks."

"Don't be so free with your appreciation," she said, and, peeking out one more time, dashed across the street, crossing into the neighborhood and away from Central Park.

FIFTEEN
SAV

A low headache had begun at the base of my skull. Morgan's instructions to return home were beginning to chafe, but it was just the excuse I needed to pull off this new plan. I would probably die or end up in someone's dungeon, but once the idea came to me, I couldn't shake it. It was simple. Trade Jack for the prisoners. Risky, but doable—if I could get him into Faerie. Willingly, if possible. Bound if not.

With the might of a fae army at my back, how could Dane refuse?

Now I just needed to convince one of the courts to lend me their army. I didn't trust the truth of who Jack was to any of them, but if they learned how abominably our kind was being treated, they'd have to do something.

I would have preferred to see Dane rot on a spike, but knowing the fae royals as I did, they'd never agree to something that might risk our alliance. I'd play along and when we freed the fae, I would plot Dane's death on my own.

Sending a prayer to Mab that Juniper would be alive when we came for her, I crossed the street, lifting my chin. This far from Central Park, they wouldn't be looking for me.

I didn't have to look back to know Jack still followed. He fancied himself a hero. That would be the key to keeping him with me long enough to secure a trade.

The memory of his breath against my neck and his warm chest pressing me into the wall flashed in my mind. Icy dread washed over me. My enemy's son had pressed me into a wall, and I hadn't immediately killed him. Worse, I hadn't hated it. *Stop it, Sav. He's a vile, disgusting human playing hero instead of doing anything truly helpful.*

I crossed Manhattan Ave, turning left on Amsterdam Ave.

"Hey! Wait up." Jack caught up to me, matching my stride.

"Balls feeling better?"

"I was just trying to keep you safe."

I narrowed my eyes at him.

He tucked a strand of raven hair behind his ear, and a dimple appeared in his cheek. "Okay, I lingered." At least he owned it. "How do you know how to get into Faerie?"

My gaze shot forward as I picked up speed. I didn't have an answer for that. Why did humans always have questions for everything?

The quickest path to the Seelie Court was along the North Meadow, but the heaviest concentration of AFF also swarmed that area. Humans still feared the Unseelie enough to avoid Bow Bridge and Conservatory Waters. I'd try that first.

Jack's long strides ate up the pavement beside me as he matched my pace and asked again: "How do you know how to get into Faerie?"

"A fairy told me," I said between pants, feigning catching my breath.

Jack gave me a quizzical look, but I picked up speed, jogging down the street. Maybe if I ran faster, he'd be out of breath, and that would put an end to his questions.

Several long minutes later, I cut left on Seventy-Fourth Street, sprinting through an intersection as blaring horns threatened to run me down if I didn't move a little faster, and dipped behind a Crumbl bakery. Humans didn't do most food well, but the heavenly smells wafting from this pastry shop had my mouth watering and reminded me my last meal was on the floor of the bar bathroom.

Jack stopped beside me. His shirt rode up, exposing a line of bronze skin and well defined hip bones that scattered rational thought.

I looked up—cheeks burning—into eyes that were already on me.

He grinned, and it was the self-assured sort of smile usually reserved for members of the high fae court.

"Got any money?" I asked, ignoring the fact that I'd just been caught staring.

"Sure."

I considered smacking the cocky grin off his face for all of half a second before he pulled a money clip out of his pocket and my gaze fell on the thick wad folded under a silver clip. That much money could buy me all the Crumbl pastries I dreamed of. Where had he gotten so much cash? "Did you rob a bank?"

He laughed, sliding several twenties out from under the clip and handing them to me.

I frowned. "What do you want for it?" In Faerie, nothing was free. In the human realm, that was doubly true.

Jack's grin slid away. "Nothing."

I folded my arms across my chest and eyed him.

"Sally. Seriously. I don't want anything." He rubbed a hand over his face. "Look, I'm not sure what sort of people you normally hang out with, but I'm not the kind of guy who expects anything for a favor."

My ear twitched. Ah. So, the human was trading his cash for a favor. To be determined at a later time. Favors were the worst kind of bargain. Never advantageous to the one who had to pay in the end.

"No deal. Keep your money."

"What?"

A couple in matching sweats jogged by, and I stepped out behind them. I guess Crumbl wasn't on the menu today.

"Sally!" Jack darted out of the alley after me. "Wait!"

The smell of crystalized sugar and cinnamon wafted on a phantom breeze and my traitorous stomach demanded we go back. But no favor was worth that delicious scent.

As I neared Central Park, a chill made the hairs on my arms rise. This close to the park, the buildings were empty; no people ventured near, and in a city teaming with humans, the silence was unsettling.

I stepped through the barrier into Unseelie territory, feeling the slightest pressure against my skin as the pads of my bare feet touched grass, and I let out a soft exhale. It was darker here—colder—the air tinged with the crisp scent of Winter.

Although both the winter and autumn court were Unseelie, Autumn had not agreed to the Inter Species Human Fae Alliance laws, instead, sending their emissary to live among the humans and choosing to allow none of its other citizens to dwell in the human realm. For that reason, unlike the Seelie side of Central Park, whose wards were shared by Spring and Summer, only the winter court barrier protected the Unseelie side.

The air shimmered with the energy of the wards the winter court had erected around the south side of Central Park, and a dusting of snow tugged low branches toward the rye grass blanketing the park.

It wasn't until I came to Earth that I experienced changing weather in one place. Once—I'd heard—Faerie was like Earth. Weather changed and courts did not have to depend on one another for their goods. But Mab had put an end to it long before my time, ensuring our kind were forced to rely on one another to survive. The addition of the sea courts controlling water access, ensured no one kingdom would ever grow too powerful over another.

Although we were in Unseelie territory, the barriers erected to block out all human sounds and smells welcomed me home and I nearly dropped to my knees and wept. It was blessedly quiet and free of iron, rot and radio waves bisecting my brain in a steady hum.

I glanced at Jack. He held a hand up to the iridescent air shield, wonder on his face. I hadn't ever considered whether humans could see the barrier, but my lips quirked at his elation.

In three years, I had not been allowed to set foot in Faerie. I'd forgotten just how peaceful it was. Of course, this bubble inside Central Park wasn't actually my realm. It was a mere prelude, and to enter, I'd have to get past one of the guardians. But thanks to Morgan's summons, I had a loophole at long last.

I jogged around the lake, stopping beside Bow Bridge, and peered along the undergrowth. If Trym, the troll guardian of the autumn court's entrance, was awake, I would have better luck with the naiads.

Jack stopped beside me, silent as he took in the scene before him.

Cattails bobbed in a light breeze along the riverbank, tickling my palms.

A distant cousin who'd lived among the humans for some time in the late nineteen eighties told me humans once littered this part of Central Park. Now, it was still and silent apart from the rustling breeze and the occasional tree branch depositing its dusting of snow on the ground.

Thorns as thick as my arm wove along man-made paths and covered old lamp posts and benches, devouring all traces of humanity and claiming this place for Faerie.

Movement in a shadowy corner of Bow Bridge had me squinting to peer through snowflakes falling heaviest where the pocket entrance to Autumn lay beneath the bridge.

"What is that?" Jack asked, disturbing the silence.

"That's a troll." I chewed my bottom lip. I had hoped that with the autumn court entrance being dormant, Trym would be asleep, but it seemed luck wasn't with me today. "Can you swim?"

Jack snorted. "You want to go for a swim? Now?" He held his hand out, collecting snowflakes and raising his brow at me for emphasis.

I rolled my eyes, marching through the cattails to the lake.

"Sally. Stop." Jack was right behind me, making far more noise than necessary, considering we were treading on damp earth.

At the edge of the lake—ignoring Jack's protests—I secured my bag over a shoulder, already wrapped in a bit of magic to keep the contents dry, and trudged in.

"Sally!"

I grimaced, the muck below the water squishing between my toes. In

Faerie, the lake beds were all filled with smooth rocks and bits of rounded glass. On Earth, lakes were murky beasts of mud and filth.

Jack splashed in behind me, as I knew he would.

Something sliced into my ankle, and I hissed. It gave a sharp yank, and I grounded my feet in the mud, turning to Jack. "Turn back."

"No. Sally, this is mad. We can't swim here. There are...things...in the water."

As if to emphasize his point, nails bit into my calf and I stifled a cry, leaning down and wrapping a fist around the slick scaley arm attempting to pull me under. "Not today, Naiad," I seethed, squeezing until her thin bones cracked. She wriggled wildly in my grasp, but a second set of nails dug into my arm, then a third. Damn naiads. I wasn't getting into Faerie this way.

Shaking them off, I turned, slogging through the mud. "Go Jack."

He hesitated, glancing between my bloody arm and the writhing water behind me. "Go!"

A naiad leaped from the water, swiping for me, and I ducked out of her way, crashing against Jack's chest. "Move before they eat us."

Finally, he backed up, trudging out of the lake, and spun around, holding out a hand. I took it and he pulled me up.

"Sally, you're hurt." Jack's grip tightened on my arm, and he lifted it. "This will get infected if we don't treat it. There's no telling what bacteria is in that lake. Not to mention what sort of poison those animals might have in their talons."

I pulled my arm free from his grip, scowling at him. "I'll be fine." *Poison. Animals.* Just the reminder I needed that he was the son of the leader of the AFF. No pretty face was enough to erase that fact.

Jack held out his hand again. "You're bleeding. Please. Let me help."

I stepped around him, but he moved, blocking my path. "Sally."

I sighed. It was a useless exercise, considering the wounds were half healed already, but I held out my arm for him to inspect. Warm fingers wrapped around my wrist, and a slight shock of electricity jolted through me. I started, backing up, but he held me in place. I looked up, studying his face as raven brows bunched in confusion.

I'd felt nothing like that in another's touch. The energy humming in my veins where he touched me was intoxicating, making me want to lean into it.

His calloused finger brushed over red lines that would be gone within the hour. I hadn't considered how slowly a human healed, but as he leaned close, my heart clattered against my ribs as his head dipped lower, inspecting what remained of the gashes. He wiped away the smear of blood left behind, and I tensed in his hold.

He looked up, emerald eyes burning as he searched my face. There was no fear or disgust, only an intense interest and maybe...I shook my head. I was cold and wet. His hands were unusually warm. That was all.

"It seems you don't need my help." He released me, stepping back to let me pass.

A shiver danced along my spine, and I stood frozen for a moment.

Jack cleared his throat. "Sally."

All the heat building in my chest fled, a stone settling in my stomach. It was one word, but every muscle in my body tensed, sensing the danger in it. Should I run? What would he do if he knew I wasn't like him? The clatter of my heart became a drumbeat.

"I know you're not...Human."

My veins iced. *Should have run.*

"I'm not upset," he hurried to say. "I think we can help each other."

I exhaled slowly. I had two options: attempt to keep up the ruse or come clean and give him enough truth to convince him to come along. And if he wouldn't come, I would just have to force him. I went with option b.

"How did you know?"

The tension building in the air dissipated, and a laugh punctuated his exhale. "I'll admit, you had me fooled for a while, but humans don't run that fast or," he glanced down at my arm. "Heal that quickly. Not to mention, no human would think of going to the fairy courts for help. The only information I have about the courts is that they're based on the seasons, and I live with a man who's obsessed with you guys."

The dimple appeared in his cheek as his lips tipped up.

A small smile crept onto my face as my heart found its normal rhythm. "No one else knew."

His smile fell. "Dane did. I should have realized it sooner. He wouldn't have chained a human up that way. He was playing some game with you. I don't know what," he ground out. "I'm just glad you got out of there before something happened."

I swallowed. If everything I'd been through didn't qualify as *something*, I'd hate to think how Jack defined the word. "So why help me in the bar?" I backed up, leaving the lakeshore and moving along the trail to Turtle Pond, bare feet freezing on the thin sheet of ice coating our path.

Jack followed. "No one deserves to be treated the way Dane treats your kind."

"My kind..."

Jack grimaced. "Anyone. Regardless of species."

"I see." I swatted blades of grass so long they brushed my thighs and wriggled my toes to keep the feeling alive in them. "So, it's not because you like the way I look? You would have helped anyone in my position." I glanced back. Jack was slowing. This could go south quickly. I needed to think of a reason for him to want to come.

He stuffed his hands into his pockets. "I would have done something for your friend if I could have without..." He trailed off, not finishing his thought.

The memory of that betrayal stung, but I hadn't stayed to save her either. "You still can. Come with me to Faerie. If they hear from a human how the fae are being treated, they'll have to believe it." I spun around, pressing my palms against Jack's chest.

He stopped, looking up. "Faerie isn't a place for people. I don't heal as easily as you do. You're safe there, but I wouldn't be." His gaze dropped to my now unmarred arms.

"You'd be with me. You would be fine."

Jack searched my face, lips tipping up, and his dimple made another appearance. "Is there some sort of protection for traveling in Faerie with a high fairy?"

"What makes you think I'm high fae?"

"You look human. It's only the high fairies that look human, right?"

I dropped my hands. Was I making a huge mistake? He was Dane Clyde's son after all, and he called me fairy instead of fae, reminding me of the divide between our species. What if *I* was the one being played here? What if this was a ploy to learn how to get into Faerie? I was about to show him exactly how to do it.

"Why didn't you give me away in the bar?"

Jack's brows furrowed, and he pulled a hand out of his pocket, running it through inky hair dusted in snowflakes. It fell in long strands over his jaw, hiding the smooth cheek that no longer held his dimple. "I didn't know what you were then."

My brows dipped. "So what? If you had, you would have left me to be recaptured by Dane?"

He reached for my hand, and I flinched away from him.

His fingers scraped through his hair again, and he met my gaze. "No. I would have helped you no matter what. I don't care that we're different."

I turned, resuming my walk along the path. Jack wanted to be a hero. He was the son of the vilest human alive, but I couldn't believe he was the same cunning, devious sort of man. I may be making the greatest mistake of my life, but I believed him. If I was wrong, it might end up costing the fae everything.

-●-) (∨-●-∧-◆-●●-

As we neared Turtle Pond, an eerie quiet settled over the park.

"Sally...I can't..." Jack started, but I held a finger to my lips as goose-bumps pebbled my arms. Whatever he'd been about to say could wait. Now, the only thing that mattered was not disturbing the silence.

He must have sensed the danger because he nodded, pressing his lips together, and I leaned down, plucking a snowdrop blossom from the mound of snow at my feet. It wilted the moment I pulled it from the magic-laced earth, unable to sustain life outside of Faerie. In Faerie, snow-drops dotted the winter court, blooming year-round, even in their frigid climate. A bit of magic was all they needed to thrive in the bitter cold.

I plucked a second blossom and handed it to Jack. "There's no going back now. She'll kill you the moment you try to run. Watch my feet and no matter what, don't make eye contact."

Jack swallowed, his Adam's apple bobbing. "Who?"

"The Bitter Wraith."

Jack's gaze darted to his feet, and his heart beat a frantic rhythm in his chest. Good. He knew who she was.

The snow flecked ground became a sheet of ice as we stepped onto the frozen pond, and my bare feet screamed in pain. "Hold your stem out."

I glanced sideways, watching Jack's big hand cup the delicate flower as he held it up. His eyes lifted to mine, and I shook my head furiously, mouthing. "Look down."

His gaze dropped just as an ear-splitting scream rent the air.

The hairs on the back of my neck rose, but I kept my gaze trained on the frozen pond at my feet.

Abruptly, the terror-inducing scream cut off, and the stem was plucked from my grasp. Slowly, I lifted my chin, meeting the Bitter Wraith's black eyes. Her inky, almond-shaped orbs narrowed on me, and she sniffed the air.

I leaned back as she pressed her nose to my neck and inhaled deeply. Her gaze moved to Jack, and I sucked in a breath. His snowdrop was trem-bling in his grip, but he kept his eyes trained dutifully on his shoes. He was a fast learner.

The Bitter Wraith moved, closing in on Jack, and my heart climbed into my throat. I needed him alive.

Pressing her nose against his collarbone, her midnight tongue darted out, licking up the column of his throat. She leaned back, leaving his offering in place. Her gaze darted back to me. "No passage for you." Her voice, harsh from disuse, grated against my ears.

"Wraith. I must go to Faerie. They're killing the folk. We have to stop them."

Her eyes gleamed in the moonlight. "What do I care for their plight?"

Her words were oddly metallic as the magic coated my mouth. "They killed the Winter Hag," I whispered.

Her head jerked back to Jack. And I threw up my hand. "Don't harm him. I need him."

She quirked one snowy brow, the motion camouflaged by her matching white skin. Baring her teeth, she snapped at his outstretched hand, now trembling violently. The scent of his fear was inciting her. In a moment, I would lose control of the situation.

I took one step back, and the ice across the pond cracked. I took another, and a massive fissure zigzagged over the frozen pond. The air grew thick with the scent of ozone. My lungs refused to expand as if she were commanding me not to breathe.

"Jack," I whispered. "When I tell you, run."

He glanced up, only for a moment, but it was enough. An ear-splitting wail erupted, sending several small creatures flying in every direction.

Grabbing Jack's hand, I turned, damning formality and yanked him after me. A spattering of tinks erupted into the air, and the leathery flap of a harpy's wings raced behind us as the Bitter Wraith stepped out of the pond.

Jack's heavy footfall and the warmth of his hand in mine were my only reassurance that he was behind me as we ran. I gave up all pretense at humanity, running at fae speed, not stopping until the Wraith's screeching cry was nothing but an echo in my eardrums.

Sliding behind a large oak tree, I tugged Jack with me, and he leaned into the tree, sucking in air. He had struggled that time to keep up, but he had impressive stamina for a human.

"You okay?"

"Still breathing." He met my gaze. "Barely."

"She denied our passage."

"Yeah, I noticed."

I smirked. "You handled it better than I expected."

He pushed off the tree, straightening, and took another large gulp of air. "Do cab drivers and doormen scare you? It's a part of life now. You get used to it."

I raised an eyebrow. "Have you had many run-ins with creatures like the Wraith?"

Jack tucked his hands into his jeans pockets and looked away. After a long pause, his gaze trailed back to me. "I've been helping the ones trapped by Dane. I've spent a little time among them. Sometimes the scariest ones were the kindest." His eyes ran over my face. "And the prettiest ones were often the worst."

Sixteen

Jack

I had the irrational urge to reach out and tuck a stray curl behind Sally's ear. Anything to see her face. Which was ridiculous. I barely knew her.

I wanted to laugh at the face she made when I told her I knew she was a fairy. Her act might have fooled me in the compound, but the moment she set foot in Central Park, she was more at home than I'd seen her anywhere else. Even the flowers seemed to bend toward her as she moved.

Sally pushed off the tree, crowding closer, and I caught a whiff of her floral, dewy scent. It was nothing like I'd ever smelled before, and it stirred something deep inside me. Something I couldn't name.

"Come on. We're not getting in this way. We'll have to find a way in through the Seelie court."

"Sally."

She glanced over her shoulder at me but kept walking.

Like an idiot, I followed, knowing I couldn't go with her. Knowing I'd have to stay behind. My plan to stop Dane depended on me being here. I couldn't traipse into Faerie with the beautiful fairy. Even if it meant saying goodbye to her. Yet when she moved, I trailed her, unable or unwilling to part ways just yet.

We left the Unseelie side of Central Park, pushed through the shimmering shield that kept Faerie from truly spilling over onto Earth, and crossed into the area of the park on the periphery of the protective barrier, but that was still fairy territory. In Dane's reeducation classes, we learned that the low fairies, ogres, fawns, orcs, satyrs, and the like lived outside the shield, while only guardians and high fairies resided inside the shield.

From what I'd just seen, only the guardians and fairy wildlife were inside the barrier. I saw no housing or high fairies inside. The fairies living outside the wards must truly miss their home. It was a small taste of what Faerie would be like, but it was breathtaking and something in the very air sang to my soul. Some selfish part of me longed to see it. Even if only once.

Sally moved like a cat, balancing on the pads of her feet, and her steps made no sound as she traced a path alongside a small stream. Her skirt bunched as she walked, showing long swaths of skin, and I noted the smoothness of it. It looked so *human*.

Eyes trailing down to her ankles, I marveled at their perfectly unmarred surface. Even a human would have chafed under the rough chains around them. A glamour. It was the only explanation. But I'd never seen a fairy with the ability to glamour away iron injuries.

I'd also never seen a high fairy in real life.

Sally stopped, and my gaze moved up the length of her again, dragging painfully over the swell of her ass and up to the eyes glaring daggers at me.

"Eyes up here, Romeo."

My cheeks burned as our gazes met. "Sorry."

Her eyes twinkled in a way that said she hadn't minded as much as she pretended. "Any ideas on how we can break through the perimeter of your father's patrol and reach the entrance to the Seelie Court?"

I tugged my hand out of my pocket and ran it through my hair. "Connor patrols the Seelie side of the park. He won't go near the creatures on the Unseelie side, but Dane culled all the Seelie fairies living outside the Seelie shield, so he runs a pretty tight patrol."

"Culled is an apt word for it," she bit out. Before I could open my mouth to apologize, she spoke again. "How often between guards?"

"Three minutes. Five tops." It was exactly the reason I had planned nothing that would mean traveling this way. "There's only one spot unguarded by patrol, but I'm sure they're all over that place at present. You're better off waiting till Dane stages another riot. Then at least he'll have all his men present to stir up unrest in the crowd."

She swore softly, sliding her bottom lip between her teeth. I tried and failed not to watch the motion. All fairies were beautiful in their strange, deadly way—even the ones who looked like trees or had delicate horns curling from their hair—but confronted with someone so human-looking, if a human could have such perfect curves and sparkling eyes, it was disorienting to my senses.

"I can't wait that long." She tucked a strand of hair behind her ear. "Every moment I waste is one Juniper and the others are being tortured. Killed."

I leaned against a tree, brows furrowing. If her fairy army would truly come to Earth and free them, that would give me time to learn how Janet was involved with my father, and if the alliance was also a part of it. It might be just what I needed to free the creatures without alerting Dane to my involvement.

"If you're going back, there's something you should know."

Sally looked up, meeting my gaze. "What?"

"Dane has other prisons around the city."

Sally's face went pale. "How many?"

"Fourteen that I know of."

"Fourteen?" she breathed.

"Most only have a few prisoners in them, but they're much more heavily guarded than headquarters. You'll need that army."

Sally swayed on her feet, pressing a hand against my chest to catch herself. Warmth erupted under her touch, and I straightened, wrapping my arms under hers to steady her. "Whoa. Are you okay?" I was hit with a wave of her scent, and my head swam.

She backed up, tugging out of my hold, and full pink lips moved as she spoke. It took a moment for her words to register. "If you brought me through Dane's patrol, claiming I was your prisoner, would they let you pass?"

I backed up, attempting to clear her intoxicating scent from my lungs. "No. And I wouldn't put you in that kind of danger."

Sally was unnaturally still, another tell she probably didn't realize she had, but at this, she fidgeted, rubbing a palm absently over her thigh. I kept my eyes resolutely on her face and her forehead wrinkled, auburn brows dipping low as she puzzled something out.

"How close are we to their perimeter?"

"Far enough they won't see us yet, but we shouldn't get much closer."

She squatted down and leaned over the stream, splashing water on her face. I tracked the movement as droplets traced a path along her jaw, dripping off her chin. Her dark lashes rested against tanned cheeks as she splashed another handful of water over her face.

Sally's eyes flew open as scaled arms, hued in blue, erupted from the water, sparkling in the moonlight, and wrapped around her forearms, yanking her into the shallow stream.

"Sally!" I lunged forward, but my foot sank uselessly into mud. She was gone—vanished beneath the surface like she'd never been there. My heart picked up speed as I searched the shallow water. Had another of the fairy beasts that attacked her in the lake just taken her?

I dropped to my knees, nails digging into mud, but it was solid with no way through. What the hell had just happened?

I pulled my phone out, checking the time. One-fifteen a.m. Sally had been gone for more than an hour and there was no trace she'd ever been there at all.

My heart rate had finally slowed, and after a careful search along the stream, tracing it all the way back to the pond we'd come from, I had to accept she wasn't coming back. I only hoped those scaled arms had been friend and not foe. Anger flared through me. It was irrational considering we had only met the night before, but from the moment I'd laid eyes on her—prisoner in my father's stronghold—held against her will for trying to help the other creatures, I'd felt something...different. A protectiveness I'd never felt for anyone. And now she was gone.

I trudged alongside the water toward Dane's camp, scanning the murky darkness for any sign she might have gone this way instead.

"Jackie. Is that you?" My jaw tightened at the nickname as I approached the invisible line Dane had drawn as the border of AFF territory. "Ooooeee. Your dad's mad at you. Better run back before he sends Grif out to get you."

I marched past him, saying nothing. I fucking hated Jim.

"Jack? You're okay?" Alice raced forward, crashing into me, and my arms came up automatically. She hugged me fiercely. The need to shove her off was overwhelming, but I stood, holding her rigidly. Alice's adoration for my father bordered on obsession, and I often wondered if her crush was born of a desire to be closer to him.

I released her and inhaled sharply when I saw the tears streaming down her cheeks. "Hey. Alice. I'm fine."

She sniffled. "I thought that awful fairy did something to you."

"What awful fairy?"

She wiped her eyes. "Sally, or whatever her true name is. Those creatures never have people names."

I would have laughed, but she meant every word of what she said. She was so brainwashed; she assumed any amount of time in the company of fairies might mean our death. A shiver rolled down my spine at the memory of the Wraith. Perhaps with some fairies it was warranted.

"Sally's human, Alice." I crossed my arms over my chest.

Alice leaned forward, lifting her fingers to my cheek. I fought the urge to smack it away. "Oh, Jack, you're too trusting. It's your best and worst quality. She was lying to us. Your dad told me."

My jaw tensed as I bit down on a response to her ludicrous words and snatched her hand before she touched my face again. Of course Dane had told them. When she escaped, it no longer amused him to use her in whatever game he was playing. Now he just wanted her dead. "Sally's not a fairy. I took her home. She has a roommate and a cat. She's as human as you and me."

Alice's nose wrinkled, and for the briefest moment, I thought she'd make up her own mind, but she shook her head, Dane's brainwashing winning out. "No. Jack, she had a glamour. The entire apartment was probably glamoured. Who knows what sort of fairy animal you really met in that apartment. You're lucky you're still breathing."

I ground my teeth, stepping back. "Where's Dane?"

Alice's face fell, her gaze drifting to my shoes. "A fairy died while you were gone. I guess it was one he wanted to keep alive. For a demonstration or something. He's looking for another like it." Alice looked up, watery eyes meeting mine. "I'm just glad you're safe."

Guilt roiled in my gut. I had to hope Sally was okay and safely back in Faerie, but I wouldn't waste any more time waiting on her. For a moment, I'd thought the universe had sent me a bit of luck when Sally mentioned a fairy army. But she was gone, and there was no telling if she would ever return with them.

A sharp psst sliced through the dark. I turned—and there she was. Warmth bloomed in my chest at the sight of her. She was safe. And she had come back. *For me.*

"I'll see you later, Alice." Not waiting for a reply, I turned, striding away from her.

SEVENTEEN

SAV

Of all the inopportune times to run into Kaspar, of course it was when I was close to convincing Jack to come with me. But in the end, it was a blessing in disguise, my once oldest friend had a way of popping up when I needed him most. He may not be a guardian to the pocket entrances of Faerie on land, but the prince of lakes and streams had his own access between realms. That I had been actively avoiding speaking to him for three years hadn't deterred him in the least from offering his aid.

Jack crunched over dried leaves as he approached from an entirely different direction than I'd seen him before. At least he was smart enough not to come directly to me and give us away. I ducked behind the massive oak, exhaling slowly. Of course the mousy girl with limp hair had found him the moment I left him alone. The twisting feeling in my gut when I'd spied them wrapped together in an embrace could only be because I hadn't eaten in hours. It had absolutely nothing to do with Jack.

"Hey," Jack said.

"Let's go. I found a way into Faerie."

I peeked out from behind the tree, spying Alice disappearing into the darkness. One of the three little pigs was headed in our direction, a gun strapped over his chest, and some distance away, the outline of another human was approaching.

"This way." I darted out from behind the tree, but warm fingers wrapped around my arm, spinning me back to him. My heart picked up speed as energy thrummed through me at his touch.

"No. Sally. Listen to me."

My eyes widened as I took in Jack's broad frame. There was a stubborn set to his chin that said he wasn't going anywhere with me until I heard him out. I straightened, glancing over his shoulder and nodded once. "Please, Jack. I have to go. Be quick."

His dark brows lifted slightly as he searched my face. "I can't drop everything to go with you to Faerie. I'm in the middle of something." He folded his arms over his chest.

I stepped closer, laying a hand on his muscled forearm. Whatever it was he thought he was doing, I had to convince him I needed him more. "I need your help. Please?" His gaze dropped to my hand on his forearm and his jaw flexed. When he looked up, I raised both eyebrows. "You know where the prisons are."

Jack's mouth pressed into a flat line. "I can draw you a map. You don't need me."

I bit my lip. This would be harder than I thought. "I don't have a good relationship with the courts. It will take more than my word for them to believe what's happening here. A human—speaking on behalf of the fae—would be accepted as truth." I pulled my hand back, rubbing my bare arms. "And, I thought you wanted to help me. After you let them take Juniper." I glanced past him at another approaching human. He was wasting time I didn't have. I took a step back, putting distance between us. "But. If you can't go."

His eyes rolled to the sky, obviously fighting a battle with himself. "Fine," he sighed, resignation in his voice. "But I can't be gone long. I have things in motion here."

Voices in the distance were drawing near, and I frowned, darting another glance over Jack's shoulder, heart thrumming in my chest. "Of course. We'll go straight to the court, ask for their aid and return."

"Hey! Look!" Someone shouted. "It's the fairy lover!"

I swore. "Time's up," I said, grabbing Jack's hand and tugging him behind me. Lunging over a hedge, I heard his muffled humph behind me as he followed. I glanced back. "Hurry!" I shouted as several armed men closed the distance behind us.

Jack picked up speed and we ran faster.

A massive aquamarine-hued kelpie appeared beside us in the stream, sailing over the water as we ran beside him. His immense blue eyes flashed to me, and I nodded. He tossed his head sideways at Jack, and those large horse eyes seemed to narrow on me.

I ran faster, and in moments, Jack began to lag behind. A bullet whizzed past my head, then another, dangerously close.

"Kaspar, pick him up! They'll shoot him!"

The kelpie whinnied and nipped at Jack who shouted in protest, slowing down.

"Jack, get on. He's taking us to Faerie."

Jack eyed the beast warily, but another gunshot cracked, and he dove onto Kaspar's back.

Kaspar leaned his powerful neck around and snapped pointed teeth at Jack.

Jack nearly toppled off his back as he scrambled away from his bite.

"Scoot up," I shouted.

Jack managed to right himself, swinging a leg over the kelpie's back and I leaped into the air, landing behind him as three more bullets sailed past.

"Dive Kaspar," I begged.

Waves swelled around us, and he sank beneath the water. I wrapped my arms tightly around Jack's waist and my legs around Kaspar's sides as I whispered into Jack's ear before we were fully submerged: "Hold your breath."

We were swallowed by dark, frigid water as Kaspar dove below the surface of the stream for just a moment before he rose back up.

Jack inhaled a heaving breath, and we sank again. This time, Kaspar moved swiftly, aiming straight for the shimmering chasm at the bottom. We were cheating, using the prince of lakes and streams to take us through the rift between worlds, but we would know in a moment whether Faerie would accept Jack or not, and there would be nothing I could do if it didn't.

EIGHTEEN
JACK

Veins bulged along my neck and my lungs screamed for air, but the fear was nothing compared to the sight before me.

Scaled creatures raced for us, sharp fangs extended, talons outstretched as they tried to beat us to the strange rainbow bisecting the bottom of an expansive lake. We wouldn't make it. I wouldn't make it, and the urge to open my mouth and suck in precious, life-giving air was a frantic chant in my mind.

As navy-scaled creatures approached, unearthly screams filled the water, and I closed my eyes, praying my last few moments wouldn't be painful ones.

Hands touched my face, startling my eyes open, and Sally twisted my head to hers. Soft, warm lips pressed against mine, and pressure built. My mouth opened and hot bubbles slid inside. I swallowed them down greedily as my lungs expanded.

Sally smiled, releasing me, and a flash of searing ice sliced through me as we fell into complete darkness.

◆→)(◡◆♠◆●◆

I opened my eyes, finding the pain in my lungs diminished somehow.

Exhaling a slow breath, bubbles floated up, stretching for a surface we were rapidly approaching.

Sally's lips met mine again, and I opened my mouth for her precious gift, inhaling deeply this time. I wanted to slip my tongue inside her mouth—taste her sweet tongue—inhale not just her air but her essence, but she pulled back, and my lips slid closed, locking the bubbles in.

Sparkling scales along the sea horse's flank reflected in the sunlight and in moments, we broke the surface, and I gasped, sucking in the overly sweet air of Faerie.

The horse began swimming toward a shore that seemed impossibly far away.

I leaned down, stroking his mane. Sure, he'd tried to bite me, but he was a good boy and saved my life. His head shook and he let out an angry snort.

"You don't like that, Buddy?" I crooned, running a hand over his shining blue mane of seaweed.

Sally cackled, and I spun to look at her.

"I don't think anyone has even pet Kaspar before. Much less called him Buddy." She stifled another laugh but sobered quickly when she saw my gaze lingering on her soft, pink, life-giving lips. The seahorse shook all over and I slid sideways, nearly tipping off his back. Sally's iron grip came around me and pulled me up. "Kaspar, stop that. The naiads will eat him if he falls in."

I tensed, digging my heels into the seahorse's sides. "Naiads?"

Her warmth pressed into my back, setting my skin on fire even through the layers of our wet clothes. Hot breath tickled my ear as she whispered, "the creatures with pointy teeth and sharp nails, chasing us on the other side of the pocket."

My racing heart stuttered between desire and fear as her words mingled with her closeness. Waves crashing over a blue-tinged lakeshore speckled my face, and in a moment, the view stole my focus. We had left Earth after two a.m., but here it was morning. A soft golden sun glittered across granules of sand so white they could have been snowflakes.

The seahorse's long tail transformed beneath me and bright, metallic hooves galloped over tightly packed sand as the lake disappeared behind us and we approached a forest unlike any in my wildest dreams.

Trees of every shade stretched far overhead, some curving at strange and unnatural angles as they fought for competing space along the canopy. Between them, moss-covered vines dotted with bright purple and green-capped mushrooms hung in an interlacing pattern, forming a web on which odd and fantastical creatures perched.

I gaped as our aquamarine horse galloped past a creature shaped like a monkey who was the color of a banana. Its matching eyes blinked once, revealing false blue eyes on its lids. I imagined how it would have looked asleep—appearing wide eyed—and smiled.

An animal not unlike an owl took flight, spreading its wings and revealed several tiny, winged fairies clinging to the insides of its feathers. I stretched my head back, watching as they hung to the creature for dear life when it tipped sideways, banking left.

"Magical," I breathed.

My eyes adjusted to the darkening landscape as our horse slowed to a trot and the light dappled forest floor came into focus. When the ground was no longer a blur of greens and oranges, my gaze traveled over every unfamiliar sight, drinking it up greedily. Was I the first person to enter Faerie? I must have been. If other humans had witnessed the splendor of this place, they could never believe its inhabitants were evil.

Sally's hold around my waist loosened, and the cold absence that followed made me shiver. Our horse stuttered to a stop, and she slid off.

I peered down the considerable distance to the ground. Swinging my leg over, I slid down the side of the massive horse. His back legs kicked up as I dismounted, sending me sprawling. I landed in a soft bed of undergrowth, spongy to the touch, and exhaled a "humph." When I sucked in a pained breath, it was spicy—a mix of cinnamon and cedar.

Sally came to my side, holding out a hand. I reached for it, and she tugged me up.

"Thanks," I said, dusting off my shirt and pants, turning in a slow circle, tipping my head back. Leaves in orange, yellow, red and green formed a cornucopia of color overhead.

"Your human is ill-equipped for our land."

The words dragged my focus to a man who wasn't a man. His skin was teal-tinged, and his hair, a bright shade of vermilion, almost floated on a phantom wind, obscuring a silver crown spiked with seashells. Below his ears, on either side of his throat, tiny, fine lines ran along his neck. As though someone had tried to slit it several times but failed. His unearthly eyes were a perfect match for his hair.

None of this was what made him most inhuman. His bare chest was speckled with turquoise scales, shimmering in the light, the exact shade of the ones covering the seahorse's body.

"Kaspar?"

His eyes went round. "It's Prince Kaspar of the lakes and streams to you, Peasant."

I gaped. A prince. I had ridden on a prince.

NINETEEN

SAV

"You have my gratitude for everything Kas. I'll take it from here," I said, moving to pass him.

"Not so fast. What's your name?" A smirk played on Kaspar's lips. "Sally? You will not trek all the way to the Spring Court on your own. It's not safe."

I rolled my eyes. "I can handle myself. Besides, I have Jack."

Kaspar's gaze shot to Jack, roving up and down his sodden, human form. "Do you plan to feed him to your enemies to make your escape?"

I let out a small laugh. "No. He's trained for battle. Quite a fighter."

"Really." The words dripped off Kaspar's tongue with interest. I'd meant to give him a little taste of his own medicine, but I'd only piqued his interest. Figured. He moved as though he were still underwater, a trait I'd never grown used to. "Tell me Jack." He closed the distance between them, getting right in Jack's face.

To Jack's credit, he didn't back down. Jack seemed to have a weakness for alluring fae though, perhaps he didn't know the threat that stood before him.

"Could you take me?"

Jack's nostrils flared, eyes narrowing, and he squared his shoulders, standing several inches taller. "I'd hate to dent your pretty crown, it looks expensive, but I would."

The corners of Kaspar's lips tipped up and he spun around to face me. "Oh, I like him. I see why you want to keep him."

"I'm not keeping him," I scoffed. "He wanted to come."

Kaspar's attention drifted back to Jack. "Is it true, Jack? Did you come of your own free will?"

His words held that lilting edge meant to entrance a human into divulging their truth and I grimaced, moving to push Kaspar aside. Jack's eyes were blazing with a fire that said he was about to make good on his promise. Much as I'd love to see someone put Kaspar in his place for once in his life, I didn't think a magicless human would be the one to do it.

"Enough. We're not going to Spring. We're going to Winter to beg for their aid."

Kaspar's lip curled. "Good luck. I regret I won't be joining you, my..." his gaze shifted back to Jack. "*Sally*. Enjoy your time in Winter."

He dipped his head to me. To Jack he bared his teeth. "Careful not to touch what doesn't belong to you, human. Many things in Faerie have sharp teeth." He winked at me and sauntered away, pants slung low on his hips, and I stared after him shaking my head.

We hadn't seen the last of Prince Kaspar, of that I was certain.

After several hours and a comprehensive list of things Jack couldn't eat while in Faerie, I could admit I was impressed. I never had to show him the same plant twice. He stored each lesson away and even began pointing out the ones I'd said were for medicinal purposes.

We stopped beside a stream, and I sank down, cupping my hands in the water. He followed, watching warily for a moment before he scooped handfuls of the cool liquid into his palms, bringing them up and drinking as if his life depended on it.

A bead of sweat trickled down Jack's chin, rolling over his Adam's apple and dipping below his too-small t-shirt. I sat back, my gaze tracking the movement of the droplet, watching as his throat swallowed several times. An image flashed in my mind of Jack between my thighs, lapping up an entirely different kind of liquid. I looked away, cheeks burning.

"Let's rest here a while." I stood, turning away from him and scolding myself for the thought. I needed to put a bit of distance between us. Clear my head. The last thing I needed was a distraction that could get me killed just for thinking it. Wiping slick palms on my skirt, I searched the forest. We needed food. It was as good a reason as any to escape his suffocating presence. "Stay here. I'll be back."

It was a risk entering Faerie through the Summer Court. Technically, our two courts were at war and that made me a trespasser, but as I'd been banished from mine, I hoped if we were found here, I could beg the mercy of a courtless fae. If Summer offered such clemency.

The sounds of Jack's slurping followed me as I moved between massive

Ash and Oak trees, and I shook my head. *Don't think about his raven curls buried between my thighs. Don't. Just don't.* The pep talk with myself was having the opposite effect for some unknown reason. Spying a green vine wrapped securely around a tall Cedar tree, I moved to it, pulling plump black berries from their tendrils.

He was probably terrible at pleasuring a woman. Not that I would ever find out. He was in Faerie for one reason and one reason only.

My shirt was stained dark purple and overflowing with fruit when I had plucked every berry from its vine. I smiled, picturing Jack's reaction to tasting them for the first time. Blackberries were native to Faerie, but somehow the little stowaways had found their way into the human realm. Since arriving on Earth, I'd heard many humans remark on their flavor, but the berries on Earth had lost their magical luster. They were nothing compared to what we had here.

I found Jack reclining against a moss-covered tree, eyes closed, breath coming in and out in a slow, steady rhythm. Stopping beside him, I dropped to the ground, tugged a large yellow leaf free from its branch, and poured the berries in. Popping a few in my mouth, my gaze drifted to his face. In sleep he looked peaceful, the tightness in his jaw relaxed, and I resisted the urge to sweep a raven curl from his face.

I let out a little moan as the mix of sweet and bitter juices burst over my tongue. It had been three years since I tasted true Faerie fruit. On Earth, I'd only tried them once. Flavorless as they were, they were a bitter reminder of all I'd lost.

Jack's heart rate increased, and I glanced over as his eyelids twitched furiously. A dream. Were his dreams full of hideous creatures and monstrous fae or did he dream of a world without our kind in it?

Biting my lip, I reached a tentative finger out, brushing the hair back from his face. His heart rate slowed, eyelids calming and his breathing steadied again. His skin was smooth, unmarred by the hardships so many had endured since Earth and Faerie collided. A perk of being the son of the man in charge of so much pain and suffering.

His eyes flew open and I snatched my hand back.

A soft smile curved his lips. "Were you watching me sleep?"

"No."

He sat up. "You were. It's okay. You can admit it."

My lips fell into a flat line. "In your dreams."

A dimple appeared in Jack's cheek and he lifted an arm behind his head, a grin plastered on his face. "If you say so." He closed his eyes again. "Go ahead. Take another look."

I blew out a breath and got to my feet. "I need water."

His laugh followed me as I retraced my steps into the forest. What had

I been thinking? No good would come of entertaining a... friendship... with Jack. He was my enemy. He was pretty, but so were Lily-of-the-valleys and that made them no less deadly.

I wandered aimlessly, letting the vegetation–bursting with life–soaked in magic, bleed strength into my limbs. It had been three years of iron infested, smog filled, torture and though I was sure returning home brought its own trouble, I was glad to be back.

⬤➔〔◡◆⋏◆●⬤

When enough time had passed that he must be asleep again, I returned to the place I'd left him. My pack was resting beside me, but the berries were gone and so was Jack. *He must have eaten the berries and gone to relieve himself.*

Small three-leaf-clovers dotted the ground at my feet, and I leaned down, plucking one of their leaves. A shrill cry emanated from the tiny creature and a small green head erupted from its center. A tirade of curses poured forth and I waited for it to finish. Its tiny cheeks huffed and puffed, and a small leafy hand shot out.

"I'll give it back when you tell me what I want to know." I said in Elvish.

Miniature eyebrows climbed up its head and it huffed several times before nodding.

"Did you see the human sleeping here?"

A single nod.

"Where did he go?"

A tiny green tongue darted out of its mouth, bits of spittle flying as it blew a raspberry at me.

I reached for a second petal around its head and it squeaked, holding up three leafy hands in a placating gesture.

"Where?"

The clover fairy spun its stem around, pointing deeper into the forest, not toward the Winter Court, but in the direction of the Autumn Court and my stomach dropped. "Are you sure?"

It nodded emphatically and I handed back its petal, patting it on the head.

It began another series of curses as I picked up my bag and stepped carefully around the family of clovers, in search of Jack.

TWENTY

JACK

A soft hand caressed my cheek, and I grinned lazily.

"Do you like that, my sweet?"

I nodded, leaning back and turning my head as Sally's mouth found mine. My lips parted, granting her admittance, and her tongue, soft and tasting of honey, swept in. I sucked it, wanting to taste her, to devour every bit of her she would give.

A warm hand wrapped around me, running up the underside of my shirt, tracing the line up the center of my stomach to my chest. There, her fingers circled my nipples, pinching each when it pebbled. A second hand slid south, dipping beneath my pants. It found the hard length of my arousal and stroked.

"I want you," I tried to say, tipping my head back to give her better access, but Sally had my tongue between her teeth and was biting playfully so my words were garbled.

A third hand traced a line up my arm, wrapping around my biceps and tugging my back against her solid chest.

Her tongue probed into my mouth again and her languorous strokes beneath my pants grew insistent, coaxing me to a quick climax, and it was all I could do to hold back the orgasm long enough to ensure she felt pleasure too.

But I wasn't touching her. I wasn't giving her any of the pleasure she was giving me. With my free hand, I reached behind me, running a hand over her rough skin.

My eyes flew open, and I glanced down.

My body was wrapped tightly in thick branches, one snaking inside my pants and choking my rapidly deflating shaft. I gagged, spitting bits of bark and sap from my mouth, and wriggled to free myself, but every movement only made the tree creature wrap tighter.

Another small, tongue-shaped branch darted against my mouth, and I pressed my lips tightly together.

"Come on, Jack. We were having so much fun," the gravely creature's voice rasped in my ear.

The branches wrapped around my cock squeezed and I screamed as bark flooded into my mouth, cutting off the sound. I pushed reflexively with my tongue, forcing it back. Biting down savagely, I tasted sap and spit out the bits of bark no longer wriggling between my teeth.

The creature's hold slackened for a moment, and I reached across my chest, tearing away the branch securing my other arm.

A scream like the dying embers of a fire burst in my eardrum and I released the branch, covering my ears. The pressure in my head was building as I tugged uselessly at the rock-hard grip around my middle.

"Jack!"

Sally's voice, clear in my mind after the delusional state I'd just been in, roused some of my senses and I fought the creature's hold again, ripping bark from my body. Its screams were an unending cacophony of sounds exploding through my head, and the world darkened as the sound overwhelmed me and I slumped forward, losing the fight.

"Jack!"

Sally's voice was closer this time and the pressure around my waist and between my legs eased and I gasped at the sharp pain in my side. I was dragged away from the tree creature and laid out on a soft bed of grass. I stared dazedly up at the sky and darkness obscured my vision before Sally's face came into focus.

Some of the wild panic in my chest calmed. Her dark lashes—shrouding eyes the color of amethysts—blinked several times, and my heart slowed, moving in time with the motion. A lock of her thick auburn hair fell across her face, and I lifted a hand, tucking it behind her ear and running my thumb over her mouth to assure myself it was really her this time. Her full, pink lips moved, saying something I couldn't understand.

My breathing slowed—calm settled over me—and as my eyes drifted closed, her face burned into my retinas.

I exhaled a long sigh. "Beautiful."

TWENTY-ONE

SAV

The human was definitely going to die here.

A simple dryad, one of the easiest creatures to evade, had trapped him. They rarely bothered folk outside of their mating cycle. Still, even young fae were almost never ensnared by such basic magic. If Jack were to have any chance of surviving in Faerie, I'd need to teach him some of the rules.

He groaned, and I looked over, narrowing my eyes. "You're still alive then."

He pressed a hand to his head, and the other ran down his body, cupping his pants.

"It's still there."

"Did you check?" He asked in a rasping voice.

How close had the dryad come to implanting her seed in him? What a liability he was turning out to be. How had this species survived so long? "You did, the last two times you woke up. Are you going to stay awake this time, or should I call on Kaspar to give us a ride?"

Jack's eyelids fluttered, and he turned to look at me. Dark purple had begun to mottle his throat and collarbone, and I was sure if I lifted his shirt, I would find bruising there as well. My brows flattened even as the tension in my chest eased each time he woke. Our kinds didn't mix because of this weakness. Their short lifespans and lack of common sense were incompatible with a superior species.

I laid a hand on his chest, feeling its slow rise and fall. Something uncomfortable twisted in my gut. I'd been worried about him. More than I should have been. True, dryads rarely killed their victims. They only wanted to propagate their kind, but humans were fragile.

"No more rides from your boyfriend," he whispered, eyes closing again. In a few moments, soft snores slid through his lips, and I relaxed.

He'd slipped in and out of consciousness for more than an hour, but his eyes weren't turning brown, and his heart beat steadily. He would recover. I licked my lips, glancing at my hand as it moved with the rise and fall of his chest before scanning the area. I couldn't wait for Jack to wake again. When we crossed the border into Winter, it would be frigid at mid-day, but at night, it would be deadly.

Standing and stalking into the tree line, but not letting Jack out of sight, I found two large maple leaves and, after testing several branches, pulled out a pair that appeared sturdy enough to hold his weight and dragged them back. I set my bag on the ground and tugged out a spool of skink worm thread. It was my last spool, a final remnant of my old life, and one of the few things I'd been able to take with me when I left Faerie.

Pulling a long needle out of the tufted top of the spool, I strung it along the leaves, looping them when I reached a branch and doubling back across the makeshift cot. When I'd strung enough thread to hold the leaves in place between two sturdy branches, I bit the end of the thread, wrapping it securely around the spool—silently mourning the small bit remaining—and tied it off at the end.

"Jack. Get up."

He mumbled something incoherent and began snoring again. He must have ingested more of the dryad's sap than I first thought. With no toad's blood to counteract its effects, though, my best option was to get him to the winter court as soon as possible. Their healer would have herbs to aid him.

I hefted him up, dragged him onto the stretcher, bent his knees, and pulled.

He was heavy, even for me. After several hours dragging him over mossy stones and soft grass, I paused, wiping a hand across my forehead and peered through the foliage and trunks, searching for any sign that we were near the winter kingdom.

My feet stung and my back ached, but the oppressive canopy of Summer's flora was giving way to taller, thinner trees and finally—finally—I stepped over the line into Winter and soft flurries of snow dusted my cheeks.

Stopping to lean against the white-striped bark of a birch tree, I exhaled a sigh. The sun had dipped low, and I swallowed as I realized we wouldn't make it to the castle before dark at this pace. The short skirt I was still wearing would do nothing to protect against the elements, but it wasn't me I feared for in the cold. Jack would be an issue if we didn't get indoors soon.

Lifting his stretcher once more, I sped up, knees lifted higher as snow blanketed the ground and my feet grew numb. A chill settled over my bones as the weather dipped from cold to freezing, and I glanced back to see Jack's mouth turning blue, frigid air puffing between his lips. A bitter wind picked up, whipping flurries of snow around my face, and my stomach dipped.

Hefting the branches under each arm, I jogged, sinking nearly to my knees in the snow. Pain radiated up the soles of my feet and, more worryingly, I no longer felt my toes. Daggers speared my lungs with each breath and my frozen fingers slipped more than once, but I kept going. There was no turning back now.

"Ho there!"

I spun around, dropping my stretcher, and gasped out a sob of relief. "Help us," I pleaded, sinking down into the snow.

TWENTY-TWO

DANE

Papers flew from my desk as Brian, my third in command, scurried out of my office. My son was a damn fool, but perhaps it was my fault. He thought I wasn't aware of his little trips to my prison to care for the creatures down there. Now, after explicit instructions to avoid the one I'd brought into our headquarters, he was missing.

I wished I could fear the worst, that he'd been kidnapped, but I knew my son. The creature, disguised as a human, was too pretty for her own good. And a damn good actress. One simpering look at Jack and he'd fallen all over himself. It didn't take a genius to know he had gone willingly.

I slammed a fist on the desk. The high fae, Sally, she called herself, was in my grasp. Why had I wasted time on Janet's petty mission? I owed ISHFA nothing, and I was tired of playing their games. I should have made a deal with the royals and traded her as I'd originally intended. Now, she was gone and with far more valuable collateral than she realized.

"Sir."

I looked up, swallowing the rage swimming in my veins. "Yes, Alice. Come in."

She glanced around at the papers scattered on the floor and I bit my tongue before I said something I'd regret later. Stopping on the other side of the desk, she placed a silver money clip and black leather wallet on the sleek metal surface. "Connor found them beside a stream just outside our perimeter."

I swiped the wallet, flipping it open. A younger version of my son grinned up at me. He'd taken that picture before the fae invaded. Before his mother had shown her true colors. Before everything had changed. The innocence twinkling in eyes so like his mother's it hurt to look at them, was gone now.

A piece of me died the day she betrayed us. The piece that housed my compassion. She had deceived me. Deceived us all and, in the end, it cost me everything. I would never tell Jack the extent of her lies. I let him believe the best. Some glimmer of humanity lived in me after all, because I still yearned to keep the worst world offered from him a little longer.

I tucked the wallet into my pocket. "Thank you. Have we questioned all the fairies who may have seen something?"

Alice nodded, tucking her hands into her pockets. "Everyone we had was already down there when she escaped. Grif thinks we should target the guardians."

Ice pebbled my skin. The guardians of the pocket entrances to Faerie. Access points that could apparently move, but that had always existed on Earth, were now all conveniently in New York City. Why the fae chose our city, I'd likely never learn, but fae royals who conducted business with our leaders used them freely to travel back and forth.

Morgan, the autumn court's emissary, had permanently relocated to our realm. Unlike the other royals, who remained in Faerie, she was regularly seen on our streets and in our cafes. She enjoyed the luxuries of human life all while touting the ISHFA principles of co-existence.

I hated her more than the rest. She and the other high fae who looked so like us but would never be our equals.

"The Bitter Wraith never leaves the water, but we would have the prince of lakes and streams' entire army to contend with if we made a move on her. Have Grif round up our strongest and meet me in command. Our best option is Trym."

Alice paled, taking a step back. Her weak stomach made her a nuisance at the best of times and dangerous to my cause at the worst. "Are you sure? The king of the trolls."

I ground my teeth. "Are you questioning me?"

She swallowed audibly. "No."

"Get Grif and send him to me. There's more I need to discuss with him."

She nodded and saluted. I waved her off, sending her out.

Alone in my office, I leaned against the desk, pulling Jack's wallet out again. I flipped it open, staring at his wide, goofy grin. "Oh, son. I should have better prepared you for what's coming."

Grif appeared at my door and knocked once.

"Enter."

"Alice said you asked me to meet you in command, but I was in the hall. I knew you were still in here."

I raised a brow. "Spying on me?" I knew someone in my faction was a spy for ISHFA, but I hadn't yet rooted out the culprit. I never would have suspected Grif. Orphaned by this war, no one had more reason to be here than him.

His lips quirked up, and he chuckled. "Nah. I was following Alice."

I smiled, wrapping my knuckles on my desk, and slid Jack's wallet back into my pocket. That's what I liked about Grif. He was never afraid to go after what he wanted. "Did she relent?"

His grin fell. "Not yet. But I'll wear her down."

I rounded my desk laying a hand on Grif's shoulder. "Come. It's time I share more of my plan with you."

TWENTY-THREE
JACK

S oft humming filled my ears, and my heart banged frantically against my ribcage. The last time I heard that sound...I grabbed my neck, running a hand over my bare chest and down to my pants, where my fingers slipped under my waistband and felt for the appendage that had been so severely abused by the dryad.

"You're alright, Jack," a soft voice crooned.

My eyes slid open, staring up at a high stone ceiling. I glanced left and searing pain shot up my neck. I hissed, turning back to face the ceiling.

A warm, wet cloth came down on my forehead. "There, there, sweet child. Don't fret. Mother Mahonia is here." Her gentle humming resumed, but no rough bark or strangling hold wrapped around my body, and I relaxed, muddled thoughts trying to piece together where I was and what was happening.

"You will not tell him, or I'll call in my favor," Sally hissed from the hall. It was low and menacing in a way I'd never heard. The hairs on the back of my neck rose. I had known her sweet innocence was an act, but since entering Faerie, something savage had begun to show itself in her.

Dane's words echoed in my head. "They have no soul and no remorse. They will bribe, steal, and kill to get what they want. They are animals."

I shook the thought away.

"You're alive."

Sally's dry voice seemed to suggest I had survived despite my best efforts not to. And maybe she was right. Though I hadn't pieced it all together, I remembered the soft singing I'd thought was Sally's and my eagerness to follow and see where it led.

In my haste to meet a very naked, very alluring, Sally beneath the tree, I hadn't asked myself, even for a second, if it made sense that she was nude and dancing seductively under this tree, when she'd marched away a scowl twisting her lips at my teasing. Lured by the promise of all that soft flesh and the wanton desire in her eyes, I'd tripped over myself to get to her. That was idiotic.

With some effort, I turned my head again, wincing as I took in her angry gaze. Was she upset with me for nearly dying or for surviving?

"Must be. Death wouldn't hurt this much." I grunted the words as each one sent shocks of pain through my chest.

She rolled her eyes, coming to stand over me. "You look like shit."

I snorted, then groaned at the fire in my lungs.

"So, this is your human?" Another woman stepped into the room. She looked less like my kind than Sally, not the least of which because of the fluffy tail curled around her wrist, but her shocking green eyes, luminescent and feline, were a more vivid version of the ones I stared at in the mirror every day.

Our similarities ended there. Where my hair was black as night, hers was white as ice, falling in a sheet down her back. Her skin was several shades darker than mine, a rich brown that reminded me painfully of my mother. I had inherited little from her, including her beautiful dark skin, but we shared the same green eyes with this stranger.

The severe contrasts between hair, eyes and skin made her striking to look at. My gaze trailed down her finely made gown. I wanted to laugh at the intricate designs woven through the fabric in the shape of polar bears. I might have asked her if she was on her way to the Renaissance festival, but when I looked at Sally, her gaze had narrowed to slits, and I sobered.

"He's not *my* anything."

The other woman came to stand beside her, and they both scrutinized me like a lab specimen on a table. "If you don't want him, I'll take him."

Sally's head whipped to the left, and she bared her teeth. It was the most inhuman gesture I'd ever seen her make. If there had been any lingering doubts about her nature, they were erased by that movement. "He's not yours to claim."

"Ladies," I wheezed. "Don't fight...I'm enough man...for you both."

Both their gazes darted to me, eyes narrowing in similar expressions of feral rage. My cock shrank in my pants.

A low chuckle broke the chilling silence and Mother Mahonia pushed out of her chair, shuffling closer. "Go on, girls, leave the patient to recover. He's still delirious."

I exhaled a shaky breath, wondering if Mother Mahonia had just saved my life.

They turned, letting her shuffle them out of the room, but Sally glanced back, giving me another seething look before the door closed and I was blessedly alone.

As my muscles eased, breath coming easier, my mind settled on Sally's words again. "You will not tell him, or I'll call in my favor."

TWENTY-FOUR
SAV

T hough I was glad to be out of the summer court and away from its prince, the ice in my veins hadn't relented since arriving in winter, making my teeth chatter. I'd groaned in absolute ecstasy when one of the staff showed me to the baths. Now, I slid down, dipping below the surface, and let the warm water sink into my bones. It warmed my frost-bitten toes and fingers, bleeding life into my frozen limbs.

Underwater, my eyes fluttered closed, and I frowned when my mind drifted to Jack. Seeing him recovered enough to open his eyes—and ogle Hazel—a tightness in my chest had eased. Even if the urge to kill him had doubled when he opened his mouth.

Breaking the surface, I inhaled the scent of mint and peony and sighed, banishing thoughts of the human. Though it was freezing year-round, there was something soothing about the winter court. Perhaps because this was Mab's kingdom, the birthplace of high fae and the root of all high magic.

Low fae had existed long before we came to be, but their magic was wild, tied to the land, and it fed the cycle rather than controlling it. Ours was a magic made to change. It affected the seasons, drew a soft blanket over Faerie when it grew too hot or called down a balmy rain when the soil was parched. Our magic had consequences and, in the wrong hands, could devastate.

But what did it matter now? When the realm continued shrinking every day, forcing more creatures into the human realm as their land was eaten up by whatever magic was destroying Faerie. What good was all that power if we weren't able to save ourselves?

Bubbles erupted from the bath, and I jumped back as a dripping wet head emerged from between my thighs. I scrambled away. "Kaspar, what are you doing here? This isn't a lake or stream." Although the baths weren't private here like in the human realm, sharing one was typically reserved for one's lover.

Water ran in rivulets over his faintly luminescent skin as his navy lips spread in a wide grin. "These baths are fed by a natural hot spring." I shoved his chest, pushing him away as the rest of his fully nude form materialized in the tub. "Can't your betrothed share a bath? It's so cold in this kingdom."

I scowled at him. "I rejected the suit. You're nothing to me."

His hand flew to his scaled chest, mock outrage written across his face. "You wound me, Princess."

"Don't call me that." Kaspar always knew just what to say to get under my skin. Titles, unearned and undeserved, were like ice water dumped on me. That he knew that and used them anyway only showed how cold and unfeeling he truly was.

He leaned back in the tub, arms resting along the lip as he surveyed me. "Look at you, my lady, reduced to this weak form, hardly any magic at your disposal, lugging around a human plaything."

My gaze whipped around the space. "Don't say that."

He held up a hand. "I apologize."

"I mean it, Kaspar—"

"Forgive me, *Sav.*"

I exhaled slowly, letting my gaze drop. Much as I wanted to be angry with him for appearing in my bath and expecting me to be civil to him after what he'd done, Kaspar was, at his core, a water fae. They simply didn't think or feel the way we did. "What are you doing here? You hate the winter court."

"I had to be sure they were looking after you."

"Why?"

Kaspar leaned forward, reaching for my fingers and tugging them to his mouth. "Are we not long acquaintances?" Cool lips brushed over my knuckles. "And am I not allowed to ensure my betrothed has been looked after?"

I yanked my hand back. "I'm not your betrothed. How many times do I have to tell you? Are you so desperate to align yourself with a court that you would pursue me even when you know I loathe you?"

He laughed. It was musical and lilting with so much magic he couldn't contain it. "Yours is not the only court with eligible females I could partner with. Hazel would have me this instant if I offered. You would be trapped in this state forever. Is that what you truly want?"

I scowled. "You hate Winter."

"She's beautiful, though. I bet she does all sorts of kinky things with that tail."

I chewed my bottom lip, and my shoulders curled in. "I can't. I can't give myself away for a political alliance."

Kaspar leaned forward, and his cool breath tickled my nose. "We could be happy." His bright eyes bored into mine, searching for some answer I didn't have.

In another life, one where I wasn't so broken, perhaps I might have convinced myself to settle for what Kaspar offered. Security, safety, companionship. "You know what I want," I whispered.

He released a shuddering breath and slid back, looking away. "I'm not like you, Sav. This cold heart doesn't love."

"I know," I murmured. "I don't blame you. But..."

"But you won't marry for anything less."

I nodded, and with one final resigned sigh, he dipped below the water and was gone.

TWENTY-FIVE

JACK

I leaned against the wall, heart hammering in my chest. Princess. *Sav.* Engaged. Not Engaged. My head swam with everything I had just learned. The man with blue skin wasn't just a friend who offered to help her, he was something more. He wanted to be *much* more. Why did the thought of them together have heat searing in my veins? Had I expected someone so beautiful, confident, and brave to be single?

Acknowledging that fact did nothing to ease the tightness in my chest. And she wasn't just a high fairy, she was a princess. No wonder she counted on the court to lend her an army. She commanded it. But what had she been doing on Earth?

Sloshing water in the bath drew my focus, and I held my breath. Soft, wet footfall in the next room moved toward the door, and I turned, nearly colliding with the other woman who visited me in the infirmary.

She grinned, a long snow leopard-like tail whipping behind her.

I backed up. "Excuse me..." I paused.

"I'm Hazel."

My gaze dipped to the spotted tail, coiling and uncoiling from her wrist, the prince's words coming back to me. *I bet she does all sorts of kinky things with that tail.*

"You must be the princess of winter." I glanced around the hall. Was there a way I was supposed to address a princess in Faerie? I had done nothing special with Kaspar, but I hadn't known what he was.

Her grin widened. "Eavesdropping, Jack?"

"I guess you were, too."

Her eyes twinkled as she appraised me, coming to some decision. "I'm no princess. I am the winter court emissary and third cousin to Queen Mab." She moved closer. "But, Jack, Kaspar wasn't wrong." She lifted a finger, trailing one long blue fingernail down my chest. "My tail is good for lots of things."

I swallowed, taking a step back. "I came here with Sav. Remember?" That was idiotic. Hazel likely knew about the betrothal. Not betrothal. And that there could be nothing between us when the woman I'd come here with had a prince chasing after her.

Hazel glanced over my shoulder and back at me. "You know. The best way to find out if someone is interested is to make them jealous." She winked at me and turned, hips swaying as her tail swished behind her.

I stared after her, considering her words. I'd never had to work for a woman's attention before. It was usually them vying for mine. But Sav wasn't like the other women I had met. *Sav.* The name fit her so much better than Sally. It was strong, sophisticated. A name fit for a princess.

"Jack."

I started turning to face Sav. I hadn't heard the door open or her footsteps approaching, too lost in thoughts of the creature standing in front of me now. My gaze trailed up the powder blue fabric of her gown, lingering on her curves before moving up to the collarbone, delicately framed by silver thread. Her hair was pulled up, curls framing her flushed cheeks, still dewy from her bath. Our eyes met and heat flared to life in my chest.

"Sav," I said.

The hunger in her eyes—mirroring my own—deflated, gaze growing wary. "What did you hear?"

"Nothing. Hazel told me your name."

"Hazel!" she shouted. Hazel continued down the hall, ignoring us.

Sav's gaze darted back to me and ran over my body. "Feeling better?"

"Yes. Mother Mahonia gave me some sort of healing tonic that worked wonders."

Satisfied by my answer and my much-recovered state, she answered. "Yes. My name is Sav. It didn't seem like a human enough name for the cult and there's power in names. But you can use it. I detest Sally."

I snorted, marveling at how little it hurt only a few hours after taking the healing tonic. "Sav. I like it." A faint smile touched her mouth. If I didn't know better, I'd think she enjoyed hearing her true name on my lips. I wanted to say more. I wanted to demand answers, but she owed me nothing and who was I to a princess?

"Come on. Let's go. We have an audience with the winter court."

I frowned, glancing down. "Should I change?"

Sav looked me over. "Why?"

"I'm still wearing this Fae'z in Harlem t-shirt and there's dirt and blood all over it." I eyed her clean appearance and new clothes.

"You're fine. We have no time to waste." She grabbed my hand, dragging me behind her, and we moved down a long, strangely lit, stone corridor, lined on either side by rows of armored statues. Each held a sword stoically in place, staring straight ahead.

I tugged out of her grip and stopped to admire one. A low growl erupted from somewhere within the metal facade and I stumbled back.

Sav laughed, grabbing my hand again. "Come on, don't mess with the wolves."

"Wolves?"

She said nothing, dragging me at a clipped pace. We reached the end of the corridor, and she squared her shoulders as massive wooden doors swung wide. I glanced sideways, expecting to see someone holding them ajar, but no one was there. I had no time to ask what was happening before we stepped into an expansive stone room and Sav pulled me forward.

We walked along a purple rug, woven with golden polar bears, through the center of the room. The space was empty apart from the armored wolf creatures circling it, the enormous portraits of what must have been former monarchs, each standing beside a polar bear, and the fairy seated atop a white marble throne.

Sav's pace increased till we were jogging toward the throne. We stopped several feet away, and she dipped her chin to her chest. I glanced sideways and did the same.

"Bow," Sav hissed, and I bent awkwardly at the waist.

"Rise," a bored voice said, and I straightened.

I looked up and nearly choked. Robin Goodfellow, the actor, sat looking regal atop his seat, draped in heavy furs and wearing a gold circlet in his auburn curls, the same shade as Sav's.

"What brings you to the winter court, House Spring? Have you reconciled with your court?"

Sav glanced at me but turned back to Robin Freaking Goodfellow. I could admit it, I was starstruck. Was there a man alive who hadn't seen at least one of his movies? He was a legend. An Icon. He was...the king of the winter court?

"Goodfellow, I had expected to find one of Mab's relations on the throne in her stead."

His flat stare was chilling. "I am acting as goodwill ambassador until such time as Mab returns or an heir is declared."

"And Spring? You've left us for some indeterminate period?"

"Rest assured, the profits of my contribution fund our court." He arched a brow at Sav in challenge, even as his tone dripped with tedium.

Sav dipped her head, appearing flustered for the first time since I'd met her. "Very well. I come to beg aid from the winter court to free several fae who are being held by Dane Clyde and his fanatics. Their conditions are dire. Many have died, The Winter Hag included."

Robin's gaze sharpened, violet-colored eyes assessing her. "Where did you come by this intel?"

If I squinted, I could just imagine him reprising his role in *Fury* the moment when he was preparing to interrogate his captive.

"I was their prisoner."

"Yet you escaped?"

"Yes, but only with the aid of this human. The others have no such support."

Robin's gaze fell on me. He took in every filthy streak of mud and dark stain and his lip curled. "You have the audacity to bring this mortal before me in rags. Have you lost all your fae etiquette? Centuries of courtly training and three years among humans is all it takes to make you one of them?"

"I..." Sav bit her bottom lip.

"And to appear here, rather than in your own court first. Have you forgotten your place?"

Sav's freckled cheeks burned crimson, and she closed her mouth.

Goodfellow's auburn brows were slashes across his tanned face and his eyes narrowed on her, promising punishment for some actions I couldn't name. "This insolence will not be tolerated."

His lips parted, preparing to berate Sav further, but I stepped forward, squaring my shoulders and met his gaze. "Your highness. It's my fault. The conditions are dire, as she said. We wasted no time getting here, knowing every second could mean another fairy death."

Robin's brows rose, and I straightened to my full height. In the pregnant silence, a bead of sweat ran down my back, but I would not sit by and watch as he spoke to her that way.

Then, he opened his mouth and laughed.

TWENTY-SIX

SAV

Robin laughed and laughed, and I would have soundly cursed him for laughing at our situation, but my uncle was never one to shirk courtly duty and he'd beheaded creatures for far less severe offenses than speaking disrespectfully to someone in a position of power. Although he was only sitting in the highest seat in Faerie in Mab's absence, he certainly outranked me at present.

Much had changed in Faerie in my banishment. What had my uncle done to gain this seat and what did it mean for my chance to receive aid?

Something flared to life in my chest as my gaze traced the broad line of Jack's shoulders. When I had been cowed by my family, he'd chosen that moment to show courage. Warmth radiated from Jack as he stood facing my uncle in a foreign land, and I reached for his hand, squeezing it, meeting my uncle's gaze as I waited for his next words.

It had been a small thing to stand up for me, and certainly Jack didn't know the threat my uncle posed, but none of that mattered to my heart. It was swelling, pulsing in time to some invisible tune that seemed to sing whenever he was near. If I wasn't careful, I'd listen to it.

"Go, prepare yourselves in the proper attire," Robin said. "Dress for the evening. Tonight, you will sup with us and attend my ball. In the morning, you will return to make your request."

I dipped my chin and Jack bowed. We backed away, not giving my uncle our backs in a show of deference.

My step was light as I dragged Jack to our rooms. If I impressed him tonight—proved to him I was still a member of the court—there was a chance he would grant my request. He could have sent me back to Earth the moment I set foot in the throne room. Instead, he had given me this one chance. Because of Jack.

"Hazel will have someone appointed to assist you. Bathe and find something nice to wear for dinner." I spun to face him, giddiness riding my every word. "Jack. This is important. The impression we make tonight will decide what happens next. Do your best to blend in."

Jack's bright green eyes searched my face for a long moment. "I won't let you down, Sav."

A nervous flutter erupted in my stomach, and I swallowed, backing away from his door. It was anticipation of returning to a fae court, seeing my uncle, the hope that we would have our army. It was *not* Jack.

In my room, I sat on the massive bed beside the fireplace, running a hand over the soft woolen blanket–forest green with golden vines stitched along its edges—magicked to represent my court's colors. A minor detail meant to put the occupant at ease, but it only reminded me of a home I wasn't welcome in.

I rubbed my arms, staring at the low fire. Once, I would have flicked a finger and set the wood ablaze. Now, with hardly any magic at my disposal, I was forced to stand, grab a poker, and stoke the fire by hand. I stared into the embers, lost in my own thoughts. Jack needed a bath, and a shave, and dinner wouldn't be for some time. That left me with a racing mind and growing anxiety.

If my uncle refused to assist me, if he sent me away, there was only one other place I could go. Even the heat of a toasty fire wasn't enough to keep the chill leaching into my belly at bay. It had been three years since I'd been home. Three years since my magic had been bound, and she had cast me out of Faerie. It was the last place I wanted to go, but if my uncle wouldn't help me, what other choice did I have?

When my skin was blisteringly hot, lips chapped from the heat, I left the fire, went to the boudoir and slid aside several pale blue gowns. The court adorned every wardrobe with clothes magically designed to fit your exact measurements, but they were also in winter court colors. My uncle would expect me to wear something that represented Spring. Even if they had cast me out.

Reaching in the back, I pulled a dark green gown off its hanger, tugging the rope beside me and a fae with ice blue skin and bright green eyes rushed through a door beside me, bobbing into a curtsey.

"Yes, Lady?"

"Would you help me dress..."

"Corylus, Lady."

"Corylus. And would you help with my hair?" She looked up, surprise registering on her face as she took in my round ears. She recovered quickly, nodding and I undressed, letting the powder blue gown I had borrowed from the bathing chamber fall to the floor.

I stepped into velvety soft fabric and held out my arms. Corylus worked quickly, fastening each button up my back and led me to a table in the room's corner.

"How would you like it?" she asked, leaving off the lady this time.

"Half up. Ringlets. Is that still the style in Winter?"

Corylus's eyes met mine in the mirror. "You've been here before?"

"Only a few times," I said, glancing down to hide the emotion brimming behind my eyes as memories of the time I'd spent here rushed to the surface, threatening to send me into a dark place.

Once, years ago, I sat in a chair very like this one while someone dressed me for the evening. Then, I'd sat in giddy anticipation of the evening to come. An evening of dancing in the arms of the male I loved. Stolen kisses in a dark alcove around the ballroom and lovemaking in a bed that would be ours when we were wed.

I laced my fingers together in my lap, working to quell the memories of Bracken, of Foxglove's betrayal, of my broken heart. I stuffed them down, swallowing the lump rising in my throat. Nothing good would come of revisiting those memories.

"There you are," she said. "A princess if I ever I saw one."

"Mab, I hope not," I said, looking up. It was polite. A court gesture meant as a compliment, but it was too close to a fate I never wanted to accept. Atop the crown of my head, my hair was woven into thick braids and looped around the back, leaving several strands to curl around my face and neck. It had been three years since I'd dressed for a royal dinner; three years since I'd worn my hair in the fae style and dressed in court finery. My eyes found Corylus's. "It's a masterpiece."

Her cheeks darkened to a shade of navy, and she dipped into another curtsey. "Will that be all, Lady?"

I nodded.

"Wait, Corylus."

She turned in the doorway.

"I give you this comb in appreciation." I pulled the pearl comb I'd brought to the human realm from my bag and handed it to her. It was too great a gift for a low fae performing her duty, but I'd spent three years among them on Earth and I could no longer see them as our inferiors, our burden. We were all equal.

Her cheeks flushed again, and she bobbed low, tucking it into a pocket before darting through the door.

In the long corridor leading from my room to the dining hall, I moved on slippered feet, a chill ghosting over my skin. The last time I'd been here,

I had been prepared to give my heart and my hand to Bracken, a male I believed was deserving of it. That thought sent another spear of pain through my chest.

"Wow."

I spun, heat crawling up my neck as Jack strode toward me, dressed head to toe in black, a navy sash hugging his hip, golden threads adorning the sleeves of his coat and breeches. A cream silk shirt peeked between the folds of his jacket, accentuating his tanned skin. His raven hair was tied back, exposing his strong jaw.

My gaze met his, and a spark of electricity jolted down my spine. Those eyes were inhuman.

"You look...Like a princess." He reached for my hand, lifting it to his mouth, but instead of pressing a kiss to my knuckles, warm fingers twisted my hand, and he leaned down, lips grazing my wrist. The thrum of my heartbeat against his mouth picked up speed, and I tugged my hand from his hold.

He released it easily, bright eyes devouring me as I stepped back.

"I'm not."

The heat in his gaze simmered, and his brows furrowed. "What?"

"I'm not a princess."

He held out his elbow, and I slid a shimmering gloved hand through the crook of his arm. "I meant, you look beautiful."

There it was again, that word. He'd said it before, even if he was delirious. I tucked a loose ringlet behind my ear, the side of my face burning under his stare. He was a human; and not just any human, the son of my enemy, and that made him my enemy, too. I couldn't let a pretty face and court finery distract me from that fact.

We reached the dining hall, and a thrill of nervous energy ran through me. Jack's arm squeezed my hand as the doors swung open and he ushered me in. I moved into the room, leaning into his warmth, and nearly fainted as the smell of all that decadent fae food invaded my senses. It had been too long since I tasted the flaky pastries, smooth, rich jams and flavorful spices of Faerie.

I released Jack, slipping into the seat beside Hazel—as I had every time I visited Winter. At least there was one friendly face in this place, even if we hadn't stayed in touch after my last visit to her court. My gaze traveled over the lush spread, mouth watering as I imagined the divine flavors that would soon explode across my tongue.

"Sit by me, Jack."

Snapping out of my food-induced daze, I glanced up to see Jack move past me to Hazel's other side. My appetite vanished, gaze narrowing as Hazel's bare hand landed on Jack's leg, sliding up his thigh and squeezing.

TWENTY-SEVEN

JACK

I looked nervously beyond Hazel as Sav's gaze narrowed on the hand massaging my thigh and moved to push it away.

Hazel squeezed, and I shoved her hand harder, bumping my plate. "Stop." I hissed. A few eyes around the table glanced my way. Hazel winked at me, and I ground my teeth, prying her fingers from my leg. This woman would be trouble. She stuck out her bottom lip, but I ignored it, peeling her hand free and letting it drop beside her.

"So, Jack, do you want a tour of the castle? I could show you all the best dark corners." By her words, one would never know she had just tried to feel me up under the table.

I grimaced, glancing at Sav again. When Hazel had suggested making her friend jealous, something uncomfortable had settled in my gut. Now, I knew it wasn't the best path to winning Sav over. "I don't think I'll be here long enough to see much of the castle." I raised my brows at her, mouthing: *knock it off*.

"Be sure to show him the alcove beside the library where you gave your first blow job, Hazel. Jack would love to see that." Sav's biting tone sent a chill down my spine, but Hazel didn't miss a beat.

"It is a good place for blow jobs, Jack. Do you like those?"

She licked her lips, and I leaned away from her. This had been a terrible idea. The fairy was clearly interested in more than her friend's jealousy. What was I even supposed to say to that? Of course I liked blowjobs. But not from her. My gaze darted back to Sav, whose cheeks were blotchy.

I opened my mouth, but Sav spoke again. "Better yet, why don't you show him the aviary where you had three guys at once."

I swallowed, wishing I hadn't sat beside the fairy. Not that there had been a spot beside Sav. There wasn't an empty seat at the massive banquette table and around us, fairies were turning their heads and whispering as the women to my left grew louder.

Hazel's eyes danced with delight. "Oh, good idea. Jack. Do you like foursomes?"

Sav's fork scraped her plate.

"Cousin, how are you enjoying your first fae meal in three years?" Robin's voice carried from much farther down the table, and my head swiveled between the king of the winter court and Sav.

The king was her cousin?

"It's very fine, Uncle. The best meal I've had in a long time." Sav's cheeks were returning to their normal shade, and she made a show of taking a bite of her potato. At least, I thought it was a potato.

The king's eyes were on us, and I straightened, looking down at my plate. The food in this kingdom resembled food one might find on Earth, with some differences. Carrots were arranged in a neat row on my plate, in colors of yellow, green and purple. Something shaped like cauliflower but bright orange was sliced like a steak and seasoned with yellow and blue specks that appeared to be like pepper.

I picked up my fork and knife, eyeing a woman in a shimmering ice-blue gown across from me. She slid her knife through her cauliflower steak, spearing a bite with her fork and bringing it to her mouth. A bit of nervous tension left me knowing their dining etiquette was the same as ours.

Something furry brushed my arm, and I glanced to my left, spying a fluffy white and black spotted tail sliding into my lap.

Frowning, I slid my fork under the table, glancing again at the king. I was certain making a scene wasn't the way to impress these nobles, but I'd had enough of the fairy's games.

"Hazel, I hope you'll be accommodating to our guests during their stay," Robin said.

Hazel's tail inched up my thigh. "Of course, Regent. I look forward to showing them all our court has to offer."

I lifted my fork and stabbed at fur. It was thicker than I'd first thought, and I missed the solid part of her tail on my first try.

"It has been many years since Lady Briar has been to Winter. She will be impressed with the improvements I've made in my time as regent."

Regent. So not a king, but a member of the royal family, no doubt.

Hazel's tail slid higher on my leg, and I stabbed again, hitting the meaty part. She hissed, and Sav's gaze shot to my lap.

The fluffy tail, flecked with dots of red, dropped from my thigh, and I smirked.

Green eyes met mine and Hazel bared her teeth, but instead of an angry glare, her lips stretched into a grin and her gaze heated.

What the hell? It seemed the fluffy-tailed fairy liked a little blood play. Too bad for her, I wasn't interested in anything she offered.

Twenty-Eight
Sav

I swallowed cold potatoes that tasted like cardboard as I stared ahead. Across from me, a male grinned in my direction. Under other circumstances, I might have found him handsome. Handsome enough to send a flirtatious smile, but he was grinning at Hazel—showing Jack exactly why she kept that tail on display at all times—not at me.

My grip tightened around the silverware, fingers aching as I forced them still. I pressed my lips into an imitation of a pleasant smile. Hazel was the closest thing I still had a friend in Faerie. Her flirtation wouldn't change that.

When Bracken broke my heart, Hazel had been there to help me pick up the pieces. She'd helped me find my way when I thought I'd never recover. *Mab*, that was a long time ago. A lot had changed since then and even more had changed since our world collided with Earth.

In truth, Hazel was just being Hazel. She enjoyed casual flings with no strings, and a dalliance with a human would be just that. Anything more would mean death. It was a reminder that nothing could ever happen between me and Jack. I needed a distraction. Someone to take my mind off the man.

I scanned the length of the expansive table, eyes landing on a handsome male who was already watching me. My lips tipped up.

He raised a glass, and I mimicked the action before taking a sip. He lifted a fork to his mouth and wrapped full lips around the metal. He ran his tongue over its grooves before setting it down. His gaze dipped to my plate and slid back up—over my cleavage—crawling slowly to my face.

Picking up a spoon, I dipped it into a bowl of pudding and brought the chocolaty substance to my lips, sucking the spoon in and out of my mouth. I licked along the metal until it was clean.

His eyes lit with amusement, and he lifted his glass again.

I returned the gesture, reached for my napkin, wiping my mouth when he turned to speak to the person beside him.

"Watch out for Heath. He has a bit of a reputation," Hazel whispered in my ear.

"Did he get it from bedding you?"

Hazel's ice blue lips tipped up. "Careful, Sav. I might think this human means something to you. And the rules in Faerie, on that account at least, do not differ from in the human realm."

"I'm not sure what you mean," I whisper hissed.

"Good. Then you won't mind if I call dibs tonight."

"Haven't you already satisfied your curiosity?"

Hazel laughed, her shock of white hair cascading over her shoulder as she leaned closer. "I haven't scratched the surface of what I want to do to this human."

Red tinged the edges of my vision, but I swallowed the emotion and smirked. "Good luck," I said, glancing at Jack, who was glaring down the table at the male I'd just been flirting with. As if he had any right to be upset after Hazel had just put her hands and tail all over him at the banquet table.

"He doesn't look like he can keep up with your appetites."

Hazel's mouth flattened into a line. "We'll see."

"Guests. Members of the royal court." Robin said, standing. "Let us take our leave and regroup in the ballroom." His gaze met mine. "I hope to see you in your finest." He dipped his head and swept from the room.

Though he'd come to dinner dressed as a king in his own right, Robin did nothing by half, and none had missed his subtle reminder that dinner attire was not appropriate for a ball.

I ran a hand down the velvety fabric that split dangerously high on my thigh and inhaled deeply.

In this dress, my intentions would be clear. Was I being idiotic? Planning to take someone to my bed? The male I had flirted with at dinner was a stranger, and I had never been one to lie with a random fae, but it had been so long since I'd had anyone between my legs, Kaspar's incident in the bath notwithstanding, and Hazel was right about one thing. My strange attraction to the human was dangerous. It needed to be snuffed out before it took root.

Tonight was a dance. One that would mean the difference between the fae trapped at the AFF's freedom or their slow death at the hand of a sadist. Acting as a member of court would go a long way toward proving I deserved my place here. Even if that meant putting on a show for my uncle. And just because the show was to help the folk trapped on Earth, didn't mean I couldn't have a little fun.

Frost clung to the archways, delicate as lace, never melting. The stone floors pulsed faintly beneath my heels—alive with Mab's magic. Overhead, flickering faelight glowed blue and white, weaving melodies that lifted the tension from my limbs and soon I was moving swiftly toward the ball-room. I narrowed my eyes as I passed Jack's door. Let him find his own way.

Guests exited their rooms, joining me in a lilting step toward the grand finale to the evening. As one, we passed long rows of wolves, created solely for guarding the realm. Unlike shifters, they could not change, but the magic of the land bound them to an erect form when guarding the palace. I wasn't sure they were alive, not in the way folk were. They were an extension of Mab's magic, never aging or dying. That they were still here to guard us meant she must be alive. Somewhere.

In the winter court, the final ball of each cycle sealed the court's magic for the season. Each step of the dance fed power into the land, high and low fae working in concert. My court followed a similar tradition, and I'd been raised on nightshade wine and dance from an early age.

Around me, fae pressed close, eager to join the revelry and a scent so reminiscent of my youth that I nearly stumbled, invaded my senses as I was hit with such a pang of homesickness my vision blurred.

I swept through grand arched doors on a tide of euphoria as partygoers raced into the room, buzzing with anticipation. A haunting melody swelled, then crashed into its crescendo, making my chest ache.

Fae, low and high, wasted no time clasping hands and falling into a lively dance as they entered. Others crowded around the long banquet tables at the far end of the room. My favorite thing about Winter was that all fae, no matter their station, were welcome to attend balls. Dressed in their finery, they came to celebrate as one, feeding their magic to the land as it gave back.

A grin split my face as the Barbegazi took to the floor, twinkling snowflakes wafting off him as he spun, adding to the magical allure of the winter court. It was good to know he had not disappeared, as so many others had with the shrinking of the realm. How I had missed this.

My feet tapped a giddy rhythm to the tune as I approached a table, lifting a dark, jammy-scented glass to my lips. Where my court delighted in nightshade and henbane wines, the winter court preferred wolfsbane.

A swath of raven hair—taller than many of the revelers—entered and began weaving through the crowd toward me. My toes stopped tapping, coldness dimming some of the magic's sway on my mood as Jack stepped between a group of giggling females and stopped before me.

"Sav," he dipped his head in some misguided attempt at fae civility, and I would have laughed if I found anything about him amusing at the moment. "I wanted to speak with you, but you rushed out at dinner. It wasn't what it looked like. I—"

"It looked like you were enjoying Hazel's company and her attention." I lifted my glass, downing its contents in one swallow. "I suppose I could have been mistaken." Turning, I set my glass on the table and grabbed another, darker than the first. Stronger.

"No. I'm not—"

"You don't need my permission to sleep with Hazel, Jack." I cut him off.

Jack's sharp cheekbones flushed, darkening, and he glanced around the crowded room.

Several revelers watched our exchange. Word would certainly get back to Hazel, but if it found its way to my uncle's ear, it would be disastrous. Forcing a smile onto my face, I tipped forward, my hand landing on his hard chest. "Enjoy her while you have her attention. She moves on quickly."

Sweeping past him, I downed my second glass. It burned going down, numbing my lips, making my heart beat unsteadily. I could feel the magic in it, old and insistent—pulling memories I'd long buried to the surface. The room dimmed, going out of focus, and the folk wrapped in swaths of blue and navy fabric blurred into a tableau resembling a tempest of waves crashing against one another. After only three years of abstaining from fae wine, it seemed my tolerance was severely diminished, but it wasn't as if I could get henbane wine in the human realm. They'd never allow something deadly to them in the hands of the fae.

That stopped me mid-stride. *Jack.* It would be poisonous to him. I spun around.

His tall, smudged outline solidified as I squinted, and Hazel came into focus beside him. She snatched a cup out of his hand and whispered in his ear.

Right. He was Hazel's problem tonight. If she got the human killed, I'd just have to find another bargaining chip.

Music halted, and my gaze trailed to the door. Four wolves in shining gold armor marched in, fanning out to make space. Robin entered with the easy grace of someone born to rule. Whispered voices followed him. Some dropped into a bow as he passed. Others simply watched, eyes glassy with awe.

Unmated, unmarried, and wealthy, both from his inherited estates and his earnings on Earth, Robin was a catch by all standards. It was rumored he'd once had a long-standing affair with a human actor, but those rumors would have been tantamount to a death sentence if proven, and no one ever had.

Seated atop a sapphire-encrusted throne, he turned, fur brushing his cheek as he nodded to the musicians, and they resumed playing. Dancers took to the floor with renewed fervor now that the regent's eye was upon them and their acrobatics, intended to show their prowess in the bedroom, intensified.

A warm finger ran down my bare shoulder, and I turned. "If you're back to—" the words died on my lips.

The male from dinner, Heath, Hazel had said, met my stare, jade eyes alight with that same amusement from before. "Would you care to dance?"

My gaze skimmed the room behind him, landing on a pair sitting in one of the darkened alcoves, heads bowed together. "I'd love to."

Heath extended a hand, and I took it, letting him spin me onto the floor. His hand found my lower back and soft fingers slid beneath the fabric of my dress, skimming low.

He wasted no time making his desire clear. That was just fine. I knew what game I'd been playing when I invited his attention. Lifting my arm to rest on his shoulder, my gaze traveled up the length of his broad chest, noting his coat was a deep shade of indigo marking him as a member of this court.

His hand tightened around mine, and he spun us. My breath caught as he pressed closer, dipping me so far backward I relied upon him not to fall. When we came up, his hand slid lower, cupping my ass beneath my dress. Pulling me closer to his chest, his lips pressed against my ear.

"How long will your uncle expect you to remain in attendance this evening?" His hot tongue licked along my neck, sending shocks of warmth to my core.

"Long enough to show deference," I said breathlessly, leaning my head back as he tipped me once more. I didn't know Heath, but it seemed he knew exactly who I was.

The music picked up speed and my vision dimmed as the wine swam in my veins. My stomach swirled, heat licking along my thighs where his arousal pressed against the thin fabric of my dress and on his next dip, my body slid along the length of him, creating delicious friction.

It was getting hot in here. My heart pounded and when we spun by the throne, I dipped back and my gaze landed on the alcove directly behind it. A shimmering silver dress writhed atop velvet-clad legs in the darkened space. I came up, my eyes met Heath's and the heat raging in his eyes turned my stomach. That same intense stare that had been so flattering at dinner now felt predatory. Invasive.

"I'm sorry," I gasped, pulling free of his grasp and dashing off the dance floor, not looking back.

I reached the door and tugged it open, stepping into a cool, dark hallway and leaned against the wall, heart racing. The room spun and my stomach threatened to heave up the contents of my dinner. Another breath in and out, and the room stopped spinning. After a third calming inhale, my mind cleared.

Go back in there, and fuck Heath, I told myself. I pushed off the wall, squaring my shoulders, and grabbed the door handle. Locked. Damn.

I trailed the dark hall, some of my anxiety settling as I continued to suck in the cool air.

Rounding the corner to the main hall, I stumbled to a halt.

A tall male with ash brown hair, cut short, swayed to the faintly playing music coming from the ballroom. A young girl was perched atop his shoes, and he guided her through the steps. She giggled and stepped off his shoes, spinning in a circle.

I was frozen, my heart thrashing wildly in my chest. The air fled my lungs, and for a moment, I was this very hall several years earlier, Bracken breaking my heart.

His gaze landed on me, and I backed up.

"Sav?"

My limbs were stone as I tried to move. To run from him.

"Sav. Is that you?"

His voice soothed some of my terror, as it always had, and I swallowed, tugging at the obscenely high slit running up my thigh, but it was no use. My leg was on full display. I crossed my arms, hiding my cleavage. Finding my voice, I said, "I didn't mean to interrupt."

"No. You didn't. It's good to see you."

I stared at the male I'd nearly given my heart to for the rest of our very long existence. Memories of a life we would have had battered my already ravaged heart. I'd thought it would be okay coming here; I'd thought I was over him and the heartbreak. Had it truly been over a decade ago now? Seeing him, it felt like things had just ended all over again.

The room swayed, from the wine or the swell of buried emotions I'd locked away, I wasn't sure.

Old wounds resurfaced as I took him in, reminding me why I'd never sought love again. Reminding me of the pain that followed the inevitable disappointment. He was the same tall, lean male I'd fallen in love with, hair still cropped short the way the royal guard wore it, but the creases at the corners of his eyes were new, and the circles under them.

Were they from nights spent worrying over his family? His mate and the child who clung to his arm now? Some small part of me wondered if he'd lost any sleep over me, the way I had over him.

I exhaled slowly. That was long ago. Long enough that my anger had died, leaving only my heartbreak behind. But even that was fading.

"This is Jasmine." Bracken glanced down at the girl beside him.

My gaze moved to the child. "Hi, Jasmine. I'm Sav."

The girl's white hair swayed behind her as she rushed forward. She stopped in time to avoid crashing into me, and straightened her shoulders, staring down her nose imperiously. "So good to meet you, Sav."

She said my name as if she were tasting it for any bit of magic. They trained them young in the winter court.

"It's very nice to meet you, Jasmine." I looked up at Bracken. "Where's Camellia?"

Pain ghosted over Bracken's features before he swallowed it down and came to stand beside Jasmine, taking her hand. "She's...No longer with us."

The agony in his words sliced into me. "I'm so sorry, Bracken."

He swallowed thickly.

"She's with Mab. Searching for a way to heal Faerie," Jasmine said, beaming up at me.

I smiled sadly. The girl was young, and Bracken had shielded her from the truth. In the end, I didn't think it would do her any favors, but it wasn't my place to say so.

"That's very brave of her."

Jasmine's gaze moved between us. "How do you know my daddy? I've never met you before. I know all Daddy's friends."

The girl had so much of Bracken in her features, but her white sheet of hair and thin aquiline nose were decidedly her mother's. Some spiteful part of me wanted to be happy he was free again, but I felt only sorrow for the loss of Bracken's mate. For a mate would never leave their partner unless they were called beyond the veil.

It was a fate I wouldn't imagine for my worst enemy, and Bracken, though he'd broken my heart once, was a good male.

I held out a hand, and he took it. "I hope you find the peace you deserve."

He stepped forward, wrapping his arms around me, and crushed me to him.

I held him, whispering kind words as he let out a low whimper. Even as I comforted him, some of my pain leached away. Once, our touches were fevered and passionate. Now, his embrace was one of a dear friend. A bit of my hardened heart cracked.

He held back tears, but his voice broke as he whispered in my ear. "It's torture every day. I wish I had never found her."

"Bracken." I rubbed his back. "At least you had some time with her. Some people never get that. And you have a daughter."

He squeezed tighter. "I can't bear it."

My hand tightened reflexively around, him holding him together with the last thread of who we used to be. Once, I'd loved Bracken's ability to be so vulnerable in a place where emotion might be used against you like a weapon. Now, I wondered if it would be the thing to break him. "Your daughter needs you. You're all she has."

Something tugged at my sleeve, and I looked down. The cherubic creature stared up at me with bright green eyes brimming with tears. "I'll take daddy," she said. Her tiny voice was strong for such a young fae.

Another piece of my heart cracked, a memory from early childhood slipping free. I tamped it down, pressing hard against the memory of my childhood, of two small girls alone in the world with a father who was too heartbroken to care for us.

TWENTY-NINE
DANE

The satyr didn't make a sound as she fell on the cold linoleum floor. She was tougher even than some orcs we'd brought up to be interrogated. It wasn't because satyrs were resilient. They broke easily enough. *She* was the daughter of Ajisai, former leader of the wood clan, a most fearsome warrior.

And though Morgan had made it clear she wasn't to be killed; I would wipe them all from our planet if I didn't get answers about my son's whereabouts soon.

Her slitted, golden eyes dilated in the harsh fluorescent light as I tugged the bag off her head, and it took her a moment to register where she was and who held her. When her vision cleared, her gaze narrowed on me, dark lashes obscuring the hate in her eyes. Good. I wanted her to know who made her bleed.

She spat at my feet, and I grinned, looking up to meet the eyes of each of the AFF initiates. "You see. They are animals, uncouth and untamed."

Several heads nodded, and I tipped the toe of my boot under her chin and forced her gaze up. Dark green blood stained the side of her face, still not fully healed from her last interrogation. I'd gone too easy on her, and every day my son was missing was another day he could be dead, or worse.

"Satyr. Tell me where my son is. Tell me where your *friend* took him."

She couldn't hide the grimace of pain as she leaned back and iron cuffs slid down her arm, sizzling across tufted skin. But if she was afraid of a repeat of last time, she didn't show it. She clenched her jaw tightly, glaring at me, ignoring everyone else in the room, and meeting my gaze with a confidence I'd rarely seen in anyone.

She had balls, I'd give her that.

Pulling my hand back, I sent it crashing across her face. The heat of her soft cheek blazed in my palm, and she fell hard, taking some time to recover before positioning herself in my direct line of sight and narrowing her eyes at me again. Still, she said nothing.

I stood to my full height, spinning to face the room. "When dealing with a stubborn animal, you must be firm. Remind the creature of its place." I met each of their eyes in turn. "But also, be willing to show kindness, lest it forget that its master ultimately wants what's best for it."

One of the newest initiates, Alex, had a hungry look in his eye as he stared with a sick sort of satisfaction at the green blood welling on the satyr's newly split lip. I would need to keep an eye on him. Breaking the creatures was a job that required finesse and if I hadn't let my emotions get the better of me, I wouldn't have taken such a harsh approach with this one. I made a mental note to have Alice reassign him to a mundane duty that wouldn't put him near enough to the creatures to do permanent damage.

We needed most of them alive. For now.

I knelt down beside the satyr, Juniper, she was called, and ran a hand over her cheek. It burned where the imprint of my hand remained, and I chuckled as she flinched from my kindness when she hadn't from my violence. She was a fighter, and they were my favorite kind to break.

I marched down the hall at a clipped pace, resisting the urge to punch something.

"Dane."

I ground my teeth, schooling my features before spinning to face Alice. "Yes?"

She halted behind me, too close, and a chill rushed down my spine at her stealth. It was her best quality and my least favorite. "Were you successful? Did you find out where Jack is?"

I resisted the urge to roll my eyes. Her obsession with my son was unnatural, especially considering I'd seen his dismissal of her more than a few times. "No. She is refusing to speak."

Alice wrapped her arms over her chest, hugging them against her torso and making herself seem smaller. "I have an idea."

I studied her, noting the pink tinging her cheeks and the jump of her rapid pulse at her throat. "Go on."

"What if you brought her up to the compound? Made her feel safe. If someone could get close to her, maybe they could get information from her."

"Like you did with the high fae?" I scoffed.

Her pink cheeks flamed crimson. "Sally was only here one night. I had no time—"

"You let your feelings for my son cloud your judgment. She would have never trusted you."

Alice squared her shoulders, standing taller, and met my gaze. "Jack's not here now, so there's no risk of *that* happening again, and I want him back as much as you do."

I narrowed my gaze on Alice, meeting her stare for long moments. When she didn't look away, I nodded. "Very well. Tell Grif to have her brought up. She rooms with you." I leaned closer, getting into her space. "And make sure you don't let your true feelings for the creatures show."

Alice's brows lifted, and I half expected her to break into a giddy laugh and throw her arms around me. She was young. Too young to act as my spy, but she tested far above the others who had joined my ranks in terms of psychological prowess and deception. She was my best option when none of my interrogation efforts had been successful thus far.

My gaze darted past her as Connor, commander of my Central Park perimeter guard, appeared at the end of the hall, and I dismissed her with a nod, turning to him. "What is it?"

He watched her go, waiting until she was out of earshot. "We've seen movement from the orc general. His second led another attack. They hit the AFF building in the Bronx. Successfully retrieved all the prisoners being held there."

"Damnit," I swore. "How did they get by us?"

"They have help from wild animals."

I rubbed my forehead, heat boiling in my veins. Another fucking prison raided. Another success on their side. I was growing tired of the orc who had managed half a dozen successful attacks in as many months. And no matter how many new recruits I brought in or how many men I stationed around the prisoners, they got by us every time.

"What do you mean, animals?"

Connor took a step back, sensing my rage. "All I know is, there's animals sniffin' around the place each time before it happens and then they come out of nowhere, when we're least guarded and take the fairies out with minimal casualties." He scratched his head. "Honestly, I can't figure it out."

I growled in frustration. They'd started as a nuisance, but they were quickly becoming a thorn in my side. "Get Grif. I want a demonstration staged tonight. How many prisoners did we lose?"

Connor swallowed. "Fifteen."

"Then we take thirty. We show them that every time they attack, we make them pay for it."

Spittle landed on Connor's face and he swiped it off, eyes widening, but he only nodded, turning and jogging down the hall.

Teeth grinding together, I slammed a fist into the wall. Our staged raid had gone well. We'd incited the people—driven them to act—and soon they had taken up their own makeshift weapons and brought down the creatures remaining in the park themselves. But we needed more. We needed something bigger to truly shift the tide.

But the cost of these incidents had never been my flesh and blood before and that was a price I wasn't willing to pay.

THIRTY

JACK

I leaned back, breathing shallowly around Hazel's cloying perfume. "I need to talk to her."

Hazel's razor-sharp nail found my jaw and dug into my cheek as she pinched my face and turned it to hers. "You can't be seen with her in front of the regent. In Faerie, just as on Earth, the rule is clear. Never fall in love with a human. The way she was looking at you at dinner was enough to sign her death warrant."

I tore my chin out of her grip. "You said you would help me. What you did was unforgivable."

"I'm trying to protect you. Both of you."

I said nothing, grinding my teeth together. When she'd dragged me into this alcove, I had been seconds away from forgoing common decency and shoving her aside to find Sav and make her listen, but Hazel had said the one thing that made me pause. My actions could get Sav killed.

Hazel leaned back against the cushion, knowing her words fulfilled their purpose.

In the enormous stone ballroom, fairies of all shapes and sizes crowded the low-lit space, moving to music that tugged at my heart, making me feel a strange sort of elation even through the anger simmering after my last encounter with Sav. It wasn't her I was angry at, though. It was myself for considering going along with Hazel's plan. I searched the crowd of mingling fae for a head of auburn hair, coiled like a crown, leaving only tendrils to frame her face and trail down her back.

Seeing her in that dress had nearly been my undoing. She was gorgeous in a dirty tee and leather skirt, but the midnight gown she'd worn tonight had been selected from my dreams, or perhaps my nightmares. One perfectly tanned thigh was exposed almost to the hip and the back of her dress hung low, showing off perfect skin all the way to the dip of her waist.

A single tattoo ran down her spine. An arrow pointing south. As if I needed guidance. Her perfect ass curved under the folds of velvet cinched over her hips and left very little to the imagination. But imagine I had. It was all I could do. And she hated me now. I'd seen it in her face when I came to explain.

My gaze halted on a lithe form moving so seductively, my slacks tented under the hard length of what was sure to be the bluest balls of my life.

The man who had been eye fucking Sav at dinner was wrapped around her, moving to the rhythm of the erotic music somehow amplified through the room. They moved and were momentarily obscured from view by a pair of fawns, laughing and spinning drunkenly. I sat up, tracking their progress on the circular dance floor and when they spun by again, his hand slid below the fabric of her dress and heat flared to life in my veins. I was possessed with the urge to shove him off her; to claim her for myself.

Hazel's palm pressed against my chest and began a slow descent down my front. It was like a bucket of ice dumped on my skin.

I grabbed her wrist. "The regent can't see you in here. No need to play a part." My gaze darted to hers and she huffed, lips forming a pout.

"Can't we at least have a little fun?"

"No." The heat in my veins was burning me alive, and I released my hold on her arm and dipped my head out of the alcove. I had to get away from her before the anger overwhelmed me. I was overreacting to the situation, I knew it, but I couldn't seem to get these raging emotions under control.

Hazel followed my gaze to the woman sliding up another man's body and the fire burning through me exploded into an inferno. The man's hand slid farther below her dress, and I climbed out of the alcove.

"Hey," Hazel called behind me.

I ignored her, weaving through scantily clad guests, halting at the edge of the dance floor. I watched as his lips pressed against her ear and his tongue ran down the side of her neck. If I opened my mouth, I was sure I would breathe fire. I stepped forward, but an iron grip clamped around my biceps.

"Go out there, and it will be her death."

I halted, turning to search Hazel's face. "She's going to fuck him, and it's your fault. I never should have listened to you."

"She won't. I've known Sav a long time."

I wrenched my arm from her hold but stood rigidly, crossing my arms over my chest.

"Come on, let's get some air."

"No," I growled.

"You'll only torture yourself if you stay."

My hands fisted under my arms as Sav dipped again and her full cleavage was in my direct line of sight. I was torn between racing onto the dance floor to tear her from the creature's hold and running from the room so I didn't have to watch anymore.

"Why don't you wait in her room? Finding you there would put an end to any fun she was planning."

I slid my gaze reluctantly from Sav's graceful form to Hazel. I'd thought part of Sav's allure must have been her fairy nature, but staring at Hazel, an attractive woman to be sure, and having seen all the other high fairies at court, I knew it was something else that drew me to her. She wasn't just beautiful; she was perfect. The very image of the woman I longed for. The one I'd imagined sharing my life with but had yet to claim.

Hazel's fingers looped under my crossed arm and she tugged. "Come on. Let's go before you draw too much attention."

I glanced around at the eyes darting between me and Sav, some of my anger banking. They stared hungrily between the four of us as if hoping a fight would break out. Reluctantly, I turned, letting Hazel pull me with her.

We left the ballroom, stepping into a much cooler hall. Away from the scents of perfume and the oppressive lilt of music refracting off every surface, my head cleared a little. I'd been about to do something foolish. And why? Sav hadn't promised me anything.

A coy smile tugged at Hazel's blue-tinted lips. Green eyes, strange against her skin, were hooded as she appraised me. "Sav's been around a long time. She's been hurt by the people she cared for most. It would take a lot for her to trust someone, especially a male. Go slow with her."

I wasn't dumb enough to think she truly wanted me—a human with nothing to offer—but there had been something between us. I felt it, and I would let her use me in any way she wanted, just so long as those plum-colored eyes were on me instead of another man.

Not waiting for any reply, Hazel turned, hips swaying as she moved down the hall back to the ballroom.

THIRTY-ONE

SAV

I peeled off my shoes and padded barefoot through the hall. The scent of hearth smoke guided me faster. I needed silence and blankets. I stepped into my room and sighed. My heart hurt for Bracken's pain, but some piece of my soul had lightened, knowing I no longer carried the burning resentment that had lived with me so long.

Bracken's name still lingered in my thoughts. I'd loved him before his mate appeared—and after. But the bond had already wrapped its roots around his heart.

Mates were rare enough in Faerie that no one waited for them. In our very long lives, one may find their mate when they were centuries old or never. Bracken had been lucky to find his after only three hundred years. My mood darkened. Or unlucky. Now, he would spend another seven hundred years without her. Father's tormented face flashed in my mind.

I hadn't waited for exactly that reason. Hadn't been looking.

I thought Bracken and I understood each other. Thought we wanted the same things, but who could resist the pull of a mate when it found you?

Letting my dress pool on the floor, I stepped on the pads of my feet, moving to my bed and tugged back the blanket, sliding in and exhaling a long breath. Beech sheets from the autumn wood caressed my skin, smoothing away the memory of the scratchy, harsh material used in the human realm.

I rolled onto my belly, sliding a hand over smooth sheets and closed my eyes. Jack's face appeared in my mind and I squeezed my lids tighter, conjuring images of Heath, Bracken, even Kaspar to shove him out.

Another image of the alcove and Hazel's sparkling dress moving atop velvet pants came unbidden into my head, and my eyes flew open.

I sat up. Embers hissed, casting long shadows. One of them breathed. A body—stretched out near the hearth. Red and orange sparks sizzled, casting the room in a low light as my gaze traveled the expanse of him. The slow rise and fall of his back told me he was asleep.

I grabbed the robe beside my bed, wrapped it over my shoulders and crossed the space, staring down at the man sleeping on my floor. I frowned. What was he doing in my room? I'd been sure he was with Hazel, finishing what they started at dinner. It certainly looked like they'd been enjoying themselves in the ballroom.

"Jack." I bit the words, and he started, groaning something but his head remained firmly against his arm. "Wake up."

He twitched. "Sav?" he said groggily.

"Jack. Get up."

His head lifted, and he turned over, peering up at nothing. His weak human eyesight couldn't make me out in the dark. I sent a tiny spark of barely there magic to the fire and it flared to life, casting strange shadows over the room. The flame leaped in Jack's glassy eyes and, for a moment, they looked as though they glowed.

"What are you doing here?"

He sat up, running a hand over his face. His gaze dipped, heat igniting in his eyes.

I pulled the robe tighter around my frame, unusually self-conscious under the white-hot desire sparking in his stare.

His swallow was audible in the silent room.

"I looked for you," he said, eyes closing slowly before they opened again and some of the heat had banked.

"I ran into an old friend." I didn't hold back the bite in my next words. "You seemed perfectly well occupied."

Jack leaned forward. "Sav. I was an idiot, but I swear nothing happened with Hazel."

I stared down at him, biting my lip. I was overreacting; I knew it. If he found her attention appealing, who was I to say otherwise? My stomach dropped as I thought of Hazel's hand trailing up Jack's leg at dinner, but I swallowed it down. It wasn't as if I had any claim on him. He may find me attractive, but that didn't mean there were true feelings behind it. For a man, lust and love were very different things. I had to keep reminding myself of that fact.

I dropped to my knees. "We're all idiots when we're young."

He snorted. "This is where you tell me you're some hundred years old being, wizened by experience and I'm just an ignorant twenty-five-year-old man?"

"Fae barely begin to experience our magic at twenty-five. When you live as long as we do, twenty-five is a blink.

He smiled, a dimple appearing in his cheek, and it did something funny to my belly.

"So, how old are you?"

"You first. Why are you in my room?"

His grin fell, and he looked away.

"I don't believe in leaving things for the morning. Never go to bed angry. That's what my mom always said, and you were angry."

I swallowed. "I wasn't."

Jack's brows dipped low. "You were. Angry enough to let some stranger put his hands all over you. I didn't like it. But I deserved it."

My heart rate ticked up as his possessive tone washed over me. *Lust*, I reminded myself. I shook my head. "Look. We can't be...anything...to one another. In Faerie, if they even suspect something other than casual sex, we would both be dead." I shouldn't pose it that way, but I wanted him to tell me it was just sex he was after. Needed him to prove me right so I could write him off as just another male who saw me as an object.

Jack's mouth flattened into a thin line. "They have the same laws on Earth. But who would actually enforce a rule like that?"

My heart was beating faster. Why hadn't he taken the bait? Why wasn't he asking for something casual?

"My uncle. Anyone in my family really."

Jack leaned toward me, and I caught a whiff of his wintergreen scent. "I heard your conversation in the bath. With the prince."

I met his gaze, swallowing. "That's not what this is about. Kaspar is... was...a friend."

"I get it. Your life is complicated. We all have complications, but I don't want there to be any confusion between us. I'm not interested in Hazel." His eyes darkened. "If you and the prince are together, tell me now."

The heat was back in his gaze, and butterflies erupted in my belly. *Lust. It's just lust.*

He leaned in, so close his scent enveloped me, drawing me closer and all my senses flared to life at his nearness. His hand came up, brushing a curl from my face, and warmth bloomed along my cheek. "Because I'd like to know who my competition is."

There was an involuntary tug in my chest, and my body strained to be closer. His fiery nearness was a bonfire, burning me from the inside. I released a scalding breath, trying and failing to convince myself he was just a damn talented actor.

His finger grazed my jaw, tipping my chin up. My breath hitched. Heat pooled low as he leaned in—close enough to burn me.

A loud knock sounded at the door.

My stomach flipped, and I jumped back, forcing a calming breath. I had almost kissed Jack! I had almost kissed the son of my enemy. A human. But that knock at the door had saved me. Hazel, coming to check on me.

"Stay here." I hopped to my feet, shaking out the tension in my limbs, and crossed the room. I slid the door open. "Hazel, I—"

I looked up into the unfocused gaze of the male I'd danced with exactly one time. He leaned heavily against the frame. "Not Hazel." His words slurred together, and he dipped his forehead toward me, nose bumping my cheek.

"Heath," I said, backing up a step. His breath reeked of wine and desire. "Leave. Now."

"Come on, baby. Don't be a tease."

I took another step backward, intent on closing the door in his face, but he wedged his foot in, stopping me. His gaze darkened, brows slashing low over green eyes that flashed with malice. "I don't think so. You embarrassed me in front of Regent Goodfellow."

I shoved the door hard against his foot.

"Bitch," he seethed, wedging his shoulder against the door.

Heat pressed into my back. "Sav's not available," a deep voice rumbled behind me and I spun, finding Jack right behind me, a dangerous glint in his eye. I gaped at him, but his focus was solely on the male attempting to push his way into my room. "Find someone else tonight, friend."

A thrill raced along my spine as I turned back to Heath. Jack's dark, possessive words had me reminding myself again that he was Dane Clyde's son, and not someone who should be turning my knees weak.

Heath stumbled back, glaring over my shoulder at the man towering behind me.

Jack stepped around me, slammed the door in the drunk fae's face, and leaned back, watching me with a feral sort of hunger I'd never seen in a human.

"Are you sure you're human?" I asked, my voice coming out higher than I wanted.

Jack pushed off the door, stalking toward me, and I backed up. "I don't like him."

I nodded, continuing backward into the room.

"I don't want him to touch you again."

I flinched at the words, halting. "You don't get to decide who touches me."

He continued forward, but I held my ground. When we were close enough that I smelled the sweet wintergreen of his breath, he stopped. "I know, but I think I've made my intentions clear. And Sav, I don't like sharing."

Something uncomfortable jolted through me. I turned, and his hand snaked out, gripping my arm as he spun me back to him.

We collided as his arms came around the thin fabric of my robe, warm fingers gripping my biceps and his lips found mine, pressing roughly against my mouth. Fire burst to life in my belly, licking up my spine and for one agonizing moment, I let the feeling sweep over me, giving in to the kiss before I tamped it down and pressed my hands into his chest, shoving.

He let me go, and I backed up. "You should go," I said, turning so I didn't have to see his face. My insides were blisteringly hot from one kiss and it wasn't hard to imagine what it would feel like to do more, but I wouldn't. Couldn't. Seeing Bracken tonight, remembering my childhood with a father broken by his mate's death, I wanted nothing with someone I could never be with. Our kinds were too different, not to mention the literal death sentence it would be.

I had been foolish for entertaining the idea.

"Sav."

My true name said so mournfully, cut deep into a place I'd buried. "Go, Jack."

"You don't have to be afraid of this." His fingers brushed my shoulder over fabric, but I didn't turn. "You can trust me. I won't hurt you."

A chill slid down my spine as I tried to block out the words. I had to turn these feelings off. I didn't want them. "Go," I whispered. I held my breath. After several long seconds, the door creaked open, then clicked shut, and I exhaled slowly.

THIRTY-TWO

SAV

I dressed quickly. Even with three magical alarms, I'd overslept. It felt as though I had closed my eyes for a moment before I was cracking them once more. I had lain in bed—running the pad of my thumb over my mouth—for hours, unable to banish the memory of his lips on mine from my mind. Now, I'd be lucky to make the last morning audience. I couldn't spend another day in this court. Juniper, the dryad who'd helped me, and all the other fae trapped by Dane, were counting on me and I was dancing with males and making googly eyes at humans.

A sharp knock at the door made me pause. Nothing good came from a knock at my door.

"Sav. Hurry!"

I exhaled, rushed forward, and swung the door wide.

Hazel stepped in, glowering at me. "After all I did," she railed, wasting no time with greetings. "To make you look innocent."

"What?" I smoothed my skirts, glancing at my reflection in the mirror.

Hazel spun to face me, sparkling eyes narrowing. "I went to great lengths to ensure the folk of this court believed there was nothing between the two of you. You came in smelling like each other, for Mab's sake, and you threw it all away."

I moved to the corner, pulling a plain gold comb from my bag. "Hazel, you're not making sense."

"I draped myself over him at the table so Robin wouldn't be suspicious of the way you were eye fucking each other. But you couldn't keep it in your pants until your uncle granted your request and now? Now you'll be lucky to leave with your head."

I forced down the knot of tension rising in me and crossed the space, grabbing her shoulders. "Hazel, what are you talking about?"

"Heath reported you."

A cold stone settled in my stomach. Heath. Heath had seen Jack in my room and assumed we were together. Not just for the night. But...*together*.

"Mab."

"I know. Regent Goodfellow is in a foul mood over it."

"Hazel. This is bad."

She nodded in exasperation.

"Jack?" My throat constricted. Had they already arrested him? Had I slept comfortably in my bed while he met some horrible fate?

"He's with Mother Mahonia. She's giving him the last of his medicine. I asked her to keep him busy while we sort this out. If you must run, I'll get him out and meet you."

I nodded, all the misplaced anger I'd had the night before gone. Hazel was a better friend than I deserved.

"I need to go to the baths."

Hazel's nose scrunched in confusion before her eyes widened. "Kaspar." Hazel had only visited my court a handful of times after Bracken, but she was there the day Kaspar's betrothal request was announced. She knew better than anyone what it would cost me to ask him for anything, but there was no judgment in her tone. Uncle or not, if Robin thought I had feelings for the human, both our lives were in danger.

I nodded. "I need the prince."

We raced down the corridor, avoiding eye contact with any of the guards who might decide to take me into custody at any moment and escort me to my execution.

I sank to my knees beside a tub and ran my hand through the bubbling water. "Kaspar. Come at once. It's urgent." Hazel watched the door, turning back to me every few moments. "I'll owe you a favor."

The water rippled, and I swore under my breath. Of course. He'd come for nothing less. The ripples grew into tiny waves and I sat up as liquid sloshed over the lip of the tub. Bubbles burst along the surface, and a crown of seashells broke through, followed by waves of aquamarine hair. Cerulean eyes that perfectly matched his mane—and a lake glistening on a hot summer day—met mine.

"My lady calls?

"Kaspar. I don't have time. Name your favor and dress for an audience with my uncle."

He stepped out of the tub, water dripping to the floor, as velvet slacks materialized around his waist, slung low, exposing an expanse of scaled skin along his torso and up his sides. Swirling blue designs trailed up his arms, circling his pecs and ended just below his neck.

"You'll need a shirt and coat. Regent Goodfellow will see you in nothing less." With any luck, his presence would be all I needed to convince my uncle there was nothing between me and a human.

A midnight blue overcoat appeared, rolling down Kaspar's back in tails, and a bright teal silk shirt unfurled into navy tipped cuffs and collar. He grinned as my gaze dipped to his feet.

"Do you have any shoes, Cinderella?"

Kaspar coughed a laugh that turned into an easy smile. "I do. Have you nothing to say about the effort I'm making for my fiancé?"

I groaned, and Hazel motioned to her wrist. "Kaspar, your favor. Name it."

Shining, pointed shoes materialized as he held out an arm. I took it, rising from the ground, and Hazel escorted us from the room at a clipped pace.

He moved with a fluid grace reserved for the water folk and that calming presence I'd so adored before I was to be sold to him settled in my bones. It would be okay. With Kaspar by my side, my uncle couldn't accuse me of anything.

"I ask very little of my fiancé for this favor. Only that you maintain our friendship, no matter where our paths take us."

I eyed him as we reached the entrance to the throne room. "My friendship. That's your price?"

He nodded.

"My friendship and nothing more?"

Kaspar's head tipped toward me, mouth stretching wide to expose two rows of sharp teeth. There was something dangerously beautiful in that smile. I trusted him. Despite myself, I believed he wouldn't stab me in the back if it came down to it. Once, I might have corrected Kaspar. I might have told him friendship wasn't something to be bargained for and that he already had mine, but I wasn't feeling so charitable toward the male these days.

"It's a bargain."

His arm squeezed my hand as the magic hit my chest and he tugged me forward, turning into the throne room. The line was short, most of those who had come to see my uncle having arrived far earlier than we had.

A nervous thrill shot through me, and I leaned into Kaspar.

"I've got you, princess," he said, standing straighter on his human legs.

My breath caught as my heart gave a few small thumps. I didn't want to take comfort in those words, but they were ones I'd never heard from my father or any of the males in my life.

Robin sat up in his chair when he spied us. "I see we're graced with true royalty today." He beckoned us to pass the others waiting in line.

Kaspar tugged me forward.

I cast apologetic glances at the low fae who had likely waited hours for this audience. If Kaspar noticed their scowls, he was unaffected as he marched toward my uncle with all the pomp of a royal, fully expecting the treatment his title afforded.

Robin dipped his chin to Kaspar, then cast his disapproving gaze to me. "Niece. I see you came to your senses with no enticement from me."

I dipped my chin. "Uncle. It's time my fiancé joins me at court."

Kaspar stood taller.

"I take this to mean the rumors of your refusal are untrue?" My uncle had never been one to mince words.

"Kaspar and I are still negotiating terms, Regent Goodfellow."

My uncle's brows fell, auburn slashes severe on his handsome face. "What is there to negotiate?"

I swallowed, glancing at Kaspar. "Well. I cannot survive under the water and Kaspar, Prince Kaspar of the lakes and streams, does not wish to live on land—"

"What are these but semantics?" Robin's gaze was hard. He wasn't asking. He was demanding.

"You're right, Uncle."

"Don't placate me, girl. Is the date set?"

I glanced at Kaspar again. His gaze was fixed on someone at the back of the room, but feeling my stare on him, he faced my uncle, not missing a beat. "I have affairs to attend to before my court is prepared to welcome their new princess."

Robin seemed mollified by this answer. He nodded. "Very well. Lady Briar, you have tarried in the winter court long enough. Return to Spring and make amends. A prince cannot expect his princess to join him with her magic bound. See that you resolve the matter so you may proceed as planned."

Everything I'd hoped to achieve in coming here, lost because of one fae male's ego. I would not receive aid from the winter court. I was only leaving with my head because of the male at my side. Heat boiled my veins at the injustice. One of my closest relations cared only for his own family's ambitions. I had been naïve to assume anything else.

My uncle dipped his head in respect to the creature with the grandest title in the room and my fake fiancé smiled, turning and giving his back to my uncle. I backed up, but he tugged me around and several hisses scalded my back as we left.

In the corridor, I whirled on Kaspar. "What did you mean by making me disrespect my uncle by turning my back on him like that? You may be a royal, but I'm not."

Kaspar's bored gaze dipped to me. "You're expected to be a princess soon. Start acting like it or no one will believe you. My people will not bow to a female who won't show spine to her own titleless male relative."

My mouth dropped open. "Titleless? He's regent to the most powerful court in Faerie. Until Mab returns, he rules this land."

"Sav!"

My gaze snapped up, meeting burning emerald eyes, and my stomach dropped. "Jack. You can't be here. My uncle could have ordered your death. Might still."

Kaspar made a noise that was suspiciously like a horse's whinny. "You haven't eaten the human yet? I thought you brought him as a snack."

Jack scowled at Kaspar but ignored his comment. "I was with the healer when Hazel arrived and offered me another tour of the palace. We all know I don't need another tour. What's going on?"

I frowned. "We need to leave. Now." He wasn't dumb. I'd give him that. To Kaspar, I said, "He's not a snack, he's my friend."

The words snagged Kaspar's attention. "Friend." His bright blue eyes swiveled to Jack. "Did you make a bargain with her?"

I sighed in exasperation, but I couldn't blame the water fae. They didn't understand the nuances of relationships the way we did. "You don't have to bargain for friendship. Friendship is given freely, or it's not worth anything."

He hissed, the gills along his neck ruffling open and closed. "You tricked me! We made a bargain."

Jack's eyebrows climbed up his forehead and he crossed his arms over his chest but said nothing.

"Jack. Give us a minute?"

He frowned. "I need to talk to you."

I shook my head. "Later. You need to get out of these halls. I don't trust my uncle not to arrest you." Jack's dark brows were slashes across his face and he eyed Kaspar as though he were sizing up a threat. "Jack. Go."

Hazel appeared from some dark corner and tucked her arm through Jack's.

I backed up, pulling Kaspar with me. "Come on, Kaspar, it's time for you to go."

He watched Jack and Hazel moving down the hall. "You're attached to the human."

"It isn't what you think." I tugged him back the way we'd come.

"I should like to stay awhile."

I bit back a dozen replies, pulling more insistently on his arm. His skin was cold even through his jacket and I shivered. When we were young, I was closer to Kaspar than just about anyone, except maybe my twin, but over the centuries—me on land and him underwater—we rarely saw one another and eventually, we became strangers. As children, he had always wished to be a part of our world and his had fascinated me. But things were different now, and we could no more fit in each other's world than I did in the human one.

"That won't be necessary, and I'm sure your subjects need you."

We trailed the long hall, and I glanced nervously at the wolves as we passed. Robin had seemed to buy our story, but we weren't truly safe until we were gone from the winter court.

Outside the baths, he stopped. "I want to stay. I want to experience your world a little longer."

I released his arm, turning to face him. "Kaspar, be serious. The land is dry and cutthroat. You would hate it."

His blue hair moved on an invisible breeze and he rocked slowly as he stood outside the door, searching my face. "I fear for you among the ruthless land courts. With me by your side, no one will dare harm you."

An unwelcome emotion crashed over me. Gratitude. I didn't want to be grateful for the male who had colluded with my sister to steal my freedom and cause my banishment to the human realm. He didn't get to make me feel anything after his betrayal. But after a lifetime of learning that those who were closest to you had the most power to hurt you, I shouldn't have been surprised. Still, that day lived with me, never far from the surface. Even knowing Kaspar wasn't like the land fae, his cold skin a mirror to his icy heart, his deception had scarred. Was it worse that he didn't understand my pain? Wasn't capable of comprehending the depths of his treachery?

"Your offer means a great deal to me, but the price of your aid was friendship, and I gave it. Was the payment not sufficient?"

Kaspar's ocean eyes swam with some dark emotion I couldn't decipher. "I have named my price. I ask for nothing more."

I nodded, and he searched my face, coming to some decision before turning to march down the hall, clothes dissolving as he went. His bare ass shook as he pushed the door to the baths open, disappearing from view.

THIRTY-THREE

JACK

"Take Sav and get out of this court while you can. But, Jack..." Hazel's eyes flashed dangerously. "When you are in Spring, don't trust anyone and don't you dare put Sav in danger. You'll be dealing with true royals in their court."

I swallowed, scanning the hall behind Hazel. There were too many things I didn't understand about fairies and their courts, but one thing was as true here as it had been on Earth. No one wanted to see a fairy and a human together.

There *had* been something between us in her room last night. I wasn't imagining it, but this morning, I'd slipped into the throne room just in time to hear Sav tell her uncle she and Kaspar *were* engaged. Had she kissed me last night and agreed to marry this fish the next morning? The callousness of her actions cut deep. But even if she'd chosen him, I wouldn't do anything to endanger her.

I nodded. "I won't hurt her."

Hazel snorted, her tail whipping behind her. "You hurt her by joining her in Faerie. Just try not to get her killed when you go to Spring."

A countdown clock had begun ticking in my mind the moment we arrived in Faerie. Leo and Grace wouldn't make a move without me and every day I was here, Dane pushed his agenda forward with no one there to stop him. My phone hadn't made the journey to Faerie, not that I thought it would work here, but I was anxious to learn what new information Leo had on Janet as well.

We'd come to court and played whatever game Sav needed to gain an army, but this morning she hadn't asked for help for the prisoners. She'd informed her uncle of her betrothal. I didn't want to believe she'd been lying to me, but the proof had spilled from her own lips. What other reason could she have for dragging me with her into Faerie?

I had no time left to wait and see. I needed to get back to Earth, where I could be free of this court and these fairies whose deceptions muddled my judgment. An ache settled in my chest at the thought of leaving Sav, but I'd laid out my feelings, giving her honesty and she had sent me away, choosing her prince instead.

"I should leave."

Hazel backed up as she barked a laugh. "You wouldn't survive a day in our world without Sav to protect you."

The memory of the creature in the woods, rough arms wrapped tightly around me, flashed in my mind, and I shuddered. Could I make it to one of the pocket entrances on my own? I'd been unconscious for part of our trek and had no idea where to go. Would any of the fairies here tell me the way? I shook my head. I was at the mercy of this world until Sav was ready to return. That truth sunk like a stone in my stomach.

Hazel narrowed her eyes at me. "Just keep your feelings to yourself until you leave the spring court. If they think there's nothing between you, she'll be fine."

Hazel had said she was one of Sav's best friends, but everything Hazel did seemed to serve her own agenda, though I didn't know what that was. Were these the people Sav had needed to put her trust in all her life? It was no wonder she wore such thick armor.

"You're not dressed yet?" Sav's voice carried down the hall. She appeared around a corner moments later, marching past me to her room, and glanced back as she stepped through her door. "Change into the warmest garment you can find, but dress in layers. When we breach the border of Winter, you'll melt in these thick clothes."

"Sav. I'm not going with you to Spring."

As usual, she ignored me, turning to Hazel. "Can you give us a ride? The bears hate me."

I ground my teeth, speaking up. "I came with you to winter as we agreed, but it's time I go home."

Hazel grimaced. "Have you seen your human? He's a beast. The two of you would break my back."

Was I fucking invisible?

Sav's mouth curled up at the corners. "Hazel Elm can't handle two at once. Who'd have guessed?"

"Don't you dare say my name like that," Hazel hissed. "I won't be bound to do your bidding. Or any others."

Sav's mouth split in a full grin. "Fine. I'll ride you. We'll find a bear for Jack."

"Hey!" I shouted. The pair turned their stares on me and some of the heat in my veins cooled. "I can't go with you." I bit the words out. "Tell me how to get home."

"Jack..." Sav crossed her arms over her chest. "I don't have time for this." She turned in her door frame.

"Make time."

She spun back to me. "What's changed? I thought you wanted to help me? We didn't get what we needed here, but I can still ask for aid in Spring." Her eyes widened as she saw how serious I was. "There's a pocket entrance in all the realms. The moment we have our army, we'll go back."

Balled fists at my sides loosened as I searched her face. Was it another lie? I wanted to believe her, to trust that she wasn't using me for some game I had yet to see, but her face was a mask I couldn't read.

"You said you came to winter for an army. But you didn't ask your uncle for an army this morning. You announced your betrothal."

Hazel backed up and Sav swiveled her gaze to her friend. "Don't leave. We're going to Spring."

Hazel froze, looking between us. "This seems like a private discussion" Not waiting for either of us to respond, she turned and fled.

My focus returned to Sav.

"You really want to do this now? In front of the guards?"

I flicked a glance to the motionless, armored statues lining the walls. "Why are we truly here?"

Sav's eyes rolled to the ceiling. "I told you. I need an army to save the folk trapped by—" she glanced around the hall and pitched her voice lower. "Dane. Heath reported us to my uncle, and I had to do something. Kaspar is my friend. He saved both our lives this morning." She stepped closer. "I realize now, my uncle would never have helped. Our only hope is my former court."

It had been on the tip of her tongue to say my dad, and my stomach sank. She was putting a lot of faith in the son of a man who tortured and killed her kind, and cared enough for my safety to swear my identity to secrecy. I had given her very little of my trust.

I swallowed, nodding. "And you swear once we meet with the prince of spring and get your army, you'll show me the way back?"

She met my gaze. "I swear." Something burned in my chest, and I rubbed absently at the lingering bit of pain. "Now get dressed. I'll meet you in the stables in fifteen minutes. Hazel will show you the way."

—●→(∪◆∩●●—

I was sweating when we reached the stables. Digging my fingers into the collar of a thick fur-lined coat, I exhaled a hot breath. I would suffocate soon. Rounding the corner of the long corridor, I gasped as I took in a massive frozen structure built into the side of the castle.

I supposed in a kingdom this frigid, everything must have interconnecting passages, but it wasn't the marvel of ice lined halls that stole my breath. In the oversized stalls, instead of horses, each held a mammoth fluffy white beast. Truly beast was the word for them, for a polar bear held nothing to the creatures exhaling grumbling breaths in the long wooden pens.

I moved tentatively forward, holding my fingers out toward the nearest creature. Hot, wet steam blazed across my skin as a massive black nose leaned closer. My lips twitched up. "There, you see. I'm your friend," I whispered.

He chuffed something that sounded like a laugh before pressing his nose into my palm.

"Damn!" Hazel exhaled, moving up behind me. "I've never seen Axallar do that with anyone."

I glanced back. "He knows good people when he meets them."

His nose pushed harder into my hand, knocking me back, and he leaned against his pen, getting closer. I slid my hands through the bars.

"I wouldn't do that," Sav cautioned as she stepped through the door.

Axallar, the world's largest polar bear, pressed against my hand, rubbing his furry muzzle up my arm. Something resembling a purr erupted in his chest.

"Huh." Sav said, stopping beside me. "I guess we found your ride."

Standing so close, her scent wrapped around me, climbing under my skin as a new heat enveloped me, twice as hot as the thick coat and clothes suffocating me. But her presence wasn't stifling. Instead, it tugged me toward her, begging me to close the space between us.

Axallar growled and yanked his head back. His solid black eyes fell on Sav and he spread his lips wide, roaring loud enough to make my ears ring. I pulled my hand out of his pen and backed up as he pawed the ground, grunting and exhaling steaming breaths. "He doesn't seem to be a fan of yours," I smirked.

Sav's eyes narrowed. "I'm not a fan of males with poor taste. You can have each other."

"I didn't know you had such a low opinion of redheads with freckles. If you want, I can help you dye that mane of yours. But you should know, red's my favorite color." I winked.

The corner of Sav's lip lifted a fraction and my heart warmed at the sight of it. Behind her, Hazel shook her head at me.

"Come on," Sav said, sliding the straps of her bag over her fur-clad shoulders. "The earlier we leave, the better our chances of making it out of Winter before dark."

Hazel moved past us, unhooking a massive latch that should have been far too heavy for her, but if there was one thing I was learning about creatures in this realm, it was that they were all deadlier than they looked.

THIRTY-FOUR

SAV

W e reached the Winterwood at midday, and even with full sunlight and no hint of snow flurries in the air; the chill had sunk into my bones. I glanced back and snorted. A thin line of frost clung to the five o'clock shadow coming in on Jack's chin and he was huddled so deeply into his coat and furs, only his nose and mouth were visible.

"We may need to break and set a fire for a few hours. Jack doesn't look like he's going to make it."

Hazel rolled her massive spotted shoulder, shaking her head. In this form, we couldn't communicate, but her intent was clear enough. She wasn't stopping.

"Jack!" I called to him. A shudder rolled through him, but his gaze shot to me. "Can you make it a few more hours?"

He wrapped his coat tightly around himself and nodded. His lips were pale, and he looked as though he might topple off his bear at any moment, but he leaned down and hugged Axallar as the bear lumbered on.

"Maybe we should go faster," I suggested.

Hazel made a hissing sound, but she picked up her pace, and Axallar trudged after us.

Several hours later, the sun had begun its slow descent and snow dripped off branches, flaking down as we ran. The chill was leaching into my very marrow and Jack hadn't said a word in more than an hour. This close to the edge of Winter, there was nothing left to do but run and hope we weren't carting a dead human behind us.

A shadow swept overhead, and I glanced up, my throat going dry. "Shit."

Hazel twisted her large, furry head to stare up at the sky and ran faster.

Axallar bellowed loudly, and I looked back at the pair. "Run Axallar! Don't wait for us!"

The massive bear didn't have to be told twice. He barreled past us, breaking into a true run, and Hazel chased him as the shadow passed overhead, and circled around.

"He's coming back!" I shouted.

Hazel loped through the snow at full speed and I wrapped my hands in her fur as wind whipped my face.

Ahead, Jack was still atop Axallar and the pair were disappearing into the distance at a rapid pace. If they crossed over the border, they would be safe. I said a mental prayer to Mab that they made it moments before a screech sounded overhead and clumps of snow toppled down around us.

The tree line broke, leaving us fully exposed to the creature above. Unlike Axallar, and Jack's white coat, Hazel's spotted fur and my dark cloak would stand out against the snow. From the break in the tree line to Spring's border, it was less than two hundred yards, but that was plenty of time for the bird to make his move.

The bird's dark shadow disappeared, and I exhaled in a moment of relief as Hazel gave it her all, running flat out. Her huge paws struck snow, sinking in with the force of her speed and every beat against the ground struck in time with my racing heart.

A field of pink flowers stretched out ahead, and I could almost smell their floral scent.

Darkness swept overhead, and I screamed as massive talons wrapped around me, wrenching me off Hazel's back.

The sound of wings flapping drowned out my scream and I twisted in the creature's claw, thanking Mab only my bag had been punctured by razor sharp talons. Slipping out of the straps, my stomach flew into my throat as I had a second of relief before I was in freefall.

I rotated around, prepared to smack earth, but bile rose in my throat when I saw how much farther I had to fall.

Stretching my arms wide, I grabbed the edges of my cloak, catching some of the wind screaming against my face. I had thought I was cold before but with my cloak spread—icy wind pelting against me—needles stung my chest and stomach, sucking the frigid air from my lungs and blackening my vision.

Every muscle went taught as I braced for impact, but nothing could have prepared me for the pain that erupted through my body as I slammed into snow. Air was shoved from my lungs and the loud crack that sounded upon my landing said at least one of my ribs was broken. I lay for a moment, breathless and disoriented, before groaning and pressing my tingling arms under my chest to push up.

When the buzzing in my head subsided and sound returned, my name —screamed in Jack's desperate voice—filled my ears. Pushing to sit up, I stared dazedly around at the blanket of snow I'd landed in.

A line of crimson dotted the snow, leading to an ocean of pink. My vision solidified, making sense of the shapes around me and Jack—waving his arms overhead, mouth wide as he shouted—came into view. Axallar had boxed him in, stopping him from stepping into the winter court. Beside them, my gaze fell on a naked, broken body.

"Hazel," I breathed.

Climbing unsteadily to my feet, I stumbled on shaky legs toward them. Jack was shouting and pointing. I glanced up and some distant voice in my mind registered the danger. *Run*, it said. *Run!* My legs moved, buckling once before they stretched out in the snow, and soon I was running at speed for the safety of the spring court.

THIRTY-FIVE
JACK

"Sav! Run!"

I shoved Axallar with all my strength, but he was immovable and I screamed in terror as Sav shook herself out of her stupor and finally ran. The massive white bird that had dragged her off Hazel's back, intent on carrying her away, had circled around, dropping her pack, and was closing fast.

She wasn't going to make it.

I bellowed and shoved the giant bear with everything I had. He growled in my face, spittle flying across my cheek, but when our eyes met, he blinked. I met his stare, cold fury in my gaze. He took a step back, over the line that separated the two courts, then another.

I raced forward, wrapping an arm under Sav's, and dragged her with me across the border.

The enormous bird's blood-flecked claws swiped low, catching my coat and yanking me backward.

Sav dropped to her knees on her side of the border and even as I was dragged away, I exhaled a sigh. Safe. She was safe.

The gigantic bird lifted into the sky, talons wrapped around my coat, and air rushed from my lungs as I was yanked off the ground.

"Jack!" Sav yelled.

I reached for the buckles fastening the garment across my body, and began undoing them as I rose higher. Too slow, I was moving too slow. My heart beat painfully in my chest as I tried to get my breathing under control and steady my fingers enough to finish undoing the clasps. Years of training under my dad's intensive tutelage were finally paying off.

Maybe...

At some height, the fall would kill me.

Pain lanced through my leg—then I was yanked back to earth. Axallar had my calf in his jaws. He hit the ground hard, dragging me with him. The bird shrieked, but before I could blink, claws and fur collided.

"Jack get back. They'll kill you!"

I glanced at Sav, then to the bear and bird, equally matched in size and in deadly talons and teeth. She was right. I should run, but I couldn't leave him to die after he'd saved my life.

"Jack!"

Ignoring her, I searched for a stick or rock. Spying a massive branch protruding from the snow, I yanked it free and charged the bird, waving it overhead.

Axallar dove in front of me, and the bird's beak speared his side. He let out a bellow of pain and swiped his huge paw across the bird's face. It shrieked, taking flight.

Sav halted beside me and set her hand on the branch. Flames flared to life along its frozen bark and I waved it in the air, stabbing at the bird. It squawked again, glancing between the three of us.

Deciding it was outmatched, the creature flapped enormous white wings, climbing until it was a distant speck in the sky.

I turned to Sav, throwing my arms around her. "Why did you come back out here!"

Her cheeks were flushed from the cold and she pushed out of my hold, eyes narrowing as she looked me over, finding only the tiny wound on my arm and bloodstained pant leg from where Axallar's molars had cut into skin.

I grimaced. "It's nothing. I can walk."

She searched my face, looking for a lie in my words. "Don't do that again!"

"Do what?"

"Risk yourself to save me."

"You did the same–"

The crack of her slap stung my cheek and I gaped at her as she marched out of the snow and back to Hazel's side. She fell down beside the creature who had shifted from a snow leopard back to fairy and was lying naked in a field of pink flowers.

"Hazel," I whispered, rushing toward her.

Axallar stepped into my path and I moved to dart around him, but the coppery scent of blood stung my nose, and I inhaled sharply. Dark crimson soaked his coat where the bird had speared him. I pressed a hand to the wound, and he moaned in pain.

"I'm sorry, buddy. Shhh. Come on, let me see it."

He stretched his mouth wide, roaring, and I backed up a step. His black eyes searched mine a moment before he dipped his head and shoved me toward the border.

"I'll help you," I told him.

He gave me another shove, checking to be sure I was across the invisible line before turning and running back into the snowy forest. I stared after him, something in my chest cracking as I watched him go. He had saved me and now I feared he would die with no one to care for his injuries.

"Jack, get over here. I need your help."

On my knees, my stomach hollowed at the sight. It was so much worse than I'd thought. The bird had hooked his claws in her and in her naked human state I saw how deep the wounds were. A slow trickle of dark blood pooled at her side and the slow rise and fall of her chest rumbled in such a way that I knew a lung had been punctured.

If she didn't see a doctor soon, she wouldn't make it.

Sav rested a hand over the wounds. "Damnit."

"What is it?" I pressed two fingers to Hazel's throat, counting out the rhythm of her heartbeat. It was incredibly slow. So slow I wasn't sure how she was alive. But what did I know about fairies? Were their hearts slower? Was this a flesh wound for them? I had taken several pre-med classes in preparation to become a doctor one day, but none had prepared me to save the life of a fairy.

"My magic doesn't work. I can't help her." Sav looked up, brushing a strand of auburn hair back from her face, streaking crimson across her cheek.

I lifted a finger, wiping the blood away, and watched her eyes for any sign of concussion. Both pupils were slightly dilated but nothing too concerning after such a fall.

She flinched at my touch but didn't stop me.

I let my finger trail her temple, tucking the hair behind her ear when it came loose again. "We need to clear her lungs. If we do that, we can stabilize her. How far are we from the nearest town?"

Her soft hazel eyes blinked at me as if she struggled to comprehend my words, but I knew that couldn't be the case. Sav was nothing if not cunning. Something else had rendered her speechless. A flicker of something like hope trickled in, threatening to give wings to the emotion, but I dared not allow that feeling to grow.

THIRTY-SIX
SAV

J ack worked long, dexterous fingers in some approximation of magic as he took a reed he'd freed from a pond, and tapped it below Hazel's rib. He tapped again, harder this time, and the reed punctured skin.

In moments, liquid filled the tube, spilling out onto the ground. The rattling breaths she'd been struggling to suck in cleared, and she inhaled a deep breath. Her chest rose and fell and I listened to her slow, even heartbeat. Her body was in stasis. An unfortunate side effect of our kind when we needed to heal rapidly from a potentially fatal injury.

"We'll need to carry her and leave the tube inserted in case any more blood fills her lungs."

I nodded, watching him work. In the past several hours, Jack had proven all the ways I'd been wrong about humans. He was brave, selfless, and competent.

I scanned the surrounding area, finding two sturdy branches and a few broad, flat leaves. "This is the second time I'm making a stretcher in less than a week. Perhaps I should open a business."

Jack looked up from his patient. "Was that a joke? Did you make a joke, Savage?"

"Savage?"

"Only a savage would choose the moment their friend was gravely injured to make a joke." He smiled, a dimple appearing in his cheek. "How did I ever let you convince me to come to this hellish place?"

I frowned. "This is my home. I lived here longer than you've been alive."

"So you're...thirty? Thirty-five?"

I grimaced. "I'm older than your grandfather." I speared the final leaf through the pair of branches and dragged the makeshift stretcher over to Jack, glaring at him. It would have held together better with my thread, but my pack was buried somewhere in the snow and we couldn't waste time looking for it now.

"Oh," Jack said, motioning for me to help him lift Hazel onto the leaves. "Your age is a sore subject."

"It's none of your business, Jackass."

His lips split into a wide grin. "Clever."

"If I'm a savage, then you're a jackass." He laughed. Tending to Hazel had loosened his tongue and oddly, I found I liked it. "You enjoy caring for others, don't you?"

He sobered, glancing down at Hazel as he lifted the two sturdy branches. I moved behind him, hefting the branches at her feet, and we began our march into the Maywood.

When the silence had stretched for some time, my question nearly forgotten, Jack spoke.

"My mom was sick most of my childhood. I was young when her sickness started, but I remember how afraid she was to go to the doctor. She said they didn't know the first thing about healing." He paused, and my gaze caught on his raven curls as they rustled in a soft breeze. "When I was nine, I asked her why she didn't take medicine like the other moms who got sick. She said there wasn't a medicine out there that would heal what was wrong with her."

I rolled my shoulders, shaking out some of the fatigue. Blue jays chirped overhead and the scent of new flowers in bloom invaded my senses. All at once, I was hit with nostalgia for my home, and my vision blurred.

Jack looked over his shoulder at me. "I'm sorry. I didn't mean to make you upset."

I cleared my throat, swallowing down the emotion choking me, and met his gaze. "We've both lost those we loved." I looked away, hoping he wouldn't share any more of his story with me. I didn't want to know we shared this pain. I didn't want to feel *anything* for him. The sooner we made it to the spring court, the sooner I could make the trade and we could both go back to our separate lives.

Crunching loudly over dried leaves, we stepped onto a well-trodden path and Jack slowed as we reached Ferndell, the small village outside the spring court's castle.

"We'll find aid here," I said as we moved under an arched trellis.

Wooded forest gave way to a row of ground-level treehouses built between massive trunks. In the human realm, they called them townhouses, and I supposed it was an apt name considering this was one of the few towns in my court.

Most low fae preferred to dwell among nature rather than carve a place for themselves from it, but those who worked in the castle and their families had grown accustomed to court life. Small villages had cropped up over the centuries and the soldiers' wives and children lived in relative comfort not far from their spouses. In my youth, I had visited Ferndell many times.

An eerie silence hung over the village and I glanced through dark windows, not spying any movement inside. No smoke from chimneys wafted in the air, and the hairs on my arms rose as we entered the town's center, setting Hazel down on leaf-strewn cobblestones.

Jack looked at me, brows raised.

I shrugged a shoulder, at a loss. Three years ago, the village had bustled with life. I couldn't fathom where everyone had gone. Circling around the stone table that served as the focal point for feasts and celebrations, I followed the path to Ivy's door and knocked. The village healer had mended a scrape or two over the years and there was a pang in my chest. Had she disappeared? Like the others.

Her young boy, Qaden, was only eight when I left. Too young to be taken by the curse that stole our land and our folk. Not that anyone deserved whatever fate had befallen them, but children had yet to experience life, to know what it was to wield magic, to dance, to love. They, least of all, deserved what was happening in Faerie.

I knocked again. "Ivy?"

The silence sent a chill down my spine.

Jack appeared beside me. "Where is everyone?"

I looked up, biting my lip, holding back the emotion threatening to spill out. "Gone."

Jack's arms came around me and I stiffened. "Were you close to them?"

For a moment, just a moment, I allowed his warmth to soothe some of the ache.

When the moment had stretched uncomfortably long, I pressed a hand against his chest and wriggled out of his grip. "I wasn't close to anyone in Faerie."

His eyes softened in a look of sympathy that made my stomach churn. "Sav."

My spine straightened at the tenderness in the word. In my long life, kindness and empathy were weapons used to disarm your opponent. I narrowed my gaze on him, tensing in anticipation of his next move. He stood, shoulders rigid, and there was so much affection in his gaze I nearly turned and ran.

The moment stretched, and he didn't move; didn't say a word.

Slowly, I released the dagger my fingers had found their way around at my hip, and motioned for him to go before me, unwilling to give him my back. "Come on. There's a healer at the castle. We need to hurry. For Hazel."

THIRTY-SEVEN

DANE

I didn't agree with many of Janet Glassdon's methods, but mind-altering medications had their purpose, and the satyr was progressing nicely. After only a few slips in doses, she'd begun taking her medication as prescribed and was already showing signs of compliance. I hadn't expected her to share anything with Alice, but I had hoped we could sharpen her into something useful and it looked like I would be right on both counts.

Although my nerves grew more frayed every day Jack was missing, I'd grown more certain Juniper didn't know where he was or why the high fae had taken him. Still, she was beginning to respond to my commands. Today, I had instructed her to sit still for three hours, saying nothing while I played dog training videos. At the end, I'd asked her what she learned, and she simply glanced glassy-eyed at the clock, and waited until the third hour struck.

When it had, in an eerily monotone voice, she'd said. "Animals require a firm hand to ensure obedience."

Good. Very good.

Grif wrapped his knuckles on the wall beside my open door. "Come in."

He stepped through the door, scanning my neatly organized desk and grinned. "Alice keeping you straight?"

My brows pinched over the bridge of my nose. "I don't have time for chit-chat today Grif. Did you have something to report?"

He straightened, coming to attention. "Yes, sir."

"Report."

"Sixteen captured in last night's raid. Five were orcs but none were the group we're looking for." Grif's gaze fell on the image behind my head, and he faltered for a moment before continuing. "Three fairy businesses burned to the ground. Four dead. Three fairies and one human."

I ran my hand over my chin, scraping stubble. "Who authorized those attacks?"

Grif's eyes darted to me. "They weren't us, sir. Rioters have gotten brave, but this might set us back. If ISHFA does anything to retaliate, especially with a human death, people might get scared."

I nodded. "At ease."

Grif relaxed his posture, running a hand over the holster at his hip. "Permission to speak freely?"

I nodded.

"If we blame the orc general, it could work in our favor, but it could also strike fear in the people. I think we cover it up."

I stood, coming around my desk to lean against it. "You see what I'm working on?"

Grif's gaze darted to my wall again. "I didn't see anything, sir."

I lifted a hand, resting it on Grif's shoulder. He tensed. "You're a good guy, Grif. You have nothing to fear from me."

His throat bobbed, but he swallowed. I sometimes forgot how young he was. Even before he'd come to live at the compound, Grif had lived on the streets for more than a year. Both parents had died, falling victim to the need for more of the power that Xcess gave them. His life had been a hard one, aging him far beyond his years and making him wise in ways I hadn't been at his age.

My own son had six years on him and no matter how I'd trained him in preparation for the eventual war we'd find ourselves in, I wasn't sure he'd ever be ready. Grif wasn't afraid to get his hands dirty if it meant living in a world that was safe for all of us. All of us humans that is.

"Do it. Take Connor and Will."

"William?" Grif choked on the word.

My grip tightened on Grif's shoulder, and I pulled him around the desk to stare at the image pinned to the center of my board. All around it was a map of Central Park and the surrounding several blocks, blown up so each detail could be labeled. X's marked our locations, whether they be living quarters, prisons or lookouts.

Bisecting the map were several pins, marking off the areas where fae lived, worked and frequently traveled. Along the edges, I'd taped blurry images of the orc general's top men and one shadowy outline of the general himself. They had been my targets these many weeks and though my demonstrations served to incite the populous, I had one goal.

Draw out my enemy.

Now, I had a new target. Someone I wanted dead more than any of the rest. Sav.

Only one person at HQ knew fae lore. Once, William's mind was sharp. But softness had crept in. I needed him scared.

Grif stared at the clear image of a female who looked very much like a human woman, but who was anything but. She was leaning against a counter, smiling at a fawn she'd worked with whom I had questioned until her last breath, and across her shirt, in glaring red letters Fae'z in Harlem do it better, was stretched over her chest.

I had let my temper get the better of me and perhaps it had cost me valuable information, but in the end, I didn't think the fawn she worked with knew any more about her than the rest of them. One by one everyone in her building had fallen. One by one, they had squealed about every petty grievance they had with their neighbors, this city, humans, but not one knew anything about who she truly was.

They'd proved useful enough in testing the new medicine Janet sent over but were a complete waste of my time when it came to extracting anything useful. Now, after all my efforts, I only had a first name. Nothing to tell me what court she might have fled to or what trouble might be on our doorstep in the coming days.

I tapped a finger against the image, my heart pounding a rhythm in time with the beat of my finger against her face. "Do you see this woman?" Grif swallowed, shoulders bunching as I pushed him forward, shoving his face against the wall, but he didn't speak. Veins stood out along my fore-arm, and I leaned closer, pressing my lips to his ear. "This is our mission. Find out what we can about her and get my son back."

Spittle landed on the side of Grif's face, still pressed against the wall and I released him, exhaling a ragged breath. I straightened my shirt, running a hand over the thin scar at my wrist. *Calm*, Aconite would have said. *Calm, Dane.*

The memory of her soft voice played in my mind, and I inhaled slowly, four, three, two...

When my breathing was even, the steady beat of my heart relaxed, I cleared my throat.

Wisely, Grif had remained silent, eyes fixed on the image.

"When we find her, she'll be yours to do with as you wish." My finger traced the scar again and again, stroking along its ridges. This time I would exercise caution. I would not let my temper get the better of me. But just to be safe, I would let someone else do the torturing, so long as her screams would be heard all the way in Faerie.

THIRTY-EIGHT

JACK

We left the small village, traveling a well worn path that grew thinner the farther we went. It was overgrown by thorny brambles, and as any semblance of a trail disappeared, it became clear Sav knew the way.

A whistle broke through the trees and my gaze darted to a thick patch of thorns wound around massive oaks. I had only a moment to register the sound before pain speared my chest and I stumbled backward, dropping the stretcher. *An attack.* I turned lunging for Sav as the sound of another arrow whizzed overhead and we crashed to the ground.

"You're safe," I breathed as my vision darkened at the edges, tunneling to the small flecks of purple in her eyes before the world went dark.

Something soft tickled my nose. I rubbed it, feeling the fur lining of my coat pulled up high. I'd been hanging on to the huge polar bear, freezing cold biting into my skin as he raced over a snowy landscape and then... What?

Eyes fluttering open, my fuzzy mind puzzled over the room coming into focus. It was dark; deep walnut and chocolate walls, interspersed with foliage in shades of chartreuse, forest green and olive surrounding me. Tiny pink and yellow blooms burst from vines trailing the aged wood as they lazily surveyed the room.

With some effort, I turned my head to the side, and several of the blossoms jerked toward me, tracking the movement. My gaze met Hazel's bright eyes, and I struggled to make sense of where I was and what was happening.

"I'm glad you made it." Hazel's ice blue lips tipped up, and she leaned down, pressing them against mine.

"Hazel," I tried to say against her mouth. Her tail came up, wrapping around my wrist, pinning it in place. I jerked my free hand up to shove her off, but scalding pain burned my chest and I groaned, letting it fall to my side.

"Shhh," she whispered against my mouth.

I pressed my lips firmly together, glaring at her snowy eyelashes resting against her cheeks. Fire boiled my veins as I shrugged her off, wincing as the movement sent searing pain through my middle.

Hazel sat up and the room behind her came into focus once more. Sav. Sav was there, watching the whole thing. I tried to sit up, but Hazel pressed me back and she gave me a look that said be silent or die. It had been on the tip of my tongue to call Sav, to tell her it wasn't what it looked like, *again*, but Hazel's nails dug into my tender flesh and white hot pain stole my breath.

My eyes went wide as I breathed around it, truly taking Sav in. But it wasn't Sav. She was her twin in features, but everything else about her was different, and she held herself like a woman who knew exactly where her place in life was—the top.

Her pointed ears dripped with jewels large enough to feed ten families for a year. Her eyes, the same shape as Sav's, were bright purple and held the same luminescence as all the other creatures I'd met in Faerie. Her gown, delicate like the petals of a flower, was the same soft shade of pink I'd seen in the field on our entrance to the spring court... The spring court, the giant bird. Axallar. It all rushed back.

I glanced at Hazel, noting her glowing skin and bright eyes. Healed. She dipped her chin a fraction of a centimeter and I understood.

All her warnings before we left her court. They were for this woman. They looked so alike they could have been twins.

The fairy woman stepped into the room and the air shifted, every flower woven between the vines along the walls turning in her direction. The very world around us was moved by her presence. I couldn't say what it was exactly, only that it was power, undiluted and intoxicating. I had felt nothing like it when in front of the winter court regent or any of the other fairies.

"I see our invalid lives." She cast her gaze over me, a look of disdain plain on her face. "You've truly attached yourself to this creature, Hazel?" Her attention shifted to the white-haired woman by my side.

Hazel trailed a nail down my bare chest, careful to avoid my injury this time. "Well look at him, Majesty. Who wouldn't want a creature like this as my attendant?" Her fingers wrapped around my wrist, nails digging in sharply, warning me again to be silent.

"My soldiers tell me he dove in front of an arrow to save you." The woman's cruel smile told me she would have been fine with that arrow finding its mark.

Hazel's gaze dipped to me once more. "He did. I've promised him a good life in my service in exchange."

Sav's doppelgänger wrinkled her brow. "What you could expect to gain from a human I don't pretend to comprehend, Emissary, but you can see we've met the demands of your court. My healer, Ivy, has given him the best possible care. You may return to Winter at once."

Hazel snorted, pinning me down as I struggled to sit up. "My attendant was given human care. He would not survive the journey through my court in this condition. Sending us away is akin to sentencing him to death. Which is very much *not* in accordance with our terms."

The other woman huffed. "Very well. Send for your healer and when he is recovered, depart. You have one week and not a moment longer." Not waiting for a reply, she spun on her heel, gliding from the room, and Hazel let out a soft exhale.

She grinned at me. "That was close. I thought you'd say something foolish and fuck it up for all of us. Again."

"Where's Sav?" I sat up, wincing at the burning pain in my chest.

"She's dealing with family matters. It's best for both of you if you don't see each other. I may have tricked her uncle, but the princess of spring won't be so easily fooled by my flirtation. The moment you're in a room together, she'll read Sav like a book." She waggled her brows at me.

I scooted back. "I need to see her."

Hazel laughed. "Not a chance. Looks like I'm not leaving Spring without you. The two of you would get yourselves killed, if not for me." She stood, glancing down at my bandaged chest. "Look what happens when I'm unconscious for a few moments."

I lifted a hand to my bandages. "What happened?"

Hazel's tail curled up into her hand and she stroked it absently. "The spring court soldiers spotted you in the woods near the castle and thought you were Summer, sneaking in." Her gaze flicked up. "I can see why. Your hair is black as pitch. They have orders to shoot on sight."

She moved to the doorframe, peering into the hall, and her long, pointed ear twitched before she continued. "I had to remove their true memories." She shook her head. "I swear you both have a death wish. It's lucky I woke before we reached the castle. With Sav's magic bound, they would have marched straight in here and told the true story."

"Bound?" A memory of the night I'd overheard Sav and Kaspar talking flashed in my mind. He'd said something similar. "She has magic?"

Hazel pursed her lips, returning to my bedside. "Sav wouldn't want me telling her stories, but the more you know about her court, the better protected you'll be." She sat. "I changed everyone's memory, so they believed you've been glamoured by me. You're a human who found his way into Faerie through my court and per the rules of Faerie, that makes you mine."

She dropped her hand to my chest, running her fingers over the curve of my abs, and I batted it away. "I had planned to kill you, but you saved me and now I can't bear to part with you. As the emissary to the winter court, you're under the same protection I am. Your actions also reflect on my court."

She lifted her fingers again, and I grabbed her wrist with my good hand before she could touch me, but she was faster pinching my nipple with the other hand.

"Ow."

"Remember that before you go doing anything foolish here. The amity between our two courts rests on our behavior. Don't do something that would put us at odds."

I tore her hand away from my tender skin. "Okay, got it. What about Sav? Her magic?"

"You're like a dog with a bone." She sighed, rolling her eyes. "Sav's magic was bound when she refused the engagement to Prince Kaspar. Her twin sister, the lovely lady you just met, planned the marriage for more than a decade, but Kaspar only agreed to it three years ago."

"Her sister is the princess?" I scratched the area around the bandage that both hurt and itched simultaneously. "So she *is* royalty."

"Her sister wed the Hawthorn Prince, making her a princess, but they weren't royal by birth. Their social climbing mother and uncle plotted advantageous alliances for both girls. Sav and the princess spent their childhood at court, shoved into the lap of every noble who glanced their way. It wasn't until Sage—Princess Hawthorn—was old enough to marry that she was finally freed of their political games."

A bitter taste settled on my tongue as I thought of two girls treated like bargaining chips and the vile creatures I'd encountered at court. Men like Heath, who had put their hands all over her, and expected more at the end of the night.

My gut twisted. "She refused to marry him and they bound her? That's cruel."

"You don't know the half of it. She was cast out of her court and Faerie, made to live with the low fae in the human realm. She hasn't set foot here in three years. The punishment for returning without a summons is death."

"What?" Ice slid down my spine as I pushed back the covers. Pain seared through my chest, but I ignored it as I slid my legs over the side of the bed. Why? Why would she risk coming here if it could mean her death? The fairies at Dane's compound. She was risking her life to save them.

A cold stone settled in my stomach. She'd refused to marry for herself. But she'd sign away her freedom for them. For the fae I had failed to save. Guilt burned under my ribs like a second wound.

"Hold on, prince charming. She's alive." Hazel pressed a hand to my left peck, holding me in place. "She has accepted the betrothal. At least that's what she claims, and has fallen on the mercy of Prince Alder, begging him to send aid to the fae trapped in your realm."

I sat back, exhaling slowly, finally understanding what was really going on between Sav and the prince. A spear of pain twisted in my gut. I'd been so quick to judge her in the winter court when I knew nothing of her troubles. "She wouldn't marry him for her own life, but she'll do it in exchange for the fairies who are imprisoned by my..."

Hazel arched a white eyebrow. "Your?"

"People."

Her lips tipped up in a feline smile that told me she didn't think I'd meant to say *people* at all. "She always had a soft spot for lesser creatures." As she said it, Hazel's gaze trailed the length of me.

My chest expanded painfully as I dragged in a breath. Alive. She was alive, but she was giving up her one chance at happiness because I had been too slow to do anything against my father. "I can't let her do it."

"It's done, Sweets. She meets with the prince and princess in a few hours to sign the contract.

THIRTY-NINE
SAV

I stared out my bedroom window, another bout of nostalgia sweeping over me. It was bittersweet being here, in the room I'd lived in since my sister married Alder. Once, I'd only wanted to please my family. I had done whatever they asked, hopeful that one day, I'd do something good enough, brave enough, to earn their love.

Refusing Kaspar had been the first time I'd ever gone against their wishes. I exhaled a long, slow sigh.

I hadn't been to see Jack today. The day we'd come in covered in his blood, Hazel had slapped me hard to shake me from my panic, reminding me what was at stake if I showed any emotion toward the human in this court. Here, it wasn't only the law forbidding a relationship. Here, my sister would take matters into her own hands if she thought for the briefest moment anyone would get in the way of her plans.

She wanted Kaspar's army; his network of spies. And she would do unspeakable things to get what she wanted.

For three nights, I'd left his bedside late, sneaking down the hall to my old room after watching him for more hours than I could count. He was heavily sedated, still recovering from his injury, and I stared at his chest, making sure it continued to rise and fall until my vision blurred.

When the arrow struck him, it felt like I'd been hit, too. I'd never experienced visceral pain for another, but in that moment, I could have sworn I was the one bleeding out. I was frozen, helpless to move and when the second arrow flew, Jack had moved faster than ever before, knocking me to the ground.

The action had likely caused more damage to his mortal body, but the memory replayed in my mind a dozen times. His terror... for me. Something uncomfortable lodged itself in my chest. I cleared my throat.

He'd been lucky. Only a few inches to the left and the arrow would have pierced his heart. When Ivy came to tend him, an unexpected flood of relief washed over me. Though the healer and I weren't close, she was one of the few fae in the spring court I trusted.

Not many folk would cross my sister. Jack would live. Ivy had treated him, even if she wasn't allowed to use magic to do it. It would be weeks before he recovered, but he *would* live.

Just as long as my sister didn't execute him.

I owed Hazel a debt. Her favor was now and forever paid. When the soldiers found us, bowing and scraping, begging forgiveness for shooting at the princess's sister, I had pushed Jack's unconscious body off me, convinced I'd sentenced us both to death.

If Hazel hadn't woken. If she hadn't changed their memories, I shuddered to think what my sister might have done. Hazel was right. Whether I wanted to admit it or not, there was something there. Feelings I didn't want to accept and they would get me killed if I didn't get them under control.

My attention drifted to the forest beyond the manicured lawn out my window when a small orange and black creature darted across the grass, diving beneath a bush. A smile crept onto my face and my spirits lifted just a fraction as his ears appeared above a grassy ridge. His shiny black nose rose into the air, sniffing before he bounded away.

It was good to know Faerie hadn't shrunk so much that the woodland creatures no longer existed in my court. Foxes were my favorite of all the woodland animals. The little hunter would never know how much he'd brightened my day.

A knock came at my door and my stomach hollowed out. Nothing good ever followed a knock. "Yes?"

"His Majesty, Prince Alder Hawthorn of the spring court, will see you."

I nodded to the fawn hovering in the doorway. She bowed low, tawny curls tipping over tufted, speckled ears as she backed out of the room. Her deference frayed my nerves. Another reminder of the path I was now on.

If I signed the agreement, I would be bound to the courts in a new way. I would belong to the prince of lakes and streams and my court would be secure against the threat from Summer—our neighbor to the west. This bargain would also ensure armies were sent to save the fae trapped in Dane's headquarters.

I swallowed the anger simmering in my veins. I'd held out the first two days at court, entreating my sister to find it in her heart to help the folk, but Sage had only threatened to toss the winter emissary and "her pet" out and lock me in her prison if I didn't relent. At least I had something to barter. So many others would have been helpless.

If the cost was my one wish for the freedom to choose love, it was worth it. Hadn't I seen what came of love? Bracken, my father, even Creig —the former general of the spring court army, the father I'd always wished for—had been broken by it. Love had ruined them. Perhaps Prince Kaspar understood something I did not when it came to marriage. A love match only ended in pain.

And maybe this way, my family would finally be proud.

I stood, brushing out the folds of my deep green gown, and straightened my bodice, tugging silver laces to loosen them a fraction. Where the fashion in Winter was all soft fabrics that fell over the skin like butter, Spring favored layers and tight, form fitting clothing. If you could breathe, your gown was too forgiving. I had *not* missed the fashion here.

I stepped into the hall and moved with a light breeze carrying me to the throne room. All along the lilac walls, vines curved and looped, winding together to form a cage around the occupants of this overgrown court. Blooms tipped in my direction, and a pang of sadness speared through me. My magic was in there. The flowers sensed it, even if I couldn't access it. The scent of lavender and ripe strawberries hung heavy in the air, and though it dredged up fond memories, darker ones crept in beside them.

Straightening my shoulders, I stepped into the throne room.

My sister's voice rang out in the space, clear for all to hear. "Have them sent to the mines to work off their debts. I won't hear of any more complaints from the low fae about their inability to keep their bargains."

A soldier dipped his head, nearly resting it on his chin, and backed up. I glanced at him as I marched toward the twin seats.

Sage sat rigidly atop a throne of silver vines, interspersed with budding blooms in shades of fuchsia, indigo, and white. As I approached, my steps grew heavy, and I fought the urge to turn and run from this court, from my family, and the expectation that weighed heavily on me.

Her perfect curls, held in place by massive ruby combs, were tame by comparison to my wild mane plated into a loose braid and tossed over my shoulder. Her long, pointed ears, tapered at the tips to points—cuffed in gold—twitched forward when she spied me. Her narrowed amethyst eyes, growing thinner as I approached, held no love for me, but I'd stopped looking for any love from my sister more than a century ago.

My steps faltered as pain sliced through me. She was a mirror of all I'd lost. A terrible reminder of the gifts I'd been forced to give up. My gaze dipped to her nose, and I began counting the freckles there. It was our one difference—before I was bound—where I had ninety-seven freckles on my nose, cheeks and chest, my sister had more than two hundred.

No one ever noticed but us. We used to sit up at night, loudly counting each other's freckles to drown out the sound of Father's crying.

Beside Sage, Alder was less composed, leaning against the arm of his woven throne, eyeing one of the courtiers who was licking her lips in a clear invitation. If my sister noticed, she gave no outward indication of the male she'd sworn to love ogling the creature several steps down.

Alder's gaze never left the female's as I approached.

"Sister," Sage said, standing and blocking her husband's view of the other female. "So good of you to join us." She cast her gaze around the room at the handful of fae gathered to hear her daily decrees. Though I'd been in court several days now, I hadn't been allowed to leave my room until I'd agreed to Kaspar's betrothal. "I hope your long respite has returned you to us hale, and hearty."

I dipped my chin a fraction, unwilling to give her the deference befitting her station.

Sage glanced to Alder, who had leaned back now that his personal show was over and was staring out over the crowd with a bored expression. "Are you not pleased to see my dear sister returned to us, Husband?"

Alder's gaze snapped to my sister before landing on me. He looked me up and down, lingering far too long on my breasts before meeting my gaze. Something in his eyes danced with amusement when I didn't look away. He stood, moving from his perch with predatory swiftness to stand before me, and leaned close, breathing in my scent. "You look well, Lady Briar."

My stomach roiled at his nearness, but I dipped my chin lower than I had for my sister, if only because Prince Alder was known to make examples of his subjects when he was in an off mood or when some lover or other had jilted him.

His fingers skimmed over my bare shoulder, brushing my mane of hair back to expose my lightly freckled chest. His nose bumped the collar of my throat as he inhaled my scent once more. "Not bedding anyone at present, it seems."

I shuddered under his intrusive touch and sharp words, turning my head away. A light patter of rain beat against long oval windows to the right. The rain in Spring began at midday and midnight each and every day falling for several hours. Now, though, its presence brimmed with a foreboding that sent a chill down my spine.

"No sense wasting time on frivolity," Sage said, clapping her hands together. Her narrowed gaze never left the back of her husband's head as she continued. "Iris, bring the contract forward."

Sage's head lady-in-waiting, spy master, and assassin, rushed from the shadows, producing a long slender tube from under her arm. The intricate seashell artwork running down its side marked it as a relic of one of the sea courts.

My gaze darted from the prince, glaring up at my sister, to the tube. The chill in my spine sharpened to a spear of ice. I had been banking on one thing to save me from this mad plan. One last ditch effort to escape my fate. I would fall at Kaspar's mercy and beg him to call the whole thing off. I would ask this favor of a friend and pray to Mab he agreed. But if Kaspar had been the one to draw up the contract, that meant he'd already signed it. Once I pressed my signature to the paper, it was binding.

Whether the wedding was in one year or one hundred. It was done.

I swallowed, glancing at Alder. He'd backed up a step at the reminder of my reason for returning to court. It seemed even he wasn't willing to risk Kaspar's wrath by damaging what belonged to him. He moved to his seat, lounging there to stare out over the crowd listlessly, as though he hadn't just announced my lack of sexual partners to everyone in attendance.

I fisted my hands at my sides and marched forward. This had always been a possibility. There were worse things than marrying Kaspar. Even if he'd betrayed me, there were some advantages to the marriage. He lived in water. I lived on land. I'd rarely have to see him.

I took another step, sweat slicking my palms. At least Kaspar was an old friend. It was more than I could say for some of the males who'd warmed my sheets over my lifetime.

Sage held out a pen, and I grabbed it, my throat going dry.

She twisted the silver cap on the tube and slid a long sheet of paper out, unrolling it. Without looking at any of her attendants, she snapped her fingers, and a fawn rushed forward with a small table, setting it beside her.

Sage set the parchment down on the table and looked up at me expectantly.

I glanced around the room, licking my lips. I recognized several of their leering faces. They all wanted this; the protection my marriage brought them. With Autumn in marriage talks with the prince of oceans and seas, we needed this more than I'd been willing to admit.

It wasn't only the low fae trapped in the human realm who needed my help. These fae lived in fear every day without any protection. Our alliance with Winter was tentative at best, and we had none of their harsh climate defenses to keep the other courts at bay. With Faerie shrinking, everyone stared longingly across their borders and wondered what they could do with the extra land if they marched on their neighbor and simply took it.

My gaze landed on Raine, the orc commander of our army, and anger stole through me. His stoic expression, unreadable as always, gave nothing away. His presence was a reminder that my once dear friend, Creig, no longer held the position.

How I hated him for all he'd taken from my friend. Hated the injustice of a world where no one truly got what they deserved and the best of us were forced to give up everything if we weren't willing to play the right games.

I looked up, searching my sister's burning eyes. Did she crave power so much that she would sell me for it? Was there any part of her that still cared for me?

"Sage," I bit my lip. "Please don't make me do it. Do you care nothing for our kind? Will you not consider sending your army without payment? They are suffering. Dying. Is it not your duty as their sovereign to aid them?"

My sister's cheeks flamed deep crimson, and she shot to her feet. "I am Princess Hawthorn of the spring court and you are my titleless subject. You dare address me so informally in my own court, among my subjects, many of whom are your superior in every way?"

I snapped my mouth shut, swallowing down the bitter taste of the words threatening to spew from my lips. Who had I been fooling when I hoped to appeal to the cold-hearted royal armored in the glittering jewels she wore to distract the court from her own self-loathing?

How had I ever thought I could appeal to a monster?

I nodded once and lifted the pen, scanning the document for the space where my name would go. My stomach roiled as I looked down, Sage's angry stare burning hot on my face.

The contents of my last meal threatened to resurface as I found, in perfect scrawling script, Kaspar's full name—glamoured so only I could see it. As husband and wife, we would have each other's full names. A trust exercise meant to show just how much we loved one another. If someone made a poor match, put their faith in the wrong fae, it meant one might use that name for unspeakable things, could force their spouse to do any depraved act imaginable.

I held the pen between trembling fingers. I had known Kaspar almost my entire life, but did I trust him enough to give him such power over me? What choice did I have? It was me or everyone else.

The moment I pressed my name to paper, Kaspar would have power over me no one else ever had. Not my mother or father. Not even Sage.

FORTY

JACK

"Jack! Stop!"

I raced down the hall, ignoring Hazel. I wouldn't let Sav do this. Damn the consequences. She couldn't throw her life away. I shoved the doors to the throne room wide, wincing as pain sliced down my arm, and glanced around the grand—entirely empty—space, spinning in a full circle.

I stopped as Hazel entered and faced her. "You lied."

Her shoulders rose and fell. "You couldn't have stopped it, and it wasn't your choice."

Something in my chest fractured. "I'm too late?"

"She signed the contract an hour ago." Hazel moved into the room, tail curling behind her.

I backed up, holding up a hand. "What's wrong with you?"

Hazel's lower lip jutted out. "You couldn't have stopped it. This marriage was planned years ago. It was going to happen. The only reason she's not dead for her disobedience is because Kaspar forbade any interference while she decided. It was important to him she choose him without coercion."

"But she *was* coerced. She did it to save the fairies trapped at the AFF."

Hazel shrugged. "Maybe he got tired of waiting."

I stormed past her, leaving the throne room and marching down the long hall, boxed in by creeping vines. Where Winter had been a frigid place, beautiful for its starkness, this castle was wild and overgrown, a feeling of being smothered as the forest seeped in through every crack and crevice, overwhelming my senses as I fled the empty throne room in search of Sav.

I wanted to call out to her, but I feared what would happen if they heard me.

Rain beat against the glass, caging me in. It had been raining for hours, since mid-day, and it seemed like it would never end. This place was nothing but a prison of pretty flowers and deceptive floral scents. Though it was cloying, a bit of Sav's natural scent lingered among the botanical blooms. I couldn't imagine someone as brave and hard-edged as her growing up here, but there was a lethal beauty to the place that couldn't be overlooked.

"Come. I'll take you to her room."

I spun, finding Hazel right behind me. I eyed her warily. She had claimed to be on my side, on Sav's side, but from the moment I'd met her, she had only made things worse. "No thanks. I'll find her myself."

Hazel rolled her eyes, planting a hand on her ice-blue, velvet clad hip. "Think whatever you want of me, but you'll never find her wandering the halls of the spring court. It's a maze." Not waiting for my reply, she turned around, going back the way we'd come. "I sent a raven to my court. Mother Mahonia will be here tomorrow. In the meantime, try not to get yourself run through by any more Spring court soldiers," she called over a shoulder.

I crossed my arms over my chest, watching her go.

She stopped, realizing I hadn't followed, and turned. Her bright green eyes softened, and she glanced around the empty hall before moving back to my side. Unlike Winter, where the halls were lined with guards and fairies moved about at all hours, I hadn't seen a soul in Spring apart from Hazel and the princess.

Hazel stepped closer, pitching her voice in a way that oddly made it clearer even though it was quieter. "Sav is fond of you, whether she's admitted it to herself yet or not. She wouldn't leave your side for two days. I had to sit with her to pretend she was consoling me instead of the other way around." She shook her head. "You don't trust me, but trust that I know my friend."

Warmth swelled in my chest. A memory of Sav's eyes, wild with terror, flashed in my mind. She *had* cared. I'd seen it. I just needed her to admit it to herself.

"Come on. She'll want to know you're awake."

Hazel resumed her silent walk, and I moved, my step lighter than it had been in days. I had been a tumult of unexplainable emotions since that night she answered the door to Alice's room and our eyes met. I had feared for days now that I was making a fool of myself, that her tentative glances and jealousy had been all in my mind. That she cared for the blue-skinned man who had laid claim to her, but I was finally beginning to understand.

Sav hid her feelings behind a mask of cold confidence and half-truths to leave you unsure of where you stood with her, but underneath it all, she cared deeply. It was there in every selfless act, in the things she didn't say. And some of that big heart of hers had been reserved for me.

We reached a large arched door, painted green, and I stared for a moment at the contrast to all the others in the hall. Where each was plain wood, this one was a deep forest green. I smiled. Her minor act of defiance in a pretty floral cage. My chest gave a small spasm. How I understood her need to defy her captors in a cage of her own making.

Hazel knocked, and Sav's clear voice spoke through the door.

"Come in."

A feral sort of energy thrummed in my veins. I longed to step through the door and sweep her into my arms, claim her lips with mine, and reassure her I was fine. That I was grateful to her for saving me. That I was furious with her for agreeing to marry someone to gain an army. That there was still time to undo her reckless decision.

Hazel turned the knob, and we stepped into a large room. On the opposite wall, an expansive window exposing neatly trimmed hedges and rows upon rows of tulips, expertly cultivated by color, formed a bright backdrop to the sparse space.

Movement at the edge of my vision caught my eye, and all my focus shifted to Sav. She stood, running a hand down rich green fabric as she tracked my approach. Her auburn hair was loose around her shoulders, cascading in waves down her back, and I counted several freckles on her bare shoulders before my gaze trailed up the line of her slender neck to soft pink lips, finally landing on sparkling hazel eyes.

Since arriving in Faerie, they had brightened and today, in her home court, they seemed more purple than brown. Thick, dark lashes blinked, her chest rising and falling as I strode through the room, closing the distance between us.

She made no move, but her keen eyes scoured the bandage wrapped around my chest, before burning a line up my body to my face. For the briefest moment, I glimpsed concern in her eyes before it banked, locked away behind her walls, and her eyes met mine in passive indifference. I had planned to say so many things when I saw her, but those eyes were like ice, and they froze me in place.

We stood for long seconds, neither saying a word, and the air was charged with magnetic energy, our bodies leaning toward one another.

"He knows about the marriage contract." Hazel said, shattering the silence.

I exhaled a puff of air as the electricity fizzled between us.

Sav's gaze narrowed on her before it turned back to me. "And? Why would Jack care about my impending marriage?"

"Why would Jack care?" I asked, shoulders tensing as I squared them. "Jack is right here."

Sav's mouth flattened into a line. "And still alive. Surprisingly."

Her terse words sparked fire in my blood. "How could you marry him?"

She turned, fully facing me, crimson staining her cheeks. "Why do you care?!"

Heat simmered in my veins, and I closed the distance between us as my eyes narrowed and I stared down at her. She met my gaze with one of defiance, daring me to answer the question.

"You know exactly why I care," I seethed, crowding into her space. "I made myself clear in the winter court."

Another flash of emotion, there and gone, slid over Sav's face, but I couldn't discern it. There was a scent in the air, something that smelled like fear, though I couldn't say how I knew that, and the anger blazing through me banked.

Stumbling back, I inhaled a sharp breath. Red dots bloomed on the bandage at my chest and my head swam. I was dizzy from being on my feet so quickly after the injury. I couldn't smell emotion. It was blood loss.

I shook my head, trying to clear the dangerous thoughts running through my mind. Thoughts of the violent things I wanted to do to the man who Sav would marry. I had to get out of this room, away from this woman, before I forgot every oath I'd ever planned to take. "I should go... rest." I turned, hearing a sharp inhale behind me, but she said nothing. Didn't stop me as I stormed out.

Outside her door, I leaned heavily against the vines running down the wall. Dainty white and yellow petals were crushed under my forearm as I sagged into them, attempting to catch my breath. What was happening to me? Why was I allowing this woman to shred my common sense and why did I feel so...off? The magic in this place had affected me somehow.

Was it dangerous for a human to remain in Faerie so long?

The anger bubbling under the surface was far too similar to the snaps of rage my father was prone to and shame washed over me. What would my mom say if she saw me now? Knew the vile thoughts racing through my mind? She had always calmed my father, but nothing about the woman in the next room calmed me. I was a tempest of scalding emotions, and they burned hot, threatening to scar my soul.

Something was wrong with me. I could feel it in my blood, thick and strange. In this place, anger was a poison infecting me from the inside. Blooms stretched their petals toward me, reaching for my bare arms, and I pushed off the wall, backing up. They were lovely delicate things, like Sav, but I had no doubt if I got too close they would bite.

FORTY-ONE

SAV

I pressed a hand to my throat, forcing my heart to slow.

"It doesn't matter what he thinks," Hazel said to my back.

I stared out the window, swallowing hard. Was he angry I was marrying someone else, or that I was doing it for the wrong reasons? The rage in the air made it hard to think.

Relief flickered at seeing him on his feet—then his presence hit me, and regret surged. As if I needed more reasons to regret my choice. As if I wasn't already drowning in them.

I didn't want to spend another night in this room. In this court. Three years in the human realm had been meant as a punishment. To show me what I'd lose if I stepped out of line, but despite the binding, the demeaning work and humans like Dane Clyde, I'd known freedom for the first time.

Coming here had reminded me of all the reasons I hadn't regretted giving up this life. Kaspar's proposal wasn't freedom. It was another pretty cage. And Jack—

Hurt shone in his emerald eyes, and it lanced through me. He masked it with fury. But I knew that trick. I wrapped my arms around myself, running my fingers over the goosebumps sprouting over my skin, and my stomach sank. I didn't owe him anything, so why did it sting knowing I'd caused his pain?

"Sav."

I shuddered, spinning around to face Hazel. I had forgotten she was there. "My sister will expect me at the ball. I need to get ready. You're not required to attend. It would probably be better if you didn't."

She searched my face, but didn't move to comfort me. She knew me better than that. "I have a few things to attend to on behalf of my court, but I'm happy to come with you. Say the word."

I shook my head, letting my arms fall to my sides. "No. I can handle one night in my own court. Find me in the morning."

Hazel nodded. "He'll get over it."

A twinge of panic ran up my spine, but I bit down hard on the emotion, schooling my features. "He's not my problem."

Hazel's green eyes narrowed at the edges, but she said nothing, nodding again. "If you need me, you know where I'm staying."

When she was gone, I scanned the bare room, noting the slight discoloration where frames had once hung on the walls. Not seeing my parents' faces had been a relief—but the bare walls only reminded me this would never be my home again.

Another of Sage's fawns I didn't recognize helped me dress, pulling my corset tight. How had I not noticed before that all the folk I was closest to were gone now? Creig had left for his own reasons, but Primrose and Daffodil? Rosemary? All the folk I'd grown close to over the many decades at court were missing.

Since I had been back, not one friendly face had graced my door frame. True, most were likely avoiding me for fear of retaliation. My sister could call it a respite all she liked, but everyone knew what happened to me three years ago. I didn't blame them, but I'd expected Rosemary to dress me at least. She had been my attendant for nearly five decades. The fawn carefully arranging my hair into soft finger curls was a stranger.

She stepped back, the clack of her hooves the only sound in my room. "Will there be anything else, Lady?"

I shook my head, unable to meet her eyes. I couldn't stand the pity in them.

When she left, I glanced down at the glimmering jewels Sage had laid out for me. She wanted me to play the part of a dutiful sister. Sparkle and shine. Let them look. Let them touch. Queasiness settled in my stomach. A betrothal to a prince wouldn't save me from my family's scheming. Even the protection he would afford our court wasn't enough to keep their expectations at bay.

I glared at the jewels. Nothing but a glittering leash.

My mind snapped to the night I finally told them no. The night I chose myself. I'd thought nothing could hurt more than their disappointment.

I was wrong.

The binding was agony. I wouldn't wish it on an enemy. Phantom pain ghosted over my skin all the places where the bindings still sat, invisible, but no less suffocating.

My gaze darted to something moving at the edge of my window. I stepped to the glass. Moonlight silvered the garden, and in the tulips, a pair of black ears twitched.

I almost smiled—until he looked up.

Too-bright eyes met mine. Not an animal. A spy.

"Shapeshifter," I hissed, yanking the curtain shut. My fists clenched. Even here, my sister's eyes were everywhere.

A soft melody drifted down the hall, beckoning all to join the revel. It was so familiar, like slipping on an old coat. I glanced back at the jewels again. I itched to throw them into a bin and show my sister I was not her puppet, but I needed her army and until I had it, I would have to play along.

I slipped the mask I'd learned to wear over centuries of Briar manipulation on, securing it as one would a broach and prepared for a ball in my sister's court, leaving the jewels behind.

I scanned the long table, searching for a lighter shade of henbane wine to take the edge off. Nothing strong enough to dull my senses, just enough to get through the night. Voices rose and fell around me, some in merriment, some in low deceit.

The lords spoke freely of their latest conquests to one another and the hairs on the back of my neck prickled when a group turned their attention to me.

"I heard she's stuck in human form until the prince has her wedded and bedded."

"Perhaps even then he'll keep her magic bound."

"Too wild for her own good."

"Someone should have broken her a long time ago."

Changing my mind, I kept my back to them, reaching for a dark glass and knocked it back. I needed a strong drink to get through this night. I grabbed another glass and left the table, skirting the edge of the ballroom until I found a tangle of vines against the wall and leaned into them.

Taking small sips, my gaze trailed the mob of partygoers, many of whom were already glassy eyed and swaying. Females and males moved with the music, sipping from their glasses and laughing.

Unlike in Winter, none of the low court fae were present here. Only the orc army and their general attended court functions and even they didn't hold positions of power. Autumn held many of our rigid traditions, separating the high fae from the low and none of their low court fae held any positions of importance. Only Summer was a mystery to me.

"Would you care to dance, Lady Briar?"

Ice shot down my spine and I bumped the vines at my back, moving to get away from that voice. I looked up, meeting vile amethyst eyes, and wine sloshed over the side of my cup as my fingers began to tremble. I swallowed, trying to find the words to speak. To scream at him, but none came.

Lord Banyan held out a hand, and I flinched back.

His saccharine smile quirked higher on his lips and bile rose in my throat at the memory of those lips on my body. He leaned toward me and I found my voice.

"No."

"Come now, Lady. Fae are watching. Don't make a scene."

I tore my eyes from his, spying several creatures eyeing us curiously. Lord Banyan was a well-respected member of this court and once, he'd been my potential suitor. My family never let me forget the shame I brought to our name when he declined the proposal.

I glanced down at his outstretched hand and another memory shot into my mind. His hands wrapped around my throat as he held me in place, grip too strong for a young fae to fight. *You're not that girl anymore,* I told myself, straightening my spine.

I exhaled through my nose, tipped the wine glass to my lips, swallowing it down, and grabbed his hand, nails digging into his meaty palm as I led him to the dance floor.

His arm went taut as he snapped me back, and a muscle ticked in his jaw.

Sweat tickled the nape of my neck at the memory of what happened when someone displeased Lord Banyan and I let him move in front of me, tugging me onto the dance floor. He wrapped a hand around my back, and only sheer will kept me from jerking out of his hold.

As with all fae balls, the music never truly began or ended. When the beat caught us in its sway, he pulled me into the dance and we were carried along its current.

He leaned toward me, hot, too-sweet breath brushing against my cheek. "I hear congratulations are in order."

I ignored him, vision blurring as the second glass of wine hit me and the music carried my feet as my mind drifted to another place. A place I hadn't needed to go in years. My safe place. There, my body was a vessel, and I existed apart from it.

When his palm slid lower, tightening in a possessive hold, I didn't feel it. I was in a forest, head tipped back as rain tickled my face and bare skin.

Those weren't hands pawing at me, they were the caresses of nature. The wind whipping over my body; the rain trailing over exposed flesh.

Lord Banyan had said something else, but I wasn't listening.

The song swelled, moving into a rhythm, one that was slower, and I was jarred into the present when his body pressed into mine and his arousal became evident.

I lost my step and stumbled back, but his grip was bruising as he held me against him, grinding against my stomach. I gagged and yanked my hand from his.

"Don't embarrass me, or you'll pay for it later," he whispered against my ear and try as I might to retreat back to my safe place, the room spun at a dizzying pace.

"Let her go," a voice I hardly recognized said, as Lord Banyan's arm was wrenched from around my waist and Jack stopped us in the middle of our dance.

Dressed in a cobalt suit, hair pulled back to expose his strong jawline and almost a head taller than Lord Banyan, he looked intimidating. But all my earlier fears about his weakness after being injured rushed in when Lord Banyan shoved Jack off the dance floor, causing him to slide several feet.

Banyan grabbed my wrist, yanking me toward him, but Jack was back, so close the heat of his rage radiated off him. "Get your hands off her."

Lord Banyan's eyes flashed with pure malice, but he glanced around the room at the other dancers, most of whom had stopped to watch, and he marched away, not glancing back at either of us.

Jack's cheeks were a dark shade of red, shoulders rigid, and he looked ready to kill someone. But in an instant, his gaze shifted to me and everything softened.

"You shouldn't be here," I breathed. Some of the terror thawing in his presence.

He searched my face for a long time. Long enough that I felt everyone's gazes on us and tugged him into a dance. We had made a scene. The only thing to do now was try to be forgotten.

The music washed over us, and to my surprise, Jack was carried with it, moving as if he was born of Faerie. We spun, eyes locked and slowly, the ice melted from my veins, my stomach settling.

With each circle around the floor, my steps grew lighter. The sour taste in my mouth dissipated and my breath came easier. I was aware of how close we were, but his arm on my waist didn't feel suffocating. It was a warm embrace. The heat from his body didn't overwhelm or terrify me. It was safe and warm.

I looked up into eyes that were already on me and my chest swelled. "You're injured. You shouldn't overexert yourself."

"Mother Mahonia arrived less than an hour ago." A dimple appeared in Jack's cheek, all the darkness I'd seen in him gone. "I'm good as new."

My heart thrummed in my chest as my gaze traced the outline of his lips as they moved. Calloused fingers drew a slow circle on my lower back, sending tingles down my spine. His touch was soothing, erasing the phantom marks burned into my skin where Banyan had dug his nails in.

On our next spin around the dance floor, my breath caught in my throat as Jack pressed closer, and every part of me came alive with his nearness. We were the only two in the room and nothing and no one else mattered. For this moment, it was just us.

A commotion on the other side of the ballroom dragged my gaze from Jack's and my hand slipped from his as the spring court general and a dozen of his soldiers marched in.

Fear shot through me and my gaze shifted from them to Jack. I grabbed his hand, dragging him toward an exit.

"Halt, Lady Briar, or we will be forced to shoot."

I froze, ice sliding down my spine, and dropped Jack's hand as if it were on fire. Slowly, I turned, facing Raine. "What is this about, General?"

Raine lifted a thick ebony brow and motioned to his soldiers. Two of them charged forward, wrapping their arms around Jack's. His gaze narrowed, but wisely he didn't fight.

"The Princess has requested an audience with you both in her chambers."

I swallowed. "What does she need the emissary's pet for? Surely she only wants to see me." I glanced around, wishing Hazel had come after all.

Raine closed the distance between us, and fae scattered to get out of his way. He stood a full head above most creatures. Only his soldiers—and Jack—were close to his height. He leaned down, a whisper sliding between green, scarred lips. "Trying to make me spill family secrets, Lady?"

Jack struggled in his captors' hold, a low growl erupting from his chest. I gave him a warning look and turned my gaze to Raine, smiling—all teeth. Raine didn't frighten me. He never had. He was more afraid of my sister than any self-respecting male ought to be. "One can dream."

He barked a laugh, long canines on display. "Let's go,"

The crowd parted as we were marched from the ballroom, every eye on us.

FORTY-TWO

JACK

Sav's fingers were clenched so tight her knuckles were white.

I mirrored her posture, marching between two towering orcs, but my attention was fixed on the general—the one she hadn't flinched from. He was imposing, but she hadn't backed down. It was the reason I'd thrown all Hazel's warnings aside and raced onto the dancefloor.

I knew that look in her eyes back in the ballroom—raw panic. Her vulnerability toward another had sparked thoughts of violence and death. I hadn't hesitated. I'd grabbed that bastard by the arm intent on murder.

I hated what this place was turning me into. Or maybe I just hated realizing it had always been inside me—the fury, the willingness to burn the world for those I cared for.

Nothing but her touch, her hand in mine, tugging me into a dance, could have calmed the fury scorching me.

High musical voices carried on a phantom breeze as we approached a large set of double doors. The towering orc who had burst into the party, interrupting our dance, knocked, deceptively light against wood.

"Enter," a voice similar, yet entirely different from Sav's, replied.

We stepped through a wide arched door into an expansive room. The guards stopped in the hall, ushering us forward. My gaze went to Sav, but she ignored me as she strode inside. I trailed her, eyeing the enormous space.

Ivy crept up the walls to the circular room, intertwining at the ceiling, and hung down the center, forming a cage. Inside the cage, small, bright birds fluttered and flapped, landing on vine perches only to launch into the air once more. They were the size of hummingbirds but in every color of the rainbow. When they moved, iridescent shimmers refracted from their wings and a sprinkling of dust scattered over the floor beneath them.

Stopping beside them, I stared in. This close, I could see not all the creatures were birds. They might have been butterflies if not for their human-shaped bodies. The tiny beings were familiar and all at once, I remembered the pixie Sav had been trying to save. It was bigger and not as bright as these, but there were enough similarities that I was sure they were the same kind of fairy.

"They'll grant you a wish in exchange for a drop of your blood," a voice like honey said in my ear.

I spun, staring into a much brighter version of Sav's violet eyes.

I bowed. "Princess."

Her high musical laugh rang in my ears and the tiny pixies in their cage mimicked her sound, matching it with eerie perfection. "Pet of the winter emissary."

Sav's gaze darted between us, landing on the princess. "Why did you have me forcibly removed from the ball, Sage? And with the human, no less. Did you hope to cause a scandal?"

The princess's eyes narrowed in an all too familiar glare. I would have laughed under other circumstances, but the tension between these two was palpable and their similarities gave me whiplash.

"You embarrassed us by making a scene with Lord Banyan," the princess said, crossing her arms over her chest.

Sav mimicked her sister, mouth pressing into a firm line. Sav's greatest weapon was silence, and she was preparing to unleash it on the princess. Her twin moved to stand beside her, and I exhaled sharply. Being so close to all that power made a light sweat break out on my brow.

"Don't give me that look. He's a member of my court and as such, welcome to attend all our functions."

Sav's arms tightened over her chest and her cheeks flushed.

"May I speak?"

Both women turned to me, one wide-eyed, the other cunning. Sav looked like she wanted to stop me, but I was done watching her fight alone.

"I know Sav wasn't supposed to return," I said carefully. "But she came for a reason. To free the fairies being held captive in the human realm and I can help."

I hadn't completely thought this plan through yet, but when I learned of all she was prepared to give up to save her people, I'd realized I had a card to play as well. One that would free her from marriage to the cold prince.

The princess's brows climbed into her hairline. "You are well informed of my sister's situation."

Sav narrowed her eyes, glaring daggers at me, but I barreled on. "Hazel filled me in." I glanced at the cage. "Should we go somewhere private?"

The princess laughed. "My creatures never leave their prison."

I nodded, avoiding Sav's gaze as I continued. "I can help you free them. She doesn't have to marry the prince. I'll offer myself in trade and Dane will return the creatures he has captured."

Sav went rigid.

The princess stepped closer, tilting her head to study me. "You have unusual eyes for a human. Has anyone ever told you that?" I met her stare, not backing down. Her strange power pressed against my skin, prodding, searching for weakness. "And why would the rebel leader trade his slew of captives for one human?"

I swallowed, sweat trickling down my spine.

"Because I'm his son."

FORTY-THREE
KASPAR

Blood bloomed in the water, a deep indigo cloud drifting from my sister Mira's wound. Sightless eyes stared at nothing as it spread, blocking the light. I reached for her–

I woke with a gasp, eyes flying wide as I took in my surroundings.

My rooms, nestled safely within the walls of my underwater castle, were lined in smooth stone, and each was more expansive than the next, but the dream never changed. In it, I was trapped in a horrific version of my castle, sharp coral closing in around me, demanding more of my time, attention, and magic, until there was nothing left of me to give.

I ran a hand over my face, clearing the thought, and swam to the door. If I couldn't sleep, I would at least get some work done.

Stepping through the air shield, my tail split, forming legs and my feet touched smooth stone as I dried before magicking a robe on and moving to my desk. I didn't expect visitors in my private wing of the castle at this hour, but any number of social climbing sea creatures had made a bid to place me in compromising positions over the years in an effort to entrap me.

Even here, snares lurked. More than one scheming mother had tried to cage me with a midnight liaison. But tonight, I wanted no one's company.

There were only a handful of rooms in the palace with air bubbles in them, my office, to ensure the myriad of documents remained safe, the rooms I'd carved for my future bride, and the training room, used by the folk of my court to prepare for their time on land. In my court, spying was the expected occupation. Any ancillary duties came second, and most fae here could, with some practice, move about on the surface.

"Sire."

I looked up from my desk. "Yes, Memphe. Come in."

My second in command, and most trusted advisor, hopped through the air shield, drying as he moved. "I have it."

Eyes widening, my gaze dipped to his satchel. "Truly? Bring it here."

Memphe reached me, withdrawing a slender silver tube—magicked to protect the contents from becoming waterlogged—from his bag, and handed it to me.

A slow grin tugged at my lips. Tapping my fingers on the tube, I glanced up. It was not yet midnight on the surface; most land dwellers would still be awake. I longed to go to her at once, but she would be at a ball, dancing with the members of her court. "Thank you, Memphe. Go. Ensure her rooms are prepared."

Memphe backed away, bowing as he went, but he stopped before stepping through the door.

I held it a moment, inhaling her lingering scent. Finally, after two centuries, she would be mine and I would keep my promise to save her from her wretched family.

I popped the silver lid on the tube, peering inside.

"Prince Kaspar."

I looked up, finding Memphe still waiting inside the door. "What?"

"What answer shall I give Prince Alder?"

"Answer to what question?"

He dipped his head low. "The date, for the wedding and the army you promised to send."

I waved him off, and he bowed again, disappearing from my rooms.

I lifted the parchment to my nose, inhaling the pungent scent. There were so few creatures in this world who deserved my loyalty or my favor. Sav had earned it ten times over, but if I knew one thing about her, it was that she wouldn't give in so easily. Something had pushed her to agree. If I was a gambler, my money would have been on the human.

They reeked of each other. I could overlook a crush, a human's passing infatuation, but something in me chilled, a sense of foreboding I couldn't shake.

I had waited for her. Protected her. She was mine.

I tugged the delicate paper from the tube, unrolling it just enough to read the terms of the agreement. Sav's name was written on this scroll. It took an act of faith to entrust such power to another and though I knew she would give it eventually, I hadn't expected it to come so easily. Something uncomfortable twisted in my gut. Could the human mean so much to her that she'd give in without a fight to save him from some foolish act?

Rolling the paper up, I slid it back inside the silver tube and snapped the lid shut. This parchment was now the most valuable thing I owned. Though the magic sealing our bargain would obscure our true names from any other who looked upon it, I had only to read it, to know her full name, and Sav would be entirely at my mercy.

I wanted to count it as a win, but after centuries of court politics and maneuvering, I had to be sure the one good thing in my life was genuine.

Alone, my mind drifted to the day Sav had grabbed my hand. I'd yanked it back, but she held fast, wrapping curling vines around my finger. "When we're old and alone and have had our fill of adventure, we'll marry each other so no one can use us ever again."

I touched my naked finger where her vine had once curled like a promise. It had dissolved in days. But the vow had rooted in me.

I had waited two hundred years to call in that promise.

My days of adventuring were long over and it was time hers were too.

FORTY-FOUR

SAV

J ack threw a punch that dropped one of the orcs, but Raine was faster —steel flashing, blade pressed to Jack's throat.

I couldn't breathe. My feet wouldn't move. They were going to take him and bury him in the spring court dungeon where he would never again see daylight. "You can't hurt him! He's an emissary."

Sage arched a brow. "The human is no emissary."

Jack cleared his throat around the blade at his neck. "He'll want me back. If we tell him I was kidnapped, I'm sure he'll agree."

I glared at Jack, all thoughts of him being strong, evaporating. He was an idiot. An idiot who was going to get himself killed. Had I planned to do the very same thing? Yes. But my plan didn't involve telling a manipulative, backstabbing, power hungry fae court royal who he was.

"Raine. Take the human to the prison." Sage snapped her fingers and Raine motioned to his soldiers. They wrestled Jack's arms behind his back, but he'd stopped fighting, a thin line of crimson running down his neck.

"You're making a mistake. He will trade them for me." Jack shouted as he was dragged through the door.

My heart was in my throat as I watched them go. I had to do something. I couldn't let her keep him.

Sage rushed forward, grabbing my hands.

I frowned, glancing down at our clasped hands. My sister's wild mood swings made her dangerous. She never did anything without reason, but the reason was anyone's guess. This false sisterly affection she was displaying only set the hairs on the back of my neck on end.

"Talk with your friend, sister. Make the emissary understand his value to our court. We need him."

I fought to get the terror under control, trying desperately to think clearly, and tore my hands from her grasp, moving away from her. "Why would I do anything to help you?"

Sage's brows lowered and her lips formed a pout. "I suppose you wouldn't. You've never cared much for your court or the fae in it."

"I'm here for them! Just because you don't consider the low fae a part of your court doesn't make them any less a part of it!" I exclaimed, my heart rate picking up speed. In a matter of moments, I'd lost control of the situation. "I'm marrying a male I don't love to save them. Or have you forgotten?" I exhaled a long breath, trying to calm my racing heart. Even now, they were dragging Jack to the prison and I had no way of stopping it.

"This is the reason you signed my contract?" Kaspar's smooth voice, tipped in ice, sent another chill down my spine as he stepped through the doorway into the room. He had appeared from nowhere, as if the mere mention of our impending wedding called him.

I looked past my sister to the prince clad only in a pair of thin trousers, hanging off his hips. His clear sign of disrespect at dressing so informally would have made me laugh, but the sight of him, knowing he must have my true name by now, had dread pooling in my gut and only intensified my rising panic. *I trust him. I trust him.* I repeated the chant in my mind several times, willing it to be true.

"Your highness." My sister dropped her chin.

"I'll marry you if she won't." Hazel's seductive voice drifted in behind Kaspar as she stepped into the room. Of course Hazel chose this moment to appear. I swore the pair of them spied on me, waiting for the worst possible moments to crash into my life. My chest was tightening as everything began to spin out of control.

Could I rely on my two friends to help me now? *They* hadn't been jailed for sneaking supplies from the castle to the low fae in their lands or for the lingering attentions of a wayward husband, seeking his wife's sister's bed, even if his advances were unwanted. I sucked in sharp pained breaths, trying to tamp down the memories as the panic clawed at me.

"Hazel," I began, but my throat constricted and my heart thrashed against my chest.

A memory hit me like a punch to the gut. The last time I'd been trapped down there. After my sister had learned of my secret betrothal to Bracken, a guard with no power or title, she'd left me alone in a cell with nothing but my broken heart for months.

My skin crawled. They didn't know what it meant to be locked away here. To be forgotten. Starved. Broken. Shallow breaths were darkening the edges of my vision, but no one seemed to notice the room closing in on me or the way I gasped desperately for air.

Kaspar's terrible, cold eyes met mine, piercing my very soul, but where I'd hoped for reprieve in them, I found none. "Sav, tell me now. Did you sign our agreement to save the fae in the human realm?"

The question pushed back some of the panic and I remembered why we were doing this. For the folk who were imprisoned in far worse conditions than I ever had been. I had to keep my head. I wouldn't let my sister win. Meeting his sea foam eyes, burning with some emotion I couldn't read, I dragged in a long breath, feeling my thrumming pulse begin to slow. I wouldn't lie to him, just as he had never lied to me.

"Yes."

The room steadied.

His expression fell. " Why didn't you ask me? Why beg your sister for aid when I would have given it freely?"

Hazel cleared her throat. "This seems personal. If you'll excuse me."

"Wait," I called as Hazel attempted to dart past Kaspar. I needed to speak with her. If any part of our friendship had ever been true, I needed to know I could rely on that friendship now. "Sage has your pet."

FORTY-FIVE

JACK

I kicked a rock against the wall of my cell and slumped back on the mossy floor. I'd meant to help Sav. Instead, I'd handed myself over like an idiot.

The orc with the knives had smiled when I surrendered. That smile had told me everything I needed to know: I wasn't a player in this game. I was a piece.

The cell smelled of mold and damp soil. But even this place was better than Dane's dungeons. At least I had a window. Through it, trees loomed —impossibly tall, blooming with white, pink, and red flowers that pulsed faintly in the dark. Tiny fairy lights floated among the branches like living stars.

I was watching a flicker of orange dart through the woods when her voice came.

"Jack!"

I shot to my feet, heart pounding. "I'm here!"

She appeared around a corner, the blue-haired prince who would soon be her husband trailing her, and my jaw clenched. Did he never wear a shirt?

Sav reached the cell, fingers sliding between the vines, and I met her halfway, lacing my hands through hers. Her touch seared through me like a promise I didn't deserve.

"Why did you do it?" she whispered.

"I couldn't let you sacrifice your freedom."

My gaze darted past her to the prince who was watching me like he was imagining my death. The feeling was mutual. I tightened my grip.

"We'll get you out," she said. But there was panic in her eyes.

"No," I said. "Don't promise them anything else."

She pulled out of my grip as her sister rounded the corner and her gaze darted to the two of us. Guilt twisted my gut as Sav's cold mask slid into place. She had already bargained away her freedom for the fairies trapped by Dane. What would she offer for me?

I couldn't let her do it. I wouldn't let her sell anymore of herself. Not for me.

There was no taking back my truth, but there must be something else I could offer to relieve some of the crushing burden she felt over my imprisonment. If only I could make her understand that I would remain in this dungeon forever, as long as it meant she wouldn't give any more of herself away.

"Sav," I whispered.

She ignored me, spinning around to face her sister, putting herself between us.

Hazel came last, shaking her head at me, facing the princess. "Release him."

Sage raised a brow. "I don't think I will. He's the perfect bait to draw out the AFF leader."

"You can't keep him," Sav snapped. "He's under Winter's protection."

"I see no reason to release him. He's the son of our enemy." Sage shrugged. "Besides, my uncle is regent in Winter. He wouldn't risk war for a pet."

I clenched my fists. They were all talking like I wasn't here. Like I wasn't a person. Like I wasn't a threat.

Heat curled beneath my skin, a flicker, then a flare.

Sav and Hazel traded barbs with the spring court princess, who seemed no more inclined to release her hostage now than she had when a wicked gleam entered her eye upon learning who I was.

My hands, fisted at my sides, sparked red hot. Heat sizzled in the air, smoke wafting off my knuckles. I stretched my fingers out at my sides, shaking them and glancing up at the room.

No one paid me any attention, flinging accusations back and forth, and I shook my hands out as the air shimmered from the heat coming off my fingers. What the hell?

I tried to shove it down. But rage pulsed through me, hotter than before.

The discussion escalated—Sav demanded the spring court's aid, Kaspar offered his own army, playing hero, inching closer to her—and the fire inside me *spiked*.

"Stop!" My voice echoed strangely in the small space.

All eyes swiveled to me.

A torch inside me burst to life, consuming me from the inside. It licked up my spine, burning a path straight for my heart. My gaze met the prince's, and his eyes widened. He moved to put himself between me and Sav, and that action made the fire burn hotter. I was a living, breathing inferno and my rage could not be contained.

Raising both hands to the vines caging me in, I grabbed hold and tore them apart. They blackened in my hold, giving easily, and I stepped through, eyes burning as I stared at each of them, gaze finally landing on Sav.

FORTY-SIX

SAV

"Jack?" His eyes were bright, fae bright, and my stomach flipped as he shredded his bars and stepped through them.

"What is this trickery?" Sage demanded, backing up. "He's no human son of the AFF leader."

Jack prowled forward, leaving scorched footprints in his wake, crossing the distance to stand before me.

Kaspar moved, blocking his path.

I'd felt the heat in his skin before; thought it was adrenaline. But this... this was magic.

Jack lunged. Kaspar raised a wall of water with a snap of his fingers— mist hissed, steam rose, and the air between them crackled as fire and water collided.

"Raine," Sage shouted. "Guards!"

Kaspar raised his arms and fog poured from his skin like smoke. It blanketed the hall in seconds. It was dense and disorienting.

Then his hand gripped mine. *"Run."*

"Jack. We can't leave Jack."

"I'm here," he said in the thick fog. "Sav. I'm sorry."

I shuddered, not entirely sure if he was apologizing for lying about what he was or for getting us into this mess. Something in my chest loosened now that Jack was free of his cage.

I jogged, knowing the way even without sight. "What about Hazel?"

"Here," she called from behind me.

Safe. We were all safe.

"Saaaaaaaaav." The walls groaned. Roots burst from the floor, thorns gleaming with poison tips as the castle came alive with Sage's rage.

"Kaspar," I breathed. "You have to get him out of here."

He glanced at me and nodded, shifting quickly into his kelpie form. His shimmering turquoise hide disappeared into the fog, and I heard more than saw Jack's shout of protest.

Sage's magic bled into the land, feeding her court, and *it* responded, coming alive. She may not be as fast as me, but her magic was so much faster, especially when I couldn't reach mine. Vines writhed along our path, blooms growing heavy with her magic. Tiny thorns twisted over every surface, spiking along the walls. Purple poisoned tips gleamed in the light as the last of Kaspar's fog dissolved into nothing.

He could have done more, could have called on the might of the lakes surrounding the castle to aid us, but to use such offensive magic in her court would have been considered an act of war. And after all he'd done to secure an alliance between our kingdoms, I knew he wouldn't be willing to throw that away for Jack.

Jack...Who was showing all the signs of coming into his magic for a high fae turning twenty-five. But it wasn't possible. Unless he was...a changeling. Those eyes had been alight with flame, sparking red, a sign of the autumn court, or of a fae coming into their fire magic.

A memory of when I had gained my magic flashed through my mind. Unlike the heat that radiated from Jack's fingertips, I'd set an entire room on fire the first time I lost my temper. The control it took to keep your fire at bay when it first manifested was nothing short of extraordinary.

Jack had said very little about his mother. Could she have been a fae hiding in the human realm? But he shared so many of his father's traits. It made no sense.

A sunflower the size of a shield tilted its head toward us. Its golden center opened like a mouth and spat a stream of seeds in rapid succession. One whizzed past my ear.

Hazel blurred past on all fours, a flash of white and black fur. I bolted after her, spiked vines a breath behind.

We weren't free yet.

FORTY-SEVEN
DANE

I tucked the newspaper under my arm and crossed the street to the coffee shop just across from AFF headquarters. The owner of the small shop, Jack's *friend*, looked up and gave me a nod.

I pulled my baseball cap low and moved to the counter.

"Morning, Dane."

Resting an arm on the counter, I leaned toward him. "Can you spare a minute?"

He looked around the nearly empty shop. It was too early for most of the regular patrons. Nodding to a table at the back, he moved around the counter and I followed, glancing at the door.

Sitting, he whipped a towel over his shoulder and eyed me. "What can I do for ya?"

"I'm looking for Jack." I kept my tone light, like I was asking about the weather—not my missing son.

Leo didn't answer right away. His eyes drifted to the back room. He thought he was subtle. He wasn't. "Not like Jack to stay away so long." His gaze darted to the back room again. Where he kept the food stores he and Jack used to feed my prisoners.

I had let it slide to appease Jack and keep him compliant. After all, it wasn't as though it did anything other than prolong their suffering. They deserved every moment of agony I tore from them.

I set my newspaper on the counter, pushing it toward Leo.

He glanced down at it and back to me. "What's that?"

"Open it."

Leo peeled back the paper, blinked at the bills inside. "Dane, I—"

"This is a good shop," I said. "It would be a shame if something... happened."

His shoulders tensed and he nodded.

That was all I needed.

"Leo."

He looked up, eyes burning with shame.

"I would never harm my son. I only want to know he's safe."

He nodded, looking away again.

I stood. "I'd like a coffee. Black."

Leo slid his chair back, curling the newspaper under his arm, and moved behind the counter once more, setting it inside the box where he kept his guns. Although he'd been a war hero in another life, I knew he hadn't started keeping guns in his shop until the fae arrived.

He may enjoy my son's company. He may have even derived some satisfaction from helping the creatures in my prison, but deep down, Leo was no different from the rest of us. He would put himself above the fae if it was his life on the line. And our lives were all on the line.

Handing a cup across the counter, he met my eyes hesitantly. "On the house."

I laughed. "I should hope so."

He grimaced, turning away from me.

Taking my coffee, I left his shop, turning right, away from headquarters, and toward ISHFA. It was time I pay Janet Glassdon, ISHFA president, a visit. We needed a fresh dose of meds to feed to the satyr who was exceptionally receptive to their mind-altering qualities. More than that, Janet owed me for allowing her to experiment on my prisoners. And I intended to collect.

—•→(∪◆∩◆••—

I pushed open the glass doors to ISHFA headquarters and grinned at the petite blonde receptionist who always wore too much lipstick and never remembered to wipe it off her teeth.

"Hi, Dane." Her lips tipped into a seductive grin, out of place on her youthful face. She tried too hard. A sign of insecurity that made her less attractive.

I nodded, removing my baseball cap and running a hand through my hair. "Morning Leslie. Is Janet in?"

She leaned forward, giving me a full view of her cleavage. "Sorry, Dane. She's out, but Morgan's here."

I ground my teeth. Working with the autumn court emissary was a necessary evil if I wanted to continue receiving funding—and intel—from

228

ISHFA, but that didn't mean I had to give Morgan the respect she thought she deserved. Her kind would never be my equal.

"That's alright. I'll come back later."

"Dane Clyde," a husky voice called overhead.

I tipped my head back, staring up at the golden-haired fae with strange crimson eyes whose blood-red nails matched her business suit. She wasn't wearing her wings today. She kept them tucked away among so many people in an effort to appear more human. Even her pointed ears seemed blunted, as if she'd subtly glamoured them to lull us into a false sense of trust.

But something was going on in the autumn court, something Morgan was keeping secret, and she had only to open her mouth for me to know she was lying.

"You missed your chance to speak with Janet," Morgan said, descending the stairs with regal authority. I had no doubt she was a member of her royal court in Faerie. "But perhaps I can help." Her crimson eyes glinted menacingly. "I hear you're looking for your son. I may have information you'll find interesting. You certainly have something *I* want. Shall we make a bargain?"

FORTY-EIGHT

JACK

Vines slammed into the hallway floor behind us, the stone groaning as it cracked beneath their weight. The air was thick with pollen and spores, and the walls seemed to breathe with Sage's fury. Ahead, Hazel bounded for the exit. Beside me, Sav sprinted faster than I'd ever seen her move.

"Hurry," Sav shouted as she darted past us.

"Wait! Sav!"

Kaspar's massive black teeth snapped at my outstretched hand, and I tucked it back, gaping at the woman running at breakneck speed. I wrapped my fingers into the roping seaweed hair on the prince's nape as he galloped and I stared in awe as Sav moved, hair streaming at her back.

"Lookout!" I shouted as blooms burst open along the walls, firing darts like arrows. He picked up speed. We caught up with Sav and I reached down, wrapping an arm around her waist and swinging her up into my lap. My arm tightened around her and she glanced over her shoulder, a look of feral delight in her eyes.

I squeezed her tightly to me, blocking her from the arsenal of flowers firing at us. "I'll keep you safe," I breathed in her ear.

Her arms locked around me. She was trusting me—*finally*, fully—and I swore in that moment, I'd take anything this realm threw at me if it meant keeping her safe.

A sting lanced my shoulder. Ice spread beneath my skin, but almost as quickly, heat flared to life in my veins and the pain evaporated. I should've been afraid of whatever I'd just done. But in that moment, all I could feel was *alive*.

Sav's hair blew behind her, blocking my view, but I didn't care, lost in her scent and the warmth of her body pressed against mine. I held on tighter, never wanting to let her go. I would shield her from any danger that came for her, but even as warmth spread through my middle, a cold stone settled in my stomach.

That moment my cage burned. It hadn't been fury. It had been power. *Freedom.* And I'd liked it.

That terrified me more than the poison.

Because I didn't know what I was becoming.

And I didn't know if the thing Sav needed protection from was... me.

FORTY-NINE

SAV

I leaned against Jack, hugging him to me, feeling his racing heart beat against my back in time with my own.

My sister's court, and the magic she commanded, fell away as Kaspar slowed his pace. This far from Sage she would have to expend a great deal of energy to reach us and though she'd put in some effort to chase us, it was a fraction of what my sister was capable of. Had she let us go to ensure Kaspar didn't break our treaty, or did some small piece of her heart still care for me?

Hazel slowed, falling into step beside us, and I loosened my hold on Jack. In the moment, when all I'd cared about was escaping Spring with our heads, I hadn't had any time to dwell on everything that had happened.

Now, faced with this new truth, one I didn't fully understand yet, my stomach sank as I released the strong arms wrapped around me.

Hazel's large green eyes peered up at us and she gave me a toothy grin. I didn't have to be a mind reader to know what she was thinking, and I glared at her. Jack's eyes burned into the back of my head and the overwhelming heat radiating from him reminded me of the secret that lay between us.

I'd just begun to trust him—then he burned through prison bars and shattered my certainty.

Unless...

I hardly dared feed the tiny hope threatening to break through, but try as I might to tamp it down, it demanded to be heard. It begged me to accept that he hadn't known. But how? How could he not know? He owed me answers and I would have them soon, but first, we needed a plan and I needed Hazel's help finding my lost satchel.

"Hazel. I lost my bag near your border. Where we were attacked. Can you find it for me?"

Hazel dipped her chin, looping through the forest and shifting direction toward Winter.

Kaspar snorted, following Hazel's lead.

Jack's hot breath blazed against my ear as he remained curled around me even after the danger had passed, and though I didn't trust him, I was loath to push him away. *Just a little while*, I told myself. Until we reach the border and continue on foot.

On the horizon, a blanket of snow spread out, and I exhaled slowly. My emotions were a dangerous mix of raw vulnerability and terror, both from my sister's latest betrayal and the fresher one at my back. The anxiety threatening to drown me in Sage's prison had been dashed against the adrenaline pumping through my veins as we fled the spring court.

Something orange and black flashed in my periphery and I glanced to the side, spying the fox with purple eyes racing beside us. He wasn't fast enough to keep up with a snow leopard, but he tried.

I leaned down, whispering in Kaspar's ear. "We have a Spring Court tail. Lose him."

Kaspar picked up speed and soon the fox's pointed ears were nothing but a memory of my short-lived return home.

Barreling across the border between Spring and Winter, Hazel slid to a halt in deep snow and spun around.

Kaspar hovered just on the spring side of the line, steam puffing out in long exhales.

I swung my leg over his side and hopped down quickly. When I looked up, Jack sat motionless, a wild look in his eyes. Our gazes met for a moment before I broke our stare, scanning the forest behind him for any sign of Raine or his weapon clad army, but nothing and no one appeared on the horizon.

Kaspar snapped at Jack, shaking him out of his daze, and he moved, sliding off the kelpie's back.

"Sav—"

My gaze moved from Kaspar's sparkling flank to Jack, searching his face. His eyes were normal again and the heat he'd been radiating before had vanished. If I hadn't seen it myself, I might not have believed it. Where high fae began manifesting their gifts and retaining them, Jack had seamlessly slipped back into human form. What did it mean? I would give him one chance to come clean. One chance to be honest. But first, I had to put things right with Kaspar.

Kaspar's form rippled as he shifted into fae form and turned to leave. "Kaspar, wait."

"Sav," Jack said again.

I spun around. "Jack. I need a minute."

His eyes darkened, sliding to Kaspar, but he said nothing, moving past me and crossing the border into Winter. He stopped beside Hazel, running a hand along her coat.

Turning back to Kaspar, I frowned, taking in his cold expression. He was never warm, never sweet, but something in his cool gaze was alive in a way I'd never seen before.

"I'm sorry," I whispered. "I'm sorry if I hurt you."

His turquoise eyes gave nothing away, impassive as always, but I sensed the utter betrayal he was unwilling to give voice to. I reached for his hand, rubbing my thumb over his palm.

He glanced down, studying our clasped hands, saying nothing. When he looked up, that alien emotion I'd thought I'd seen was gone. "The free army is on Earth. Your former general, Creig, leads them."

"What?"

His fingers tightened around mine. "I will offer them reprieve in my court if they aid you. I know the water is no place for land fae, but, if they desire to return to Faerie. There is a place for them. Offer them this and you may find a willing ally."

"Kaspar."

He dipped his head, pressing cool lips to my knuckles.

I squeezed his hand, warmth spreading from my chest and along my limbs. "You know why I don't want your help with saving the humans. Don't you?"

He swayed on an invisible breeze, his cool facade firmly in place. "You care for my safety and that of my people."

I nodded. Those were the words I'd said to him after I was bound. When my sister sent me to live on Earth and he had offered to come with me to keep me safe. Even then, even when I hated him for putting me in that situation, I couldn't let him risk his life for mine.

The words were no less true now, but I wasn't sure if he understood what they meant. He was my oldest friend, dear to me in a way no one else ever had been. If something happened to him, I would never forgive myself. I couldn't protect him from everything, but I could keep him safe from the humans. The memory of the emaciated kelpie rotting in Dane's cage flashed in my mind and my stomach flipped. I clasped his hand more tightly. "I need you," I said honestly.

He shuddered and released my hand, stepping back. "If you're in danger, call for me."

The air rippled and in a blink, he was my favorite kelpie once more. The one who had taken me on wild adventures when we were young, racing through the forest when it seemed to stretch forever. He swung around, lashing his tail as he wove between massive trees.

Kaspar had been a lot of things to me in my life, best friend, confidant, fellow explorer and once, in my darkest hour, he'd been my hero. When he'd agreed to my sister's terms, knowing my wishes, I'd thought our friendship had ended, but as I watched him go, admiration settled in my chest.

I exhaled a breath turning back to Hazel and Jack. We'd been lucky. My sister wouldn't give up so easily now that she thought Jack was valuable, but she wouldn't stray so far from her castle for a prize.

"We need to find Creig and enlist him in our cause. I know you're needed here Hazel. Please find my bag. I'll come back for it."

She eyed me as if she wanted to ask more about it, but nodded.

I glanced to Jack. "This close to the border, our best option is traveling through the Seelie Court."

Hazel closed the distance between us. "I'll find it." She pulled me in for a hug, pressing her nose to my ear. "Come find me when this is all over. I've missed you. You have a place in my court, no matter what your sister says." Her arms tightened around me and I hugged her back, my vision blurring.

"I've missed you."

She squeezed once more, then released me. "Take care of my pet. I want him back in one piece."

I grinned at her teasing tone. "You know I won't give him back."

She smiled, wiping snow off my cheek. "I know."

I grabbed Jack's hand, shocked at the warmth of his fingers. Answers. He would give me answers now.

"Are you sure we should go back to the spring court?" he whispered.

Continuing forward, I sighed as we crossed the border and the temperature increased by several degrees. Releasing Jack's hand, I wiped my slick palm on my skirts. Truly, his hands were burning. "Getting into the human realm is easier through a Seelie entrance."

Jack looked dubious but trailed behind me as I marched deeper into the Maywood.

I glanced back when we were far enough from the Winter border that I was sure he wouldn't catch cold. "Start talking."

Jack crashed to a halt. "I would tell you whatever you want to know, but I swear, I have no idea what happened in the prison."

I stopped, spinning around to face him, and let my gaze trail the length of him. Hadn't I thought he looked like one of us when we first met? But he had none of our gifts, apart from his ability to nearly keep up with my speed and whatever happened in my sister's prison.

"Tell me about your mother." I turned around. "But walk and talk. We need to get back to Earth."

Jack moved, footsteps lighter than before. He was silent for a long time as we moved through the Maywood. It was more than a day's trek from here to the spring pocket entrance to Earth. There were four in total, one for each court, but why the points of access were so far from the castles in Faerie I didn't know.

The ones in the Seelie court were strangely close to one another and it would mean coming dangerously close to Summer's border, but it couldn't be helped.

"My mom was amazing." Jack said after a considerable silence.

I said nothing, listening to the steady beat of his heart.

"She used to call me her little prince." He laughed. "Not that I was little for long. I was taller than her by fifth grade."

There was so much warmth in his words that my heart ached for a love I'd never felt. "So, you've always lived in the human realm?"

He glanced up. "You think I'm not human?"

I shrugged, running my fingers along an unfurling fern leaf. Its blades caressed the pads of my fingers, bleeding strength into my limbs. After a full day and night on my feet, I needed the boost and silently gave my gratitude to the land for sharing its energy with me.

"I'm not like you," he said, watching the exchange in fascination. "I don't affect the plants. I can't see in the dark or hear exceptionally well." His gaze dropped to my slippered feet. "I'm not silent when I move or extremely fast."

I bit my lip, considering his words. He *was* fast. Not as fast as me, but no one was as fast as me in fae form. "And you're sure Dane is your father?"

He grimaced, stuffing a hand in his pocket. A habit I'd come to realize meant he didn't like the subject. "I wish I could say he wasn't."

I nodded, knowing the chances of them looking so similar but being unrelated was highly unlikely. "Has anything like that ever happened to you before?"

Jack snorted. "Like burning cage bars and making a water fairy's magic steam?"

I frowned as he caught up to me, walking by my side. "Like calling elemental magic to aid you when you need it."

He swatted at a low-hanging branch. "No. And don't forget, I've been around iron all my life and it doesn't burn me."

I paused at that, stopping to stare at him again. He was right. No fae, not one, was immune to iron. The closest were orcs. They had a higher tolerance than the rest of us, but immune? No.

"Do you feel the magic in your veins now?"

He considered my words, resuming walking. I glanced down at his fingers curling and uncurling at his sides.

"No. I don't feel anything. But...When we were running, one of the poison darts struck me." He looked up. "Something inside me dissolved the poison. I felt it."

We fell into silence again as I rolled all the information he'd shared around in my head. He wasn't fae. There were no exceptions to the iron rule. But what did that make him? Some new species? A creature from another realm our kind was yet unaware of? We'd always known about Earth. It was so intertwined with our world that I wasn't sure we'd ever existed without it.

Who was I to say then, that there weren't other worlds? Other creatures unlike either of us? A mix of us both?

At the end of a long day, we stopped in the Ash Wood as the sun dipped low and I looked up, watching Luna slowly wake, unfurling glowing wings to light the night sky. I'd puzzled over his words, the steady beat of his heart and everything I'd witnessed since we met. He wasn't lying. I was sure of it. He didn't know what he was any more than I did.

Some of the bitter resentment that had built between us eased as I accepted it. Realized that I wanted it to be true. I wanted to trust Jack, and that terrified me a little.

"We'll have to sleep under the stars tonight."

Jack dropped heavily onto the carpet of thick moss blanketing the forest floor, leaning back against the trunk of a tree, and looked up. "It's beautiful here." He grinned. "I mean, it's deadly, but there's something about this place."

I nodded, sitting across from him and pulling back layers of skirts, tugging off thin slippers, still damp from our trek through the snow, rubbing my aching feet.

Jack leaned forward, lifting my foot into his lap. I resisted the urge to pull away, exhaustion washing over me. He dug his thumbs into the arch of my foot, and I moaned as he worked the knots loose, tipping my head back against the tree.

The dusting of stars blanketing our sky had begun to twinkle, and I sighed, some of the day's tension bleeding away. I glanced down at Jack and my lips twitched at the contented look he gave me. If rubbing feet was his thing, I would not say no.

When he'd rubbed every knot out and my feet were jelly, my eyes drifted closed and I smiled, more content in this moment than I had been in a long time. "When I was a child, I thought Faerie was endless," I said. "I believed it was possible to continue exploring and having new adventures forever and you'd never reach the end of it." I felt his eyes on me, and my lashes fluttered open.

Jack searched my face, his expression open. "I would have liked to meet you back then."

My smile fell, and I cast my gaze up.

Tiny sparkling stars shone brightly in an effort to gain Luna's attention, but as with every night, she had eyes only for us. We were her favorite. Blessed because of the shifters who graced our lands. Luna had a special place in her heart for creatures, but especially those with dual natures. As a Gemini, Luna represented all shifter folk.

All creatures in Faerie, no matter their kind or station, could be shifters. If you were born under the Gemini constellation, on your tenth birthday, your dual nature would be revealed and you would forever have the gift.

Geminis weren't the only blessed signs. Leos had an affinity for fire and Pisces found themselves drawn to water, choosing to live near lakes or the sea. In my own court, earth signs were prized above all others from birth. It was the reason my sister's match was planned the moment her due date was named.

Though we were twins, I'd been born several hours before Sage, making me a Leo.

In Spring, Virgos ruled supreme and my sister's sun, moon and rising sign were all in Virgo. Destined to be one of the most powerful life-giving fae in our time, she'd proven the seers right, wielding her gift like a weapon and feeding the land to strengthen the court the moment she ascended.

Spring would have been well positioned to lead after Mab disappeared, if not for Fero. Unlike the other courts, Summer tested all their children and proclaimed their prince or princess by power alone. At any time, a ruler might be forced to cede their position if someone new held a greater ability.

This often meant, in the summer court, rulers only lasted a few decades. To remain in power for a full century was nearly unheard of, but in four centuries, Fero's power had never been surpassed.

Some said he must have descended from Mab herself. It wasn't only the strength of his ability, it was that Fero had strong affinities for both air and water. Born at midnight on the cusp of Libra and Scorpio, he'd been granted both.

In the history of Faerie, he was the first Summer court prince to hold his position so long and the only fae ruler besides Mab with more than one affinity at his disposal.

"I'm sorry," Jack said, and I shuddered, returning to the present.

"What for?"

He stretched an arm up and rested his head in his palm. "Bringing up old wounds."

My tired gaze shifted from the outline of those muscles, straining against silken fabric to his full mouth, then darted up to meet his eyes. "Ancient history. All that matters now is finding Creig and offering Kaspar's reprieve. With any luck, he'll already have the weapons we need. We might have Juniper and the others out by tomorrow night."

We lapsed into silence once more and I resisted the urge to glance again at his muscled arm, wrapping my hands around myself to stave off the bite of cool night air. Bark bit into my back and I shifted uncomfortably.

"I'm a lot softer than a tree."

"I've slept outside before." I shot back.

"I'm also a lot warmer."

As if his words brought the evening chill, the temperature dipped, and a shiver rolled down my spine. I hugged myself tighter, moving to avoid the knob digging into my back. A gust of wind tore through the tree, slicing through my gown, and I eyed Jack's inviting arm.

He grinned, his dimple cutting through smooth bronzed skin.

I scooted over, leaning into Jack's warmth just as another gust of wind whipped my hair around my face and I pressed into his side, wrestling my wild mane into a knot. His arm came around me, tucking me into the warmth of his side. He squeezed me tighter, that damn muscled arm a furnace against my skin, and I inhaled his wintergreen scent.

"Sav?"

"Yeah?"

"Thanks for coming to find me in that prison cell."

I tilted my head to look up at him. A lock of raven hair fell over his face, obscuring the strong line of his jaw. His dark lashes rested heavily against his cheeks. I studied his face. He was human, but something other lurked beneath his skin.

He cracked a lid, eyeing me under his lashes, and I glanced away.

"I mean it. You could have left me in the spring court, so thank you."

"What have I told you about giving people your thanks?"

His full mouth tilted up at the corners and his eyes closed once more. "Well, I owe you, so what will it be? What favor do you ask of me?"

I smiled, tucking a strand of hair behind my ear. "You saved yourself. Now, if only we knew what else you could do with that gift of yours. Maybe you could help us free the fae in Dane's compound."

He opened his eyes, shifting at my side and his expression was earnest as he met my gaze. "Magic or no magic—I'm not sitting out of this fight. I won't let him take you again."

I exhaled a long breath and closed my eyes. "Let's talk about it in the morning."

His weight shifted as he pulled me closer and I settled against his side, my heart slowing to match the rhythm of his. It soothed the riot of emotions I was still coming down from and I relaxed into the feeling. Just for tonight. Just this once.

FIFTY

JACK

Something warm and heavy pressed into my chest, and my eyes flew open. Long auburn hair tumbled around my face, and I gently brushed it aside, inhaling her sweet, floral scent. Sav. Her head rested on my shoulder, one arm draped across my waist. My body was warm everywhere she touched me. My left arm tingled beneath her head, but I would sooner let it go numb than move it and risk waking her.

We were still beneath the tree where we'd settled the night before, her body curled against mine like it had always belonged there. My heartbeat slowed to match hers, and my eyes drifted shut again.

"Jack. Get up."

I blinked, looking up at her standing a few feet away, her arms crossed. My gaze followed her curves, halting on narrowed eyes and the glint of steel in her hand.

I sat up. "What happened?"

"Your hands were all over me."

I glanced down and groaned. "Sav, I swear—I was asleep. I didn't mean to..."

Something sharp whizzed past my head embedding in the tree behind me with a thunk.

"Whoa!" I threw my hands up.

Her smirk faded. "In Faerie, we don't touch a female without her permission. Ever."

Another blade zipped past, slicing the edge of my ear. I touched it and my finger came away red.

"Understood," I said, holding perfectly still. "Truly. I hope you believe I'd never do anything without consent. Even asleep."

Her lips twitched upward, and she sauntered toward me. My back hit the bark as she leaned in, her fingers gliding up my chest and along the side of my face. Her mouth brushed my ear.

"I'll hold you to that."

She yanked the dagger from the tree and spun, her hair whipping me in the face before she disappeared into the forest.

I followed, groggy and frustrated, to a nearby stream. I cupped water in my hands, splashing it over my face and trying not to replay the moment her body had been wrapped around mine. Or the way she'd flung those blades. Or how something about her fury was... maddeningly attractive.

She stood and straightened her skirts. "Come on. We need to make better time today."

I wiped my hands on my shirt, cleared my throat. Walking anywhere right now was going to be a challenge.

"Should we... get breakfast?"

She shot me a look. "They don't have Starbucks in Faerie, Jack. If I see any edible berries, I'll let you know."

So we weren't going to talk about it. Fine.

As we trekked, I kept my wary gaze on the stream to our right, half expecting a sudden appearance from the shirtless prince. A thought struck me. It was his arms I'd seen grabbing Sav back on Earth. Even then, he'd been protecting her. He was a fairy prince, meant for this realm. He was the logical choice for Sav.

And what was I? Not fae. Not human it turned out. And I didn't know what that meant. Unless it was the magic of Faerie affecting me somehow.

A flicker of orange caught my eye. A fox, its fur streaked with black, watched us from behind a log. One glowing purple eye met mine before it dipped out of sight.

"Sav," I whispered.

She looked up from the stream. "What?"

I tipped my chin toward the log and mouthed, "Fox."

Her gaze sharpened. "Where?"

I pointed. She nodded and crept forward, slipping a dagger from her belt. Silent. Even the leaves didn't rustle beneath her feet.

"Sav, don't!" I hissed.

The fox darted from cover and vanished into the woods. She swore, rounding on me.

"Why did you do that?"

"You were going to kill it. Even if it was spying, that doesn't mean it deserves to die."

She sheathed her dagger with a sigh. "I wouldn't have killed it. I was going to *injure* it so it couldn't follow us."

Somehow Sav thought that meant it was okay. I would never understand her logic.

We walked on until the trees began to change. They grew taller, their bark smoother, and sunlight began to trickle through the canopy. The ground shimmered with hazy orange light, and rows of brilliant yellow flowers burst into view.

They were mesmerizing.

I stepped toward one, drawn in by the scent. It was the most intoxicating thing I'd ever inhaled. I reached for the petals.

"Jack! Stop!"

Sav slammed into me, tackling me to the ground. My head hit the mossy earth, shaking me from my dazed state. Her sweet scent and the warmth of her body pressed against mine stole my focus for a moment before my gaze snagged on the yellow blooms I'd been so drawn to. Before my eyes, the flowers morphed into rows of snarling, snapping creatures. Tiny dragon-like beasts with thorned petals and needle-sharp teeth.

"What the hell are *those*?"

"SnapDragons," she said, standing over me. "Flower fae. Guardians of the summer court."

"They don't *look* like flowers."

"They *did* a moment ago."

I scrambled to my feet. "How?"

"Glamour. Most fae have it—the ability to change their appearance and lure others in."

She turned and walked ahead, her red hair refracting like fire in the light.

Glamour. A mask. Just like everything else here. Just like everything about her.

And yet... I wanted to know what lay beneath.

FIFTY-ONE

SAV

We snaked along the border between Spring and Summer, moving far enough away that Jack wouldn't be ensnared again. No true fae would fall for glamour. Unless they'd never set foot in Faerie, I supposed.

My sister would have tested him. Used her magic to drag out the truth, no matter what it cost him to learn it. I shuddered. How had she and I shared a womb? Now, though, knowing Jack wasn't just a human, I questioned the soundness of my plan.

He'd as good as said the words I had been thinking aloud, albeit without the threatening army at his back. So why did thoughts of making the trade twist something in my gut?

I frowned, gaze darting to the left. The fox had managed to stay with us the entire trip. Whoever it was, would likely report to my sister the moment we crossed realms. If I saw it again, I'd string it up by its tail.

We were closing in on the path to Earth and I wiped my palms on my skirts. Our plan was half hatched at best and relied entirely on Creig's aid. If he refused me, I needed to come up with something else. How foolish would it be to make the trade without the might of Sage's army at my back? Did Dane want his son badly enough and if so, what would stop him from simply killing me and taking him? Would I be putting Jack in danger if I sent him back to the humans?

"Lady Briar."

The blood in my veins froze as power crackled over my skin. I turned, already knowing who I'd see.

We were still on the spring side of the border, but nothing and no one was strong enough to stop the prince of summer from stepping over the line and ending me if he wanted.

I searched the forest behind him and realized with some surprise he was alone. But with power like his, what did he need an army for? I dipped my head, praying to Mab Jack was bowing as nonmembers of a fae court were expected to do, but couldn't spare him the glance. To look away was tantamount to death.

"What brings you this far from your palace?"

I lifted my chin, not breaking his stare. Every inch of his honed, golden skin was bare, all the way to his feet, showing off the perfectly sculpted physique of our realm's closest thing to a deity with Mab gone. It reminded me of our very first meeting.

"And with a human?" he continued.

I met his eye. "I'm merely shoring up our borders, your highness."

Prince Fero barked a laugh. "Come now, Briar. You can't think rumors of your binding haven't reached me in Summer."

I bit the inside of my cheek, hiding a grimace. Though we hadn't spent a great deal of time together when he visited our court, he held one card over me that, even now, had my stomach twisting into a knot. If he wanted the truth, he could demand it. "There's more than one way to protect a border, your highness."

"Surely, your sister has more than enough magic for the task. Or," he searched the forest. "Has her power weakened of late?"

"She has plenty of power."

I squeezed my eyes shut at Jack's words as Fero's gaze moved to Jack for the first time.

"Your pet speaks so freely, Lady Briar. You should keep him on a tighter leash."

I begged Mab to seal Jack's mouth and thanked her when he said nothing else.

Fero's flaming eyes, the color of autumn leaves, returned to me, looking me over.

I stood perfectly still, letting him drink his fill. His perusal would have given my uncle great joy if it meant he could use it to his advantage, and years of training had me frozen in place, rather than speaking against it. Letting my mind wander to the place it went in situations like these, I was surprised when it went instead to my sister's prison and the moment Jack had burned the bars of his cage. I'd looked into eyes flaming with a feral sort of rage that sent the hairs on my arms standing on end. Had they been orange, like Summer?

"I hear congratulations are in order. What will your sister do now that she has the might of the lakes and streams at her command?"

"The alliance doesn't secure my sister over Prince Kaspar, and I'd recommend never making such a statement in his presence."

Fero chuckled. "Glad to see he hasn't curbed your wicked tongue. I miss our days together at court, Lady."

He said lady with enough derision, there was no confusing his insinuation at how I'd received my title.

"Princess, soon enough."

Fero shifted on his feet, and I kept my eyes on his face, studiously ignoring the impressive length hanging between toned thighs. "Ah yes. Has the happy date been set?"

My fingers slid to my waistband, running absently over the daggers rimming my corset. He could ensure my sister never received the aid she desired right now if he wished, and though my blades would be of no use against Fero's magic, I wouldn't go down without a fight.

"We're working out the details," I said, searching the tree line to gauge the sun's position in the sky. Any moment the rain would begin in Spring. Perhaps it would be enough to send Fero away, but somehow, I doubted it. "I'll be sure you receive an invitation, your highness."

Fero's raven eyebrow quirked up. "Will the festivities be held in your new sovereign's court or did you just extend an invitation into Spring?" His right leg twitched as if he planned to take me at my word and step over this moment.

"We seek a neutral venue." A deceptively cool voice replied behind me. Fero's attention shifted past me and I glanced to my left, swearing under my breath as Kaspar approached and took my hand. "I want my betrothed to feel comfortable to invite whomever she likes to our nuptials." He brought my fingers to his lips and pressed a kiss to my knuckles.

Sweat ran down my back. Kaspar had timed his entrance well, as usual. I fought the urge to sneak a look at Jack, wondering why he was so silent, but unwilling to risk drawing attention to him.

Fero was content to spend the rest of eternity chatting, or at least until I divulged too much information. What did he need spies for when he need only needle things from me? "Something neutral sounds perfect, my prince," I said, painting on a false smile.

Kaspar's attention drifted from me to Fero as he looked the male over, clearly unimpressed. For the first time, I wondered if Kaspar's power might rival the prince of summer. We'd never talked about his gifts. In all the years I'd known him, he'd never mentioned them at all. Perhaps that was because, unlike most land courts, the sea courts didn't choose royals based on power. Kaspar was destined to rule whether he had a drop of magic or an ocean full.

Fero met Kaspar's cool gaze with one of his own and the two males sized each other up for long moments before Fero's gaze broke first, nearly making me gasp. "You know, Lady Briar, things would have gone differently if your sister and her husband had accepted my marriage suit. We might all be friends now, rather than preparing for war."

Fero turned, giving us all his back, and Kaspar hissed at the insult. He crested a hill on his side of the border and disappeared over it. Jack let out a grunt behind me.

I heard the sounds they made, but they were background noise, drowned by the screaming in my own head. Fero? Prince Fero had requested my hand and my sister had declined? The forest spun at dizzying speed. Why had she never told me? Why had no one ever told me? I wrenched my hand free from Kaspar's, whirling to face him.

"Did you know? Was that why you offered your suit?"

Jack moved, pressing into my back, and my world steadied. I leaned against him, drawing on his comforting warmth, but my gaze remained fixed on Kaspar, a knife buried in my chest as I waited for his reply.

Kaspar watched me impassively, even as my heart thrashed under my ribcage. His lips were pressed firmly together and his gaze shifted over my shoulder to the man at my back. His eyes narrowed.

"If you hope to gain my lady's affections, you'll need to do more than–."

"I don't have a title to throw around, but make no mistake, I won't back down from a fight." Jack cut him off, stepping around me, towering several inches over the prince.

"Enough!" Heat flared to life in my veins, and tiny sparks fizzled along my fingertips. "Both of you!" I spun on my heel, marching away from all the testosterone clouding my nostrils.

"Sav, wait!"

I didn't wait for Jack or Kaspar or any more men who thought they had a claim on me. So much might have been different if anyone had bothered to ask me what I wanted. I wanted love, they knew, but if I'd been given the opportunity to make peace between two rival courts at war for centuries, I might have taken it.

I marched blindly, not caring where I went, suddenly feeling my mission to save a few fae was a pebble, sending a tiny ripple across a great lake. I might succeed in saving a few today, but what would become of the rest of my kind? In Faerie, on Earth? Fero may have been willing to open his borders to the low fae. I might have found them a place that didn't involve assimilation and degradation on Earth.

My breathing had calmed, but my temper hadn't. I longed in this moment for a taste of my magic so I could expel some of the heat burning through me. I glanced over my shoulder. Jack was crashing through the brush in an attempt to keep up. Kaspar was nowhere to be seen.

I continued on, reaching the place we'd been trekking to all day. Now that I was here, I wasn't sure what to do. Even if Kaspar offered asylum, the low fae couldn't survive underwater. His offer might have bought us an army and the ability to spy on our neighbors, but there were so many things Summer offered. So many things my sister apparently didn't want. But why? Why choose an alliance that guaranteed war when there had been another option? One that would have strengthened us.

I leaned against a tree, grinding my teeth.

Jack halted beside me, breathing loudly.

My gaze hardened on him. Who did he think he was challenging a prince of Faerie? And who did Kaspar think he was, deciding my fate for me? These males and their egos would drive me to violence.

He straightened unusually quickly, catching his breath far too fast for a human, reminding me he was no normal man. A thrill of fear shot through me. I had been too hasty in my plan to deliver Jack to Dane. I had no idea what he was or what he was capable of, and once Dane had him, he would know how to get into Faerie.

I couldn't do it. Not when giving him up might hand Dane the key to everything and destroy what was left of Faerie.

FIFTY-TWO

JACK

Sav pushed off the tree. "We're going to Earth. Together."

Saying nothing else, she locked her gaze on the path ahead, jaw set so tight a muscle twitched in her cheek.

I wanted to tell her I wasn't like the people who sought to use her here, but right now, I was just another man in her way. Much as I was loath to put any space between us and even though all I really wanted was to be closer, I had to give her time to process her latest revelations.

"Getting to Earth is simple. Put the place you want to go in your mind and don't deviate from that thought." She narrowed her eyes at me as if accusing me of getting this wrong before I'd even tried. "But we must think of the same place or we won't end up together."

I straightened, breathing easier. I wanted to apologize again. It was clear she was hurt by the prince of summer's declaration. I'd never felt so much power coming off a creature in my life. Not that I had much experience with fairies.

The most powerful creature I'd met before him was the princess of spring. Her power had seemed endless, but when the male on the summer side of the border—naked as the day he was born—made his presence known. It was like a wall crashed down and all that terrible power bowled over me.

I'd struggled to speak—to move—and his strange magic held me in place. But even as it wrapped around me, something inside me rose to meet it, fighting to throw off his hold. When I could finally say something, I got out one sentence before his magic was back, choking my very lungs.

I was tiring of people calling me a pet, but the hurt on Sav's face when he told her he'd asked for her hand punched a hole straight through my chest. Did she have feelings for him? I couldn't tell, but the news had shaken her. Was there anyone in this forsaken place who didn't want to marry Sav?

Jealousy burned low in my gut. I shoved it down, reminding myself I was the one she'd remained with through this journey. I was the one she chose repeatedly. A tiny voice in the back of my head said it was only because she, like Hazel, didn't think I'd survive on my own, but I ignored that voice. Soon we would be back on Earth and then I'd know the truth.

"Where are we going?"

Sav twisted her hair into a knot, tying the loose strands in place. "I don't want to come out near the AFF. Seelie portals aren't like Unseelie ones. We can divert from the main access point by a slight distance if we picture a place in our mind." Her brow furrowed. "The farthest we can go is Times Square. There's a wide alley behind Hershey's Chocolate World. Have you been there? You'll have to picture it."

My lips tipped up. "Of course I have."

She nodded. "Good. To get to the human realm, you'll have to walk this path." She pointed to a long trail—lined in bowed branches—that shimmered at the end, seeming to disappear into some invisible distance. "Think of your destination and no matter what, think of nothing else. Don't be distracted by anything you see, hear, or think. Your senses can't be trusted once you enter."

Her eyes met mine. "Jack. I mean it. No pretty flowers, no trees singing you songs. You must picture your destination in your mind and leave it there. Once we're on the path, we won't be aware of one another. The time it takes depends entirely on how determined you are to get there."

She looked away, glancing over her shoulder. "Creatures have died on the path, lost and unable to find their way."

A light coating of sweat prickled my brow, and it wasn't entirely because of the heat near the summer border.

"Don't worry. Just put everything else out of your mind and focus on going home."

Home. Was that what Earth was for me now? Did I belong there? Dane certainly would have locked me up in one of his cages if he'd seen me in the spring court prison. But Sav wasn't sure what I was, and that meant Faerie wasn't my home either. Earth was the place I needed to go to stop Dane, to help the creatures he'd trapped and take him down. Whether it was home or not, it was where I needed to be.

I nodded.

She searched my face. "You go first. I don't want to step in there, and some new fae creature snatches you up before you enter."

I deserved that.

I stared down the path, exhaling a long breath, knowing when we reached Earth everything would be different. All the moments we'd shared in Faerie, good or bad, were ours. Leaving felt like abandoning what we'd experienced here together.

I spun, meeting hazel eyes that sparkled in the midday sun. "Thank you for not giving up on me."

She stepped forward, and I moved, meeting her halfway and wrapped my arms around her, dipping to press my nose to her hair. I let her scent envelop me, cocooning me in a place I never wanted to leave. If I belonged anywhere, it was here.

"Be careful, okay?" Her words sunk into my chest, nestling deep.

-●-> (˅◆ᴖ◆●●-

The moment my foot touched sun-flecked earth, the sounds and smells of Faerie evaporated. Here, no wind rustled the leaves; no birds chirped. It was unnaturally still and silent. I took another step, staring straight ahead, and pictured the Hershey Chocolate Factory.

A memory, long buried, rushed in. Mom held my hand, tugging me through the door. "Anything you want, my little prince."

I smiled up at her. Her face flickered in my memory, changing from the one I'd always known—the face that looked at me with so much love. It was distorted at the edges and her hair, normally as black as mine, shimmered in the light, appearing silver.

I tugged my hand out of hers.

"What is it, my sweet Jacaranda?"

I blinked, the name warming something in my chest, and shook my head. My mother was always doing silly things like that. Calling me fun made up names or telling me wild stories of lands we'd never traveled to.

When I looked up again, her face had returned to its natural shape, her hair dark, like mine. Only her eyes remained different, still green, but brighter than they ought to be.

"I'm excited about candy!"

She grinned and held out her hand.

I took it, and we stepped into the store. My eyes went round as I spied rows and rows of chocolate and high overhead, the largest candy bar I'd ever seen hung from invisible wires.

My mother pressed her hand to her temple.

"What's wrong, Mom?"

She shook her head. "Nothing, my love. Go. Pick out some candy. Anything my prince wants for his birthday."

I laughed, darted into the store, and grabbed a plastic bag. I scooped up chocolates of all shapes and size, filling my bag to bursting.

Glancing back, I frowned at my mom standing outside the store. When her eyes met mine, she dropped her hand from her temple and waved. We had driven into the city for my birthday. It was our annual tradition, but this year I didn't know if she was up for it.

I hefted two full bags to the counter, beckoning her inside. The sooner we left, the sooner we could find a place for her to sit and rest. She joined me at the counter, leaning down to dig in her purse.

The salesclerk weighed my bags and looked up. "That'll be forty-nine, twenty-five."

"Of course. One moment." My mother fished around in her purse and pulled out a long, slender leaf.

I snorted, waiting for her to pull out real money, but the salesclerk took the leaf, holding it up to the light. He pressed a few buttons on his register and it slid open. He reached in, pulling out three quarters and held them out.

My gaze swiveled between the man and my mother waiting for someone to shout: "Gotcha!" or "Surprise!" but my mom just turned to me.

"Jack, these quarters are for you. An extra present on your birthday."

I shuffled forward, holding out my hand, and the salesclerk dropped three shiny objects into my outstretched palm. Mom watched me expectantly, and I swallowed, forcing a smile onto my face. "Thanks, mom."

Her brows furrowed, but she said nothing, grabbing my bags of candy and motioning for us to leave the store. I trailed her, desperately trying to make sense of what I'd just seen.

She glanced back, beaming. "Do you want to take your candy to the park and enjoy it there?"

I nodded slowly, searching her face. She seemed to feel better. We turned toward Central Park. Mom slowed, waiting for me to catch up, and handed me a bag. "Will you share a piece with your mother?"

I smiled, already knowing which she'd ask for. It was the reason I'd put so many of the peppermint chocolate kisses in the second bag. My mom loved anything to do with Christmas, and her chocolate preferences were no exception.

She untied the bag, fished out the candy, and unwrapped it.

We walked the fifty blocks from Times Square to Central Park, racing one another to see who could eat the most candy before we got there. When we reached the park, my mom stopped and reached into the bag again. "Here Jack. I have something special for you. You'll need it for what's coming."

She held out her hand, and I opened my fingers. Instead of a candy as I'd expected, a ball of glowing light pressed into my palm. She closed her hand around mine, squeezing tight.

I looked up. "What is it?"

The scene before me glitched—some other version of the park overlaying the one from my distant memory.

It was jarring, and it jolted me back to reality. I had left my path and had deviated. I had to turn around before it was too late. I spun, but my mom's hand snaked out, locking me in an iron grip.

"Ow." I yanked against her hold, but she didn't release me.

"Let's go, Jack. To your father. To Central Park, where everyone who cares about you is waiting."

I pulled harder as her face changed, morphing before my eyes into my father's. My legs gave out before I could move. I hit the floor hard, scrambling backward on my hands as if I could claw my way out of the vision.

"Come home, Son. We miss you."

"No. I hate you and I'll stop you."

Dane's lips split into a vicious grin, and his grip tightened. "You think the little fairy bitch cares for you? You think killing me and your fellow humans will earn you any points with her?"

"No. I—"

"Come to me, Jack. I'll protect you. Just like I always have."

A vision flashed across my mind. Something too horrible to put into words, and I wrenched my arm from his grasp, stumbling to the ground.

The scene changed, and we were in our old apartment in Jersey. He came for me, a manic gleam in his eye, but when I held up a hand to ward him off, it wasn't my hand. A simple gold band encircled my left ring finger, and I touched my face, running a finger over soft lips that had kissed my forehead so many times before.

Dane lifted his arm, a long, rusted pipe gripped tightly between his fingers. "Did you think you could keep it from me?" He swung.

"No!" I screamed, wrapping my arms over my head, waiting for the blow.

When it didn't come, I opened my eyes and exhaled a shaky breath. I was in Central Park, just a few blocks from the AFF compound. I blinked, unsure whether this was still in my mind or if I had made it out the other side.

"You don't belong here," a sickly-sweet voice said.

I shot to my feet, searching the dark for the owner of the voice.

"You aren't allowed on the Seelie side," a second voice, similar to the first, said.

"Who's there?"

A set of barking laughs that grated against my spine rang out near the tree that seemed to be bisected by the path I'd just tumbled out of. I inched closer but froze when two sets of faces came into focus. They leaned against the trunk. But that wasn't right. They were attached to it somehow.

Each on either side of the path.

Dryads. "No, no, no," I said, backing up. "Stay back."

They laughed again, and I turned, darting away from them as memories of rough, bark-like hands scraping over my skin resurfaced. Following the same path I had in my strange vision, I stopped outside the Hershey store in Times Square.

Something shimmered from an alley behind the store. I moved toward it and leaned close. Tentatively, I held out a hand. Inky darkness latched onto my arm, yanking me forward. I was pulled through an invisible wall and when my feet touched solid ground, the world exploded with sounds and smells.

Around me, car horns, music and advertisements overwhelmed my senses. Cooked meat and corn, mixed with bodies doused in perfume or their own natural odors, assaulted me, and I gagged. Was this how the fairies who came here felt when they arrived? After so long in a place so quiet, with only the subtlest hints of flora and snow, Earth must have seemed like a nightmare.

"Sav!"

I glanced around the dark alley. Nothing guarded this entrance and now that I had come through it, I could no longer see it. I struggled to process everything that had happened on my trip. It was meant to pull me from my destination. Meant to force me off the path. Those last memories weren't memories at all, but nightmares that would have left me trapped forever. It had seemed like a few hours, but how did time work when crossing between realms?

How long had I been in Faerie? A week? Two? There were stretches of days I couldn't remember or hadn't been conscious for.

I whipped around in the dark. Surely Sav, a fairy who had traveled through pockets before, would have made it through faster than I had. "Sav," I whispered again.

In the silence of the dank alley, my chest constricted. Was she coming, or had it been her plan all along to send me here—away from the danger— while she went looking for the former spring court general? I'd wanted this test. To see if the feelings we shared were strong enough to bring us across realms. And now I feared I had my answer.

I ran a hand through my hair. Turning in a circle, searching the alley one last time.

It was no one's fault but my own that she couldn't put her trust in me. I may not be much help in Faerie, but here, I could do something.

I glanced down at my strange clothes. First, I'd need a change of outfit. Stepping out of the alley into Times Square, I breathed shallowly and scanned the stores. Looking both ways, I darted across the street, narrowly avoiding a cab as he laid on the horn. I reached the other side and stepped into the Ralph Lauren store.

Scanning the shelves, I briefly considered how I'd get out with my new outfit. My wallet—and all my money—was somewhere in Faerie. A tee shirt would have been easier to steal, but after my brief stay in the winter and spring courts, I had to up my wardrobe if I hoped to compete for a fairy royal's attention.

"Excuse me."

A man looked up, gaze scanning my outfit. His eyes were strangely illuminated and for a moment I wondered if he was a glamoured fairy or if I was losing my mind. "Yes?"

"I'm new to buying button downs. How do you choose the right fit?"

The man's eyes twinkled, and he sized me up. His gaze roved over the rows of black shirts and he grabbed one handing it to me. "Planning a date night?"

"No." I scoffed. "The woman I care for isn't happy with me at the moment."

The man's brow rose as he eyed me with interest. He reached out, touching the material of my spring court shirt. "This is fine fabric. Where did you get it?"

I laughed. "You wouldn't believe me if I told you."

He leaned closer. "Try me."

Those strange eyes were luminescent, and I tilted back. "I have a better idea. We're close enough in size. You'd only have to shorten the inseam a few inches. Buy me a new outfit and this one's yours."

He grinned. "What's your name?"

"Jack."

"Pleased to meet you, Jack. I'm Simon."

FIFTY-THREE

SAV

I tumbled onto rough pavement cursing as I crashed into a dingy brick wall. Piss and some other horrid stench drenched the area and I scrambled back, climbing to my feet. I glanced around the alley behind the Hershey's store and sighed.

A buzzing had already begun in my ears and all around me intrusive sounds and smells clattered against my skull. I hadn't missed this place for a second.

The sun hung low in the sky, but even this late in the day, it radiated heat. I hadn't expected it to take so long to travel the path. Every shadow whispered a memory—my sister's face, my father's grief—but I gritted my teeth and pushed forward. I didn't flinch. Not this time. I'd been down the path and my past enough times.

My mother was dead, killed by a summer court assassin, my father too, dead from a broken heart when I was still very young. They were older by fae standards when they had us, choosing to wait until they found their mate before having offspring, but my father should have had at least another few centuries of life. Ultimately, the call of his mate was too strong, and he had succumbed to it.

My sister wasn't who I thought she was–reminder after reminder of all the times she'd shown her true colors and all the times I'd given her another chance–had hurtled by at speed.

I had no desire to linger in any of those memories, to watch my own past mistakes play out again.

But when I stumbled over more recent memories, ones I hadn't examined or accepted yet, my mind tried desperately to pull me off the path. I might have ended up back in Faerie beneath the moon, curled into the side of Jack's warmth if I lingered too long, but I had reminded myself of the plan. Save the other fae and return to Faerie to sort out the life I'd been putting off for too long.

The sun inched across the sky as I paced the alley, glancing toward every flicker of movement. He should be here by now. A mangy cat emerged from a trash bin hissing at me and I bared my teeth at it.

I wasn't staying in this alley to wait any longer. I stepped out onto a bustling sidewalk, packed with humans racing to get to their destinations and pushed open the door to the Hershey's store.

Blood pounded a rhythm in my head as the overwhelming amount of iron in this store crashed against my senses. Holding my head to relieve some of the pounding, I backed out and into a solid frame. Spinning around, I looked up and up. "Creig!"

Sharp cheekbones, crisscrossed with thin white lines, strained against his grin. "Sav."

I flung my arms around him, entirely uncaring of the crowd giving us a wide berth. Relief surged through me. Then guilt. I was hugging my old friend while Jack could already be dead on the path.

Releasing him, I stepped back. A pair of massive axes were wedged into his belt and his loose shirt did little to disguise the leather bands strapped to the gills with throwing knives bisecting his back. He was completely unchanged after so many years.

"What are you doing here? I was coming to find you."

"A little birdie told me where you'd be."

I glanced around the busy street, half expecting to find that damned fox, but out here we were the only oddities.

"Come on. The gang is waiting for you. Where's the human?"

"He hasn't made it through yet." I bit my lip, swallowing hard.

Creig scratched his chin, winking at a woman who was gawking at us. She gasped and scurried by. "I'll ask Murz to stay behind and keep an eye out for him. It's not safe for you on the street."

I peered into the alley, Anxiety gnawing at me. *Stupid. So stupid to let him go first.* "Murz will stay here until he arrives?"

Creig nodded and a tall, lean orc with darker than usual skin slid out from the shadows. Creig whispered orders in their native tongue and Murz dipped his chin, grinning at me before he moved into the alley I'd just come out of and disappeared from sight.

A man in an expensive looking suit, snapped a photo and began typing rapidly. Creig snatched the phone from his hand and he shouted in indignation.

"Reporting me to the ISHFA?" Creig flashed sharp teeth at the man and he backed up.

"It's... It's illegal to speak in your native tongue," he stammered.

Creig's grip on the phone tightened and it cracked under the pressure, screen going dark.

"You can't... do that." The man glanced at me, looking for support from a fellow human.

I shrugged. "Looks like he did." He glanced warily at the massive axes strapped to Creig's belt and backed up, disappearing into the crowd.

"Maybe I should stay and wait for Jack."

Creig's brows bunched over his wide nose. "You can't. Morgan's put a price on your head."

My throat went dry. "What?"

"Come on, Sav. Let's get off the street. If anyone recognizes you it could be bad." Not waiting for me, he marched down the packed sidewalk.

I raced after him, catching up as my heart bumped against my ribcage. "What reason could she possibly have for putting a bounty on me?"

Creig strode confidently and people darted to get out of his way. Envy colored my mood. I wished I had his confidence. I wished I could wear my species like a badge of honor instead of hiding. The wild urge to remove my glamour surfaced, but even if I'd wanted to, I didn't have enough magic available to undo it. I was stuck like this until my sister unbound me.

"It was reported that you were working with the AFF. That you helped plan the attack on the fae dwellings in Central Park." He cast a disapproving frown over his shoulder and kept walking.

"Why would I help my sworn enemy? Why would I kill my own kind?"

"The Inter Species Human Fae Alliance council met to discuss just that. Seems someone on their committee has a kid living at the compound. The girl said you did it for love. Love of a human."

I inhaled a sharp, disbelieving breath and my heart rate ticked up. "How do you know all this?"

"I have spies, Love."

My stomach dropped. Things were unraveling in both realms and soon I'd have nowhere safe to go.

-●→) (ᴗ●♠♠●●-

We stopped outside a row of arched tunnels in red brick.

"This is where you've been hiding out?"

Creig winked at me. "They call us animals." I followed him through the arched entrance to the Central Park Zoo abandoned since the day our realms collided, I'd heard.

We crossed the brick path to the seal pool, empty now, and Creig hopped over plexiglass and dropped into the empty pool. He disappeared behind a rock and I scrambled after him watching him vanish into a silvery pocket door. A knot twisted in my stomach. I sent a silent prayer to Mab that Jack would come through the portal soon.

I stepped through the shimmering door and my breath caught. Moss underfoot, vines in bloom, trees I hadn't seen in six years. This wasn't just a hideout. This was a stolen piece of Faerie.

"Creig. What's going on here?"

FIFTY-FOUR

KASPAR

I paced the space that would be Sav's room. The ceiling was too low. The walls too close. Sav would feel like a caged animal here.

I shoved the bedpost hard enough to splinter it.

I could expand her rooms, make more breathable areas for her.

Scowling, I turned. Nothing I did to my castle would make it livable for a creature who craved adventure.

"Sire."

"Yes?" I looked up as Memphe entered.

"I have a missive from your uncle."

I beckoned him forward and he came, pressing through the air bubble into the room. He handed me a silver tube and bowed.

Dismissing him, I slid the parchment free and unrolled it, scanning my uncle's neat handwriting.

My jaw clenched as I read the last line. The autumn princess had accepted his proposal and the date was set. Not only would he beat me at my own game, he would do it before me.

I rolled the scroll between my fingers, resisting the urge to crumple it in my fist.

I jammed it back in the tube.

Perhaps I had been too hasty in choosing Sav. I could have denied the bargain and chosen someone else to align with. If I had, she would be wed to the prince of summer now.

He wouldn't give her the freedom I would. He would trap her; force himself upon her and use her to build a stronger alliance with Spring. She would spend the rest of her long life under the thumb of very powerful royals.

Still, my uncle was making his move and the winter court heiress had been more than amenable to an alliance. She was an adequate lover and her blood was pure. Aligning with the winter court would be prudent if my uncle brought war upon us. They had the numbers and their hostile environment, even with Mab gone, made invasion unlikely.

But if the folk of my court sought shelter, whether as Faerie continued to shrink or when my uncle struck, Winter would be a harsh refuge.

Moves and countermoves were all I had. There was no room in my life for anything more when my uncle had centuries on me to set the board for his long game. I squeezed the slender tube in my hand, crushing metal in my fist. I wasn't playing, though, and this wasn't a game.

With access to Autumn blocked—by my uncle no doubt—I was blind to his intentions toward us and beginning to believe he had bigger aspirations than I'd ever dreamed. Whatever he had planned, he wouldn't make his move before his wedding. There was still time for me to secure my alliance and learn the truth of what was happening in Faerie.

FIFTY-FIVE

SAV

"Welcome to the rebellion, Love." I spun in a circle, taking in a place I thought I'd never see again. "How are we here?"

Creig held up a hand, grinning, and his oversized incisors inched over his bottom lip. "Did you really think I left my people and just fucked off to the human realm?"

"Well...Yeah."

His smile widened. "I'd never leave them behind."

"But Shel...and Raine..."

Creig's smile faltered for a moment before it slid back into place. "If you think I'd abandon my kind over a female, you don't know me at all."

My cheeks heated. I did know him. He was the father I needed when mine was lost to his despair. When he'd left nearly a decade ago, before any of our treaties with the humans, before the courtless fae were forced to live on Earth and all the rules that bound us made us little better than their chattel, I'd assumed he wasn't coming back. It seemed that no matter how old I got, Creig was still teaching me lessons.

I rushed forward wrapping my arms around his wide shoulders.

He disentangled himself from me, tipping my chin up. "I missed you little Sav."

I blinked back tears. I wanted to melt into the memory, into the safety Creig represented—but my thoughts kept circling back to Jack. To Dane. To the bounty.

He stepped back, leaning against a broad tree trunk. "Now, tell me it isn't true."

"That I tried to kill the folk?" I asked incredulously.

"That you fell in love with a human."

"I'm not an idiot," I snapped. My pulse jumped. I looked away too fast, rubbing my wrist to hide it. Creig's silence told me he'd heard it anyway.

Creig's black eyes searched my face, as a braid fell over his nose and he tucked it back. "Love isn't a bad thing. If you find it with one special enough to deserve it."

I snorted. "Are those words for you or for me?"

"Don't deflect."

My brows dipped low, hating how well he knew me. But I couldn't help wondering if this speech was him giving voice to the thoughts still plaguing him. Was he still not over his wife of more than a century leaving him? "I'm sorry about Shel."

"It couldn't be helped."

I hadn't ever heard of orcs having mates before, but I supposed every species deserved their happily ever after, even if it meant someone else's anguish. "What about Larek and Yolmar?"

"What about us?"

I spun around squealing as Larek scooped me up and hugged me. He set me down and my smile was so wide I thought my cheeks would burst. "You're here! I can't believe it. I thought you stayed with your mother."

"Dad needs us," Larek shrugged. Besides, I can't stand Raine and his rules."

Creig boxed his son's ear. "Don't talk that way about your uncle."

"Uncle, stepdad. Whatever. He sucks."

"Larek, watch your mouth."

Larek grumbled something under his breath and bumped my shoulder. "Don't feel bad for dad. He has no shortage of ladies chasing after him."

"Oh yeah? Do tell."

"Hey! Sav!" I searched the forest for the owner of that voice and raced forward meeting Yolmar halfway.

He wrapped me in a tight hug. "Okay...can't...breathe..."

He set me down, moving to stand beside his twin.

I hadn't realized how much I missed this trio until they were standing before me. Emotion welled inside me. Once, Sage would have been right here beside us, and Kaspar. Innocent children, wholly unaware of what life would bring.

Larek and Yolmar linked arms, as inseparable as ever as they moved to stand beside their father.

"Kaspar has offered you a reprieve. In exchange for helping me."

Creig clapped Larek on the shoulder, saying something in their language and both boys disappeared back into the forest. "Sav. There's a lot you don't know. I want to help, but Dane is up to more than anyone knows. And I won't go back to Faerie while so many of our kind are exiled from it."

He moved deeper into the forest, motioning for me to follow.

I chased after him, climbing over logs and vines. The farther we traveled the more convinced I was that I was still on the path and hadn't yet returned to reality. If this much of Faerie existed somewhere, was it *all* still intact? Was there room for everyone?

We crested a small hill, and a massive thatched home spread out, connected by the trees that grew within and around it. It was large enough for five families, if you weren't a royal. Creig tugged open a door made entirely of vines and stepped inside.

Like most orc things, the outside had been a deception. If it looked big before, it was a palace inside, with walls stretching up so far I could hardly make out a ceiling far overhead. Although no windows were visible from the outside, expansive circular port holes lined the walls letting in natural light. Overhead, pixies buzzed to and fro, dusting the floor in glitter. As we continued—the open space stretching into the distance—anger stirred in my gut.

"Creig, you have space for anyone forced to live among the humans. Why haven't you helped them?"

Creig stopped beside a long table covered in maps and parchments. "Come. I'll show you."

I stood beside the table scanning the various maps. Some were of the human realm, some of Faerie. My gaze lingered on several scattered smaller maps. They were bordered by nothing and seemed to be bits and pieces of Faerie. Taken from the various courts.

"Are these the missing parts of Faerie? Have you found them *all*?"

"Not all." Creig stabbed a pile with one black nail. "Summer." He pointed to another. "Winter." He laid his hand on the largest stack. "Spring."

"Where's Autumn?"

"Exactly."

I searched his face, returning my gaze to the piles of papers spread out over the table and moved to stand over a map of Faerie. In all the courts, Xs were drawn over places where corresponding new maps had been drawn.

"So you've found all these places?"

"Either I or the others helping us. But we've found nothing that belongs to Autumn."

I pursed my lips, scanning the map again. "Are all the entrances in New York? Who's creating them?"

Creig moved around the table to stand beside me. "We still don't know who's creating the pockets. Likely the same creature responsible for moving them to begin with. And no. Only Winter is exclusively in New York. Entrance points to Spring span the entire East Coast."

"What about Summer?"

"Summer's an interesting one," a refined voice said from the corner.

I looked up and reached for my dagger. "What's he doing here?"

Foxglove Hawthorn, the male who'd fed my secrets to my sister, strode across the room, straightening his coat. Magic flared in my veins, begging to be released. I flexed my fingers. If only I had access to it.

"Lady Briar. I aligned my cause to Creig's more than a decade ago."

Boiling anger flared to life in my chest and warmth licked up my spine as my gaze narrowed on the traitor claiming allegiance to Creig's rebellion. It would be a cold day in hell before I trusted any of my secrets to Foxglove Hawthorn. My gaze swiveled to Creig. "A decade. Faerie only started shrinking six years ago."

Creig's mouth flattened into a thin line. "So they would have you believe."

My gaze returned to Foxgloves and he extended a hand. "So glad to have you on our side, Lady."

Rage tingled at the ends of my fingers as my bound flames begged to be released on him; to give him the retribution he deserved for betraying me to my sister. I slapped it away, storming past him. At the door to the room, I spun facing Creig. "If you think he isn't feeding information to Sage, I can promise you're mistaken."

Perhaps this rebellion was weaker than I thought.

FIFTY-SIX

JACK

Adjusting the sleeves of my shirt, I moved back to the alley, checking one last time for any sign of Sav.

I had known she wouldn't be there. But my chest clenched when I saw the empty alley.

My mom's words danced through my mind. 'Never stop believing in people, my prince.' I wished she was here now, I'd tell her how wrong she was. *Hope is a luxury for people with two living parents*, I thought.

I'd tried calling Leo, then Grace from Simon's phone, but they hadn't answered, not that I'd expected them to answer a strange number. I'd just have to find them. Leo would be at his coffee shop. He lived in a small room in the back.

Before I'd made it half a block, I heard my name whispered on the wind. I turned around, wondering if I'd imagined it.

"Jack?"

I peered into the darkened alley. "Yes?"

Strong arms snapped out, grabbing me roughly and dragging me into the inky blackness. My heart pounded in my chest and there was a moment of searing light, then the darkness swallowed my vision once more. There was a tilting sensation in my mind, and it reminded me of the way it had felt when I stepped through the portal into Central Park. I flailed wildly, kicking out at my attacker, but his grip was like steel and he shoved me hard against a wall, scanning the distance before leaning close. "I'm here to bring you to Sav. Let's go."

I stopped struggling as the darkness fled, peering at the creature. Soft yellow light caught the side of his green cheek and a network of white lines ran over his face, and arms. I'd seen a few of his kind before. Orcs. Vicious, dangerous beasts who were notoriously hard to trap. According to Dane.

"How do I know I can trust you?"

He grunted, releasing me. "You don't." He turned, striding away.

I stared after him, contemplating my next move. I could leave now, go back to the compound and attempt to free the creatures myself, or I could put my faith in this orc and see if he led me to Sav.

"I'm coming!" I called, marching after him.

He crossed the street and continued heading in the direction of Central Park.

Fear twisted in my gut as I ran to keep up. Why would she be in Central Park? Had she been captured? But if she had, this orc wouldn't be working with Dane. I had to trust that wherever she was, she was safe.

Stepping into tall grass, I moved faster as the creature jogged at a clipped pace. I glanced up at the old arched entrance to Central Park Zoo and sped up, glimpsing the creature as he hopped over the plexiglass in the seal pool and sank below eye level.

"Wait!" I hopped the glass, landed hard on the cement, and ran around the side of a large rock.

The air shimmered around me and, like when I exited the Seelie path, and in the alley a moment ago, something caught me in it's vortex, dragging me through glittering light. When I landed on the other side, I was standing in a rainforest unlike anything I had ever seen before. I spun around, taking in my new surroundings. Was I back in Faerie?

I stumbled back, heart hammering as the largest snake I'd ever seen dropped out of a tree, hissing. I turned to run.

Thumps sounded behind me and I spun around, gaping at the snake pinned in place by two massive axes. I looked up at the orc standing on the other side of the clearing. Had he thrown those axes all the way over here and severed the snake's head so cleanly?

"Thank you," I said on a shaky exhale.

He grinned. "Do you?"

I bit down on a curse, remembering Sav's words. What sort of favor would I owe this creature for thanking him?

"No—"

"Jack!"

My gaze shifted to the streaming auburn hair racing toward me and something in my chest—something I hadn't realized had been clenched—loosened when I saw her. Warmth flooded my veins as she neared.

"Sav!"

The huge creature who had saved my life glanced between us and she slid to a halt beside him staring down at the snake.

She looked up. "You thanked him, didn't you?"

"I—"

"He sure did."

She slapped a hand to her temple, rubbing slowly. "You can't hold him to it. He doesn't know how fae bargains work."

"Did you warn him?"

She scowled up at the creature. "Yes."

"Then he owes me." Not waiting for a reply, the orc strode forward, plucking his two massive axes from the dirt, wiping the blood onto the grass, and sliding them into his belt. He held out a hand. "Creig."

"Jack," I said, wrapping my fingers around his much larger ones.

"Oh, I know who you are. And I look forward to calling in my favor."

I groaned as he yanked me forward into a hug I wasn't expecting.

Releasing me, he turned and marched back the way they had come.

Sav crossed the clearing. "You have no idea how bad that could have been."

"I know," I said, running a hand through my hair. "Is it especially poisonous? How fast would I have died?"

Sav laughed, twisting her thick hair into a braid and tossing it over a shoulder. "Not the snake. The favor. If it had been anyone other than Creig you might have been handing over your kidney right now."

Ice ran down my spine. She had to be joking. She didn't look like she was joking.

"Come on, I'll show you where we're staying."

Inside the largest ground-level treehouse I'd ever seen, Sav led me to a room down a long hall with a massive fireplace beside a cozy-looking bed and a chair. "Is this your room?"

She frowned. "It's your room."

"Right." So many emotions coursed through me at her proximity, at knowing she hadn't left me behind. But the one drowning out all the rest was relief. When I found myself back in New York City, I'd wanted nothing more than to turn around and go back to Faerie. To Sav's home. The place where she'd let her mask slip and had begun to let me in.

Wherever we were, this place felt oddly familiar and a sense of safety lingered on a phantom breeze, telling something inside me it could be trusted. Perhaps here, away from fairy royals and people like my father who wanted to see her kind dead, we could finally connect.

She faced me. "There's something you should know. It's not safe for us in the human realm." She tucked a loose curl behind her ear and I longed to do the same with the strand she'd miss. "There's a bounty on both our heads. ISHFA is offering a one hundred-thousand-dollar reward for anyone who brings in either of us." Her eyes met mine. "Dead or alive."

I reeled as if she'd struck me. "For what?"

"They're claiming we were involved in the attack on my building, and..." She looked down, her cheeks flushing. "That we're in love."

I sputtered a laugh. "They haven't seen my bloody ear. They'd know you can't stand to be in my presence most of the time."

"That's not true."

"You've thrown at least three daggers at my head since we met. One quite recently."

Sav's eyes narrowed. "It doesn't matter. What matters is that ISHFA believes it. I don't have to tell you what the penalty is if they find us guilty."

I swallowed.

One law above all others had been made clear the moment ISHFA was formed. Love between species was tantamount to death. Sav had warned me, so had Hazel, but I'd never truly thought they would act on that law.

"But you don't love me." The words barely made it out. Something twisted in my chest. Hope. I hated it. Hope would get us both killed.

She reached up, hand grazing my cheek. "Oh Jack..." Her lips trembled. I—"

"Lady Briar."

Sav backed up, yanking her hand away as though she'd been burned. I looked over at a fairy male dressed head to toe in tweed. He may as well have been in a Sherlock Holmes novel, and I was certain we had never met before. The way Sav was backing away, cheeks crimson, I could only assume it was another of her suitors.

Heat licked up my spine. Could we not have one fucking moment alone without some male in love with her bursting in to ruin it?

"General Creig asked me to fetch you to the council room."

She nodded, turning to me. "Stay here. I'll be back." She darted past the male, stopping in the doorway. "If you're hungry, find Poppy. She'll help you."

"Who's Poppy?" I called, but she was gone and the male who had come to fetch her raised an eyebrow at me before he turned, following after her. I watched him go, unease settling in my gut.

FIFTY-SEVEN

SAV

Foxglove matched my pace, glancing at me as we raced down the hall. "I would be more careful, Lady. Another might have interpreted that display quite differently."

"Run and tell my sister about it. Maybe she'll find another husband to sell me to."

Foxglove halted and despite myself I stopped, spinning to face him.

His voice softened. "You must know... I never meant you harm."

For a moment, I almost believed him. Almost. "What I know is that I might have found my place in the winter court if you hadn't told my sister about my secret betrothal to Bracken."

"He wasn't right for you. I only meant to help."

My hands landed on my hips and I planted my feet, determined not to rush forward and tear his eyes out. "Well you didn't. None of you Hawthorns ever do." I turned away, before he could say more, not wanting to hear another word from the male I thought I could trust all those years ago.

I stopped beside Creig, ignoring Foxglove as he entered the room and stood on Creig's other side.

"What is it?"

Creig pointed a sharp nail at a spot on the map of Earth. "We found another pocket. It leads to a piece of the summer court. That makes them even with us."

I looked up, searching Creig's hard expression. "Creig...Do you think." I bit my lip. "Do you think Mab is in one of these pockets? One of Winter's maybe? Trapped?"

"Mab is more powerful than any of us. I'm sure she could return if she were."

I nodded. "Have you found no others in any of the missing pockets?"

"No. They've all been empty as far as we can tell."

"And you haven't lost anyone?"

He frowned. "We have."

"And you're sure none were lost to these pockets?"

He moved to the other side of the table, sliding out a map at the bottom of a pile. "Lord Hawthorn." Foxglove moved to stand beside Creig. "You sent two males to investigate this space just outside Winter's border. Regent Goodfellow reported the anomaly. They never returned."

Foxglove nodded down at the map. "True. We assumed they were being held prisoner by Autumn. Since she's closed her borders, no one has returned from her court."

"Have you sent any others to investigate missing lands along Autumn's border?"

Foxglove scanned the larger map of Faerie. "Here. Near the North Mountains."

"And?"

"They didn't make it back."

The males looked at one another, some silent conversation playing between them. Foxglove nodded and swept from the room, not sparing me another glance.

"I know this is important, Creig, but every day we wait, more of Dane's prisoners die. Please give me a few of your men and some weapons. If this mission can't spare you, I'll command them."

Creig gave me an indulgent smile, raising my hackles. "Are you prepared to lead an orc army into battle, Love?"

I scowled at him. "Yes. With weapons."

He stalked around the table, resting a hand on one of his ax handles. "And when they're captured because the laws our people bound us to don't allow them to lift a weapon against the humans? What will you do then?"

He was laughing, but there was a cunning edge to his words. A test. If I answered correctly, he would give me what I wanted. "We won't need to fight."

"Go on."

"I only need them to ensure Dane fears us. When I call a meeting, I'll offer a trade Dane can't refuse."

Creig's dark brow rose.

"His son for the prisoners." We couldn't actually allow the trade to happen. Jack knew too much, but I wasn't prepared to admit Jack might be something else to Creig yet.

Creig crossed his arms over his chest. "Do you mean your human?"

I nodded. "He was only ever a means to an end." My fingers trembled and I laced them together to stop the shaking. "I did what I had to, to keep him close."

"Savage."

I spun, cheeks and neck flaming as I took in Jack standing in the doorway. I swallowed dryness in my throat. "Jack."

His gaze hardened as he searched my face for a long moment before turning, his quick footsteps echoing down the hall.

I whirled on Creig. "You knew he was there."

He shrugged. "Better he knows what he's walking into. If we brought him under false pretenses, any number of things could go wrong. This plan only works if Jack goes along with it."

I darted from the room hating how true Creig's words were but hating myself more for hurting Jack. It had been true when I learned who he was. I *had* planned to use him; I had planned to trick him. But somewhere along the way I'd let my guard down. I'd let him in and now the words couldn't be further from the truth. But with ISHFA and my sister after us, there was only one way to keep him safe now.

When Jack arrived here; when I knew he was okay, a piece of the wall around my heart had fractured, but Jack didn't belong in my world, and he would never be safe in his so long as there was anything between us. I had to let him go; had to ensure he let me go.

His eyes had been full of pain, and I'd put it there.

I stopped outside his door. What was I doing here? I should let him believe those words. It was the easiest path forward, but my traitorous heart stuttered at the idea. I held up a fisted hand, hovering over wood. I bit my lip, indecision warring through me.

I knocked, unsure what I would say.

Silence.

"Jack." I knocked again, pressing my forehead to the door. "It was only going to be temporary. You could have left as soon as I got the others to safety. You were never in any danger with your father." Much as I wanted to take it all back, to tell him I didn't mean the things I'd said, I couldn't.

Jack's door flew open. "I offered myself to your sister. I offered you a way out." He filled the doorframe, looming over me. "You didn't have to pretend you felt something for me."

I stared into his bright green eyes and flinched at the pain in them. He wasn't upset that I wanted to use him. He was upset because he believed my lie. He believed I felt nothing for him. Mab how I understood that feeling. The pain in my chest intensified at being the one to hurt him.

Finally...Something my family would have been proud of.

"Jack...I..."

Wetness pooled along his lashes and he backed up slamming the door in my face.

FIFTY-EIGHT
DANE

My grip on my phone tightened. "I understand."

"If you understood anything, you wouldn't have burned down the last of the fae dwellings before we had everything in place. You don't have room for all the new fae you've captured." Janet's sharp tone smacked of superiority and my jaw clenched. She still believed she was in charge. Thought the money she paid to ensure my organization expanded gave her power over me.

She was wrong.

"Take the latest batch to wherever you've hidden the rest of them or I'll execute them. I'm too far along in my trials to kill the creatures I have here."

Silence crackled over the line and I knew I'd struck a nerve. Janet thought I didn't know she had prisoners. She assumed all her illicit activities were untraceable.

"The fae we've relocated were sent back to Faerie." She finally said.

"Bullshit."

Morgan's sultry voice whispered in the background, and I realized I'd been on speaker. It didn't matter. The winged fairy didn't frighten me.

Janet's muffled voice gave a clipped response before her words came through the phone more clearly. "We need Juniper. Choose the next best candidate to begin work on from your recent acquisitions and we'll be by to get the satyr tonight."

I swung my hand up, checking the time on my watch. We had another demonstration planned in less than an hour, one that required the satyr's presence. More than that, she'd made it further along in the trials than anyone else and I wanted to continue our work. "Not tonight. I need her. In fact, I have several demonstrations lined up this week. You can have her when I'm done."

I hated negotiating with Janet. With anyone, but her resources still outweighed mine and until I had ferreted out the mole at headquarters, I couldn't make a move against Janet without her being warned.

More whispered discussion between Janet and her lover before she spoke to me. "One week. We'll take any orcs you have. Get rid of the rest."

I mashed the end call button on the phone, slamming it on the desk. It was time to cut ties with Janet. Time to find my own informant. But finding someone ISHFA was willing to hire would be far more difficult than bribing someone who already worked there.

Leaning out the door to my office, my eyes narrowed on a shadow stretching away from my door. Someone had been outside. Listening.

I marched down the hall, picking up speed as I neared the exit stairwell and threw the door open glancing up, then down. The light tap of tennis shoes bounding down caught my ears and I dashed after them. Spinning around on the second-floor landing, I ran down the steps. The first-floor door clanged against metal, and I swore as I tore the door open and stepped into a mob of restless people preparing for our next rally.

"Damnit." I growled. William's gaze shot to the ground and I marched to him, gripping the collar of his shirt in my fists. I yanked him up until his toes only skimmed the floor and watery brown eyes met mine. "Did you just come from the stairwell?" I spat the words, and a vicious grin broke on my face as his turned red, then purple in my hold.

"No. Dane." he wheezed out.

"Who just came through that door?" My gaze narrowed on his as a bead of sweat ran down his temple and his eyes bulged.

He opened his mouth but no words came out. Visions of squeezing his throat, watching the light drain from his eyes as I wrung every gasp from his body, danced in my mind and I flashed a wicked grin at him.

His cheeks were mottled now and he'd pass out in a moment.

A whisper in my head: *Calm, Dane.* I exhaled. Once. Twice. Then loosened my grip, setting William on his feet.

William coughed and sputtered, sagging in my hold, but I held onto his collar, unwilling to release him until I had my answer. When his cheeks were only a few shades darker pink than usual, he gasped out another breath and mouthed: "Grif."

I released William, squeezing my hands into tight balls at my sides as my vision went red. *Grif.* Grif, whom I'd considered a son, had betrayed me. "Grif!" I shouted.

The crowd parted, people trading nervous glances with one another as they moved to get away from me. A group backed up, leaving Grif at their center. He looked up, the grin stretched over his face falling as his skin went ashen.

"Yes sir?"

I stopped several feet away from him, not trusting myself to move any closer. "Grif." His name was lead on my tongue and I spit out the putrid taste of it. "Why were you in the stairwell?"

He glanced around, searching for anyone to support him should he need it. "I was following—"

"Alice?" I cut him off, tilting my head. "Enough. Enough lies, Grif."

His eyes widened as his gaze shot to someone behind me. I didn't turn. Didn't bother looking to see who he hoped would come to his rescue. No one would. No one in this compound was dumb enough to come between me and my rage.

"Brian, Oliver, Jim. Take him to the prison."

The trio appeared beside me and rushed forward, grabbing Grif roughly. He didn't fight. Didn't say a word as they dragged him away. He knew he deserved whatever fate awaited him. Some of my racing thoughts stilled, the anger boiling in my veins simmering. I had trusted Grif more than anyone. More than my own son, and he had betrayed me.

For that, he deserved a traitor's punishment.

◆→)(◡◆∧◆●●

Outside the remaining fairy housing in Central Park, now a smoking pile of ash, I stepped up onto the makeshift platform and brought the megaphone to my mouth. "Good evening, good people of New York."

A cheer rose, incited by AFF members interspersed in the crowd of onlookers whose number seemed to grow at each rally.

I raised a hand, stretching my lips into a wide smile. "Tonight, as promised, we've taken back our city."

A roar of approval erupted from the crowd and I held my hand up again. "But destroying their housing doesn't solve the problem." I motioned to Connor and his guard and they stepped forward, tugging a silent satyr behind them. "We must domesticate the beasts if they are to live among us. Teach them their place."

The crowd whispered and murmured to one another as Juniper stepped up beside me on the platform. All eyes were on us as I directed Connor to bring one of the latest captives forward. My limbs loosened, lightness stealing through me as we came one step closer to ridding the Earth of another alien creature.

Juniper stood motionless beside me, waiting for my command.

An orc was dragged to the grassy patch of ground before us and Connor tugged a spike from his pocket, spearing it through the creature's right hand as he staked him down. Green blood oozed from the wound and his fingers flexed with each pound of the mallet, but otherwise he was still.

We had finally captured one of General Creig's men, but it had been a fruitless effort. No amount of torture had loosened his tongue and we were no closer to learning of the general's whereabouts than we had been before we'd captured the soldier. Whatever Creig did to inspire such loyalty, I would learn and I would replicate. Then perhaps I wouldn't be faced with the difficult task of ending those I'd thought were closest to me.

"Juniper. Remember what we discussed?" I said gently. "You were made for one thing."

Her glassy-eyed stare swiveled to me and a chill ran down my spine. In this state, she was a thing of beauty. A killing machine bent on seeing my justice done.

I handed her the spear. Her hands hissed, skin bubbling around the spear. She didn't flinch. She never did. Our first several times, I'd had to give her clear instructions. Now, she needed no prompting as she gripped the iron tightly in both hands. Widening her stance, she ran the spear forcefully through the motionless orc.

He jolted from the impact of her thrust, convulsing once before going limp. The spear stretched into the sky as she yanked it from his head, holding it up for the crowd. For a moment, the only sound came from the soft breeze rustling the leaves on nearby trees, then, deafening shouts, and screams of approval as all were swept up in the joy of the moment.

I reached for the spear, tugging it from Juniper's bloody palms and she released it easily, reverting to her catatonic state once more.

Holding the spear overhead, my chest expanded as I yelled with them, reveling in the glory of our hard-won battle. My voice cracked as I was caught up in the fervor for just a moment and I threw my head back, screaming to the heavens.

When some of the elation settled, the reality of what came next, sinking like a stone in my chest, I sobered, nodding to Connor.

Cheers slowly died as a pair of ogres marched through the crowd, each wearing collars of iron. A chain stretched between them, and they stopped on either side of me when the iron went taught. I held up the microphone again, clearing my throat. Now that the moment had passed, regret hung like a blanket over my shoulders, but a traitor deserved one end and no matter my personal feelings, a leader had to make hard choices.

Grif was marched out next and I met his steely gaze. Not a flicker of guilt. Not even now. What had I created?

But he wasn't my creation. Nothing I made would ever betray me the way he had.

The crowd glanced warily between the man in chains and me. This was the part I knew would be difficult. Convincing them to end fairies was easy, showing them why we had to defend ourselves even from our own kind would be harder.

"You may be shocked by this prisoner's species, but do not be fooled. Our enemies are all around."

A line of fairy creatures was marched forward, most of them from tonight's raid. Some whimpered and cried, while others stood rigidly, glaring daggers at the crowd.

"And protecting our freedom comes at a high cost when our own kind threatens our way of life."

Mumbles in the crowd and downturned lips had a light sheen of sweat trickling along my brow. What I needed was to feed their bloodlust. To incite their anger and terror.

"Gremlins do what you were made for." The gremlin on the right moved, but the one to my left stood firm. As with most of the others, I'd met this resistance often. Only Juniper had complied absolutely. "Gremlin. End the folk before they end you."

The crude command would instill the creature's fight or flight instinct and jar him into action. He moved, and together, they wrapped thick chains around the group of fairies lined up. The folk wailed and screamed as both gremlins continued squeezing until the creatures stopped fighting their hold, slumping against one another.

Fairies weren't so easily killed, though. Whipping out my pistol, I stepped off the stage and fired. Bang. Bang. Bang. The crowd had taken longer to rally this time, but one by one, with each shot to the head, a new round of cheers rose until they were frothing at the mouth for violence.

Turning, I faced them once more. "This man," I pointed my gun at Grif. "Is a traitor. What do we do with traitors?"

"Kill him!" Someone shouted. One of mine. "Hang him," someone else shouted. "Gut him!" That one from a legitimate member of the crowd. My chest swelled. I had known we would bring them around, but now that the moment had come, I couldn't drag out his end. Couldn't watch him die slowly as I'd envisioned.

"Dane," Grif said softly, only for my ears. I ignored it, and the pain clawing its way up my chest. If I gave him a chance to speak, to plead his case, I would be weak. Leveling the barrel between his eyes, I offered Grif this final gift—quick death—and pulled the trigger.

FIFTY-NINE

SAV

I trailed the long empty hall, wrapping my arms around the leather tunic the house elf, Poppy, had brought me that morning. Even soft supple leather couldn't warm the cold knot in my chest.

It was better this way. Better for Jack if he hated me, but I couldn't shake the melancholy settling in my chest.

"Sav." I glanced up, exhaling a long breath as Creig approached. "There's another way to save them. We can find another way."

I leaned against splintered wood, inhaling its pine scent and Creig stopped and tipped against the wall beside me. He laid a gentle hand on my shoulder. "We don't have to give him up if he means that much to you."

I jerked out of his touch. "I don't care about the human."

He quirked a scarred brow at me, crossing his arms over his bulging chest. "Love, I've known you since you were a girl." His gaze darted past me, searching the hall before it returned to me. "No matter how awful your family was. No matter how badly they used you." He paused, meeting my eyes. "You never became like them."

I huffed a breath, looking away.

Creig's finger found my chin, tipping it toward him.

My gaze reluctantly met his.

"You've waited your whole life to find love." My eyes narrowed, daring him to finish his sentence. He did. "Don't let anyone tell you you can't have it now."

I tore my chin away. "You think this is about ISHFA?" I pushed off the

285

wall, stalking away from him. Why did Creig always see through me so easily when no one else had. "He's Dane Clyde's spawn."

Spitting the words made them real. And that made them unforgivable. "So what?"

I spun back, facing Creig. "He's human!" Though I wasn't sure that was true, I'd keep Jack's secret as long as I could and hope word of what happened in my sister's prison didn't reach the rest of our kind. I knew Hazel and Kaspar wouldn't betray him, even if it was only for me. But the less folk who knew the truth, the safer Jack was.

"And?"

I wrapped my hands around my arms again, gaze dropping to the floor. "And he'll die before we ever get to know each other." One bit of truth to sell the lie. One fear I'd held close to my heart until this moment. But if he wasn't human... If he was something else—something *more*— what then? What excuse would I have left?

Creig straightened and wrapped his arms around me, caging me in a fierce hug. He dipped his head until it was beside my ear. In a soft voice, he breathed, "We don't choose the time we get with the ones we love, only the time we don't."

I wriggled in his hold, but he squeezed me tighter. A shudder rolled through me at the memory of all the times he'd done this when the days got too hard, and I'd been ready to give in to my family and go along with whatever cruel plan they'd devised. He'd hugged me, refusing to let me go and reminded me I wasn't like them.

A tear ran down my cheek, leaving a hot trail in its wake.

In this dark hallway, with only my own fears and Creig, I could admit the thing that held me back from giving into the feelings growing in my heart. Fear of losing someone I cared for so deeply that even now I was breaking. Watching my father crumble under the weight of his loss and seeing Bracken in the winter court, I was terrified of what a love like that would do to the last remaining shreds of my soul. And if Jack was human, his short life would be a blink in mine, and at its end, I would be left holding the shattered pieces of my heart together with no one to comfort me. But what if he wasn't human?

"Come on, Love. Meet me in the map room. I have a new strategy to propose."

Creig released his hold, and a chill settled over me. I longed to wallow in my own pain, taking back just a little time for myself, but I'd started on this path for a reason, and I needed to see it through to its end. More than that, the time for hiding from my life was over. Going back to Faerie, seeing just how dire things were for everyone, had been the wake-up I needed.

For three years, I hid from my life, my responsibilities. For three years, I ignored everything that was happening, burying my head in the sand and allowing my kind to suffer.

It was time for me to stop hiding.

-●→(◡◆▲◆●●-

Creig pointed a finger at the pocket entrance to Central Park closest to Dane's headquarters. "If we go out through here, we'll be inside their perimeter. It's a quick jog to the entrance they took you through. With any luck, we can sneak the prisoners out without Dane ever knowing."

Foxglove bent, scanning the map of Central Park.

I glared at the side of his face. I still didn't trust him, but Creig did, and I trusted Creig, so I kept my lips pressed firmly together, waiting for his insight.

"If even a few humans are guarding them, they'll sound the alarm. It's too risky."

Creig laid a hand on the head of one of his axes. "You're forgetting. I have half a dozen soldiers who never swore an oath. Nothing's stopping them from slaughtering the humans before they have time to open their mouths."

A look passed between the two males, and my heart pounded in my chest. Six males with no magic binding them was better odds than I could have imagined. Six orcs against the might of Dane's army might just make this a fair fight.

"Wait."

Both males looked at me.

"Your soldiers are our greatest weapon."

"What do you mean, Love?" Creig arched a brow.

I glanced at Foxglove. *Creig trusts him.* "If we go with my original plan—"

"Sav."

"Wait," I said. "Let me finish." They nodded and I went on. "We approach with an army, and we bring Jack." His name stuck in my throat. "We come under the guise of proposing a trade. Dane will assume our army can't harm them. They'll come expecting us to be weak. They'll try to take Jack and keep their prisoners."

My gaze darted between the two men. "While we pretend to negotiate, four soldiers free the prisoners. Two stay with us. When Dane makes his move, they remind his army we're not helpless."

I glanced between them. "The humans are only brave because they believe us weak. Let them think we could *all* harm them and they'll run screaming." I grinned madly, picturing carnage and death.

"There's one problem with your plan," Jack said, stepping into the room.

My heart skipped a beat and my palms grew clammy. He met my gaze —eyes hard—before he looked past me, speaking to Creig and Foxglove. "My dad won't be satisfied with a trade for me when he sees the orcs you plan to send with me. He'll be prepared to take your soldiers, and he knows exactly how to do it when the enemy can't fight back."

Pain lanced my chest. That dark look in his eyes had never been there before. And I had been the one to put it there.

Creig grunted, appraising Jack. "He can try and take my men."

"He's taken bigger creatures than you." His tone was calm. Too calm. Like the part of him that used to ache for me was gone.

Foxglove scanned the maps again before casting his gaze on Creig. "He's right. Dane's men took Trym."

"Trym," Creig and I gasped at the same time. "But how?" I asked. "Trym is guardian to the autumn court and the oldest Troll alive."

Foxglove shrugged. "Dane has powerful weapons and friends in high places. And more than that, Trym was too powerful to be allowed to guard the entrance without agreeing to the ISHFA laws."

I shook my head. How had our kind ever allowed a guardian meant to protect us to be bound by such a law? With Autumn's pocket entrance unguarded, anyone could wander in.

"What do you propose, Jack?" Creig asked, scratching his head with one of his daggers.

Jack leaned over the table covered in maps, scanning the one of Central Park. "Dane has more than one hundred armed guards ready to attack and an arsenal of iron weapons. You need to draw as many away as possible before you move in." His eyes met mine for the briefest moment. "Stage an attack on one of his outposts far from Central Park to draw them away, using men who are bound by ISHFA laws. I'll go alone to meet Dane." He ran a finger down the map. "If I ask him to meet me here." He stabbed a spot on the map. "Take your six and any others you can spare to free the prisoners. You'll need all the help you can get to carry out the injured. Last I counted, there are fourteen prisons holding creatures in them. If you can spare the men, you should hit them all at the same time. I can tell you where they are."

"We've already freed most of them," Creig said, and my mouth fell open.

"You have?"

"Love. Did you really think I'd leave them? We've only waited to hit

AFF headquarters because we didn't have a plan that kept my men safe while doing it. I lost a soldier last week and I swore to my men I wouldn't let that happen again."

My chest swelled, wetness brimming along my lashes. He'd always planned to help us. He *was* helping us. He just needed Jack. But sending Jack back to his father now, knowing what he could be, irrational terror stole through me. "What happens after you distract Dane?" I asked.

Green eyes burned with some intense emotion I didn't recognize as he searched my face. "Does it matter? Your people will be free, and no one will be harmed."

But what about you?

It's a good plan, Lad." Creig slapped a hand on Jack's shoulder.

Jack winced, but a smile crept onto his face.

I couldn't look away. The smile never reached his eyes.

SIXTY

JACK

I n my room, I slid the loose daggers Poppy had brought me into a leather belt around my waist. Poppy was a sweet little elf who had only glanced once at my round ears before making up her mind and welcoming me into their fairy rebellion. It was the advantage I'd needed all along. How I'd thought Leo, Grace and I could pull it off on our own, I didn't know, but learning all Creig's carefully laid plans over several years, I saw the futility in my efforts. It was as if fate had brought Sav to me so she could bring me to Creig's army.

I'd never thrown a dagger in my life, but there was something comforting about the weight of them on my hips. Like I was finally becoming the person I needed to be.

Sav's beautiful hazel eyes on me in the war room flashed in my mind, making my chest ache. The cut she left behind wasn't clean—it tore every time I breathed. Every memory of her felt like salt rubbed into a wound that wouldn't stop bleeding. None of it had been real. The stinging truth of her words sliced so deep I wasn't sure I'd ever recover. But I couldn't reconcile her words with all the heated looks she'd given me or the electricity that sparked between us when we were near each other.

The memory of her warmth pressed into my side, beneath that tree, as she shared stories of her life in Faerie, and I rubbed her aching feet, mesmerized by the twinkle in her eyes, was burned into my soul.

All an act? No one was that good of an actor. No one could fake wanting me that well. Except maybe she had.

A knock sounded at the door, and I looked up. "Come in."

The man in tweed, Lord Hawthorn, stepped in, glancing around before closing the door behind him. There was something especially other about him. I couldn't put my finger on it. He looked more human than most of the folk I'd met, but his presence dripped with other worldliness.

Standing eye to eye, he was as tall as I was, maybe taller.

"Yes?"

"I've come to warn you—"

"I know Sav is only using me." I cut him off.

He quirked a brow, lips tugging up at the corners. "I will take your word for it, but I was referring to your father."

"What about him?" I slid another dagger in the belt at my hips. Was six enough? There was room for several more, but how many daggers did a person need in a battle? Fake battle, if things went the way we planned. I'd only ever fought hand to hand in sparring sessions and I'd actively avoided learning to use guns. Strangely, I didn't have the same twinge of panic about harming Dane as I did with most other living things.

"He's working with ISHFA."

My hand hovered over another blade, and I looked up. "Explain."

Lord Hawthorn tucked his hand into his pocket and pulled out a cell phone.

"Let me show you."

I had never seen a fairy with a phone before. My mouth fell open as he swiped through images until he stopped on one of Dane leaning close to Janet Glassdon, president of ISHFA. The next picture on the phone was of Janet handing my father an envelope.

While I trusted these fairies with the plan to save the creatures Dane had kidnapped, I hadn't been prepared to share more of my secrets with them. Not yet. That they already knew this one made me wary. What would they do with the information? Could I trust them with my bigger plan? I wasn't sure yet. "So they know each other. New York isn't as big a city as you think."

He swiped again and this time my father was entering ISHFA headquarters, a baseball cap pulled low over his head.

"Each time your father led an attack on the fae, he met with Janet either before—like in the photo above, with the envelope—or after, like in the last photo. We've traced large deposits to his accounts that we believe directly correlate to his attacks."

Leo had come to the same conclusion when he followed the money trail. Hearing it confirmed from this fairy had something sinking in my gut. I'd wanted it to be a lie. With ISHFA backing Dane, it would be a lot harder to take him down.

When Lord Hawthorn left, I sank into a chair. There was no love lost between me and my father, but his single-minded focus had always been centered on one thing. Avenging my mother.

My memories of her had never aligned with Dane's, though. She hated drugs, medicine of any kind. Why would she have begun taking Xcess? The drug had surfaced several years before our realms collided, but no one knew where it had come from. It wasn't until fairies revealed themselves that we learned of its origin. Dane vowed that day to end the creatures who had been responsible for the drug that ultimately killed her.

When I was younger, I'd accepted everything my father told me as fact.

I'd believed that my whole life. But that strange vision on the path wouldn't leave me—her flinching back, the gleam of that rusted pipe. The way his eyes looked. Cold; not broken.

Every day loved ones of those who had become addicted to Xcess arrived at AFF headquarters and though all their stories were unique, they all ended the same. The person became so dependent on the drug, they would rather die than go another day without it.

It cured illness, depression, and alcoholism. Anything that ailed you could be healed with Xcess. I knew the awful truth—only because my father had devoted himself to learning what it was and how it had fallen into my mother's hands. It was made using fairy blood. One drop was enough in the beginning, but like any other drug, eventually you needed more. Addiction grew until it became too expensive or simply inaccessible.

But unlike many other drugs, there was no recovering from Xcess. Once you had a taste, you would do anything for it. It made you feel invincible when it tapped into powers humans never knew they had, granting enhanced senses and control over the elements for a short time. The pain of being utterly human, the absence of all that power was just too much. You would die trying to find that missing piece of yourself again.

None of it fit. Not the symptoms. Not the timeline. Not the truth I'd been fed.

But the alternative, this new idea tumbling around in my mind, didn't align with it either. Not to mention, my father would never raise a hand against my mother. Not that he wasn't capable of acts of violence. I had seen him enraged to the point of murder. But Aconite Clyde was my father's whole world. Before she died, I couldn't remember a time he wasn't smiling, laughing, doting on her.

My mother's death had sent me into a spiral that had taken years to come out of, but it had broken my father. The man who loved her was gone. And maybe he'd been gone a lot longer than I wanted to admit. If Dane had lied about her death, what else had he lied about?

SIXTY-ONE
SAV

I shook out my wrists, praying for a spark of fire. Nothing. Not even a flicker. That one bit of magic I'd used—wasted—on a polar bear and Jack. Now I had nothing but a flicker of glamour and the guilt twisting my insides.

Nervous energy thrummed through me. This was a bad plan. Something would go wrong. We wouldn't get into the basement. Juniper would be dead. Jack would be kidnapped. We would all be taken prisoner and I'd be forced to watch my friends die slow, painful deaths. *Snap out of it, Sav,* I commanded myself. I'd always wanted to be one of those cup-half-full fae, but when it came down to it, that glass looked half empty to me.

A knock sounded at the door and a cold stone dropped in my stomach. One day someone would knock, and it wouldn't fill me with dread. "Yes?"

"It's time."

I swallowed, pulling open the door and meeting Larek's gaze. "Are you coming?"

He nodded and a wide grin broke over his face. "Didn't Dad tell you? I'm one of the six." Larek danced into the room spinning in a circle, pulling his hands, aimed like pistols, out of pockets. Yolmar followed, doing a similar dance and the twins faked a draw, both aiming at one another and shooting. Yolmar grabbed his chest, sinking to his knees and groaning.

A smile tugged at my lips as I fell into one of our old games—shoot first, ask questions never—and pulled out my own fake pistols.

Larek held up his scarred hands, thin white lines crisscrossing them. "You win. Don't shoot."

I dropped my gun, pouting. "No fair." Just for a moment, their light moods had lifted some of my gloom, but even that small reprieve was out of my grasp.

Yolmar hopped up, tucking a braid behind his long, pointed ear, and spinning me around. "You're the best. We wouldn't stand a chance against you." He leaned down several inches, whispering close to my ear. "Sometimes you gotta know when you're beat."

I grabbed his rough, calloused hands. "If it gets dangerous, promise me you'll run. I want to save them, but if it's between you and the prisoners, save yourselves." I met each of their eyes. They were the little brothers I'd never had, even if they hadn't been smaller than me in centuries, and if anything happened to them, I'd never forgive myself.

"Don't worry, Sav." Larek said, black eyes meeting mine.

"We'll be fine against three puny humans," Yolmar finished. "Come on. Dad's waiting in the map room."

I slid my arms between each of their bulky biceps, and we left my room. Trailing the long hall, a swath of raven curls rounded a corner ahead of us.

"Jack!"

He didn't turn, didn't acknowledge me and a stone settled in my stomach. His dark stare flashed in my mind and I squeezed the twin's arms tighter.

"He'll get over it." Larek said beside me.

"Or we pummel him." Yolmar finished.

I smiled weakly at them. If only everything could be solved with a bit of violence.

Stepping into the map room, I disentangled myself from the twins and moved to stand beside Creig. He had dressed for battle, leather straps crossing his chest, a cape trailing over one shoulder. Thick lines of white paint were slashed across his cheeks and a solid black line ran down his scarred forehead to the tip of his nose.

In this attire, he was a fearsome sight. It was easy to imagine our enemies cowering before him as they had so many times at the borders of the spring court. But a memory of the ogre who had fallen in Central Park crowded into my mind, and I exhaled a slow shaky breath. Creig wasn't like that creature. He wasn't bound by ISHFA laws. If Dane and his minions attacked, *he* would fight back.

I laid a hand on his much larger one, lacing my fingers through his.

He looked up, searching my face. "I'll be alright, Love. We'll get them out and get back here safely."

I nodded, emotion swelling in my chest. I stepped forward, wrapping my arms around him. A tear slid down my cheek.

His big arms came around me, and my shoulders relaxed into his touch. The past three years came rushing back, the hurt and rejection of my family. The exile and binding of my magic. The utter loneliness I'd felt in the human world. It pressed against me, weighing me down until I sank against him and let Creig take my burdens just for a moment.

Two enormous bodies crashed into my back, squeezing me against Creig, and I laughed as we stood in the middle of the room, pressed together in one big hug.

When Larek and Yolmar released me, I freed myself from Creig, wiping my cheeks. I searched each of their beautiful, expressive faces, memorizing them and promised myself it wouldn't be another decade before I saw them again.

"No matter what else happens, promise me you'll take care of yourselves." I narrowed my eyes at Creig. "You especially. Nothing brave. If we can't get them out, we'll regroup here and come up with another plan."

"I'll make sure Dane is distracted."

I jumped, twisting to stare at Jack, hovering in the doorway. He was dressed head to toe in black. A perfectly tailored button-down shirt, rolled up to his elbows and a thin leather belt at his waist lined in knives.

His hair was pulled back, showing off the strong line of his freshly shaved jaw and my gaze lingered on his lips. They were set in that firm line he'd adopted since he learned of my deception, and when our eyes met, something jolted through me. His burned with a new intensity I hadn't seen before, and I shuddered. That fire in his eyes—it wasn't human. Not entirely. And part of me wondered, *hoped*, that he wasn't. Because if he wasn't human...

"Jack."

"Savage," he said, moving into the room.

When he stopped on the other side of the table, as far from me as he could get, a chill settled over me.

Foxglove followed, standing beside him and they tipped their heads to the map together. When had they become such good friends?

"Jack. Can I talk to you?"

His gaze snapped to mine, dark and searching. Heat flooded my chest as goosebumps prickled my skin. He didn't speak, just gave a sharp nod, excusing himself from the room, and I followed him out, my heart racing with every step.

In the hall, he spun on me, his jaw clenched tight, and for just a second, the mask he'd donned slipped. There, hidden beneath the anger simmering in his eyes, was something raw. Hurt. The kind of hurt I knew too well. My heart splintered at the sight of it. Instinctively, I raised my hand, running my fingertips along his cheek, searching for some connection.

He flinched under my touch, muscles taut, but he didn't pull away.

"I'm sorry."

The words hung in the air between us, heavy and unfinished. His eyes never left mine, as if waiting—begging—for something more.

"That's it?" he asked, his voice rough with disbelief.

I opened my mouth to respond, but nothing came. The words tangled in my throat. What could I possibly say that would fix this?

He took a step back, the distance between us widening as he shrugged away from my touch. "Unbelievable."

"Wait." The word escaped me before I could think, and Jack froze, his gaze snapping back to mine.

My lips parted, but I hesitated. The truth clawed its way up my throat. I should protect him. I should lie. But I was losing him, and I couldn't—I couldn't let him walk away. "Since we met, I've tried to see you as nothing more than a means to an end," I forced out. "Because..."

His eyes, once again on mine, were unreadable.

"Because if I didn't..." I inhaled sharply, my pulse a frantic beat beneath my skin. "If I didn't, I'd have to admit you mean something more." My voice trembled. "That you've become...a friend."

The air between us changed, the charged tension evaporating into something cold. Hard. Jack's eyes darkened, fury flickering in their depths.

"Friends." The word landed like a slap. He stepped closer, his breath a heated whisper against my skin. "I've never wanted to be your friend, Sav."

My breath hitched. Heat radiated from him, burning every inch of my skin. He was so close, and yet not close enough. His hand slid down the wall beside me, caging me in, and my pulse thundered in my ears.

"I've wanted so many things from you," Jack said, voice low and rough, his eyes tracing the shape of my lips. "So many things." His gaze flicked back to mine, searing me alive. "I've wanted to taste you. To feel your body against mine." His breath ghosted over my mouth, making me shudder. "I've wanted you to take all this tension between us and finally do something about it."

A nervous laugh escaped me and my lips touched his. A spark ignited low in my belly, and I pressed my head back against the wall, fighting the pull. "I...can't. I can't," I whispered, though every fiber of my being screamed to say the opposite.

Jack's hand hovered an inch from my face, his fingers trembling. "May I touch you?"

My heart hammered against my ribs, threatening to break free. I should say no. I should—

"Yes."

His finger brushed my cheek, gentle as a whisper, tucking a strand of hair behind my ear. He didn't stop there, though. His touch continued, tracing the line of my jaw, the curve of my neck, down to my collarbone, leaving a trail of heat in its wake. My breath hitched, and the fire he stoked within me burned hotter, fiercer, until I was set ablaze with it.

I could hear his heart pounding, matching mine, and for a moment, all I wanted was to close the gap between us. To give in to the longing, the need that had been building for so long. But fear held me still. Fear of what would happen if I let go. Fear of what it would mean for both of us.

"Do you know what I want most of all?"

"What?" I breathed.

"Your heart."

The second the words left his mouth, I was lost. I surged forward, capturing his lips with mine.

His arms wrapped around me, his grip unyielding, as he kissed me back, hard and desperate. His fingers tangled in my hair, tugging just enough to make me gasp, and I tasted the wintergreen on his breath—cool and intoxicating.

This was Jack. And I was falling. Falling too fast, too far, with no way to stop.

His kiss devoured me, swallowing me whole. I was a storm of desire and need and he was the lightning setting my very being on fire. His hand slipped to my neck, cupping my head gently and my body melted into his, as his other hand traced the line of my back, wrapping around my waist. A swell of emotion rose in me as his warmth bled over my skin, feeding a fire I'd waited my whole life to feel.

When he released me, my head fell back into his cradling hand and stars danced at the edges of my vision. Every fiber of my being radiated heat as I looked up into those bright, shimmering green eyes.

A soft smile played at the edges of his mouth, and warmth evaporated from my neck as he released my head, tucking a curl behind my ear.

"I've wanted to do that for a long time," he said, leaning back.

I went with him, loath to leave the comfort of his warmth.

His arm tightened around me and his gaze devoured me almost as hungrily as his mouth had.

A throat cleared. I froze. Jack didn't. His hand lingered on my waist, hot and unrepentant.

I spun to face Foxglove, heat creeping onto my cheeks.

Jack's warmth radiated along my back.

Foxglove's gaze dipped to my swollen lips, then trailed up over my shoulder.

I didn't turn, didn't want to know what he saw on Jack's face. I had let my selfish feelings get the better of me and the truth of those feelings was painted on my face. I'd had one chance to set Jack free–to keep him safe–and I hadn't taken it.

SIXTY-TWO

JACK

The taste of Sav's lips lingered, burned into my memory like a brand. Her soft moan, the way she melted against me—I'd never forget it. But just because that kiss had changed something in me didn't mean anything had changed for her.

"Jack."

I blinked, gaze moving from the strands of auburn hair falling over Sav's face to General Creig.

"Yes?" They were all staring at me and I cleared my throat. "I'll enter beside Central Park and call Dane. I'll tell him to meet me near Turtle Pond."

"And what's your plan for the Bitter Wraith?" Creig folded his arms over a barrage of weapons strapped to his chest. In his battle paint and war gear, he was a fearsome sight.

"I'll offer her the fairy marigolds."

"Fae marigold blossoms," Creig corrected.

"Right." I kept forgetting that only humans called them fairies. They referred to themselves as fae. I must have sounded so ignorant to them all. Why had Sav never said anything?

My gaze drifted to her once more. She whispered something to Lord Hawthorn, pointing to a map and he nodded. His finger traced the path hers had taken and when their hands brushed against one another, heat simmered in my veins. Of all the men I'd encountered in Sav's life, he was the only one who hadn't staked some claim on her. Why did that seem to make him the most dangerous?

My thoughts turned dark when Prince Kaspar's aquamarine gaze, watching her with a cold possessiveness, flashed in my mind.

"And if she rejects your gift?" General Creig prompted.

My focus shifted with some effort back to the general. "I'll leave Turtle Pond and follow the path away from the AFF compound toward Times Square."

General Creig leveled me with a heavy stare. "Remember. You want him to bring as many of his men with him as possible. Tell him exactly what I said."

I nodded. Dane was no one's fool. But his hate for the fae would twist his judgment. When I dangled an orc general in front of him, he would stop at nothing to have him and that's exactly what our group was counting on.

We left the war room, Creig heading our party. His twin sons came next, followed by two more large orcs with just as many weapons strapped over their bodies as the others. The quintet towered over all of us, looking menacing as they crowded into the hall.

I fell back—beside Sav—and glanced over at her. She had changed into tan leather pants and a matching vest lined with rows of knives. I'd thought I chose wisely when I strapped half a dozen knives to my new fae belt, but she was sporting at least fifty and as my gaze shifted to the backs of the orcs leading the way, I suddenly felt woefully unprepared.

Sav's fingers found mine, lacing them together and she squeezed.

The small act sent a rush of desire through me.

To say I had been devastated when her confession had fallen so callously from her lips would have been an understatement, but in the hall, watching her struggle to form the words I'd so desperately hoped she felt, I knew she was scared. It wasn't a cold heart that made her push people away. It was a wounded one. She had been used over and over again in her life and built a wall around her heart to protect herself. In that moment, I saw who she truly was. She cared deeply and it terrified her.

She stopped short, pulling her hand free. My heart thudded—was this where the act ended?

But when she looked up, I knew. There would be no more pretending between us.

"What's wrong?"

She tugged a stray curl from her long braid, wrapping it around her finger, and bit her lower lip. "I don't want to say it, but I'm just going to, because too much is on the line."

I reached for her hand, but she pulled it back and my stomach hollowed out.

She exhaled a long sigh. "If your father captures you, he'll want to know how to get into Faerie. He could hurt you to get that information."

I flinched. "He wouldn't." She stared, unblinking. And I was forced to accept that she may be right. I wanted to argue, memories of father son basketball games and bedtime stories resurfacing in my mind, but those had stopped long ago. "Sav, I'd never tell him. You can't think..."

Sav searched my face for long moments, her brows bunching tightly over her brow.

I held my breath, waiting to see if she was finally ready to start trusting me. I wasn't sure if my still bruised heart could take it if she knifed me again, but I was wholly dependent on her willingness to lower those walls.

I held out my hand, and this time, she took it. She looked down at our interlaced fingers and I squeezed, praying this woman wasn't about to shatter my heart again. Her brows relaxed, a small v still indenting her fore-head, but she nodded.

"Just promise me you won't tell him how to get into Faerie." Sav's eyes were so full of hope, and it did something to my heart. She'd never looked at me like she wanted anything from me before, like she trusted me enough to ask.

Hazel warned me that Sav didn't trust easily, that everyone in her life had betrayed her. But somehow, she was willing to give me that gift. It left me speechless. I nodded, swallowing the lump in my throat. "Never," I choked out, and I meant it. If the world turned on its head and Dane Clyde chose to torture his son to learn the truth, I would endure it and Sav's perfect, trusting gaze, would live in my mind through all of it.

A strange tingling sensation speared my chest and I rubbed it absently with my free hand. Sav's gaze darted to my hand, but she said nothing as we resumed walking.

As planned, Sav, Creig, Foxglove and the others went through first. We waited fifteen minutes, giving them time to make it to the side entrance of AFF headquarters before we stepped through a white, shimmering light, Larek and Yolmar grabbing my arms as we breached the pocket and returned to Earth. Portal travel was never the same. Each crossing was new —this one slammed me into Earth with such force the soles of my feet tingled on impact.

We landed inside Central Park very near the main entrance and far enough away from Sav's group that we wouldn't immediately alert any of Dane's patrol to their presence should they spot us.

A dozen rifles clicked as men shouted upon our arrival and I looked up, meeting cold grey eyes.

"Hi Dane."

SIXTY-THREE
DANE

SEVERAL HOURS EARLIER

"They're going to hit Long Island."

I folded my arms over my chest, leaning back in my chair. "Are you sure?"

"Yes. We have eyes on Yolmar and Larek. They were seen less than an hour ago traveling with an unknown orc along the eastern seaboard. If you plan to stop them, you need to get your men over there now.

Janet showing up at my compound for the first time meant one thing —she was getting too cocky. And I'd had enough of this bitch thinking she could tell me what to do.

I ran a hand over my chin, stubble scraping the calloused pads of my thumb and forefinger. "I don't like leaving the compound unguarded."

Janet slid a hand in her pocket, pulling out her phone, a photo on the screen, and set it down on the desk.

I tipped forward, uncrossing my arms as my vision went red. The fae whom I'd learned had taken Jack into Faerie and was pleading her case at the royal courts, was standing in Times Square, her arms wrapped around none other than the orc general.

I slammed a hand down on the table.

Janet's cool voice raked nails over my exposed nerves. "She's working with them."

I shot to my feet, fists flexing. My shirt strained across my shoulders as I fought the urge to put my fist through the table. "They have my son?!"

Janet's glassy eyes met mine, not an ounce of fear in them. She was showing all the signs of using, but somehow, she hadn't tipped over into madness. I'd never heard of a human taking Xcess and not losing themself to it. My once beloved wife, Aconite, would have loved to study her. To learn why this human was so unaffected while so many others could only withstand the periods of withdrawal between doses for a matter of minutes near their end.

I shoved the thought down—the sound of her beautiful laugh echoing in my mind.

"We believe he's planning to hit your warehouse tonight and clean out all your extra ammo. He means to split your forces."

"Fuck the fairy," I snapped. "Where's my son?"

Ice crept across Janet's fingers. She was using Xcess—had to be. Only a human who was using had access to fae magic. If she'd been born in Faerie, she'd be some sort of water fairy. But humans got the bastardized version when they dabbled.

I swiped the phone up, holding it to my face. There was no sign of Jack in the image and no indication he was with her, but every report coming in from my network–and Morgan–said they had been inseparable since arriving in Faerie. ISHFA had even placed a ridiculous bounty on Jack's head for claiming he'd broken law number one.

Jack wasn't dumb enough to fall for one of them. He'd fuck around, sure—but feelings? Emotional attachment? Not a chance. In twenty-five years, he'd never let a woman get that close.

"Stay close to home tonight. What you're looking for might come knocking." She leaned forward, plucking her phone from my grasp and turned, marching from the room.

I glared at the back of her raven hair as she slid through the door to my office. When she was gone, I stared down at stacks and stacks of papers on my desk. Reports, images, text chains, deep web searches of every known fairy sympathizer's recent conversations. None of it had told me anything.

Because no one could have pulled off a disappearing act like this but the orc fucking, general.

Let them come for me. I'd welcome them with a blood-soaked stage—and the satyr as my main act.

SIXTY-FOUR

SAV

B ack pressed against the wall, I watched the steady rise and fall of Creig's chest, taking comfort in his confidence. He'd led several rescue missions and was painfully familiar with Dane's movements and the movements of his troops.

Anger flared to life in me when the memory of our heated argument just before entering the portal flashed in my mind.

"You already planned this attack? I hissed, fury burning my throat.

Creig didn't flinch. "I needed to be sure about the human. If you didn't care for him, I would've used him like any other pawn."

What a fool I'd been—my feelings weren't the danger. They were the shield that kept Jack safe from those who would have used him.

Creig raised one hand, squeezing it into a fist, then stretched his fingers wide and tipped them forward. A line of orcs darted across the street, swallowed by the darkness and I balanced on the balls of my feet, preparing to follow.

"There's no shame in letting us handle this one, Love."

I glanced up, narrowing my eyes at Creig. "And let you have all the glory?"

He grinned, flashing sharp canines at me. "Didn't think so. But I had to ask." He broke into a run, and I dashed after him.

A thrill of nervous anticipation raced in my veins as, for one glorious moment, I envisioned meeting Dane in the alley outside his prison. I'd let my daggers fly, pin him to the wall and take my time removing them from his bleeding corpse. Shaking the thought, and the bloodlust, from my mind, I slammed against the wall as voices rang down the long alley.

I spared a glance at the building across from Dane's headquarters, a chill ghosting over my skin as I passed. I didn't slow. Just kept moving past the broken windows and the wrongness bleeding from that building.

We halted outside the barred door. Murz produced a wrench and twisted the bolts without a word.

I gaped as he handled the metal object. His fingers didn't burn or sizzle and my brow furrowed. The large plastic bar, painted to look metal, fell away from the door, bouncing to the ground. It made almost no sound, but I glanced around, swallowing as I searched both ends of the darkened alley. Creig frowned at Murz, but said nothing as he tugged the door open and slipped inside.

Hairs on the back of my neck rose and I prayed to Mab we weren't walking into a trap.

Foxglove had lent his phone to Jack to make the call and none of the orcs had one so we had no way of knowing what was happening with Jack and the twins. My stomach twisted as I tried to reassure myself Dane would never harm his son.

The hallway stank of scorched hair and iron. My skin prickled. My feet froze halfway down the stairs. I'd been here before. I knew what came next.

Shouts at the bottom of the stairs kicked my heart into overdrive and I reached for two daggers, palming one in each hand. The feel of them steadied me and I breathed in and out, reaching the bottom step in time to see one of the three little pigs—Jim—fly into a wall and slide down it silently.

Oliver and Brian were locked in battle, but the fight was over quickly when Murz thrust a wicked-looking knife into Oliver's neck and Creig reached Brian, yanking his head back and slicing a blade cleanly across his throat.

My gaze lingered, with sick fascination on the blood pumping rhythmically out of Brian's neck as he fell from Creig's hold to the floor. Creig gave another hand signal to two of his soldiers, wiping the back of his slick blade across his thigh and moving quickly to the back of the room.

"Clear," someone called from the top of the other stairs, and I glanced back to see another orc guarding the stairs leading back out to the street. His face was familiar and all at once I knew where I'd seen him before. The night we'd been trapped in my old building, he and another had been the ones who stepped up beside me, ensuring I and as many others as possible escaped the flames.

Creig. He'd been watching over me all along. Me and the others.

My gaze shifted to the cages at the center of the room and I let out a defeated sigh. There were less than two dozen fae standing or staring up at us. Several of the cages were empty and not one was a sandy-haired satyr with delicate curling horns.

Murz leaped into action, moving to the first cage and tearing the door wide. It spurred me forward and I lifted my dagger, prying open the first set of bars near me. Shocks of pain sparked along my fingers where they met iron, but I ignored it, moving to the next cage and doing the same. I held out a hand to a naiad whose navy scales were faded to indigo blue and she clasped my hand, pulling herself up. "Have you seen Juniper? A golden-haired satyr?"

She shook her head, running past me and the orc by the door took her hand, motioning to several others gathered nearby who could stand and led them away.

Another of Creig's soldiers positioned himself in his place and several more who could walk were freed and escorted out.

In less than a minute, we'd freed most of those who could walk without aid.

I scanned the cages, opening them as I went, but none held Juniper. My heart sank when I moved to the smaller cages, finding several gray, life-less bodies crumpled in corners. I let out a whimper as I reached the cage with the pixie I'd tried to save.

"I'm so sorry," I breathed. Her gaze was vacant, a broken wing wrapped protectively over her still form. A tear slid down my cheek as I pried her door open and lifted her tiny form from the cage. My skin popped and sizzled, but I ignored it, shoulders shaking as I carried her to the orc standing by the door. "We can't leave them. They would want to be in Faerie. They wouldn't want to spend eternity down here. In a cage."

The orc nodded and held out his hands. Gently, I laid her in his palms, sniffling as her wing twisted at an odd angle. I straightened it, holding in a sob. "Wait. Let me get the others."

I raced back to the small cages, popping each one open, a warm shoulder bumped mine and I looked left to find Murz crouching beside me. I ripped tiny doors from their hinges, reaching in to lift small bodies from the floor. A group of tiny tinks had died huddled together and I hefted them out gently, careful not to untangle any of their entwined limbs. "We were too late," I cried.

Helping me to my feet, Murz flattened his palms, and I laid all the tiny bodies I'd collected on them side by side. "We'll get them home," he promised.

I nodded, wiping the back of my hand against my cheek and watched him go, pain spearing my chest. I found the kelpie, shriveled in a corner of his cage and slid an arm under his shoulder, lifting him gingery. He grunted, wet, gurgling breaths slipping from his lips, but we moved toward the door, and soon, someone was helping him, along with several other severely injured fae, out of the basement.

A blur of movement at the top of the stairs. I froze. Was it Dane's men? And then—a tufted hand swiped for me.

"Juniper," I gasped, but her eyes were wrong. Vacant. "Juniper. It's me, Sav. Stop!"

But she wasn't stopping; she was running straight for me, blades slicing air, and I gasped as metal swiped inches from my nose.

A massive axe sailed through the air, embedding itself in the wall behind Juniper, catching her shirt sleeve, pinning her in place. I gasped in horror as the blade in her free hand swung again, and it seemed her target was...me. I backed up, giving her space and Foxglove wedged himself between us, cursing soundly as the scalpel dug into his arm. He grabbed her free wrist, pinning it down and Creig appeared beside him, yanking the axe from the wall. Foxglove grabbed the other arm, forcing her arms down.

"Juniper?"

Creig yanked out the scalpel embedded in Foxglove's arm and snatched the other from Juniper's fist.

Foxglove wrapped his arms around her tightly and held fast even as she tried to wedge her horns into his chin.

"Get her out of here. Poppy will know what to do," Creig said, and Foxglove nodded, lifting Juniper off her feet and carrying her out the way we'd come.

"What's wrong with her?" I asked, watching her go.

"I don't know, Love, but we don't have time to worry about that now."

I nodded, sparing a final glance backward as Juniper was carried from the room, my chest aching for her. What had they done to make her try to kill us all? I prayed to Mab we could reverse the damage once we got her to safety. She was alive at least. Anything else we could put right.

My focus shifted to the cages lining the room. No time. There was no time to worry about Juniper when Dane and his men could arrive at any moment. There were four of us now that Foxglove had gone, and we each worked as quickly as we could, prying open doors and dragging out limping, bloody creatures.

"Sav."

I looked up at Creig, wiping my cheeks.

"The wood nymph is too weak to move. She's asking for you."

A sob burned in my throat. She was waxen and gray, lips shriveled to reveal bark-like teeth. I wrapped a hand around her brittle branch, careful not to disturb the final remaining leaf. She expelled a long breath, eyes cracking a fraction.

"You came back for us," she croaked.

Hot tears slid down my cheek. "Too late, I think."

Her dried lips moved, bark flaking off as it dusted her exposed roots. "Did you save them?"

I glanced at the empty cages around the room. "The ones we could."

Her rough fingers wrapped around mine. "Did you unite our kind against.—" she coughed. "A tyrant?"

"We're just a group of fae." I said, swiping at my cheeks. "We haven't changed anything."

The nymph's grip tightened, and she yanked me closer. "You will."

Her chest rattled and I leaned back searching her face. I gasped as something brushed my arm and I looked down, stifling as sob as her final remaining leaf wafted lazily to the floor.

"Sav. We have to go."

I searched the nymph's face, sniffling as another tear streaked down my face. "We can't leave her."

Creig nodded, holding out his arms and gingerly, I tugged the lifeless creature out of the cage, careful not to let her touch metal. She wouldn't feel it now, but I would. As I felt the loss of every other creature we'd been too late to save.

I backed up, stepping over the lifeless form of one of the three pigs who'd dragged me down here the night I learned of this place and I spat on the ground beside him. I would have liked to be the one to run him through, all three of them, but bound as I was from harming humans, I would have to settle for being present to witness their deaths.

Creig scooped the nymph into his arms and I followed, casting a last glance around the darkened room, ensuring we weren't leaving any others behind. I wouldn't let them use the dead to strengthen their cause. Tonight, we left no one behind.

-●→(◡◆∩◆●●-

Back in the missing spring court forest, fae moved quickly, finding rooms for each of the injured folk and I scanned their faces, exhaling a long, exhausted sigh. We'd managed to save all who still lived, apart from the nymph—heaviness settled in my chest at her loss—but so many of the creatures who had been imprisoned when I left only a few weeks before were already gone.

"Have Larek and Yolmar returned with the human yet?" I asked a passing fawn. She shook her head, dashing away, arms full of bandages.

Several more fae raced by carrying pastes and salves and a group of orcs hefted a kettle filled with soup and enough bowls to feed a hundred fae.

Larek, Yolmar and Jack were all that consumed my mind and I would go mad with worry if I didn't find something to distract me until they were back. Spying Murz slinking between trees, I moved on silent feet, stopping in a clearing as he picked up a shovel, joining soldiers digging deep trenches beside a row of already-filled graves.

His eyes widened when he saw me.

"You shouldn't be here, Lady."

I'm not a healer," I said, wiping my cheeks. "But I can say goodbye to the ones we couldn't save."

"The number would have been far greater if you hadn't fought for them."

I took Murz's hand. His grip was steady—like Creig's. They'd both been there in my darkest moments, even if I hadn't seen it.

"Sav!"

I looked up, chest expanding as Larek raced for me, Yolmar close on his heels. I exhaled my first real breath since returning, seeing their uninjured faces.

Larek reached me and ice drenched my veins as I met his anguished gaze.

"What is it? What's wrong?"

Yolmar slid to a stop beside him and they both stood for a moment, frozen with some news too terrible to speak aloud.

I looked between them. *Jack.* My knees buckled.

Larek caught me.

"He's alive," Yolmar whispered.

"But ISHFA has him."

My heart stuttered in my chest. If they found out the truth about him... if he *wasn't* human, they wouldn't just imprison him. They'd dissect him. And I couldn't protect him from that.

SIXTY-FIVE
KASPAR

Memphe hopped through the air shield to my study and stood, a shudder rolling through him.

"What is it, Memphe, you know how I hate it when you hover."

"We found them," he said, webbed fingers clenched around a long silver tube.

"Where?"

"AFF headquarters. The rescue was successful." Relief flickered, then died as Memphe added, "They vanished after. Into Central Park Zoo."

"Vanished?" I stood, pacing. "And not one of my spies followed them?"

He licked his eye.

"Not Twila? Not Kila?"

"No, Your Majesty."

"Then you didn't find her. You lost her."

He flinched and I swallowed down the anger. Water fae were unaccustomed to emotion. It was a fact I knew well. Some defective part of me I'd worked hard to quell over the centuries. Still, no matter how I worked to keep the facade of cool indifference my kind was known for, it found its way to the surface.

Perhaps it was the true reason my uncle never sought to bring me into the fold. He had worked closely with my father, creating one of the most effective spy networks in history, but upon my father's death, my uncle had not continued our alliance, choosing instead to rival us without so much as an explanation.

My once soft heart had fractured at his callousness, but so many centuries later, I had finally frozen the heart our kind were never meant to have.

"Keep looking. And Memphe...Tell Twila and her sister to grow a pair of legs and search every inch of that zoo. I don't care what they have to do to find her."

He nodded, hopping away and disappeared into the castle to bring my message to my most faithful spy twins.

Dropping heavily into my chair, I unrolled the scroll reading it quickly. Another pocket entrance—gone. Five years ago, the lakes of Autumn had sealed themselves from my court, making it impossible for any of my spies to enter. I hadn't known why then.

Now, Winter's waters were closing one by one.

I crumpled the letter in my fist.

It was time to pay a visit to Hazel.

Sixty-Six

Sav

We found Creig in the map room, scanning a document. He looked up, rolling the parchment and wrapping a bit of silk around it. Larek released me, but Yolmar squeezed my arm tighter, as we came to stand beside his father.

"Creig."

He held up a hand. "I know what you're going to ask, Love, and I wish I could say yes—"

"Then say it. I won't stand by while they hurt him."

"Lord Hawthorn told you of his father's connection to them. Do you think he'll let ISHFA kill Jack?"

"Dad." Yolmar laid a hand on his father's shoulder. "We have to try."

Creig hissed through his teeth. "We don't owe the human our lives and that's what we'll be giving if we go into ISHFA headquarters bent on taking one of their prisoners."

"Dad," Larek echoed.

Creig slammed a fist down on the table. "This isn't some secret mission against humans. The ISHFA is backed by some of the most powerful fae royals. And they have Morgan. There would be nowhere we would be safe."

Yolmar and Larek glanced at me. Each harsh word he spoke was a knife to my chest, but he was right. I wouldn't trade any of them for Jack. Only I had been responsible for putting him in danger and only I could get him out of it. I nodded.

"Sav." Creig held a hand out.

I stared down at it, watching the edges blur. "You're right. I would never forgive myself if you were arrested."

"You can't go, Love."

I wiped my cheek, squaring my shoulders as I met his stare. "I understand your concern, but it's not your decision. I won't bring him here. I promise."

"A trip to ISHFA headquarters is one way, Sav."

The memory of Jack's breath, hot against my mouth as his lips crashed into mine surfaced, and my heart fractured. We'd only just begun to explore what could be between us. I couldn't leave him there to die. Maybe. Maybe it was a one-way trip, but there was something I could do to even the odds.

"I owe you, Creig. For everything you've done, and you'll never know how grateful I am that you were always there for me when no one else was."

He shook his head but made no move to stop me as I untangled my arm from Yolmar's.

"Sav, you can't go alone." Yolmar said, as I turned.

"We'll come with you." Larek called, as I reached the door.

"Like hell you will," Creig growled, and I didn't turn to see if either of the twins would argue.

I raced from the room, rounding the corner and stopping outside a door at the end of the hall. No one followed and I knocked softly before entering. "Juniper?"

I stepped in, glancing around the dark space and flipped on a light.

I dropped to my knees. "Juniper?"

She didn't blink. Her eyes locked on the wall. Her curls were brushed, the dirt and grime cleaned from her hair, as if she–or someone–had taken the time to wash away the blood and gore from the AFF, but her body was frozen.

I touched her wrist.

Quickly, too quickly for even my mind to process, she moved and I gasped at the pain. Releasing her, I wrapped my hands around cold metal protruding from my side.

Juniper moved again, grabbing another blade from the sheath around my waist and raised it to strike. I reached for her arms, but she swiped at me, just as she had at Foxglove in the prison and blood welled along my fingers.

"Juniper, stop!"

She swiped again and I ducked out of her path, grabbing two of my daggers. Creig had pinned her to the wall with one of his axes, narrowly missing skin, but I wasn't sure my aim would be as good when she moved like some possessed creature, and I threw up my blades just in time to deflect her next attack.

"Juniper. It's me. Sav. We saved you. You're not at the AFF anymore," I panted, dodging another blow.

She swiped again and I backed up, grunting as the pain in my side radiated down my leg. My finger wounds were healing quickly, but I feared the one in my side had struck something vital. She'd meant it as a killing blow.

I reached the doorframe and slipped out into the hall. "Someone, help! Help me with Juniper!"

Heavy steps sounded down the hall, and I dodged two more blows before Foxglove appeared and wrapped his arms around Juniper. She struggled in his hold and he glanced over his shoulder at me. "Get the knife."

I lunged forward, tearing it from her iron grip. It clattered to the floor and he backed her into the room, not looking back again. I watched as he sat her down in the chair, binding her in invisible magical rope. Long fingers caged her face, and he stared into her eyes.

"Juniper. Look at me. Sav is your friend. We don't harm friends."

"What's wrong with her?"

Foxglove's gaze never left Juniper's as he spoke. "She's been drugged. Something magical that implants false motivations in her mind. I've seen it before."

Gingerly, I touched my side, wincing at the searing pain radiating from the knife. "Can it be reversed?

"With time. And quiet."

I leaned against the doorframe, inhaling shallowly

Foxglove glanced at me. "Go get that taken care of. I'll stay with her."

I nodded, swallowing as I backed into the hall and frowned. Foxglove's jaw slackened as he brushed a knuckle down Juniper's cheek, his voice dropping to a whisper I barely heard. His fingers trembled.

His soothing words followed me down the hall as I stopped in the medic room, scanning the empty space. With so many injured fae in residence, I hadn't expected anyone to be here, but a fae could hope. Alone in the room, I ground my jaw. This was going to hurt.

Tearing the shirt free of the wound, I gagged as it bumped the edge of the blade protruding from my side and tossed the bits of fabric down on the counter. Scanning its surface, I found a bowl of crushed spadeleaf already prepared and scooped a handful of the paste onto my fingers.

My vision tunneled as I pulled. The pain was white hot, and for one excruciating moment, I forgot how to breathe.

I slumped against the table, inhaling shallowly as the worst of the pain ebbed. I lifted a shaking hand, scooping another handful of paste out of the bowl and smeared it over my wound.

Retracing my steps down the hall, I glanced at Juniper's room before moving to my own. I changed quickly, tightening my bodice, staring at my reflection. Soon, I'd don a crown of lies. If this was what it took to get him back, I'd wear it.

I was willing to sell my freedom—for Jack. And not just because he mattered to me. Because he'd risked his life for our kind and now he would have to pay for it.

Foxglove and Creig would help Juniper. But for what I had to do next, I'd be on my own.

SIXTY-SEVEN

SAV

As I'd known he would, Kaspar appeared moments after I stepped through the pocket entrance into Central Park Zoo. Some invisible tether I couldn't put words to made me uncomfortably aware of his nearness. It must have something to do with our newly sealed bargain.

He stalked toward me, murder in his cold eyes. "Where have you been?"

My fists clenched at my sides. "I can't tell you."

Kaspar reached me, lifting my hand to his mouth and brushing a soft kiss over my knuckles. "I was worried."

I gasped in mock shock. "Prince Kaspar has feelings?"

He squeezed my fingers. "I thought you were captured again."

I exhaled a soft sigh, something uncomfortable swimming in my chest. I had said I'd never lie to Kaspar, yet I was prepared to do just that. Was I choosing wrong? Thoughts of Jack being tortured—killed—bubbled up in my mind and I shook the guilt away. This was for Jack. If Kaspar couldn't forgive me, I'd live with it.

"No. I rescued the fae trapped by Dane and as promised, I'm prepared to follow through with our bargain."

Kaspar's brows rose. "Just like that?"

I glanced around at crumbling brick and overgrown paths. "There's nothing left for me in Faerie and I never belonged here. It's time for me to go home." The word home was sour on my tongue. I'd never thought of Kaspar's world as my home and I couldn't imagine ever thinking of it as anything other than a prison of my own making, but it was a price I'd pay to save Jack.

A pair of naiads in matching navy scales appeared behind Kaspar, walking on unsteady legs and one whispered in Kaspar's ear. His mouth flattened into a thin line and he returned his gaze to mine, releasing my hand. "Come. It's not safe here and this requires further discussion."

He turned, his two naked spies falling in line behind him and I rushed to follow. Wasting no time with explanations, he dove into a shallow stream quickly followed by the two naiads and I jumped in after.

Underwater, his cool fingers found mine, tugging me down. We sank far enough that light sifted through murky water and I glanced sideways at naiads drifting lazily. They paid us no mind as we descended, sinking until we reached the bottom and I kicked my legs, propelling myself though the entrance to Faerie and into the bright, clear water of my realm.

When we reached the shore, Kaspar dragged me from the water and I stumbled to my knees rethinking my wardrobe choice.

"What an impractical clothing choice, Salvia."

I hissed, glancing around the lakeshore.

"Calm yourself, princess. No one is near."

I struggled to my feet, glaring at Kaspar's perfectly dry pants, wishing that I had a sliver of my magic. Layers of skirts would chafe and rub as we trekked to the spring court palace. At least Kaspar had brought me through inside our border. I could take the dress off...

I reached for the sleeve, when Kaspar transformed, shifting into the beautiful kelpie I loved so dearly and snorted at me.

"I'm wet."

He huffed in exasperation. I rolled my eyes but climbed up. Every moment we wasted was a moment Jack could be suffering. Wrapping my fingers in his seaweed mane, Kaspar took off at a gallop and warm, midday sun beat down on us, as the wind whipped my clothing dry.

●→)(�W●∩◆●●

We reached the palace in less than three hours and though my hair had dried into something resembling a dark red powder puff, my clothes were only slightly damp. I left Kaspar in his appointed rooms, promising him more answers after I'd made myself presentable and raced to my room.

Swinging the door wide, I ran to the closet, tugging out the first gown I found and began stripping.

"I found your bag."

I glanced up, eyes widening. "Hazel."

She closed the door behind her, magicking it locked, and set my shredded bag on the bed. "What are you doing with Mab's crystal, Sav?"

"You looked through my bag?"

She held up her hands, sitting beside it. "You can't expect me to go searching through mountains of snow for something and not be curious about what's inside."

I glared at her, tugging my bodice over my breasts. "It was none of your business."

She shot me a look. "It absolutely *is* my business, and my court's."

I ran my fingers through my frizzy mane, trying to comb out some of the tangles. "Can you help me with these laces?"

Hazel stood, swaying her hips as she moved. "Are you truly doing it? Are you going to marry him?" She stopped behind me and I leaned against the table as she tugged my laces.

I bit my lip. "Yes."

She yanked hard, making me gasp. The knife wound was mostly healed. Mostly. "How can you do it? I know you care for Jack."

She yanked again, but this time my gasp wasn't from physical pain. "It's the only way to get my magic back." Silence fell as she finished tying the laces and stepped back. I spun to face her expecting condemnation, but instead, I saw only sadness. "What are you doing here?" I asked.

Hazel's fingers toyed with her tail. Ignoring my question, she said, "I've always been jealous of you."

"Me?" I snorted.

"Yeah. You. You could have gone along with your family's wishes. Married a prince, made them proud and lived your life in comfort." She reached forward, running a hand over my wild hair. "Instead, you chose the hard path because you believed in your dream that much."

She spun me around, running long blue nails through my unruly hair. Her angry tugs at my snarls tore at my scalp, and I opened my mouth to protest, but she continued, "If this is what you want, tell me now, and I won't say another word."

Our eyes met in the vanity mirror, and I looked away. "It's what I want."

She pulled my hair, snapping my head back. "Don't lie."

"Ow, Hazel. I'm not. I want my magic, and this is the only way to get it."

She wouldn't understand giving up freedom for a human. She didn't know the first thing about sacrifice for those you loved.

"Alright. I'm done."

"No, Hazel. Wait."

She slid her fingers from my hair and held out a hand. "Let's get you married."

--- • → (~ ♦ ʌ ♦ ●● ---

A riot of butterflies swarmed in my belly as we entered the throne room. Kaspar stood rigidly, watching me approach. Alder's gaze trailed hungrily over me, but I knew it was the power he craved. My sister sat straighter when I reached the bottom step and dipped my chin.

Hazel released my arm and backed up. Kaspar took her place frowning at me.

My sister's eyes narrowed as she took me in. Her brow rose in challenge as if even now, she expected me to have some trick up my sleeve. "So that's it. You're ready to do your duty; help your court?"

"Yes."

She opened her mouth but Alder spoke, cutting her off. "Wonderful. When is the happy date?"

"Now." I snapped.

Kaspar's arm went taught in mine and his gaze burned into the side of my face. "I'd like a moment with my betrothed."

I faced Alder, ignoring his request. "I'm ready. Give me my magic and we'll do it right now."

I tensed under Kaspar's unwavering stare but held my back straight.

"Oh, I don't think so. My terms were very clear. Marry your prince and then you'll get your magic."

My eyes narrowed on my sister. "It's done, Sage. The paperwork is signed. I will marry him the moment you unbind me."

She crossed her arms over her chest, nose lifting high. "No."

"Dew drop, don't you think you're being irrational?" Alder laid a hand on his wife's stiff arm.

Her gaze swiveled to him and her brows dropped low. "I think my sister is none of your concern."

Alder's face contorted into one of rage. Sage's eyes widened, knowing she'd gone too far. She leaned back and the air in the room grew stifling with her fear. Anger twisted in my gut. Had this man harmed my sister? I slid my hand down, searching for a knife.

"Sav," Kaspar said in the loudest voice I'd ever heard him use.

Alder's jaw clenched, but he leaned back with a curl of his lip.

Kaspar's face, normally so devoid of emotion, was a tumult of feeling. Something I'd never expected to see on my old friend's face. "I *will* speak with you."

His words brooked no argument as he turned, dragging me away.

In the hall, Kaspar spun to face me. "If this is about your magic I will demand it. I will force them to give it to you in exchange for anything they ask. Do not marry me simply to get your magic back."

I gaped at him. He'd spoken so freely and with so much feeling. This was a subject we danced around. We never said the words aloud. Shock faded as anger took its place. "You have no idea what I've been through because of you. I've been bound and cast out for three years because of your agreement. One you never asked me if I wanted."

My voice broke on the words and anger was chased by all the betrayal I had tried to bury.

His eyes widened, just a fraction and he lifted scaled fingers to my cheek.

I turned, commanding myself not to cry. My tears didn't listen. One fell, then another and I wiped my cheeks furiously. Meeting his gaze again. "Why did you do it?"

I tugged at the loose strands of my hair, searching his face for any answer that might hurt just a little less.

"Sav. I never thought your sister would do this. I never thought your banishment would last so long. And I thought you'd be safe from their scheming in the human realm."

I huffed, a disbelieving breath. "You did it to protect me?"

"I offered to marry you because they would have agreed to Summer's proposal. He would not have given you the time I did. He would have demanded you go through with it. I never would."

I knew it. I knew the moment Fero told me of his proposal, it was the reason Kaspar had made his offer. What I didn't know—still didn't know—was..."Why?"

He brushed his hand over my cheek again. "We made a bargain."

"What?" My heart beat frantically against my ribcage. "We didn't. I wouldn't." I backed into the wall, vines tangling into my hair as I pressed into them.

Kaspar didn't move. He watched me backing away, something like sadness in his eyes. "You did. You promised me, when you were done adventuring, we would marry. I made the same bargain. I can marry no one else."

My right hand flew to my left, tracing phantom vines from long ago. My head swam and the room tilted. Something silly we'd said as kids had bound us eternally. "We didn't mean it." The words were sticky in my mouth.

"I did."

He sounded so forlorn. If I didn't know better, I could have sworn there was true emotion behind his words.

I dropped my hand, pushing off the wall. Fire surged to life in my veins. "It doesn't mean the same thing to you that it does to me. We can break it. We can stop this." I hadn't meant to say it, but the words were out and my heart picked up its pace again.

Had I just ruined everything?

"You don't want this?"

"I do. I want this. I..."

He searched my face. "Give me the truth and I'll give you your magic."

I bit my lip. Kaspar didn't lie. It was my favorite thing about him. No matter what truth I told him, he would keep that promise. It was a risk, but one I had to take. "I need my magic to save Jack and my sister won't give it to me until we're married. Nothing you say will convince her."

Silence sat between us, heavy and immovable.

When I thought he would say nothing, he spoke. "Very well."

He held out a hand and I slid my fingers into his warily.

Each step towards the thrones beat like a drum against my skull, a death march toward the only inevitable end.

Kaspar began speaking before we stopped, forgoing any formality. "We have agreed. The wedding is today. I will return with my bride to collect her dowry and see that she is unbound by day's end."

I swallowed, not daring to look at Kaspar as he delivered his speech in a flat tone. I'd always thought that was his style of speaking, unfeeling as he was. Now, I wondered if it masked all the emotions he didn't want anyone to see.

SIXTY-EIGHT

KASPAR

I pulled Sav with me as we fled the throne room, working to tamp down every bit of rage boiling in my veins. She would never want this. That desperate promise between two children was nothing more than a lie. Sav and I had always been honest with one another. Or so I thought.

We halted outside the single green door in a hall of wooden ones and I released her. "Get your things. We'll move them to your new rooms before the ceremony."

She touched the handle to her door, turning to face me. "Kaspar, I—"

"Hurry. Before I change my mind."

She flinched and spun to the door, pushing it open. She left it open as she moved to the bed, grabbing a torn leather bag and swinging it over a shoulder.

"Sav!"

My gaze slid left, to the fae who had lied again and again. Hazel skirted past me, giving me a wide berth and closed the door in my face. I huffed, the heat in my veins intensifying.

Staring at painted wood, I tensed. The last night this door was unpainted had been the worst of my life. I could only imagine what it had been like for Sav. Still a young fae, it had been the night I swore to tell Sav my secret. I felt things no one else in my court ever had. I was more like her and Sage than the other sea fae.

I stepped up to a door that was the same shade of pine as all the others in the hall, holding up a fist to knock when her muffled cry came through the door.

Not thinking, I shoved it hard, knocking it off its hinges. I hardly remembered those next moments. The world was red, and I changed into the beast Sav loved and—teeth gnashing—tore through her attacker's flesh. The room was painted with his blood, and he crawled to the door, weeping.

I wasted no time on him, transforming again and wrapping my arms protectively around my friend's nude, battered body. She shook violently and only when I released her did she stop.

I sat at the edge of her bed, mute as she flicked her wrist, glamouring away the worst of the bruising on her neck and back. It would heal quickly, but some of the injuries were severe enough that only a glamour could hide them until she recovered.

She slid a thin robe over her body, wrapping it tightly around herself and the glassy vacant expression on her face as she performed the tasks necessary to cover his treachery, chilled my already cold blood.

"We have to tell the prince."

"No." Her words were dead, like those of my court and I swallowed back my rage, attempting to be whatever she needed. "Lord Banyan is in negotiation talks with Alder." Her words were clipped. "Anything we say could jeopardize that."

My mouth fell slack, indignation burning in my gut. "You can't marry him."

Her dull eyes cleared, and her gaze found mine. "I'll do what I must. As I'm obligated to do."

Try as I might to convince her otherwise, Sav refused to say anything to anyone else about what happened, swearing me to secrecy.

When I'd brought her paint from the deepest seaweed in my lake—imbued with magical properties that would only allow those the painter willed to enter—knowing it would make her feel safe in her room once more—she had hugged me and told me I was the only fae she trusted.

"No!" Sav shouted on the other side of the door, bringing me back to the present. I leaned against painted wood to listen. "I'm not asking for your help. I'm not asking for anyone's help."

"Except the prince." Hazel shot back.

Sav's reply was a whisper, and I pressed an ear to the door straining to hear her words. What I wouldn't give for one of my spies right now. My gaze snagged on a small feline slinking down the hall. Its bright eyes gave it away and I snatched it up as it tried to dart past me, holding it by the scruff of the neck.

I scrutinized twitching whiskers and oddly reddish colored eyes. Too light to be Autumn, but not orange like Summer.

"Who are you? Spring court staff?"

The creature gave a mewling cry, twisting in my grip, but I held it fast. "I have a task for you. If you complete it to my satisfaction, I'll offer one favor of your choosing from the court of lakes and streams.

The cat stilled, twitching its nose.

"Blink once if you agree." Strange eyes blinked and I set it down. "Go around and climb in through this window. Then report everything you hear back to me."

It scampered away, white and black tail bobbing as it went.

Leaning against the wall, I peered along the hall, spying no one. It was no wonder Spring was so desperate for aid; they were woefully short on guards. They must be relying solely on Princess Hawthorn's magic to keep them protected. Why then had she presented me with a proposal when she could have benefited from allying her court with its neighbor?

I'd spent so much time investigating Autumn and Summer that I hadn't considered what might be happening in the court I was soon to align myself with. It wasn't like me to be so careless.

Thoughts of Sav's empty promise drifted in. I had known her reasons for agreeing weren't aligned with mine. In truth, I'd thought she missed her home and after she'd returned to it, she'd been coaxed into seeing the benefit of our alliance.

But I was wrong once again. No matter how I tried to protect her, she put herself in harm's way. Now, she likely had some ill-conceived plan to save the human from his own kind. It would get her killed or at the very least imprisoned. But I would never stand in her way or try to control her the way everyone else did.

Why then did I feel such anger each time I thought of the reason she was so desperate to get her magic back?

Shouts rang on the other side of the door, and it cracked open. "Get out!" Sav yelled and a small black and white cat ran through the door just as a shoe smacked the wood. It was slammed again, and the cat shook itself out, transforming into a fae boy.

"You're a child."

The boy spread his lips into a wide grin. "I'm eleven. But my ears work as good as any fae's."

My lips twitched and I waved a hand. "Very well then, what did you learn?"

The boy leaned close, and I knelt as he pressed his cupped hand to my ear. "They're fighting about going to the human realm to save a man. He's trapped in ISHFA headquarters and the one with the tail says if the other one goes in, she's not coming back out."

I quirked a brow. "That's it?"

The boy's tanned cheeks grew blotchy. "No."

I waited.

"The one with the tail also said the prince is hot and she'd...take him to her room...if the other one doesn't want to."

I straightened. The shifter boy looked away, embarrassment coloring his cheeks.

"Was there anything else?"

"Nope. That's when they saw me and chased me out."

I nodded. "Very well. A bargain was struck. What favor do you ask of the court of lakes and streams?"

He swallowed. "Can I ask for two things?"

I shook my head. "Those were terms you should have negotiated up front. Our bargain was for one favor."

He looked down at his bare feet and huffed. "Okay." He exhaled another long sigh, but I was not so easily persuaded. One did not learn to rule at the same age this boy was now, by being swayed by others' disappointment. "I want you to keep my mom safe from the summer court." His oddly colored eyes met mine and he squared his shoulders.

"Who is your mom?"

"Her name is Ivy. She's an herbalist in the princess's healing ward. She's kind, but she fears Summer will come for us one day. She has nightmares about it."

I nodded gravely. "You have my word, child. My army will protect her from Summer."

"Oh. And anyone else who comes."

I pursed my lips. "That was not our deal."

The boy groaned.

"Now go, before someone sees you and knows what you've been up to."

The boy dropped to all fours, shifting into his cat form and darted away. He turned at the end of the hall, eyeing me and dipped his chin. I hadn't shown mercy in our negotiations, but it was a far greater kindness than coddling him ever would be. One day, when it mattered, he would remember this lesson and not make the same mistake twice.

The door swung wide, and I pushed off the wall. "Ready, Princess?"

Sav's dull, human eyes narrowed on me. "I'm not a princess."

"Not yet." I held out a hand and she took it. I glanced behind her. "No bags?"

"I only need this one." She tossed her chin over her shoulder. "But Hazel's coming with us."

Hazel stepped through the door and for once, her fluffy snow leopard tail didn't follow. My gaze moved to the room behind her, noting its starkness. Once, it had housed all Sav's most precious belongings. Someone had removed them. It was truly not her home anymore.

-●→(◡◆⌒◆●●-

We left the spring court, stepping into the Maywood and I wrapped my arms around both fae. "Hold your breath. This will take a moment."

Sav nodded and Hazel's eyes widened, but she inhaled deeply and together, we dove. Beneath the water, I called a current to us, rushing us along and soon we were in my court. The lake my castle resided in was surrounded on all sides but one by Spring. It made us natural allies through the centuries, but on one shore, the sparkling sandy beach of Summer lined the edge of my waters.

Fero and I had never grown close. He was more than a century old when I was born and he had never formed an alliance with my father, despite our neighboring borders. Though we'd never been to war as Winter and my court had all those centuries ago, I didn't count him as a friend.

For that reason, I regularly monitored his court, and the vast majority of my army was stationed against his border.

As we sunk lower, my gaze swiveled between my two guests, and I nearly laughed at Hazel's awestruck expression. She took in my castle with a childlike wonder. As we neared the main gate, two kelpie soldiers rushed forward, tugging dead coral doors wide. Though they couldn't live in freshwater, they made a great defensive perimeter around my home. Should any dare attack, they would be forced to cut their way through.

Inside, smooth stone walls lined our path, and I pushed forward, breaching the air bubble and setting Sav and Hazel down inside her new rooms. The pair gasped for air and gazed around the space.

"Is this your room?"

I slid pondweed stocks aside and stepped through. "It's your room."

Sav trailed me in, spinning in a slow circle.

"The receiving room will be outfitted with drying aids and submersible suits, so you don't have to worry about getting your clothes wet every time you leave." I reached for a satchel from a long row of them. "These are magicked so you can store your clothes in them and change when you're on land."

Sav ran a hand over the row of dozens of bags. She moved beyond them to a closet carved into the wall, equipped with hangers and a long rod to store all her gowns. It was empty as I had assumed she'd be bringing clothes with her. I had assumed wrong.

"And a washroom. Will I have one of those?"

I nodded, guiding them through a second set of stalks to a room specially designed with Sav's land needs in mind. A tub was carved into the floor and magical levers siphoned water in and out as needed. A sink across from the tub was fashioned with a brushing station and mirror and across from both was another arched doorway leading to the privy.

Her slow circle stopped, gaze landing on me. "How long did all of this take to build?"

I searched her face for any sign of appreciation. Finding none, I answered truthfully, though I suspected she already knew. "Years."

Sav eyed me, stepping up to the sink and waving her hand under the spout. Water, perfectly adjusted to the temperature of her preference gushed out, running through her fingers. She spun to face me. "Wow, Kaspar. This is really—"

"Make yourselves ready," I said, cutting her off, gaze not meeting hers. "I have a few things to attend to, but we can complete the ceremony here once I've finished. I know you're in a hurry."

Sixty-Nine

Jack

I lifted my chin and bit down on my tongue.

"Tell us where they are," Morgan's cold, ethereal voice demanded.

Her magic pried my lips apart, loosening my tongue, but I fought it, and satisfaction stole through me when her brows furrowed at my silence.

When I arrived in Central Park, Dane hadn't been surprised to see me. In fact, it seemed as though he'd expected it. Weapons aimed at Larek and Yolmar and safeties clicked off when Larek backed up. I threw up my hands.

"Don't shoot."

Dane grinned, closing the distance between us. He leaned close whispering so only I and the fae at my back could hear. "Thank you for bringing them to me. I'd be willing to bet good money the orc general will trade just about anything for his sons."

Terror shot through me as I swiveled my gaze around and mouthed, "Run."

They didn't.

In a desperate gamble that sure as hell shouldn't have worked, I grabbed Dane's second pistol from the holster at his hip, cocking it and held it to his head.

Shouts from behind him lifted the corners of my lips. "Let them go, Dane."

He backed up a step, a confident smile creeping over his face. "You won't do it. You've never had the stomach to harm anyone."

I looked over his shoulder at the men slowly closing in. "Put down your guns or I will shoot."

Dane hadn't brought his top men and that made me more uneasy than anything. If he knew we were coming and somehow he had, why bring random AFF members with no real training? Perhaps for once in his conniving life, Dane had miscalculated. A man set his gun down, then another.

I glanced back at Larek and Yolmar who hadn't moved. "I said, run!"

Larek tugged Yolmar's arm, and they backed up.

"Don't let them get away," Dane shouted, never breaking eye contact with me. "He won't shoot his own father."

One of the men behind Dane fired, but though his aim was wildly off, it startled Larek and Yolmar into action. They turned and another gunshot cracked.

I grimaced, lowered the gun to Dane's arm and fired. He stumbled backward and the shock on his face made my stomach roil. Realizing I would do as I promised, everyone behind Dane began setting their guns on the ground. "You too, Dane."

Dane held up his hands, but it wasn't a gun he was holding. It was a walkie-talkie. "Now. They're getting away."

My eyes widened, but I had only a moment to think of Sav and the others and hope they had already made it out before white hot pain surged through me and I fell to the ground.

My vision blurred and overhead, Morgan, Emissary of the autumn court and Fae leader of ISHFA, stood over me.

Janet Glassdon stepped through sheer glass doors as they slid silently apart. It was a marvel of engineering I might have taken more time to admire had all my energy not been focused on keeping the fae leader of ISHFA from spilling my secrets.

I'd promised Sav, no matter what, that I wouldn't tell them how to get in Faerie, but Morgan wasn't interested in Faerie. She wanted Creig and his free army.

"No progress?"

Morgan shook her head, and a mane of golden curls bounced with the movement. Shimmering wine-colored eyes met mine. "He's surprisingly difficult to break."

Janet smiled but it was all teeth. Her severe black bob was a vivid contrast to pale skin and her features were all sharp angular lines. When her gaze fell on me, my skin crawled. I'd seen that kind of madness in another's eyes only once. The day I'd visited mom when she'd been placed on suicide watch.

It was three weeks before her death and if I'd known then she would actually go through with it, I'd have fought for her to stay in that horrible, bright place. I'd give anything to have one more day with her. But that wasn't how love worked. Keeping those we loved when they no longer wished for it, was selfish.

When I visited her, her eyes were remarkably clear. None of the desperate frenzy I'd seen before they took her in. It wasn't *her* eyes Janet reminded me of now. It was the nurse in white scrubs who wheeled her into a room we weren't permitted to enter.

I knew then something was wrong, demanded they release her before the crazed nurse did something my mom would never recover from. Perhaps I was too late. Or maybe nothing anyone did could have saved her from her silent pain.

"When magic fails," Janet said, pulling me from my thoughts. "There's always good old-fashioned torture."

A bead of sweat ran down my temple even though the room was frigid. Morgan hadn't frightened me; her magic was a fraction of the power I'd felt from the summer prince or Sav's sister. It was no wonder she left her court in search of it. In her realm, she was nothing.

Janet slid a thin dagger from her belt. Metal glinted and the dagger flew before I had a chance to process the movement. It was inhumanly fast, and I blinked, exhaling a full sigh before I registered what had happened.

Glancing down, something like shock stole over me as I stared at the object protruding from my thigh. The room went silent as all my focus zeroed in on the scene. I couldn't make sense of it. I was struck. A thin line of blood welled along metal, trailing over the side of my leg and pooling in my chair. Its wetness soaked into the underside of my thigh, cooling rapidly and my brain knew I should be screaming, but instead, I felt nothing.

I looked up, blinking at Janet, and her cold smile fell.

SEVENTY

SAV

"Kaspar."

He moved past me, shoving aside vines of pondweed and leaving us to stare after him.

"This is really..." Hazel said to my back.

I turned to face her. "I think I made a mistake."

Hazel trailed a hand along smooth stone, perfectly carved to match the sinks in Spring. "Do you think—"

"He doesn't love me." I cut her off. "He said he couldn't."

Hazel raised a snowy brow. "He lied." She spun in a slow circle. "If he didn't care, would he have recreated your court baths with such attention to detail?"

I scoffed. "A pretty prison is still a prison."

Hazel held out her wrists as she stepped into the tub. "Lock me up because I would live here with hot prince forever."

I rolled my eyes, leaving the bath and returning to the expansive bedroom. It wasn't like my room, and I wondered if that was intentional. Did he know me so well? Of course. Of course he knew I didn't want a reminder of the room my sister wouldn't let me move out of after Lord Banyan.

My one small act of defiance. A reminder that I could lock them out, was painted with Kaspar's magic. It changed nothing about that night, but it gave me some power back. Kaspar was the only one who knew the truth, and since that night it seemed he had made it his mission to keep me safe.

I sat on the bed, running a hand over smooth fabric. Hazel flopped down beside me. "Look at that."

I followed her gaze to a circle of glass and outside, a lake teaming with life. We watched as creatures came and went, tails moving swiftly through clear water and I let out a startled laugh when a frog, too large to be anything but folk, spread his webbed feet wide and kicked through the water.

"He's cute," I laughed, and it cracked some of the anguish that had taken up residence in my chest from the moment I'd chosen to go through with this deception.

Hazel laid a hand over mine and I looked at her. "You don't have to marry him."

"Hazel."

She sat up. "I mean it. There are other ways to get your magic back."

I tugged my hand from hers, leaning back. "Such as?"

She reached for my pack, pulling out the object I'd kept hidden for three years. "You stole the quartz crystal from my court for a reason. Let's use it. Let's find Mab and restore order to this mad, messed up world."

"There's no time for that. Every minute we waste, Jack could be closer to death."

She exhaled a long sigh. "You care that much about him?" She searched my face. "There's no undoing this. Marriage is binding. I don't think Jack would want you to marry someone else just to save him."

I pushed up, rising and stalking away from Hazel. "We've had this conversation. He's human. I'm not doing it because I expect a future with him. I'm doing it because he was only captured in the first place because of me." I tugged a strand of my sodden hair. "I can't let him die because of me."

Hazel blew out another breath. "Are you back to believing he's human again?"

I rolled my eyes, tired of this argument. Human or not, I had to save him. "Come on. We need to change into dry clothes before we catch cold." I reached for my satchel and pulled out two sets of leather pants, my sheath of daggers, and flowing silk tops.

"You couldn't have brought me something nicer? I'm going to a wedding."

I arched a brow. "My wedding. You can't dress better than me."

"No one told you to bring pants and knives to your wedding."

I chucked the clothes at her. "Just get dressed."

—●➔(∽●∧♦♦●—

My heart had begun a nervous thrumming in my throat that only intensified with each passing moment, beating against my jaw. Kaspar had said he had matters to attend to but in this place, where sunlight filtered in through water, I had no idea if it had been thirty minutes or three hours.

I paced the room, stopping beside the window.

"Sav. Please. Stop." Hazel flung a hand over her face.

I glanced back. "I don't know how you can sleep."

"It's either that or die of boredom."

"You wanted to stay here."

She dropped her hand, glaring at me. "That was when I thought I'd be spending my time having hot sex with a prince all day."

I rolled my eyes.

The sound of water sloshing in the next room had my nerves jumping and my heart climbed into my throat. The room swayed and I inhaled a slow, deep breath. *I can do this.* I was doing this. I was marrying my best friend. Former best friend. And then I would get my magic back.

A small green creature hopped into the room and bowed low. I stifled a giggle, nerves momentarily forgotten. He was the cutest thing I'd ever seen. On land, shifters were only ever land creatures. We never got cute little frogs with webbed feet and big bulging eyes that seemed to look everywhere at once.

"Lady Briar. His Majesty, Prince Kaspar, asked me to escort you to the ballroom."

I laced my fingers together, squeezing, and Hazel stepped up beside me, looping her arm in mine. I leaned into her, thankful for her presence. I had just begun to dry, but at least in these clothes, I wouldn't drag water with me.

His words hit me. "But, how will I say vows underwater?"

The little frog slid his tongue out of his mouth, smacking it against his eye and I nearly squealed in delight, nervous tension bleeding away. "The throne room has been made ready for you."

Not waiting for my next question, he turned and hopped through the pondweed and was gone. Hazel tugged me along behind her as we followed the frog, and I gasped when we stepped into a narrow hall lined in lake stones in every shade of blue and gray. It was dry. No, not dry, but a path had been carved down the middle. A pocket of air. For me.

We moved on silent feet, the green creature ahead of us, hopping impossibly fast. At the end of the long hall, we slid to a stop. The massive two-story arches weren't blocked by any weeds this time, giving us a full view of the cavernous room. It was at least three stories tall, lined on either side by massive ovals. Unlike my rooms, the water was held back by magic and only the center of the room—leading to a stone dais—had been cleared of water.

On either side of my path, rows of sea folk floated, eyeing me as I approached.

Hazel squeezed my arm, and I moved through them, gaze landing on Kaspar, dressed in a navy suit. I looked down at shoes polished to a shine, and back up to the small pink flower tucked into his lapel. It was representative of my court and nausea overtook me. I may have rushed to make this day a reality, but Kaspar had planned for it.

Aquamarine eyes met mine.

This wasn't how a wedding should be. This wasn't how I'd imagined mine. My wedding was supposed to be a day of joy and a promise of forever. Instead, I was crushing Kaspar's dream and shackling myself to a male I would never love. A wild, selfish thought tore through me. I could leave this all behind and return to Creig's hidden pocket.

I could hide from the world and all the creatures whose lives I destroyed merely by being in it.

Hazel released my arm and I turned, wide-eyed. She nodded, giving me a small smile. I spun back to Kaspar, feeling the rush of blood to my head as he held out his hands. Mine slid into his and I watched through a fog as he gave me a small smile and nodded to the naiad standing beside us.

The creature spoke and Kaspar repeated the words.

He searched my face, and I swallowed. "I promise," I began, heart beating so loud it drowned out my words. If I couldn't hear them, did it mean they weren't true? "To remain true." My throat was dry and the room began to spin. "To put the needs of our folk first." Kaspar's grip tightened on mine and I glanced down at our clasped hands. "Never to use my husband's name for ill or in vain."

The naiad spoke again, and Kaspar repeated after her.

I cleared my throat, feeling as though a frog were stuck in it. Wild laughter bubbled up my chest at the image I'd conjured of the small creature who'd brought me here, trapped inside my mouth. I swallowed it down and cleared my throat again. "To care for all the subjects of the court of lakes and streams as if they were my own."

The room was spinning and voices blurred together. Whirling, twisting, suffocatingly close.

"I do." Everything stopped as the words left Kaspar's mouth and my gaze fell on navy lips.

It was my turn to say it. My turn to promise forever. "I..." I glanced around at all the leering faces, ice sliding down my spine. "I..."

"Salvia," Kaspar whispered. Power laced his words and my stomach hollowed out. He was going to do it. He was going to use my name to force this. I wouldn't let him. I wouldn't let him take this choice away from me. Not when every other choice in my life already had been.

"I do."

Magic swirled around us, weaving through my hair and circling our clasped hands. Invisible ribbons wove tightly, squeezing our palms together. It traveled up our arms to our shoulders, wrapping around us until we were consumed by it. A jolt of pain shot through me as the magic pierced my heart. Kaspar's mouth opened as it struck him too.

As quickly as it had come, it dissipated into nothing. It was oddly reminiscent of my binding as it settled. No longer heavy or oppressive, only a featherlight touch caressed my hand, reminding me of the promises I made today.

Kaspar loosened his grip and I tugged my hand back, holding it up. On my left ring finger, an intricately woven band of vines was tattooed in a circle. It was exactly like the one I'd given him all those years ago.

SEVENTY-ONE
FOXGLOVE

I twisted in my chair as the hairs on the back of my neck rose.

She was silent, eyes vacant, but she had found me, and that warmed something in my heart.

"Are you alright, Juniper?"

She didn't speak. She never did.

I stood, moving to her side and held out my hand. "Would you like me to escort you to the kitchens? Dinner was an hour back, but I didn't want to wake you."

Her vision cleared, gaze dropping to my outstretched hand. Lightning fast, she reached for the dagger at my hip, but I caught her wrist, careful not to touch the mottled scars at the daintiest part of her arm.

I'd hoped the medicine Poppy gave her would wipe the drug from her system and restore her to her former self—the fierce satyr I'd heard legends of all those years ago—but the drugs in her system were magical in nature and had rooted so deeply inside her nothing Poppy tried had worked. With so many wounded and nothing physically wrong with Juniper, there hadn't been time to dedicate to a cure.

I ran my thumb in slow circles over her palm.

As with each time I'd done this before, her expression glazed, honey-colored eyes softening as she stared at nothing, and the tension in her arms relaxed.

"Come. Let's eat." I tugged her forward, and pliant as a doll, she went.

We reached the kitchens and after a quick scan of the room and all its sharp objects, I thought better of releasing her to gather items. Tugging her behind me, and keeping a healthy distance from the rack of knives, I grabbed a loaf of bread and a bowl of fruit, already prepared for tomorrow's breakfast.

I could have taken her to her room, but it was sparse, unlived in, and I didn't think that was what she needed. Pressing against the door to my room with an elbow, I ushered her inside and set the bread and fruit down on a low table overlooking the missing spring forest.

When my brother became prince, I'd moved to the old advisor's room, first so I could keep a closer eye on my brother, but second because the advisor had many hidden passages by which to move throughout the castle. Though I wasn't my brother's advisor—he said he had no need for such things as he sliced a blade cleanly across the male's throat—I was his spymaster, and it benefited me greatly to have such access. The view had been the one thing I liked about that room.

There was a comfort in having my old palace view here in this missing pocket of Faerie. In knowing that though my brother no longer had access to the place, I did.

Juniper sat without prompting and I exhaled a soft breath. My room was messy, lived in, and somehow, I was sure it was just the thing to begin the long process of bringing her back to herself.

A knock sounded at the door. I glanced down at the bowl beside Juniper, lips quirking. Some sense of self-preservation lived in her still. If I'd had to feed her, I would have been truly concerned.

"Yes?"

Murz burst into the room. "Prince Kaspar and his new princess have returned to court. They've just been wed. I think you should get back there."

I straightened my collar, standing and nodding. "Stay by the door. Don't let Juniper leave before I return," I ordered. He dipped his chin and stepped back to let me pass.

—●→(∽●∩●●—

Outside the throne room, Prince Kaspar glanced around the hall with bored indifference and by his side, the princess fidgeted in her wet clothes. I reached them in three long strides and searched Sav's ashen face for any sign of injury. Seeing none, I glanced through the open doors. Dipping my chin to both, I risked impropriety and addressed my question to the princess. "Is my brother not aware of your arrival, Princess?" The way Alder ran his court was appalling—he spent more time putting our kingdom in peril than aiding it—but surely he wouldn't keep the prince waiting knowing how much his army was needed.

She jolted, eyes widening at my use of her new title and licked her lips, meeting my gaze. "He is. He's waiting for my sister to arrive."

I ground my teeth. Would this constant bid for superiority between the twins never end? "I'll find her."

"No need," Prince Kaspar drawled, glancing my way. "In ten seconds, princess or no, I'll see the Hawthorn heir and he *will* give me what's owed."

A chill settled in my veins at his cold clinical words. I wouldn't have wished this marriage on an enemy, much less someone I'd considered a friend. If I could have spared her from it, I would, but there was only one male I feared in all of Faerie and I would have offered to marry Sav myself before I saw her sold to the prince of summer.

As promised, the prince tightened his arm in Sav's and dragged her forward when ten seconds had passed. I let them go, hugging the wall of the throne room as I moved into the shadows. Several spring court soldiers lined the room. Most of the remaining army. A fact no one outside the royal family knew.

When Earth and Faerie collided, our land had begun to disappear, but unlike most of the other courts, our people disappeared with it. Each time we lost another slice of Spring, dozens of folk disappeared. Although we'd located much of the missing land, even if we couldn't find a way to reunite it with the rest of our kingdom, none of the missing fae were in it.

My attention moved to the throne. Alder was raising his hands in a placating gesture. Something I'd rarely seen him do. But he was more eager than most to have the prince's army guarding our border and whether Kaspar knew it or not, my brother would have given him just about anything to ensure it.

"You will unbind my bride immediately."

A bead of sweat dotted Alder's brow as I approached. "Brother. Shall I fetch your wife?"

He flicked an irritated glance at me. "No need. Silv is enroute and is perfectly capable."

Sav's lips were white and she trembled, but though she was still wet from her swim, I didn't think it was a chill. "I am certain the princess would prefer her sister be the one to do it." My gaze moved between the two princes. My brother was hiding something. Would Sage truly not unbind her sister? Would she go back on a bargain? No matter how jealous she was, I didn't think so.

Silv raced into the room, halting at the foot of the throne and dropped her head low. She was a satyr of no small talent and the leader of her clan, certainly capable of a normal unbinding. But the princess of spring was no weak fae. Her binding would be nearly impossible to remove without her earth magic.

I studied the satyr looking for any common traits between her and my new ward. I hadn't known Juniphera personally, but I'd heard of her. When we fought in the great war five centuries ago, she had led her clan to victory, defending our borders more fiercely than all the orc commanders combined. What had happened to her that she had been cast out of Faerie?

Silv held her hands up to either side of Sav's head, whispering softly. I had never witnessed a binding, and had been away from court when Sage had done this horrible thing to her sister. For if I had been present, I certainly would have stopped it.

Sav cried out and Prince Kaspar wrapped his hands around hers, squeezing. It was the most emotion I'd ever seen from the sea creature and I quirked a brow, studying his passive face. There was nothing in it that spoke of concern. To anyone watching, he was as indifferent in this as he had been upon learning of his parents' death. But there were small things, tells one learned when working as a spy.

The way his shoulders hunched forward, his hips angled in her direction. The stiffness in his back when he often appeared to be floating on some phantom current, lithe and carefree. He was a master at hiding it, but I had just learned a valuable secret about the ruler of lakes and streams. One that might benefit me greatly in the future.

If only his weakness was anything other than Sav.

SEVENTY-TWO

SAV

A scream tore its way up my throat, clogging my lungs and my back bowed as another ribbon of invisible power, woven through the fabric of my very being, came free and slithered through me. Silv, the clan leader of Spring's satyr tribe, dropped her hands, panting.

"Are you ready to go again?" she asked far too soon.

Kaspar gripped my trembling hands in his, jaw clenched as he squeezed. "Your sister's cruelty knows no limit."

The words skated down my skin, promising death and I would have been fearful for my sister if I had any love left for her. Alder had long since fled the room, stomach too weak to sit through any more of my torture.

"How many ribbons was that, Silv?" Foxglove asked behind me.

I wanted to shout at him to leave. Horrified that he would no doubt take the news of my suffering back to my sister wherever she was languishing, but my energy was spent, and I couldn't muster enough even to chastise him.

"One-hundred-seventy-four, Lord Hawthorn."

He growled something under his breath, then, in his polite court voice, said. "Might we take a respite to allow the princess a moment's reprieve?"

She nodded, but I pried my hand from Kaspar's latching onto her arm. "No," I ground out between clenched teeth. "Finish this."

Her bright yellow eyes were round, and her gaze darted over my shoulder to Foxglove. She opened her mouth when Kaspar spoke.

"My lady has given you a command, Satyr, and as her rank far outweighs Lord Hawthorn's, I suggest you follow it."

Sweat soaked my silk blouse as, with some effort, I released Silv's hand

and Kaspar wrapped his fingers around mine, holding them in his steel grip.

Silv raised her hands, glancing warily between Kaspar and me.

When the pain began again, my vision went dark at the edges and I leaned into Kaspar.

"I will end her for this," he seethed.

"It's...as much...your fault...as hers." I panted, digging my nails into his flesh as a ribbon of power worked its way backward, out of my chest. She'd started with my head and that had been both better and worse. With some of my magic accessible, I was healing the damage nearly as quickly as Silv inflicted it, but just as I'd remembered, each one was a new kind of torment as she worked her way down my body.

Kaspar's aquamarine gaze was cool, indifferent, but the way he squeezed my hands, holding me upright so I didn't have to writhe on the floor like a beast, told me emotion was buried somewhere under that cool facade. I was transported back to the night he'd saved me from Lord Banyan. Back to the night when, just for a moment, through my numbness, I'd thought I witnessed real feelings.

I had tried to stop the shaking, as I did now, tried to hide the pain, but I could never hide anything from him. That night had changed everything between us. I wondered how it would change again after this.

"Sav, you should rest." Foxglove said.

With great effort I turned my head as another ribbon tugged out of my middle, and my gut burned. I swallowed bile rising in my throat, attempting to answer him, but when the next ribbon slid over my spine my body jerked and I crashed to my knees.

Kaspar tugged me to my feet and Silv dropped her hands looking stricken. "I don't think you can handle anymore today," she said, in a small voice.

This would have gone so much faster if my sister had been here. Silv was working blindly, unable to call on magic that didn't belong to her and so far, she'd only unwound the outer layers. Deeper magic, wound around my heart and soul would need to be undone by my sister. The coward was going back on her promise.

I gritted my teeth. "I can take it."

Silv shook her head. "Let's rest for a few minutes. My own strength is waning."

A lie. But my knees threatened to buckle again and I relented, nodding.

Kaspar guided me to a sofa in the room's corner and I collapsed into it, breath rattling. My lungs were full of blood, but the magic in my veins rushed to heal them and I leaned over, spitting up crimson.

Foxglove surprised me, crouching low and handing me a cup of water.

Kaspar stood, saying nothing, but I felt his anger. It twisted my gut. I wished I didn't need him here. Wished I didn't need any of them, terrified to admit just how much I did.

With shaking fingers, I lifted the cup to my lips and drank. Glancing down, my vision razor sharp, I noted the tiny hairs on my arms standing on end. My fae vision had returned.

Shoes squeaked on wood in the hall, telling me my hearing had as well. Silv had done good work, releasing all of the superficial magic, but to reach my well of power, I needed the deeper bindings removed.

Setting the cup down beside me, I held up a hand and nearly cried with relief when red flames flared to life in my palm. They bloomed beautifully in my hand now that my lungs were clear of blood.

I inhaled my first real breath in three years and tasted all the emotion roiling around me. I'd never truly lost it, but now, partially unbound, Foxglove's anguish clogged my nostrils. Kaspar's blind anger and most surprisingly, Silv's shame.

My gaze snapped to her, zeroing in on her interlaced fingers, white-knuckled and squeezing together.

"Silv."

Her gaze shot up, meeting mine and another wave of shame barreled into me. The others must have scented it, but perhaps they were too clouded by their own emotions to smell anything else.

Silv dipped her chin and dropped to her knees, eye level with me. "Yes, Princess?"

"What have you done?" The magic lacing my words tasted sweet on my tongue. I should not have taken such satisfaction from using one of my gifts on the low fae, but it had been years since I could force the truth from anyone, and I reveled in it. Just a little.

Her lips parted, compelled to answer, but she fought it and her words came haltingly and grudgingly. "Princess...Hawthorn...Is...Missing." She choked on the last word, and I wrinkled my brow, not making the connection between her emotions and her words. Why would the admission cause her shame?

"I don't understand."

Silv said nothing, pressing her lips into a thin line.

"Speak."

She fought hard, standing and backing away.

"Kaspar." His name had hardly left my lips before he moved, wrapping strong fingers around her biceps and holding her in place.

She let out a small whimper, and the words tumbled free. "A whole section of the castle has disappeared, just like the rest of Faerie, and Sage has disappeared with it. Alder hoped you'd be taken too. You and the prince."

I glanced at Foxglove, silently asking the question I couldn't say aloud. Had whoever was removing pieces of Faerie taken Sage? Was it the same person who took Mab?

My thoughts were interrupted as Hazel raced into the room. "Sav."

Kaspar, Foxglove and I all looked up as she slid to a stop beside us. "We have to move. Two sections of the castle have disappeared, Prince and Princess Hawthorn with it. We're not safe here."

EPILOGUE

JANET GLASSDON

I watched Jack slumped over in his chair, a crimson Rorschach painting at his feet, through the pane of glass separating my office from the interrogation room we'd left him in. He had been surprisingly difficult to injure, and nothing we did loosened his tongue. What little I knew of fairies had me questioning their methods.

Morgan's truth magic hadn't rattled one secret from his lips.

When the knife I'd thrown landed its mark in his thigh, he hadn't flinched. Shock. It was the only explanation. Especially after I saw how well he could bleed. I'd give him a few more hours, then I'd go back to work. Eventually, everyone talked.

"Janet."

My gaze swiveled from the prisoner to my reason for living, and warmth bloomed in my chest. "Morgan." Her eyes sparkled in the false light, contrasting beautifully against porcelain skin. I could stare at those eyes forever.

She reached me in three strides and cupped my chin, teeth tugging my lower lip before her tongue found mine. Her taste was cinnamon and fire and utterly intoxicating. Her roving fingers trailed my neck, tracing the length of my body and landing possessively between my legs.

Her grip tightened, tugging me closer, and our kiss deepened as I ran my fingers through golden curls. A breathy moan escaped her, igniting a flame between my thighs, and I walked her backward, pressing her against the table in my office, and lifted her by the hips to sit atop it. Her fingers stroked between my thighs, and I grinned around her mouth, leaning her back until she was flat atop the desk as I climbed up, wedging a knee between her legs.

"Hi. Don't mind me. Two ladies. Hot."

I slid off the desk, spinning around in disbelief. Jack was sitting up on the other side of the glass, wide awake as though I hadn't just given him the beating of his life. One eye had swelled shut, and his lip was split wide. Bruises were already forming along his ribcage. We had long since discarded the shirt. I liked to see my masterpieces.

I glanced over my shoulder at Morgan. "I have to work, baby."

Her swollen pink lips formed a pout, and I longed to turn around and finish what we started, but we had a rebel insurrection to stop. There was no rest for the wicked.

The story continues in book 2—coming late 2025.